You Believers

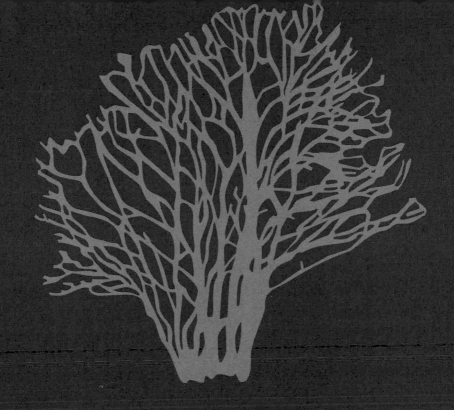

You Believers

JANE BRADLEY

Unbridled Books

Unbridled Books

Library of Congress Cataloging-in-Publication Data

Bradley, Jane.
You believers / by Jane Bradley.
p. cm.
ISBN 978-1-60953-046-4
1. Missing persons—Fiction.   2. Self-actualization (Psychology)—Fiction.   I. Title.
PS3552.R2274Y68 2011
813'.54—dc22
2010047173

1   3   5   7   9   10   8   6   4   2

Book Design by SH · CV

First Printing

*For Monica Caison
and Community United Effort,
Wilmington, North Carolina*

Set me as a seal on your heart, as a seal on your arm,
for stern as death is love, relentless as the netherworld's devotion;
its flames are a blazing force.

Song of Songs 8:6

Bodies

When Wilmington police searched for Katy Connor, they found a woman's leg, fish-belly white, gray at the crease at the back of the knee, black at the top where someone had hacked it off before tossing the leg into the stream. A blue Keds sneaker still clung to the foot in spite of the suck and pull of so much water. It wasn't Katy's leg but some other woman's leg, another woman's story we will never know. This is Katy's story. At least I think it's Katy's story. It's hard to say sometimes where one woman's story ends and another begins.

It's classic, almost. Like the story of Persephone picking flowers in a field one spring afternoon. The earth opens. Hades comes roaring up in his chariot, black horses digging up dirt with their hooves, hot breath swirling from flared nostrils. With a quick swoop of thick, muscled arm, Hades snatches the girl, drags her down to the underworld. You know the story. A mother comes to the rescue, finds her daughter has eaten six seeds of the dark fruit, pomegranate seeds that crunched between the girl's teeth, red juice running from her lips.

And the mother's world, the whole wide world, is changed.

You could say it could be anyone's story. People go missing every day. That twelve-year-old blond who disappears while waiting for her school bus one spring morning. The woman last seen turning away from an ATM camera. Sometimes we find them. Sometimes not. Most often we find remains.

My name's Shelby Waters, and you don't know me, and you might not ever want to know me because I'm a searcher. I'm the one you call when someone you love goes missing. Yes, of course you call the cops first, and you should. But once the cop is gone with his report and the profile of what went down rising up in his mind, and you've got nothing left but worry and waiting for the phone to ring, you call me.

And I listen to your sorrows and fears and speculations. And you, like everyone who's missing someone, hope for the best and fear the worst. That's a hard line to walk. So I step in and I look at your pictures, letters, whatever fragments you might have that belong or relate to the one you've lost. I try to fill in the gaps between what you think might have happened, what you fear might have happened, and what did go down and how it went. And while I'm figuring the story, I'm doing my best to make you feel you can stand and walk, and no matter what happens, you can go on and live.

It was my sister, Darly, got me started on this.

I was always the hard, shy one, but Darly, she was the popular girl. You know the kind, with blue eyes and a sweet little mouth that makes you think of cherries. All the boys liked her. The girls too. She was the kind anyone could love. Pretty and sweet, you know, not taken with her own beauty, just cheerful and helpful and good. She grew up, got married, and moved out of our little cove called Suck Creek to Chattanooga. Momma had a bad feeling, but mommas most often have bad feelings about their babies moving away. But the rest of us, well, we were proud. I mean Suck Creek isn't exactly the kind of place where people do big things in life. In the old days it was pretty much moonshiners and poor folks making do with some kind of labor. Some say there was a curse on the place for all the shooting and drinking and general meanness that went on back in the woods off the roads. Some say it was cursed by the Cherokee when they got pushed out on that old Trail of Tears.

There was a creek there, Suck Creek, looked clean and deep and just right for swimming in the summer. It sat back a little from the Tennessee River, where the rainwater runs off the mountain, just tucked back a little in the cove. It looked calm enough, but now and then there'd be this current, some said it was the pull of the river way down beneath, but something would shift, pull people under. And they'd drown. Mostly kids and drunk teenaged boys. My momma liked to say God looks after drunks and little children, but living in Suck Creek, I don't know how she could hold to that way of thinking. But she was strong on religion. Lots of folks are strong on religion back there. Momma said one day they had a revival out by that creek, and there was a woman there. Lillian Young was her name. My momma knew her, said she had some power of God working in her. She'd once stopped two boys from lynching this black boy just for riding his bike back in there. The white boy that brought him in, the redneck boys knocked his teeth out. They beat the black boy pretty bad. His face was all bashed in. They were throwing a rope over a tree limb. Had the noose tied. Some of the boys tried to keep Miss Young away, but she pushed on, saying, "I want to know what you boys are doing back there." And when she saw what they were doing, she stopped it all right, just by calling those boys down with words. She said, "God is not pleased with what you boys are doing." And they listened. They all knew Miss Young. She'd go all around there helping the old folks, teaching the young ones to read. So those boys, they quit their beating on that black boy, and she yanked him up, shoved him toward his bike, and said, "In the name of Jesus, get on that bike, get home, and never, ever, come back here." Whenever she said something in the name of Jesus, something changed in the world. Everybody believed in the powers of Lillian Young.

So after that revival, when folks were all full of faith and joy in salvation, Lillian Young decided it was time to go out and pray over that creek, pray for whatever evil lay beneath that water to vanish, in the name of Jesus, of course. She prayed, "Lord, if this creek gives you no glory, in the name of Jesus, take this creek away." They say she said that a few times, along with some others praying. And it wasn't a week later a big storm rolled through, tore up the riverbank, changed the way the rain flowed down the mountain and into the river, and that creek, it disappeared. I do not lie about this. That creek was gone. And Miss Young, well, she came to be known from Knoxville to Tuscaloosa for the holy woman she was.

I wish we had her now. And I wish we had had her to pray over Darly before she moved away. Like I said, Momma had a bad feeling, and to tell the truth I did too. I thought maybe I was worrying about being lonely for my sister, so I told Darly I was proud she was moving off and going to college to be a nurse. It wasn't long before she had a job and a husband and a house and all that stuff a woman's supposed to get in this world. And it was good for a while. Then, on her way to work one morning, Darly disappeared.

You never believe it at first. You go looking for the simplest explanation, the thing you want to believe, like she just met up with a friend and forgot to call. But they found her white nurse's cap on the shelf in a phone booth, her little white MG broken down by the side of the road. No signs of a struggle, just a car, keys hanging in the ignition. The car had had some kind of engine trouble. It was always getting her stuck on the side of the road. She'd probably be alive today if she'd done like my daddy always said to and bought a Dodge.

I had a dream the morning she disappeared. I was planting red tulips in black dirt, and Darly rode by the house in a black car. She was in the passenger seat in the dream. I didn't see the driver. She just looked at me, so sad. I straightened up from digging in the dirt and said, "Darly doesn't like this." I woke up with those words. And I wondered why I was dreaming about Darly. I mean I'd seen her around, but we'd kind of drifted apart with me still back in Suck Creek running the Quick Stop and her off being a nurse and married and all. While I was pouring my coffee that morning, my momma called, told me about the phone booth, the car, the keys still there. I knew it was bad.

After the cops investigated her husband and did a half-assed job of a search, they gave up looking. Too many other crimes to get on to, they said, or something like that. I knew we'd find her in time, not Darly, but what was left. It's a hard thing to learn to live with what's left when so much is always falling away. A year later two hunters out for deer found Darly in the brush in the north Georgia mountains where only hunters go.

Police never found the facts, just figured it was some guy saw an easy target. Such a little woman, her nurse's uniform bright in the predawn darkness. Did he snatch her from the phone booth? Or did he, smiling, offer her a ride? These are the questions that got me started. With answers I'll always want to know. I tried to talk to Darly all those months she was gone, and I sent up prayers trying to catch a sense of her spirit. But Darly never answered. I guess I'm no Lillian Young because no matter how much I cried out, God just sat silent and shadowed as those deep, dark mountains back there. Once they found her remains, I gave up on God. And I couldn't look at mountains without thinking what meanness might be going on. I used to love mountains, had no fear of any kind of wildness out there. But I got to where I couldn't even get off our porch, so my momma thought I should visit my cousin in Wilmington. He ran a bar out on the beach. No mountains, just sea and sky and sand. I needed that. And it was good for a while. All those happy tourists, big beach homes and condos and parties and money and laughter flowing in and out like the tides.

But then this little girl went missing from town, from downtown, where it's bad. Word was her momma was a crack whore, so the cops, well, you know cops. So I called and met the grandmomma, who was the one really raising that girl, who took her to church, kept her clean, made sure she did her homework. The girl deserved a search. Her name was Keisha. That was the first thing I did, make sure the city knew a nine-year-old girl named Keisha Davis was missing and needed to be found. Given the momma's way of living, I had a feeling Keisha wasn't dead; she'd just been stolen for a while. Taken by somebody who'd seen her in her momma's house, somebody who knew how to snatch a girl without a sound. And I knew with enough word on the street we'd find her. I told every little dealer, thief, and hooker I could get to listen to keep an eye out. Waved a fifty-dollar bill at 'em, then put it back in my pocket. Said, "You get me the word that finds that girl, you'll get this fifty, and you'll be my friend. And you never know when you'll need a friend like me." Maybe I do have a little Lillian Young in me 'cause I got their attention. But you gotta cover all the odds and work fast when it's a child lost. So I raised a search crew from her grandmomma's church. We put up flyers and started asking questions and searching that city, one alley, abandoned home, and Dumpster at a time. Then we stretched the search to the banks of the Cape Fear River, with me thinking if she had gotten in that river, she was gone. Turns out one of the hookers got the word, some guy told her about some girl locked up in a room, said it wasn't right doing little girls like that. Turns out it was an uncle who had her. I don't even want to count how many times it's some uncle doing these things. He had her in a house three blocks away. Another crack house, another uncle, another girl. You know the story. She was alive at least, but she was broken way past where anything could mend. I see a lot of this.

It's a calling, really, what I do. The way some folks are called to the church. When someone goes missing, people do a lot of praying, and being from Suck Creek, I know a lot about praying and sitting around and more praying when something needs to be done. And, well, that bothers me. All that *she's in God's hands* and comforting talk and a whole lot of *it'll be all rights*. There's lots of times it won't be all right. It'll be hell, and my job is to get folks through it.

But don't get me wrong, I think praying is a good thing. It's a start. It gives some kind of comfort and a little bit of hope. But like my momma used to say, "You gotta put feet on your prayers if you want something done." She said that was what Miss Young believed. And any woman who can knock two Suck Creek rednecks back from beating a boy, she's got strength. When Momma packed me off to live here, she said, "You gotta get your prayers moving across the ground, Shelby Waters. You gotta set your prayers in motion instead of just letting them go floating out there in the air."

I started my search for Keisha by raising money from the church where she went, then other churches, then just people. In time I started something that would make my momma, daddy, and Lillian Young proud. REV, I call it. Rescue Effort Volunteers. While lots around here are all about saving souls, I'd say my calling is saving lives, lives of the missing and the lives of those who get left behind. I've led those gatherings of searchers through fields, armed with guns, sticks, shovels, any kind of protection against the snakes that wait in weeds, the alligators lurking in marshes, where somewhere in miles of fields and woods and rivers and lakes a body can be found.

I always know when we'll find them. My eyes tear up like from a chemical burn, my stomach heaves, and my head gets all thick and swimmy, like my whole body is saying it doesn't want to see. But I push on through the bad feelings, keep walking, keep using my stick to push back the weeds. And then: remains, skin matted with leaves baked by the sun to the bones, ribs riddled with spiders, beetles, centipedes. And there's the shirt sometimes clinging, a watch, a ring, a shoe.

I step in between the police reports and camera crews when a family discovers a loved one is lost. I see what most don't, the story behind statistics and the news. I've seen the mother vomiting in a hotel room in the city where her daughter was last seen alive. I've seen the father who cried because he lost a flashlight while looking for the body of his son at the county dump. He was a big man, collapsed on a pile of cinder block. He sobbed the words, "I just had it in my hands. I just had it." I found his flashlight, gave him a bottle of cold water to soothe him a little. Kept moving on.

I'm trying to tell you the story, but to give you the story would be like giving you the churning blue sea one bucket at a time. You might taste the salt, feel the cold, but the weight and wave of so much water, well, it's lost.

Like Katy.

Like the woman who once walked on that leg hacked off and tossed to rot in a stream.

Bodies.

Joggers find them in the bushes by well-traveled roads.

Bodies are tossed in ditches, woods, and fields. Some are left in Dumpsters in back alleys. Some are dropped in rivers and lakes, like fish caught, thrown back, not worth keeping. Floaters, they call them, when bodies fill with gases and rise to the surface of the dark water that consumed them. Something inside stirs, expands, causes them to rise.

A parent always knows whether the child is just missing or is truly gone. And I can read it in the lines of their faces, the shadows, those sad, sad shadows in their eyes. But when I met Katy's momma, I wasn't so sure. I could see the sorrow of a child gone, but I could also see the life that comes with love, living love, hanging on. Which is another story. She's from Suck Creek too. You gotta pay attention when you run to the end of the earth to get away from Suck Creek and a little piece of Suck Creek comes drifting up, swirling around your feet. I mean that was the feeling I had when I met Olivia Baines. I kind of recognized the accent and got to asking questions. And when she said she was from Suck Creek, I got this swimmy feeling, like it was pulling me back. So of course I felt the calling, said I'd do everything in my power to find her girl.

I picked the picture for Katy's flyer, went through all those photos her fiancé had, picked the one of her smiling with this big, happy, tennis-pro kind of smile, thick dark hair unfurling in a breeze. She was looking at her fiancé, who held the camera. She was looking like a woman who had no idea just how beautiful she was. She was looking like a woman in love. And it took me back to my sister, Darly, who had that same kind of smile and wavy long hair. I wanted the whole town to fall in love with Katy Connor, to work to find her. Strangers gathered weekly for the search. Church groups, bikers, even some of the homeless climbed on the bus to help.

Katy Connor thought she was safe. She was supposed to be safe at three o'clock in the afternoon in the parking lot of a strip mall on one of the busiest streets in town. She did nothing wrong. She bought a bag of clothes and walked to her truck.

It can happen like that.

You think you're going home. And some picture of your face ends up on a grainy black-and-white flyer tacked to a phone pole. Your image fades in sunlight. The thin paper sign of you tatters, fluttering in the breeze. Strangers pass by, study your face for something

9

familiar, think maybe they've seen you somewhere. But they haven't. You are a stranger. You are lost.

Loved ones can find themselves composing you on a MISSING sign like this:

```
          MISSING
 from Wilmington, North Carolina:
    Katherine (Katy) Connor.
        5'10", 130 lbs.
   Blue eyes. Long brown hair.
 Tattoo of a cross on her shoulder.
Last seen on June 22 at the Dollar Daze
store in Briarfield Plaza. Her blue Chevy truck
with Tennessee plates found 50 miles west of
    Wilmington in Columbus County.
If you have any information, please . . .
```

Long ago they tattooed members of nomadic tribes to identify the body in case of death; the missing could be returned to the family for proper burial, to put the soul to rest. The system often worked, depending on time and the ways of weather.

Today they use a more reliable system of dental records.

But people will always go missing and prayers unanswered. Lost souls go wandering. We all know this, and bodies are calling to be found.

You could say this is a ghost story in some way. A crime story. A classic kind of tale. Biblical almost, but not quite.

Katy didn't know that day would be a story. Katy didn't know Jesse Hollowfield was watching for his chance. She didn't know that at any moment the continental plates miles underground can shift, the earth crack apart, an unseen hand reach, grip, throttle the street, sending it all tilting as someone gasps, someone screams, maybe, if there's time to comprehend the darkness reaching up, maybe to yank a whole world down. No one is ready for it when something snaps, eclipses the sweet blue world. And no one stays the same after a thing like that.

It can happen, I tell you. Like this:

You Believers

Jesse Hollowfield and Mike Carter knew which cars had automatic locks. They sat waiting just behind the strip mall, patient as lions hunkered in the reeds, heads raised to sniff the humid air while watching gazelles herd, looking for the weak, the young, the one alone. The Datsun's engine was running because when they shut it off, half the time the engine wouldn't fire again, and it was hell to roll-start a car in the North Carolina flatlands when the sun can break your back with the heat.

Katy didn't see them—she had a things-to-do list in her purse: gas station, the library to drop off books, the drug store to pick up birth-control pills. She had left a note for her fiancé on the refrigerator door: "Be back when I can." But driving by the strip mall, she saw the Dollar Daze sign and got the impulse to buy something new for her trip back home. She pulled into the side lot, where the sun wasn't directly bearing down.

Jesse gave a nod. "Check it out. That chick parked between the Dumpster and the ATM. That truck, what year is that thing? Looks old, but listen to that engine."

Mike watched the truck. The girl was bobbing her head a little, like she was singing. Mike leaned a little out his window, heard the sounds of a Bob Marley song coming from her truck. She had to be happy listening to that song. He said, "Maybe we don't want an old truck. We need a good truck."

Jesse shoved Mike's shoulder. "Listen to that engine. It's tuned. Somebody takes care of that thing." He nodded, whispered, "She'll ride all right."

Katy sat in the truck, moving to the beat. Bob Marley's music always made her think of beaches and beer.

"Come on," Jesse whispered. "Get out of the fucking truck."

Katy turned off the engine and stepped out into the sun.

Careless, Jesse thought as she dropped the keys into her unzipped purse, dangling loosely from her arm. He leaned forward, his back straight, jaw tight, eyes fixed on the woman with nothing on her mind but where she thought she was going to go. He guessed her weight: 125-130. Tall but skinny. He'd take her truck and anything she had in that piece-of-shit fake-leather shoulder bag.

Katy walked toward the store, hoping to find something cute in the racks of five-dollar tops and twenty-dollar jeans. She didn't have much cash, and her card was maxed out. But she wanted to look good for her trip. She wanted her mom to know she was doing something more than tending bar these days. She'd tell her she was learning how to hang wallpaper; she was practically an interior decorator. Her mother would want to talk about wedding plans. She would want to look at Katy's hand, touch the engagement ring as if she needed to see it was still there, proof that yes, Katy was finally settling down.

Katy stopped, stood still in the heat. She'd be married in a month. To Billy. She was leaving the one she still wanted, Frank, behind. But she didn't want to settle. And there was the new guy, Randy— Randy, who made her laugh; Randy, who'd get her high for free anytime she wanted. Randy had told her, "Sure, you go on and get married, but you and me both know you'll never really settle down. You'll always come running to Randy when you get those little bad-girl needs." No one knew anything about Randy. Billy thought his only problem was Frank back in Chattanooga. He suspected that when she went back home, it was more about seeing Frank than her mom.

"Let me take this one last trip," she'd told Billy. She would party with old friends at the marina on Lake Chickamauga, the way they always did when she returned home. Frank would be there. "I need one more trip," she had said. "One more trip back home, alone. I miss my mom."

Billy had told her she could go, but he had a bad feeling.

"What?" she'd said. "Tell me your feeling; go on and say it."

Billy had lit a joint, said, "Frank." He'd looked straight at her. "I can tell when you're lying, Katy." Then he'd left her standing in the kitchen while he'd gone on to work with a joint in his hand. Just another fight, she'd told herself. She'd take a drive, let it go. She'd make lasagna for him when she got home. He liked it when she took the time to make a real meal. He called them good-wife meals, and he'd tease her, say he saw past her wild streak, saw the happy, peaceful, good wife she wanted to be. And he was right. Maybe. She hoped he was right.

She stared at the pavement and knew Billy had a right to be jealous. She knew she hurt him, but she just couldn't resist the need sometimes to break a rule. To be a little bad. It gave her a rush, like leaping off a high dive. "I'm sorry," she said out loud. She'd told Billy that a hundred times: "I'm sorry" for something; then she'd go on and keep doing what she wanted to do. She looked to the pavement and saw that her toenail was chipped; she'd get a pedicure before heading to Randy's house. He noticed things like ragged nails. Billy didn't give a shit, but Randy—and her mother—did. She looked up, saw the clerk watching her from the window. Katy smiled, gave a little wave, and went in.

Shuffling through the racks of clothes inside, she kept thinking she shouldn't spend the money. They couldn't afford it. "I don't know, I don't know," she muttered to herself as she rifled through hangers holding tops and skirts.

Then the clerk was suddenly beside her, said, "Can I help you?"

Katy jumped. "I don't know," she said. Then she looked at the woman, smiled, reached and squeezed the woman's shoulder. "I'm sorry. It's just I'm going a little nuts. I'm about to get married and all. Prewedding jitters, I guess."

The clerk nodded and said Katy had a pretty ring.

"It was his grandmother's," Katy said. "The diamond's not that big, but I like the little designs in the gold."

"You buying stuff for your honeymoon?"

Katy shook her head and moved hangers across the rack. "Taking a little trip back home. I like it here, but sometimes I feel like Dorothy, want to click my heels, close my eyes, and go home. But then once I'm back there, I know I won't like it. I'll know I should be back here. No matter where I am, seems I always want to be someplace else." Katy looked up and sighed. "Know what I mean?"

The clerk, a sweet-looking older woman, smiled and said, "Tell me about it." The clerk offered a little white top. "This will look great with your tan."

Katy took the top. It was cute, cut to show off her shoulders. "I just don't know if I'm the marrying kind."

"Oh, you poor young girls," the clerk said. "You just have too many choices these days."

"You sound like my mom," Katy said.

"I don't mean to lecture," the clerk said. "It just seems to me these days there aren't any rules."

Jesse studied her truck. The Tennessee license plate said, "POSI-TIV." Optimistic was good. They went along easy. And it could take days before her truck got into the system back in Tennessee. Perfect. He laughed and sang in a monotone, "Over the river and through the woods . . ."

Mike lit a cigarette. "You one crazy motherfucker, man."

Jesse waved a hundred-dollar bill and motioned to Mike to move the car closer. "Now, you keep your mouth shut. If she asks, you look stupid, say we just gotta take the car to your granny's house. Now move."

Mike's hands trembled as he gripped the wheel. "Why's it got to be my granny?"

Jesse leaned forward, his eyes on the store. "Come on, we've got a job to do."

Mike nodded. He was the driver. He told himself that no matter what came of this, he was just the driver. They needed her truck to hit the pawnshop. Get guns, get cash from Jesse's friend Zeke. Then Jesse could skip town and run back to Atlanta the way he always said he'd do, and Mike would have some cash to buy groceries for his granny, maybe fix his car, score some more weed. "A simple plan, man," Jesse had said. But Jesse was always saying, *A simple plan, man.* Jesse made it all sound easy and clean. Mike knew him from juvy. Mike knew Jesse had been behind that dude in the laundry getting stabbed to death with a laundry pin. The guy was always wanting to suck somebody off for cash. But when he hit on Jesse, he hit on the wrong man. When the word got out about some fucker—even a fag—dying like that, stabbed two hundred times with a laundry pin, people said, "Man, that's fucked up, even in here." Jesse just shrugged, said, "Everything got a reason, man." Mike wished he could be like Jesse, all fire and wires and sparks inside. But cool somehow, like the cool blue of a gas flame.

16

Jesse laid the hundred-dollar bill on the dash, stretched his arms, and cracked his knuckles. With batting gloves stretched tight and smooth on his hands, he looked like he could be ready to knock a fastball out of the park.

Mike watched the glass door of the store. It didn't seem right to use his granny like bait. Jesse had said he wouldn't hurt whoever they hit, but Mike knew Jesse's need to hurt whatever he held in his hands. Except dogs—he had a thing about dogs. And kids. Little kids. Mike hoped maybe that girl inside would be lucky, have a dog in her truck. Jesse wouldn't go after a girl with a dog there beside her. Mike looked toward the truck. Then he got to wondering if the truck color was called sky blue or robin's-egg blue. He'd always liked that color on a truck. He felt Jesse staring at the side of his face. Jesse had a look that really could burn. "How do you do that, man?"

Jesse dropped back and leaned against the passenger door. "What?"

"That thing you do with your eyes."

Jesse smiled. "Told you, man. I'm the devil. Don't know why folks have such trouble believing a thing like that. They'll believe just about anything but that." In one quick move, he popped the glove box, reached under the papers, and pulled out a bag with a couple of tight little joints rolled and some loose weed. He looked Mike in the eye. "I knew you were stoned, you fucker. You get all paranoid and fucked up when you smoke. I told you, lay off this shit till the job's done."

"I don't get paranoid. I just think about things." Mike watched the storefront while Jesse shoved the weed in the pocket of his jeans.

"Here she comes," Mike said as Katy walked out of the shop. She slipped her sunglasses on.

Jesse watched her, thinking, *Ignorant, not looking where she's going, too busy digging for keys. Not seeing a damned thing.*

Jesse grabbed the hundred-dollar bill. "Amazing what some folks will do for a buck."

Katy stood outside the store, happy with what she'd bought: the little white top, a bra and panties, and a short black skirt that would show off her legs. Randy always said her legs were her best part— well, not her best part. Then he'd laugh. Katy looked back toward the store, saw the clerk standing there watching, thinking Katy was some kind of criminal or nut just because she'd wanted to use the restroom to change into the new underwear. The woman had backed off, looked at her like she was some kind of whore, said, "What kind of woman needs to change her bra and panties in a store?" Katy had just said, "Never mind," and figured she'd change at the McDonald's down the road. She knew Randy would like the matching black lace bra and panties. Randy liked it when she took extra care to dress for him. He liked most everything she did, except taking something without asking. Once it was just a cigarette from his pack on the table. And then the shirt. He'd been really pissed about her taking it when she'd left his house that night. But he was asleep, and there was a cool rain falling, and she needed something over her tank top. So she just picked up his shirt from the floor. She told him she'd return it, and he said that wasn't the point. Now it was in the truck, just picked up from the cleaners because it was a Brooks Brothers. She'd take it back, and she'd surprise him with a nice clean shirt and new black lace underwear. The clerk came out of the store, said, "Miss, why are you standing here?"

Katy laughed. "Ma'am, I'm just standing here thinking about a man. Don't you remember just standing and thinking about a man?"

"Well, I'd be more comfortable if you did your thinking some-place else." Then she gave Katy a look that meant nothing but busi-ness and went back inside.

Katy laughed and headed for her truck. She hoped Billy would work late. She'd need the time to get to Randy's, the grocery store, then home to clean up and make that lasagna and run him a bath that would make him forget they'd ever had a fight. The good wife. She'd make him the good-wife meal. Just like her mother. But she didn't want her mother's life. So what the hell was she doing?

She got in the truck, found her keys, and wished she had her cell phone. If she had her phone, she'd call Randy to say she was coming, and then maybe she'd call Billy to tell him she was making the lasagna he liked. She knew it was messed up. She looked at the keys in her hand, realized she was sitting there in a sweat, an idiot in a truck, baking in the heat.

Katy flinched when Jesse opened the passenger door and jumped in.

He tossed the hundred-dollar bill in her lap and smiled. "Mind giving me a ride?"

"What?" The plastic bag of clothes crumpled to her feet.

"I need you to follow that car. It's kind of an emergency, and taxis won't run to where we need to go."

She studied his face. Good-looking and smooth. "You're sitting on my boyfriend's shirt."

He lifted the shirt, smoothed it across his lap. "Sorry," he said. Then he smiled a smile that was just a little bit devilish. "Come on." He gave a little shrug like a boy. "It's just a little drive." Yeah, he was cute, and he knew it.

She glanced back at the white Datsun rumbling behind the Dumpster. The driver looked like a kid, soft round face, big dark eyes staring at the man beside her.

"Come on," he said. She turned and looked into his eyes, green flecked with black and looking straight at her. She'd always had a thing for green eyes. She tried to guess his age, early twenties, she figured, younger than she was, but worn. He was hard-looking, like

19

a man who didn't eat enough real meals, a man who worked out in a basement. He had a scar on his cheekbone, a little crescent shape. But what a mouth, pretty lips that curved in just the right places. The kind of mouth that knew just how to kiss. Pushy but firm and soft.

He smiled, leaned a little closer. "Yeah, I know. You like my face. I get that." He picked up the hundred-dollar bill. "But I'm not looking for a date right now. I just need you to follow that car." She liked the smell of him, clean but that man smell underneath.

"Why should I follow that car?" she asked. Katy had tended bar for years. She was used to guys wanting things. Asking questions was the best way she knew to make them stall. Men, no matter what they were after, always liked a little time to talk.

"Why?" The bill dropped into her lap, and he eased back into the seat beside her. "Don't you need the money?"

"Well, sure, but—"

"Well, sure. Yes, you need the money. The thing is, my friend there, his name is Ronald, and I'm Brad." He offered to shake her hand, and she almost took it, but she kept her hands on the steering wheel. "Okay, then, I understand your caution, some strange dude jumping in your truck—"

She laughed. "Well, yeah."

He smiled. "You see my friend there, Ronald, he's a little nervous. His granny, she's sick, and she lives way out there in Whitwell. Out by Lake Waccamaw."

Then she grinned, sat up, looked around. "Is this a joke? Where's Randy?"

"I don't know no Randy," Jesse said. "What you talking about?"

"Randy. My friend. He likes to play little tricks on me. He lives out by Lake Waccamaw. I drive out there sometimes."

"That's nice," Jesse said. "It's real pretty country out there, isn't it?"

She nodded. "Yeah, there's something pure out there. No tourists. Just trees and water and sky."

"And Randy," he said. "But I guess you just drive out there for the nature and all."

She turned to him. "Look, I'd like to help you out, but I gotta get home."

Jesse shook his head and leaned closer. There was a softness to him, but a confidence. She liked that soft confidence in a man. She breathed that scent of him. He definitely knew what he had. He sat back and looked out her windshield as if this were just another conversation. "You got a chance to do something good here. I saw your license plate—positiv.' You like to think positive, right?"

"I try," Katy said.

"You like to do good things, right?"

She nodded, looked back at the other guy in the car.

Jesse sighed. "Well, Ronald's granny, she's sick, and he's got these groceries in his trunk, and he's gotta get the stuff to her, and if he makes it there, he can get a neighbor to work on the car." He nodded, rocking in the seat beside her. "See, she's waiting, and we've got these groceries in the trunk, and it's a long ways out there through farm country. And that car, it's always stalling out, and you got no idea how bad that can be in this heat."

It sounded like a good story, but there was something off. "I need to get home," she said. "My fiancé—"

"What about Randy? Nah, Randy isn't your fiancé." He said the word mean and teasing. He lifted the hundred-dollar bill and held it to her face. "For your gas and trouble. It's just forty-five minutes from here. But then, you know that 'cause Randy lives out there, and you like to drive out and see him."

She studied her hands on the steering wheel. The engagement ring shone in the sunlight. Something was wrong. This felt like a joke. It had to be a joke. Maybe it was Billy's joke. Maybe Billy had found out about Randy. Maybe Billy somehow knew where Randy lived. "Is this a joke?"

"Nah, man," Jesse said. "This is serious. Listen to that car of his."

She listened to the chugging, staggering sound of the engine. "I'm sure it's something simple," she said. "You can just pull up there to a station. You could use some of that hundred dollars to fix his car."

He smiled again as if he were telling her a joke she just didn't understand. "Not when we can get it fixed for free. And besides, I can't keep track of the money he owes me." He opened his palms in a little helpless gesture. She studied that hundred-dollar bill. "It's the principle of the thing," he said.

"I mean why would I want to drive out to Lake Waccamaw?" she said. It was just too strange that Lake Waccamaw was exactly where she was heading as soon as she changed into that new underwear. He waved the money again, then shrugged, made a move to get out of the truck. But he didn't leave. He paused, looked back at her.

She reached for her purse. It lay open between them.

"Look," he said, "nothing funny is going on here. We just need you to go along in case the car dies. We can fix the car for nothing if we get out there. Ronald's granny, she's waiting, and if we don't hurry, that milk in the trunk is gonna turn. I need a ride, that's all." He dropped the hundred dollars into her purse, zipped it tight, and tossed the purse into her lap. "There and back," he said. "And tonight you and your fiancé, or Randy, can go have a steak dinner on me."

"I don't eat steak," she said.

"Tofu, then." He smiled. "Go have twenty tofu-bean-sprout suppers on me."

He was really good-looking when he smiled. Like some rock star. Flashing eyes, sandy hair that fell in his face. He had country-boy good looks, the kind of face that promised wild rides in fast cars though green hills. Definitely the type she liked. "Come on," he said softly. "My friend over there, his granny's waiting, and she doesn't have a phone. All you gotta do is start the engine and pull out, follow that car."

She clutched her keys and took in his clothes, Polo shirt, good jeans, Nikes that looked brand-new. At least he had good clothes. And he was polite for a guy who'd jumped into her truck. She sat back. It was a risk. But it would make a great story to tell her friends. And Randy, he'd love it that she'd taken such a risk and made money doing it.

"A hundred bucks. How else you gonna make a hundred bucks so fast?"

"All right," she said. "There and back."

"There and back." He laughed.

She started the engine, glanced over and saw the nod he gave the other guy, not happy but intent. She wished she could call Billy, tell him where she was. If she could call Billy, she wouldn't go to Randy's. If she could call Billy, she'd get rid of this guy and head straight home.

Katy backed out and pulled in behind the Datsun. Jesse cracked his knuckles and sighed. She saw the batting gloves. She mashed the brakes, kept her eyes on her hands gripping the steering wheel.

"What's wrong?"

"Why are you wearing those gloves?"

He opened his hands. "Yeah, not exactly sexy, right?"

She nodded, watched his face for a lie. He glanced at her, embarrassed. "I've got this skin condition. My palms sweat, get these bumps that open up." He gave a little shake of his head. "Not pretty, kinda like poison oak. I have to keep hydrocortisone cream on when it acts up. Keep a bandage on them. These gloves, they protect the sores."

"That's awful," she said.

He shrugged, put his hands on his thighs. "It's all right. It clears up. Just flares up with the heat." He smiled. "Now you know my secret weakness. What's yours?"

She felt herself blushing, shook her head.

He gave a little laugh. "That's all right. I can guess what your weakness is."

She smiled at him, liked that little secret game of flirting, not flirting, just working that line between yes and no. It wasn't her way of mixing drinks that made her the best bartender in town, it was her way of mixing up the men, keeping them guessing. She looked away from him. "You think you know who I am?"

"Yep." He settled back, buckled his seat belt. "Don't you buckle up for a ride? You really ought to."

Katy reached for her belt. "My mom made me have these installed. It's an old truck."

"I know," he said. "We'd all be better off if we listened to our mommas more often."

"Yeah," she said. She started to press the gas, waited.

"But mommas aren't right about everything, are they?"

"No," she said. Her momma had never approved of any guy she'd ever dated. What did she want? For Katy to marry some professor like her dad?

He nodded, looked ahead as if they were already moving. "You got to trust me on this." He reached out the window and motioned for the guy in the Datsun to move on.

"Trust you?" She laughed and pressed the gas and followed the car into traffic on the highway that would soon have them all heading out of town. She had a sick feeling in her stomach, knew what she was doing was dangerous. But she'd done dangerous before. Frank had pushed her into doing things way past anything like safety. And Randy, hell, Randy was nothing but a risk. But she liked to take risks, liked that jangling feeling in her belly and something sparking behind her eyes.

She told herself not to panic, just the way she told herself not to panic when her daddy played his hunting games with guns. They lived in the country, so nobody really worried about guns going off. Boys were often out shooting cans off logs, road signs, possums. Her daddy was just another one of those boys grown up. He would sit at the open window of what he called his office but was really his gunroom. He'd keep his eye on the garbage cans out back, just waiting for the scent to draw some roaming dog. He hated those dogs getting in his trash, making a mess in his yard. Then he got to where he liked to play a shooting game to keep them away. He'd call Katy in to test her. "Let's play a little game. I can shoot that dog there or let it go. What do you want? If he gets in the garbage, it's your job to clean it up. Or I could just shoot him. What do you say?"

Sometimes he was just testing her. He would show her sometimes that there were no bullets in the gun. He was teasing. "Let's see how much my tough little Katy can stand." But lots of times he did shoot. Sometimes the dog yelped and ran off. Sometimes it dropped to the ground. "If you cry, I'll shoot." She'd stand frozen beside him. Katy learned to chew her lip until it was bloody, but in time she learned not to make a sound.

Katy glanced at Jesse, sitting easily and looking out the window as if he were just a guy on a road trip. She told herself she'd been through much bigger dangers than this. She was a bartender, had walked to her car in the back alley hundreds of times, had talked guys out of raping her more times than she could count. The key was to make yourself human—she'd read that in a psychology class.

It had worked once when her car had broken down and she'd hitched a ride with a man who kept saying it'd be easy to rape her, leave her, and be long gone before she told. She looked him in the eye and said, "You won't do that." She told him she was on the way to the hospital, where her daddy was dying from a tumor in his head. She made the facts of her daddy's suffering real in the air. And the guy believed her. He went silent and drove. He dropped her off at the hospital door and sped off before she thought to check his license plate. She was amazed. She had spun a story of her daddy's pain to save herself when her daddy was already dead. He would have been proud of her lying like that to get to the hospital instead of ending up somewhere getting raped.

Crossing through downtown, she looked up and saw the Cape Fear River bridge. Once she crossed that bridge, she'd be in farm country. There'd be hardly anyone around. Randy would laugh at the risk she was taking. And Frank, he'd just say it was one of Katy's new adventures. Even Billy would like the cash. But her mother would be furious.

"My mother," she said thinking her mother could never hear about this.

"What about your mother?"

"Nothing," she said. "My mother," Katy said again, looking out at the suspension bridge she was about to cross. "My mother hates driving over bridges. She's a nervous type, that's all."

He laughed. "And look at you. You're not nervous at all."

Katy headed up the ramp to the bridge over the Cape Fear River and saw the dark water swirling below. She'd heard stories of all those guys thinking they could swim the river. They got caught in the crosscurrents of the river rolling out and the tidewaters of the sea rushing in. The churning force pulled them down in the river, so dark it was almost black with tannins from the vegetation that rotted on its shores. People drowned all the time in the current that whirled like a wheel. They got disoriented, couldn't see which way was up, the water so thick and dark it sucked away all light.

As the truck surged forward, the bridge seemed to shudder, but it was her own shaking inside. Her stomach clenched, and a flash of fear shot up her spine. She saw his hands now clenched in his lap while his face looked so easy and mild. She'd seen that expression of a man about to explode: face calm, body tensed. And that look just before they grabbed a beer bottle and broke it over someone's head. And she knew it. This was bad. This was stupid.

Slowly she reached under the seat for the little pocketknife she kept there, but all she'd ever used it for was to cut apples and cheese. She tried to slip it under her thigh to be ready. Maybe this was really bad.

Jesse saw the move, reached across, snapped up her wrist, and squeezed. The truck veered into oncoming traffic, and she pulled back into her lane. A car horn blared; the driver gave her the finger and rushed by.

He took the knife, put it in his pocket, and laughed. "What do you think you're doing, girl? You could've killed us back there."

"I'll give you the truck," she said.

"Really," he said with a teasing little sound.

"You can have it. I won't call the cops. You drive to his granny's house. Once we get across the river, just let me out. I'll walk home."

He smiled. "Now, why would I make you do something like that? You'll get home later."

Billy would be furious. "My fiancé, he'll be wondering where I am. He doesn't like it when I'm late coming in."

"Your fiancé." He shook his head. "And what about Randy? Girl, I'm sitting in your truck and see you got Bob Marley, Lou Reed, Tom Petty, Stones, all that old rock-and-roll shit. Don't sit there and tell me you take this fiancé shit serious." He looked her up and down and laughed. " Damn, girl, I'm betting you got two guys on the side. Don't you?"

She stared ahead at the highway unrolling, wished she hadn't stopped to buy some stupid skirt for Frank and that damned underwear for Randy. Maybe if that lady had let her change in the restroom, this guy would have jumped into someone else's car.

He was nudging her. "You get it on the side, don't you? Don't you?"

She gave a nod, eyes still on the road.

Jesse slapped her shoulder as if they were old friends. "Women. You got all the power, man. Don't give a shit about nothing but a man between your legs. My momma, my blood momma, she was like that."

Katy gripped the wheel harder, thought of yanking the car off the road, but there was nowhere to go. She glanced his way but couldn't meet his eyes. "You're not going to hurt me," she said.

"Hell, no. You can drop me off and go see Randy." He laughed, popped open the glove box. "Let's see what other music you have." He rummaged through a couple of CDs and, as if he'd known it would be there, grabbed the bag of pot. "Jackpot!"

She reached for his hand. "That's my fiancé's."

"Right," he said. "The bad shit we got always belongs to someone else." He found the papers, started rolling. "I'd say we could use a little something to relax," he said. "I knew you were into this. Smelled it the minute I got in your truck." He reached in her purse, took her lighter, and lit up.

She felt a tear slip down her face, wiped it with the back of her hand.

"Ah, don't worry, girl. It's not what you think. We've just got a little thing to do here."

She heard the hissing sound when he inhaled. She squeezed the steering wheel as they descended from the bridge. Back on solid ground she felt she'd left the world she knew behind. It was happening. Her mother had warned her: "You only think you're in control, Katy. With every little reckless thing you do . . ." Katy couldn't remember the rest of the warning. But somewhere inside she'd always known something like this would happen one day. She was Dorothy suddenly lifted by a furious wind spinning her to a terrifying new place where good really did battle evil, where a rebellious girl's only desire was to go home.

When Katy was a girl, she believed in Oz. The first time she saw the movie, she was five years old. On the overstuffed green sofa she leaned into her daddy's side, ate popcorn, and sipped Coke. She sat transfixed when the black tornado rolled across the prairie and snatched up Dorothy's house, sent it spinning in a world flying by with cows mooing, chickens flapping, the mean old lady furiously pedaling her bicycle as if anyone could really outrun a storm.

During the commercial she asked her daddy if a tornado really could lift her off to another land. "Most definitely," he said.

She asked, "Do we have tornadoes in Tennessee?"

"Sometimes," he said, "but you don't have to worry about that. Our house is made of brick. Remember the wolf? He huffed and puffed and couldn't blow the brick house down."

Katy glanced at the man beside her, now looking at the CDs she kept between the seats.

"Cool; this old truck's got a player."

"I had it installed. This was my daddy's truck."

But he wasn't listening. "You got lots of Marley." He turned on the accent. "You like da ganja, lady. I got good ganja for you." He held the joint out to her.

"I don't want any pot," she said. "I just want to get home."

He was studying a CD cover. "Yeah, Bob Marley, he's cool. Black folks, white folks, all kinds of folks dig Bob." He tossed the CD to the floor and looked out the window. She realized Randy's shirt was down on the floor. But she didn't say anything. He was watching her every move, and when he caught her eye, he just grinned. "You believe that Rasta shit 'bout Haile Selassie? I've got these black friends I do some dealing with. They talk about Selassie like he was some kind of a god."

She'd heard that. Most people didn't know about the Haile Selassie connection. Most thought Rasta was just a smoke-dope-grow-dreadlocks kind of thing. "I'm not sure they think he's a god," Katy said. "More like a messenger, I think. But don't real Rastas see a little bit of God in everything?"

Jesse laughed, his shoulders rocking as he watched the land go by. "Yeah, a messenger. I'm a messenger. Them Rasta dudes get high enough, I bet they see a little bit of God in me." He turned, gave her that soft grin she'd seen when he'd first slipped into her truck. "What I mean is, we can all be messengers. We all got something the world needs to hear."

"Yes," she said, looking at the clock. She'd be home by dinnertime. *Positive,* she thought, *think positive. The Lord didn't give us a spirit of fear, but one of power and love and soundness of mind.* It was scripture. Her mother kept it framed by her bedside table. Nice calligraphy, with a rose drawn in one corner. It was a pretty thing to wake up to, Katy guessed.

She thought of Dorothy, closing her eyes, petting little Toto, whispering, *There's no place like home.* Yes, positive. They would take her truck and leave her, and she'd find her way to Randy's house. He was always trying to get her to do reckless things, like take a plane to Vegas with him, Cancun. He lived the good life, all right. He called her a coward, teased her about being a good wife, said if she really had the nerve she liked to think she did, she'd say to hell with the good-wife thing. Maybe this guy jumping in her truck and asking her to take him out by Lake Waccamaw was a sign that Lake Waccamaw was where she was supposed to be. But she couldn't shake the feeling that this guy was dangerous. Anyone could be dangerous. She glanced at him, tried to sound casual. "How about we stop somewhere for a six-pack? I could use a cold beer. Make it like a road trip."

He laughed. "Drinking and driving. Don't you know that's against the law?" He smiled and waved the joint toward her. "Nah, we got this. You take me where I'm going, we'll burn this together. Just you and me. Let Mike go tend his granny. You and me, we'll do some shit. Then like Marley says, 'Every little thing is gonna be all right.'"

"Mike? Who's Mike?"

He looked at her. "Ronald Mike," he said. "That's his name. He likes to be called Mike, but I call him Ronald just to give him shit." He kept his eyes on her. "Relax, girl. You're going to Lake Waccamaw. You like the land out there. You like Randy. Now, why is it you really drive out there? Oh, yeah, the land, the lake, the sky, that's right."

"I do," she said. "I love the easy pace. Yeah, I do like the land and lake and sky. I like to get away from the tourists. I like it where people know how to sit back, have a drink without sinning, look at the land and relax."

"Is that what you want? A drink without sinning and relax? You're just like all those other tourists."

"No, I'm not," she said. "You don't know me."

"Yeah, I do," he said.

He looked at her, grinning. A guy with that kind of smile couldn't be too mean, could he? No, he was just a little scary. "So you from here?" she asked.

He shook his head and stared out at the Datsun ahead of them.

"So where are you from?" she said again.

"Where am I from?" he said. "Let's just call it burned bridges. You can understand that."

Billy believed in burned bridges, said that was the only way you moved forward. He told her, "You've got to burn the past, leave it all behind." He was talking about her daddy. But what he was really talking about was Frank. Billy was teaching her how to leave the past behind. If she could just choose him. Poor Billy didn't have a clue about Randy. Billy didn't have any idea he'd probably be one more burned bridge she left behind in time. "Billy," she said. "My fiancé—I can tell you don't like that word, but he likes to leave burning bridges behind too."

He yelled, "I don't give a damn about Billy, or Randy, or you, lady. I just want you to stay close behind that car and drive."

She braked and pulled to the side of the road. "I'm not going any farther," she said. "This doesn't feel right. I've got other things to do."

Jesse mashed the joint out on the dashboard. His eyes went dark. He turned, reached behind his back, then raised a gun between them. "Damn right you got things to do." He poked the barrel of the gun into her ribs, but his face was casual, almost smiling. "We need your truck, you see. We need you to follow us to Whitwell. That's all. You got that?"

She sat tight and trembling. Her body felt frozen. How could she move without cracking, without breaking to pieces all over the seat? She could feel the heat of his breath between them. She caught the scent of oil and metal. Katy sat back in her seat, tried to catch up with her breathing, which seemed to take off, running out ahead of her. She told herself to stay calm. "I don't want to," she said.

"You don't have a choice." He looked straight at her, and she saw a face she hadn't seen back in the parking lot of the mall. His eyes, empty. She thought of the alligators that sunned themselves in swamps around Lake Waccamaw, still as logs on the water, dull eyes focused on the surface, patient, blending quietly into the landscape, certain what they wanted would come within reach in time. Billy had told her to be careful walking around Lake Waccamaw. More than one hunter had been taken down by a gator waiting in the reeds. Poor Billy; he thought she just drove out there for the lake. He didn't know about the man named Randy, whom she'd met when she'd been bartender for a wedding at some rich man's house out there. Randy was handing out coke to the wedding party. He slipped her a tiny bag for a tip. "Just a taste," he said. "One little taste, and you won't want to quit." Then he grinned and said, "I'm not talking about the coke, darlin'. I'm talking about me."

Jesse nudged her lightly, as if they were old friends and she'd just lost the conversation.

"Please," he said. "How's that? Please? I promise I'm not going to shoot you. That isn't what this gun is about. Come on, we gotta stay behind Mike there. Get going and you can tell me all about your fiancé."

"I don't want to talk about my fiancé."

He touched her arm lightly. "Look here. I apologize for my brutish behavior. All right? My momma, she brought me up better than that. She's done a lot of work to teach me manners. I just slip now and then. You know how that is. Don't tell me you've never slipped." He gave her a smile again, as if they shared a secret. "Now, come on. We're halfway there. Put me out and I'm taking back that hundred-dollar bill. I know you need the cash."

Katy looked out and saw the Datsun stopped ahead. "I don't like it, but I'll do it," she said.

"Well, neither do I," he said. He sat back, more natural, relaxed. "You think I like having to take care of his ol' granny? You think I don't have better things do to with my day?"

33

He stared ahead, and they sat like two lovers worn out from a fight, caught in the lull of silence. A car rushed by on the highway, disappeared in the distance and left Katy behind. Tears ran from her eyes.

"Relax," he said. "I'm really not gonna shoot you. All I'm asking is for you to follow my friend. Look at him up there. He's waiting. We don't have much farther to go. And then you can go see Randy." He tucked the gun back in his waistband. "Now, please, this can be over in no time. And you get that hundred-dollar bill. Would you just put this truck in gear and go?"

He reached and relit the joint. "Just take a little hit and relax. There really is nothing going on here but you helping a couple guys out." He offered her the joint. "I promise."

He watched her put the joint to her lips, watched her take a hit, hold it. "All right," he said with a laugh.

Up ahead Mike rolled down the window of his car and looked back at them. Jesse reached his hand out the window, gave a thumbs-up sign.

Katy asked. "Why don't you ride with your friend in his car? Why do you need to be here with me?"

He shook his head. "You really need an answer to that question?"

"Yes."

"All right, then. My friend up there, he farts a lot. I hate riding with that man."

Katy laughed. "No, really," she said. She handed back the joint; she didn't want to get high, just needed to level her nerves.

He took a hit, nodded. "Really." He exhaled. "And, well, truth is, I guess I did want to make sure you came along. Now, would you please put this thing in gear and go?"

34

"You won't shoot me," she said.

"I swear by all that's holy and all that's not, I will not shoot you." He mashed the joint out, flicked the roach to the floor. "Can't have us getting too buzzed for the ride."

Katy drove, thinking, *The Lord didn't give us a spirit of fear.* . . . But with each passing mile she felt she was sinking into some soft, wet pit. Nothing sudden as an earthquake but a slow, steady sinking like a million-dollar glass house in the Hollywood hills, shifting, slipping slowly, quietly, in a mudslide rising like a tide from the earth.

She scanned the horizon for a car. Her hands shook on the wheel.

"Relax. Just tell yourself you're being a good little Girl Scout, doing the public some kind of good."

"I never was a Girl Scout," she said.

He shifted. "Nah, I know your type, one of those misfits. You could play the game, but I bet you never felt you really fit in. Probably always dreaming of some other life, some other place you'd rather be."

Fear hummed like a nest of bees whirling in her head. She couldn't breathe. "How do you know that?"

"I pay attention. That new-age bullshit on your tag. 'Positive.' Like you really believe thinking positive can change a thing. You believers, man. You make me laugh. And this truck of yours. It's the kind of car a girl who likes to dream of going places can afford. I bet you're saving money for trips all the time. And never go anywhere, right?"

She could feel his eyes. She blocked his view of her face with her hand. She knew he could see everything she was. "Are you a friend of Randy's? Have you been spying on me?"

"God, no, I'm telling you I just notice things. Like your fake fingernails. Fake and shiny but got dirt all under 'em. You got this thing about looking good, but you still like to spend your time playing in the dirt." He poked the back of her hand with his fingertip.

"You probably grow all those herbs healthy people eat. Basil, rosemary, dill. My mom, my legal mom, not the blood one, she grows that stuff."

Katy looked at him. She had been transplanting seedlings to the garden that morning. Like his mother. He had mentioned his mother. She felt a little relief.

"I do grow basil. I keep meaning to make pesto." She thought about the basil going to seed in her yard. She'd grown it last year too. Always talked about making pesto. Her mom made great pesto, but Katy never got around to it. She could never collect all those ingredients at the same time, so the basil kept growing until it went to seed and she'd tell herself she'd try it again with basil she could buy from the store.

"I look at you and figure, this is a woman believes in things." He shook his head. "You were one of those little girls who set out cookies for Santa Claus, thought fairy things like Tinker Bell lived in the woods and the Easter Bunny really crept around your house hiding those eggs. You probably believe in things like guardian angels too."

She looked out at the flat, empty highway. "I don't know. I did believe in fairies when I was a girl."

He looked out his window. "Me, I was always playing pirate. Eye patch, scarf on my head, stole this big ol' kitchen knife." He laughed. "I scared the shit out of some of those kids. 'Shiver me timbers,' man." He laughed and propped his foot on the dash.

She didn't want to hear about pirates and kitchen knives. She stared at his running shoes. "You an athlete?"

He laughed. "Yeah, breaking and entering—that's my sport." He lit another one of her cigarettes. "Nah, girl, I'm funning you. Football," he said. "I play football." He lifted his chin, exhaled. "Love it when the defense crumbles and you're out there, man, just running."

She looked him over, wouldn't have guessed him for football.

He was too little, too lean; she figured him for a wrestler, a runner, or some skinny guy who just buffed up with weights.

He turned to her. "I know what you're thinking. I'm too little for football, right? But I can run like a mother, and I'm stronger than you think."

Up ahead the right blinker of the Datsun flashed. "Here," he said. "Get off and follow him."

"This isn't the way to Whitwell. Lake Waccamaw is just up there."

"Shortcut," he said. "This is farm country. His granny, she lives on a farm outside Whitwell."

She followed the car, could hear her little-girl self crying inside, but she kept going. She followed his instructions, did what she was told, and the roads grew smaller, the land more empty with each passing mile. "I don't want to do this."

"But you're doing it," he said.

She trembled, wishing she had paid attention to the exit number, the route number, something. She looked out, saw some kind of abandoned factory. A power station maybe. Lots of electrical towers and power lines that seemed dead now. She'd remember this. If she just paid close attention to where she was going and could get back to this, she could get back to the highway. Lake Waccamaw wasn't too far. Randy's house was just south of the lake. If she focused, stayed steady, she'd get there. And Randy, he'd make it all right. He'd make her forget this whole stupid mess. She drove in deeper darkness and realized she'd forgotten to pay attention. While she was thinking about what she'd do later, she'd lost the sense of where she was. A dark wave rolled up from inside her, as if she'd been snatched by a current. The Cape Fear River. She had felt it then. She might have gotten help if she'd done something to get attention, but now she'd been carried too far out for anyone to hear her call.

Katy kept her eyes on the Datsun. Maybe they'd just rob her, maybe rape her, leave her to find her way home. But she was lost; she had no idea where she was. She looked out at the fields going red in the sunset and saw herself rising in the air, like Dorothy in that little house lifted by a storm. She'd get through this, like Dorothy, and she'd wake up, find herself settled in a bright new land.

Jesse flipped through her billfold. "Man, you've got no cash here. Not a dollar here."

She slapped at his hands. "Stop it. Stop going through my things like I'm not here."

He smacked her arm hard enough to make her bite her lip, grip the wheel. "Now, don't you start pissing me off."

"All right," she said, "I'll pull over. Go ahead and shoot me. I'm not scared."

He laughed, yanked the gun out and waved it in the air. "Damn gun doesn't work. It's just a prop, man." He pulled the trigger. Nothing happened. It was jammed. "Scared you, didn't I? See, I told you I wouldn't shoot you. Look here, now. It's almost over. He's turning down that dirt road."

She looked to where the Datsun was turning, west where the sky hung in purple and pink waves. *The gun doesn't work*, she thought; she'd driven all those miles for a cute guy with a smile and a gun that didn't work.

The Datsun slowed, took another turn, and Katy thought to just plow straight ahead to get to anywhere but where they were going. Jesse was shaking with quiet laughter. "All you got to do is raise a gun to somebody's face. They put the bullets in it. They see their heads blown off. All you got to do is raise the gun. Devil works likes a magician, man, half the game is sleight of hand. Most people. You believers. You do all the rest." He waved the gun in the air. "This is what you get for believing in things."

She kept driving down the narrow gravel road, saw a field of fallen trees as if a great wind had leveled the land. She remembered she was in hurricane country. Every year the coastal towns prepared for the seasonal storms that spiraled out at sea, gathering up strength like a fist rising to slam the coast.

She scanned the horizon for any sign of something she could know. Then she saw it. The radio tower, just a few miles away maybe. If she could get to that tower, she'd know where she was, and Randy's house was only a few miles from that. She sighed. She'd be all right. The tower, there it was back there, a sign that she wasn't as lost as she had thought. She followed the car down another gravel road, but it curved as if it might go someplace. She kept watching the land for a sign of a house, a tractor, a powerline, anything that looked like someone could be around. The road kept curving, surrounded by nothing but thickets and brambles and trees.

"Where the fuck is he going?" Jesse leaned forward in his seat.

Katy said, "I thought we were going to his grandmother's house." But she didn't believe the words any more than she believed in that hundred-dollar bill, which was probably a fake. She looked out at the land, thought the trees looked familiar. Then she saw a house. A little brick house. Once they stopped the truck, she could run to that. Driving on, she saw an old tire on the ground, thought maybe she'd seen that before, but in the country people were always just leaving their old stuff scattered in the fields: tires. washing machines, old cars. At least with all this junk, people couldn't be too far away. And she could run. She'd been a real good runner back in school.

Jesse leaned out the window, looked around. He yelled, "You're driving in fucking circles, man. I thought you knew where you were going." He sat back in his seat, kept his eyes on the Datsun. "The fucker is stoned," he said. "That's another reason I hate riding with him. When's he's stoned, he doesn't know what the hell he's doing." He gave her that smile. "Don't you worry. He'll get us there. It'll be all right."

The Datsun eased to a stop, then made a quick turn down a little road she could hardly see for the trees.

"See," Jesse said. "We're getting there." The rutted road led them through thickets and overhanging branches so thick she was sure there would be nothing but more trees and dirt and rocks where they were going. And the crying, that stinging ache, rose behind her eyes. The sky was shrinking to a thin patch above. She looked left, right. All she could see was trees. She wished she'd paid attention to where the sun was when she'd seen that house. She hoped the guys would do what they wanted and leave. She knew they'd take her truck. Billy had warned her to keep the doors locked. She glanced at the man sitting in her truck. He might rape her. But he might be too stoned for that. If he did, she'd go still so he wouldn't hurt her. And when she got her chance, her first chance, she'd run. She'd take whatever he did, play along, but at the first chance, she'd run. She might have to run a while. But she'd live. She'd been through worse than this. She'd live. She'd get to Randy. Maybe the whole point of this was to get to Randy, who'd give her the nerve to leave Billy behind. If she could be with Randy, she could get over Frank. There was always a reason for things. It just took time to understand. She'd never really wanted the safe guy. Poor Billy. He loved her. She wished she could want the safe guy. If she'd wanted the safe guy, she wouldn't be stuck in a truck with a guy who'd do God knew what if he got the chance. But she was stronger than he could guess. She was. And smart and fast, and she would do whatever it took to get out of this mess alive.

Sacramental Things

Livy Baines used her ring finger to dab night cream on the tissue-thin skin of her eyelids; they were bluish, sunken a little, but not as bad as they were for most women her age. She worked gently around to the crow's feet, then touched at the lines beginning to form underneath her eyes. She stepped back from the mirror and saw a face that was growing to look more like her own mother, who was buried down in Suck Creek, than like her daughter, Katy. Livy glanced at the clock. It was going on midnight. She imagined Katy tending bar now, pressing cold beers into the hands of men who smiled at the simple sight of her girl. Yes, she was a pretty girl. Everyone said so. Livy tried to remember when she'd crossed the line to looking more like her mother than her daughter, who was tall and lean with thick, curly dark hair, sapphire eyes, and a smile that made every other man who met her fall in love. She could have been a model with that face and that long, slender frame. People used to say the same thing about Livy. She looked at herself in the mirror. Not bad for her age, just an older, more filled-out version of Katy. But the last time she'd had a facial, the woman had asked if she'd considered getting rid of her "eleven."

"My what?" she asked. The girl was referring to those two creases in the middle of her forehead that ran straight down between her eyebrows. Everyone was getting them Botoxed now. Livy leaned toward the mirror, pressed her fingertips at her temples, lifted the skin back. She did look a little younger that way. But Lawrence would have a fit at the waste of such money, and Katy, she'd just shake her head and laugh and say, "Whatever makes you happy, Mom."

How long ago was it those boys had thought they were sisters at that Mexican restaurant? Livy had laughed, thanked them for the compliment, but she'd figured they where just throwing out flattery to get near Katy. She played along, bought a round of beers for the boys, and they all laughed and talked, the boys' eyes on Katy, but polite, as if they knew that to keep Katy's attention, they'd have to be nice to her mom. Those were the good years, years between being married, years when she had Katy in a life where they could be more like friends than mother and daughter. Livy had gotten a job at an insurance firm, and Katy had gone to college. On a good track, it seemed. Then Katy met Frank, who was nothing but bad, and Livy got to where she couldn't drive for the anxiety attacks. She looked in the mirror, figured it was around then that the "eleven" started digging into her face. Frank was a coke dealer. Even though Katy swore he had inherited his money, Livy knew the truth. She'd stayed with Joe all those years to keep Katy in private school, to get her ready for college. And there she was, dropping out of college and living on a boat with a coke dealer. Those times put the years on her face.

Then she met Lawrence at her shrink's office, of all things. She was signing in at the reception desk when he strolled into the waiting room as if he owned the place, the kind of walk she liked in a man. He stopped, stood still in the middle of the room, and gave her a nod that was more than a nod, something more like a bow and a smile that said, *How can a woman like you have any kind of problem that would bring her to this place?* She couldn't remember what she said to him, just remembered the warmth, the twinkling in his eyes. She couldn't remember the last time a man had looked at her like that. It turned out he was dating the shrink then, and now he was married to Livy. It was one of those see-it-got-to-have-it things. All roses and dinners and diamonds. Then marriage. Now, just outside the bathroom door, Lawrence Baines was no doubt snoring in bed already with the *Wall Street Journal* on his chest.

Oh, Katy, she thought. *Maybe you shouldn't get married yet.*

Years later, when she told Lawrence about the night those boys had taken her and Katy for sisters at that Mexican restaurant, he threw down his paper and said, "You might still look like a glamour girl, but you're too old for that kind of thing." He was furious, she knew, because his hair was thinning, his broad chest collapsing to a soft bunch of flesh at his waist, while she, well, she did have a little bit of elegance that didn't age. She just smiled at his fury. "But those boys in the Mexican restaurant, it happened years ago," she said. He stood up then, said with the kind of meanness as if she'd cheated on him, "And you're still thinking about it!" Then he walked out of the room with such fury and force, it occurred to her that that was what people meant when they said a person stormed out of the room. Joe had always been a quiet man, but Lawrence came and went like weather, so when he stormed out the door, she let him go and wondered what she'd been thinking to get married again so fast. She knew it was safety. That was why Katy was marrying Billy. And safety always meant some kind of sacrifice, so Livy let Lawrence stomp away and decided she'd make those popovers he loved to go with the roast beef for dinner. He always softened with a good meal.

Now she looked at her face in the mirror. Far from a glamour girl, but she had good bone structure, high, defined cheeks. Livy hardly wore makeup, didn't have to work to catch a glance. When

43

she was young, it was hard to keep the Suck Creek boys from grabbing at her. Being tall and filled out seemed more a curse than a gift. Then in college, after that one ballet class, she figured it out. It was all in the way you carried yourself. Livy had discovered the power to make men suck in their bellies and straighten their shoulders at the sight of her entering a room. That was what had gotten her out of Suck Creek and gotten her Joe Connor, who'd bought her a nice home halfway up Lookout Mountain. And that was what had gotten her Lawrence Baines and the five-bedroom, three-bath house on top of that mountain that was like being on top of the world in that town. Posture was everything. She used to tell Katy this. She'd touch that space between Katy's shoulder blades when she'd see her slump. *Straighten up*, Livy would say. *You don't want to look like an old woman before your time*. And Katy learned. She stood straighter, and finally walked away from Frank. At least she was marrying Billy, who lived a brick house and not some floating bar of a boat on the water.

Positive thinking and good posture. Those two things could take the years off, just maintaining a strong stance and a sweet smile. Livy had learned this from one of those self-help books she'd read. She glanced at herself in the mirror, closed her eyes, and thought, *I'm beautiful, I'm strong, I'm blessed, I'm beautiful, I'm strong, I'm blessed*. But when she opened her eyes in the harsh light of the bathroom, she saw that she was teetering on the threshold of becoming the kind of woman who disappeared in a crowd, a gray smudge who brought attention only when she was about to purchase something, the kind of face that brought attentive smiles only when she was ready to pay. Was that what Lawrence wanted?

Joe had been proud of his catch, said he'd married the best-looking woman in Hamilton County, seemed to forget she was from

Suck Creek. Joe liked to forget where she came from. He was Catholic, so she had to forget she was a Suck Creek Baptist girl, had to take classes with a priest before she got married, but that was okay then because Livy believed life was a process of continuously reinventing ourselves. She'd read that in a self-help book she'd found at the library. She was willing to reinvent, and even though it made her momma cry, she was rebaptized with a saint's name: Olivia Katherine, a little cup of holy water dribbled over her forehead at the font with no one but the priest and Joe and God and maybe the saint she was named for watching.

If it hadn't been for Katy, she might have left. Maybe. But back then she was a good Christian girl who tried to believe, so she went to her momma for help. "Life gives us crosses to bear," her momma had said. "We prove ourselves in times of trouble, not times of ease." Livy was happy that at least her momma didn't blame her bad marriage on the Catholics. When things got worse, her momma told her to go talk to her priest. He told her that love was a gift, but marriage was a sacrament, a covenant. She would have to honor that. "A sacrament is a sacrament," he said. But where was the proof of sacramental things? "It's self-evident," the priest said. "A sacrament is an outward and visible sign of an inner and spiritual grace." Yes, she knew that. But with that definition anything could be a sacrament—helping a stranger, baking a perfect cake. "It's a mystery," the priest said. "You don't walk away from God's mysteries. You embrace them. You struggle to understand, and what you don't understand, you accept." He left her there in his office, staring up at the crucifix, and she thought of Jesus, tortured on the cross like that. Jesus was a tortured man. Not a God. Just a man. That was all. She came to the conclusion that sometimes God left you to your own salvation. You had to save yourself. Now she looked in the mirror and told herself she would have to tell Katy that. She'd tell Katy to beware of believing sacramental things.

"Are you coming to bed?" Lawrence called from the bedroom. She peeked through the door, saw him sitting up. He had that look in his eyes. At least with Lawrence, the sex was good.

"I thought you were sleeping," she said.

"Oh, no," he said with a smile. "Just dreaming."

"I'll be there in a minute," she said. "You know me and my routines."

She went back to the mirror, rubbed cream in swift, light strokes up her neck and in gentle circles in her cleavage, what her aesthetician called her décolletage—there was a special cream for that. She closed that jar and reached for another for her hands.

She sat on the lid of the toilet and rubbed the cream into her skin. She liked her long fingers, good nails. And that diamond, Lord, a diamond so big it embarrassed her sometimes. Her mother would have declared it prideful. But she liked the fact that she had her mother's hands, a few scattered freckles, the Irish blood. She would have to tell Katy to be careful of the sun with her dark hair, blue eyes. Statistics suggested that Katy was a prime candidate for skin cancer. She would have to tell Katy all kinds of things before she married. *Take care*, she would say, the words whispered in her head, *take care*. *Your body is a temple*, the Bible said. *Your body's the only one you've got, so maintenance is crucial*—that's what her personal trainer said, and her aesthetician, and her doctor, and just about every self-help magazine on the stands.

She gave one last look in the mirror. Yes, she did look good, and if she didn't look good, she wouldn't have Lawrence, and she wouldn't have this house on top of Lookout Mountain instead of some prefab place in Suck Creek. But she was fading; she knew it. In the long run life wasn't about beauty at all but learning to make do when it was gone. She was glad she had taught Katy that. She had told her, "Yes, you are beautiful, but beauty passes, so be kind, Katy. That will sustain you. The world will love you long past your prime if you remember to be thoughtful and kind."

Livy turned toward her bedroom, looked in and saw Lawrence propped up on pillows, dozing with his paper scattered across the bed. Livy looked at the man she planned to spend the rest of her life with. *You used to take me dancing*, she thought. He used to smile and stand when she entered a room, as if he couldn't bear another second away from her. He used to bend a little toward her whenever she spoke, as if to catch the very breath of her words. Did all passion fade like this? She stood there, watching him, wondering if he'd wake and want her or just keep sinking deeper into the sheets. Either way it didn't matter.

Livy stood in the doorway, just feeling the room, listening to the soft whir of the central air, the soughing sigh of Lawrence's soft snores. She studied her life, the furniture solid on blue carpet in a white room with a wall of windows, drapes open to the night. A long way from Suck Creek. She thought this every night and gave thanks. She had her doubts sometimes about God and his ways in the world. But she believed in giving thanks for every day.

She crossed the room, went to the window that looked out onto a lot of nothing but trees. She'd convinced Lawrence to buy that lot so she'd always be able to stand at the window and watch the birds flitting in the branches, the squirrels digging, chattering, always a little nervous and hungry, it seemed. Other people's children played there now. She liked to watch them, hear the high, happy sounds of children playing, digging, inventing who knew what in fantasy worlds hidden in those trees. Livy loved their innocence, so rowdy and loud, pure as pups until something in the world taught them to be afraid.

She would have to warn Katy about marriage. *Maybe in the end kindness is overrated. Don't give yourself away.* She felt a surge of sorrow. Tears rushed into her eyes, a queasy feeling that made her sit. It was too late to teach Katy to be selfish. Livy had seen enough bankers, lawyers, contractors to know that even though Jesus said the meek inherit the earth, the world belonged to bankers, lawyers, and investors like Lawrence. She knew that in the world of living, it is not the meek who win.

"Livy," Lawrence called from the bed, his voice soft, curious. Livy looked up.

He squinted, leaned for a closer look at her face. "Are you all right?"

She smiled, shook her head. He was worried. This was a man who after ten years of marriage would still sometimes show up with flowers for no reason. She would have to remember that.

Livy wondered why she was feeling so selfish, so pitiful and mean. Self-pity was a sin. She'd learned that in church.

He sat up, pulled the sheets up around his waist. "Sorry I fell asleep."

She went to him, rubbed his chest, thick and hairy. She just wanted to touch him a minute. She felt the warmth of his skin, stepped back, and said, "I think I'll get some water. Want anything?"

He studied her. "Did something happen?" he asked. "I can see it in your face." Lawrence was a gambler—that was what stock traders really were. It was his business to know how to read every line and shadow, expression, even on a stranger.

"It's nothing," she said. "I just had this bad feeling. You'd think I'd be happy Katy's finally getting married. But it's just that she's so far away."

Lawrence leaned back, gave a quick glance at a headline before tossing the section of paper aside, smoothing another across his lap. "Isn't she coming up this weekend?"

"Yeah, but I've just got this bad feeling."

"Call her," he said, his attention now locked on something in the paper.

"She's working."

"She doesn't work on Mondays." Lawrence looked back to his paper and sighed. "My wife's thirty-year-old daughter works in a bar. She went to college, for God's sake."

Livy didn't want to start the old defense of the choices of her girl. "I'm calling her," she said. But Lawrence had already dropped out of the conversation by the time she turned away.

She went down the hallway to the kitchen. She settled with her glass of water at the counter, and just as she reached for the phone, it rang.

Billy's voice. She had trouble letting the meaning of his words sink in. Katy wasn't home. Katy had left a note saying, "Be back when I can," and she'd been gone all day. He said that note was a bad sign, a sign that she was still mad over a fight they'd had.

"A fight?" Livy said.

"Just an argument. Nothing real big." Billy sighed. There was a weakness in his voice. He was guilty or lying over something.

"Billy," she said, "anything you're not telling me?"

He didn't hear or pretended not to hear the question. "When things are good between us, she writes, 'Be back soon.' She only writes, 'Be back when I can' to let me know she can keep me waiting or come home. To remind me it's her choice. It's always gotta be her choice."

Livy looked at the clock on the stove: 12:14.

"She wouldn't run off?" He said it like a question. "Katy wouldn't run off. I didn't do anything wrong."

"No, Billy," she said. "Katy would never just run off."

"She's coming to see you this weekend. I just thought maybe . . ."

The kitchen shook, righted, shook again. An earthquake? The house held, but the world was slipping. Katy had said something about coming home for a visit, but nothing had seemed wrong. Livy thought it could be something with Frank, but she wouldn't mention Frank, not to Billy. "Have you tried calling her?"

"Her phone is here. You know how she tends to forget her phone."

Livy could feel panic rising in her chest. *Stay rational*, she thought. *No need for fear, not fear*. But the word and the feeling hummed in her head. "So check who she's been calling."

"She keeps her phone locked, and I don't have the code. Funny how she forgets her phone but never forgets to put the lock on."

"Have you called the police?"

His voice, she understood that weakness in it. He was high. Of course. "They say it's too early to declare her a missing person yet."

A wave of nausea rolled up. "Don't say that. She is not a missing person, Billy. She'll come home." Katy had never run off. She threatened to sometimes. The only time she'd ever done anything like run off, she'd moved to Frank's houseboat. But she'd called Livy that same day just so she wouldn't worry. Livy checked her cell phone charging on the counter. No missed calls. "This isn't like Katy. Tell her to call me as soon as she comes in," Livy said. She hung up the phone, gripped the counter for balance, then walked softly down the hallway, one hand touching the wall as if she were a blind woman feeling her way down the long corridor of an unfamiliar home.

What This World
Needs Is a Little
More Awareness

Jesse stared into the open refrigerator at Mike's granny's house. "What a waste, man. What a fucking waste of a day." He was looking for something to eat but kept seeing the pawnshop metal door going down, the "Closed" sign, and the owner, Larry, walking away. They were five minutes too late because they'd had to dump the truck on a back road out by the lake. They couldn't risk driving it back to town. He hadn't seen that the truck was on empty. He should've noticed. But no, he'd fucked up, too busy worrying about Mike up there driving stoned. He turned, saw Mike sitting at the table eating a chicken leg. Without a word, he smacked the back of his head.

"Ow!" Mike grabbed his head. "What you do that for?"

"It was the weed. I'm back there worrying about you driving stoned, and I don't think to look at her fuel gauge. Boost a truck that's out of gas. Zeke would really like that."

"Keep your voice down, man. You don't want my granny hearing this."

"I thought she was deaf."

"Half deaf," Mike said and went back to his chicken.

"We fucked up because I had to keep my eye on you, making

sure you drive straight, and there you go driving in circles and I'm trying to watch her, make sure she doesn't flip and run." Jesse turned back to the refrigerator, pushed past the foil-covered bowls. "I could use a beer. Don't y'all keep any beer in this house?"

"She's a Christian," Mike said. "There's some sweet tea there in the jar on the counter." Mike took a sip of milk. He was glad his granny was half deaf back there in her bedroom, falling asleep, staring at people on TV. She'd never liked Jesse, said he was like that Eddie Haskell kid on TV, always smiling and nodding and up to no good. He was glad she was too weak to come to the kitchen without her walker. He'd had the sense to sneak in, grab her walker, and put it right in the kitchen by the stove. He'd make sure he put the walker back once he got Jesse settled down and sleeping on the sofa.

"I don't want any sweet tea." Jesse sat, looked at the cabinets. "I need something to eat."

"Your stomach better now?"

"Yeah, I took care of it at that McDonald's back there."

"You always had that stomach thing?"

"Since I was a kid. Doctor says it's nerves." He went back to the refrigerator. "I don't have any nerves. But I do need to eat something."

"Have some fried chicken." Mike lifted the foil off the platter on the table. "It's good, man. She makes great fried chicken."

"I don't eat fried chicken."

Mike took another chicken leg. He'd grabbed the first one while Jesse was outside pissing in the yard. "I've heard you say you like fried chicken. Everybody likes fried chicken."

"I eat chicken strips," Jesse said, "nice lean chicken strips. Nothing with a bone. It's nasty."

"Nasty?"

"I had this dog once, choked on a chicken bone." Jesse glanced back, saw Mike looking at him. That was one thing he liked about Mike. He liked Jesse's stories. He could listen to Jesse's stories all day when most people didn't give a damn. Except his mom. And Jenny. She listened to his stories. Jesse went to the kitchen window, looked out at the dark. "Her name was Pup. My momma didn't want me having no dog, but I kept her, fed her scraps from my plate. I didn't know a dog could die on chicken bones. But she choked, bone got stuck in her throat, and she just laid there, twitching on the sidewalk." Jesse glanced at Mike, sitting there, just listening. "I was yelling to my mom to help her, but hell, no, she wasn't home, just this man she kept around. He just sat on the front stoop, sipping his beer and watching."

Jesse turned back to the window. "Pup finally stopped moving, and I guess I was crying or something. I was standing there, looking at Pup and all that blood. And he yells at me, 'Just put the dead bitch in the trash.' But I couldn't move. I couldn't stop looking at her. Then the bastard smacked the back of my head. Hard. It's like I went blind for a second. I heard him saying, 'Quit crying. Throw the bitch in the trash.' I wanted to bury her, but he laughed and kept hitting. So I did it. I scooped her up with a shovel, and I tossed her in the Dumpster. I knew the rats would get her by morning. And that bastard, he sat there laughing, said, 'You think that's the worse thing you ever gonna see?'"

He turned back to Mike, who was tightening the foil over the platter of chicken. "Damn, Jesse. That's about the saddest thing I ever heard."

Jesse went to the refrigerator, grabbed a hunk of cheese. "It ain't the worst thing. The bastard was right. There's always another worst thing you're gonna see." He pulled a knife from a drawer, sat at the table. With a smooth stroke of the blade, he cut a slice of cheese and slid it into his mouth. He shook his head. "You got any crackers?"

Mike got some saltines from the cabinet.

Jesse cut another slice of cheese. "Zeke was all set to move those guns from that pawnshop. And we boost a truck out of gas. We don't have shit but a fake hundred-dollar bill." Jesse put the cheese down. "This ain't real cheese. I can't eat this." He sat back, rubbed his belly. "I need something, man, something solid, something easy."

"Want me to make you a fried-egg sandwich?"

"Yeah, man. That'd be cool. Thanks."

Good, Mike thought. *He's settling down*. He'd never seen a man shift moods as fast as Jesse. You never knew what could set him off, and sometimes it took the simplest thing to calm him back down.

Mike put a skillet on the stove, scooped in some bacon fat, reached into the refrigerator for an egg. He felt Jesse watching him. "You want this on plain bread or toast?"

"Toast. No butter. Just toast. " Jesse's cell phone buzzed in his pocket. He looked. His mother. He clicked the phone off. There'd be hell to pay for this. She would yell, then cry, then give him more jobs to do around the house. Her car would be off limits for a while. He watched Mike leaning over the frying pan, studying the sizzling egg. Zeke cooked like that, studied whatever he cooked in a pot, kept leaning over it, smelling it, stirring it. Made the best fried trout Jesse'd ever had. Mike was tenderly flipping the egg. Jesse watched him. "You do that like Zeke, man. The man loves his food."

"Did you call him yet?"

"Yeah. While you were making sure your granny was in bed, I called him, said we didn't do the job."

Mike put a piece of toast on the plate, slipped the fried egg onto it. "He pissed?"

Jesse shrugged. "And lay that top piece of toast on real gentle. I don't want it all mashed down." He watched to make sure Mike did it right. "Nah, he wasn't pissed. He's too cool to get pissed. He did this repo once. A man tries to sic his dog on him, big fucking Doberman, Zeke just turns real calm to the back of his truck, pulls out a chain. The dog just studies him. And Zeke, man, he ain't scared of nothing. He just keeps looking at the man and winding that chain up, getting ready. Man keeps trying to sic that dog, gives it a kick, and it runs up to Zeke like it's gonna jump, and Zeke just stands there. Dog sniffs at his crotch. And Zeke must have some kind of magic in his crotch 'cause that dog, it just steps back and starts wagging its tail." Jesse laughed and slapped the table.

Mike put the sandwich on the plate in front of Jesse. "I guess ol' Zeke's girlfriend likes that magic in his crotch."

Jesse glared up at him. "Don't be talking about her that way. She's his wife, and she's a good woman. Nicki Lynn is the only woman in the world worth keeping, or Zeke wouldn't have her. You gotta be some hell of a woman to catch Zeke. And now they've got this baby on the way. Due any day, I guess." Jesse studied his sandwich, turned the plate to make it look just right. "Yeah, Nicki Lynn. She loves that man. Cooks, cleans, keeps his books. And Zeke, he can't keep his hands off her. Always patting her head, her ass. Now he just pats that big ol' baby belly of hers."

He studied the sandwich. "Thanks, man," he said. "You make a neat sandwich. All the edges perfect."

Mike smiled. Jesse was all right on a good day. You just had to keep on his good side. Jesse cut the sandwich in half, dabbed his finger in the yolk running on the plate, tasted it, gave a nod. He took a bite, chewed and swallowed it. "That's a good egg. Not store-bought."

Mike gestured toward the backyard. "She's got Rhode Island Reds back there. She's kinda known for selling her eggs around here."

Jesse bit again into the sandwich. He ate it all without stopping. He told Mike he'd take some sweet tea now. He sighed. "Fuck of a day, man. All that planning just to get there five minutes too late.

Have to see that Larry closing up, pulling the metal door down over his storefront, locking it up like he runs Fort Knox. We could've taken him. But no, he goes walking down that sidewalk, and a damn cop pulls over just to say hey." He took a cracker from the pack. "Some of Zeke's best customers are cops. He's good at playing both sides of the law. Says to me, 'What's the difference between a cop and a crook? Nothing, man, a cop's just a cop until he gets caught, and then he's a crook like anybody else.'" Jesse stood and looked out the kitchen window. "Hey, Larry," he whispered. "Yeah, you, Larry of Larry's Pawnshop and Trade, not you other Larrys out there. You, Larry Watts. You were one lucky bastard on this day. The blue truck, it saved your ass. And you, Larry, you just walk on down that sidewalk and talk to your cop. But they'll be another day, Larry boy."

"They'll be looking for who stole her truck," Mike said. He was doing the dishes.

Jesse ate another cracker. "Nobody gonna worry about that truck sitting by Lake Waccamaw. First thing her fiancé is gonna think is she ran off to Randy. He said the name like he hated it. Randy. Can't any bitch besides Nicki Lynn and my mom be happy with one man? And meanwhile, cops will be looking all over Lake Waccamaw. She told me herself she went there all the time." He raised a finger to Mike. "Her pattern, man. She gave it right to me. You gotta work your pattern into her pattern, that's the way you disappear."

"What about the girl?"

"What the hell is she gonna say?" Jesse shook his head. "Positive, think positive. We gonna be just fine, Michael Man."

Mike smiled. He liked the way Jesse called him Michael Man. Back in juvy, Jesse wouldn't let anybody give him shit. "That's my boy," he'd say. "Nobody gonna fuck with my boy." Then he'd call him Michael Man.

"So what's the next hit gonna be?"

Jesse kept staring out the window. "I've got another little piece of action in mind. Right there in Land Fall, just around the block." He glanced at Mike. "I'm doing this one on my own. It's a big house. Just a mom and her daughter. They gotta have all kinds of jewelry, crystal, silver. I fit it in my backpack. Zeke fences it. There you go. And that daughter, man, she's hot. Nice ass, always running around the block. Looks at me, don't even see me, man. No, the princess, she sees only what she wants to see. Jenny says nobody knows what they're looking at when they think they're looking at me."

Mike took the dishes to the sink, turned on the faucet. "Doesn't Jenny get nervous around you sometimes?"

Jesse looked at him, squinted like he was making up his mind about something. He refilled his glass with tea, took a long drink. "Not Jenny," Jesse said, "I've known her since we were kids. A hippy chick. Why would I screw things up with a girl who gives me free massages anytime I want? Says she has to practice on somebody to get her license." He smiled. "And she likes that somebody to be me."

Mike washed the dishes, set them in the drain, kept his eyes off Jesse. "So you two really have something. She ain't just some chick."

Jesse rummaged in the cabinet, found a bag of cookies. Mike knew there were just a few left. He'd been saving them for his granny "Yeah, we got a thing. None of that going-steady shit, just a thing." He shoved the last of the cookies into his mouth and rubbed the back of Mike's head the way he would a dog. "I'm staying here tonight," he said. "In the morning you gotta drive me back home."

"Man, I can't take my car. Cops might be looking for my car. I get pulled over just for being in your neighborhood in that piece of shit I drive."

"Don't worry. Nobody remembers half the shit that walks right by. They just see what they want. People don't notice anything. I thought you knew that an eyewitness is the worst lead a cop can have. How many people notice what kind of car you drive?" Jesse walked across the kitchen and looked out the window toward the lights of a distant neighbor's house. "Take you and me here. You think anybody noticed us pull up in your granny's drive? No, they're all watching some trash on the television. Shit, you think the folks in my hood see who I am?"

"You don't live in a hood."

"No, it's a gated community. I'm inside the gate keeps the bad dudes out, right? My daddy's got money. People see him, think he's my old man. People see me, think I'm one of the luckiest guys in the world."

Mike wished he had some more dope. The only weed left was in Jesse's pocket. "So," he said, "you want to finish up that weed?"

"Nah," Jesse said. "I'm saving it." He turned, stared out the kitchen window into the darkness. From where Mike sat, he could see Jesse's distorted reflection. The eyes narrowed, sharp cut of his jaw. He was good-looking, but sometimes when his face went a certain way, he looked like some kind of fiend. Mike wished he had that. If he lost some weight, worked out, maybe if he changed his hair, he could be something like Jesse: the guy the chicks wanted, the man who didn't give a damn.

Jesse exhaled a whistling breath between his teeth. "This place I'm gonna hit. Rich lady. College girl, long red hair. Nice. Drives around in this silver Sebring with the top down." Jesse leaned against the counter, rubbed his belly. "Man, my stomach still ain't right. Your granny got any Coke? I could use a Coke. That always eases me."

Mike shrugged. He knew there was one Coke in the fridge behind the milk, but that was his granny's Coke. She liked to save it for when she got a sour stomach. "Ice water might help." He took out some ice cubes, dropped them in a glass, ran the water cold. Jesse drank a few sips, ran his tongue over his teeth, and wiped his mouth with the back of his hand. "I know they got some good shit in that house, man. It'd be easy. Her momma works, spends evenings out, I'll bet in one of those I'm-rich-and-divorced-so-help-me support groups. And this chick, she's in and out of school, out with this baby-faced boyfriend. And man, she's running around in these shorts. Whew. Runs right by me, doesn't even look." Jesse rubbed his belly again, looked around the kitchen.

Mike nodded. "Just don't get caught, man. Like Zeke told you, it ain't smart to mess around in your own hood."

"My folks, they'll always cover me." Jesse grinned. "Remember that crack whore? The one they popped me for?" Jesse opened the refrigerator, and as if he knew where it was, he pushed the milk aside, grabbed the Coke. Mike knew he'd have to slip out in the morning and buy another one for his granny. Jesse twisted the top off, sipped. "Good thing she had a record. Drugs, shoplifting, bad checks, credit cards. I nearly did time for that one." He went into the living room, opened the front door, looked out, took in a long breath, let it go. "Now I've got two years suspended hanging over my head." He stood in the doorway, rolled his shoulders. "Is that fucked or what?"

Mike could see the tension in his back just by the way he moved. When he got this tight, Mike had to be careful. Jenny at the marina had to be a pretty cool chick if she was willing to rub Jesse's back. Mike took the quilt off his granny's chair, laid it on the couch. He arranged a pillow and gave Jesse a grin so he wouldn't take things too seriously. "You put her in a coma for two weeks." Jesse rolled his head to loosen his neck. Mike could hear a pop. "You scare me sometimes, the risks you take, man."

"Don't you worry." Jesse drained the Coke. He stood there, muscles bulging as he squeezed the doorframe in his hands "You ever just want to pull a house down?"

Mike shook his head.

"I want to be like the night, man. Be like the dark seeping into everything when the sun goes down." He turned, shut the door, locked it, and grinned. "What this world needs is a little more awareness."

Mike stood. "What I need right now is some sleep."

Jesse walked to the couch. "I'm crashing. Take me home in the morning."

"All right," Mike said. "I'll take you home, but I got to leave you at the gate. I don't like the way that guard looks at me. That all right with you?"

"Yeah. That'll be all right." Jesse dropped flat on the couch and closed his eyes. "Thanks, man."

Mike knew that was Jesse's way of saying goodnight. He stood in the doorway, waited until he could hear the regular deep breathing of Jesse asleep, then crept down the hallway leading to his granny's room, where he would turn off the TV, sit in the big chair at her bedside, and take comfort in the quiet sound of her breath until he sank into his own sleep, forgetting the awful mess of the day. "I'm sorry," he whispered to the darkness of his grandmother's room. She had turned off her light. Hadn't waited for him to come tuck her in the way she liked. He wanted his granny to be awake; just her voice would give a little comfort. Still, he crept into her room, sat in the chair, hoping being near his granny would make him feel all right. But there was no consolation, just the memory of that blue-truck girl. The touch of her hand on his arm. He tried to think of her running in the dark, trying to get to some guy's house. Some guy named Randy. So what if she screwed around on her fiancé? He closed his eyes and tried to see her finding her way in the dark, knocking on some guy named Randy's house. Then he felt the touch of her hand again, her saying he should know her name. It wasn't over with the blue-truck girl. He was pretty sure of that.

He shuddered, tried to shake off the feeling. But he could still see Jesse standing out in that field. Calling to the girl to come on. She stood by the car. Mike told her to go on, to do what Jesse wanted, and it would be all right. He wanted her to get away from his car, wanted to roll up the window, lock the door. He could feel her looking at him. But he wouldn't look up from his hands gripping the wheel. "Talk to me," she said. "What's your name?" He glanced up, looked away. Then she reached in, squeezed his arm. He flinched, said, "What you doing?" He pulled away from her, ducked down, leaned closer to his hands on the wheel. "My name is Katy," she said. "You need to know my name." He kept his head down, didn't want to look at her, and when he looked up, she was gone. And before he knew it, Jesse was throwing a screwdriver at him, giving him all kinds of hell.

Mike pulled the chair closer to his grandmother's bed. He told himself it was like Jesse said, there were always worse things. He leaned back in the chair, listened to the soft sound of his granny's breathing. It would be all right. Yeah, it was a waste of a day. Nothing went like they'd planned, but it would be all right. But he couldn't shake the feel of that girl's hand. There'd be no leaving that girl named Katy behind.

Just Nature She Loved, Flowers and Fangs and All

The old woman liked to watch the night from her back porch. In the old days, she did laundry there, wringer washer, hung clothes on a line out back, strung them up in the kitchen in winter months. Now she had an electric washer, dryer, heat, and air conditioners. All stuff her daughter bought her, insisted that she have. Now her daughter was trying to talk her into getting a burglar alarm. "Everybody knows you live out there by yourself. Anything could happen to you."

But the old woman wasn't worried. She'd lived a long life and seen a lot of things. Sure, she lived alone, but folks knew she had nothing in her house worth stealing, and they probably figured she had her husband's old .22. She could still see clearly and wasn't afraid of pulling a trigger.

And she loved this land. Her husband had courted her with this five acres, and before long they'd had fifty. It was a home built on love, and much as her daughter wanted to her to sell and move to be with her in Poughkeepsie, she wasn't budging. She knew she'd freeze half to death up there. This was her land, and the only way they'd get her out was in a box. Or a bag, she guessed. She watched police shows. They used black bags these days.

She walked down into the yard to look up at the sky. Saw the Big Dipper. The top end of Scorpio and the other one she liked, Orion's belt. Her husband had taught her to see these things.

A hoot owl swooped in moonlight, grabbed something up and rose. She figured it had to be a field mouse scurrying toward the brambles out by the trash heap. She liked the predatory birds. Ospreys, red-tailed hawks, owls that sometimes looked big as boys sitting up in those trees. She'd watched a show on Discovery about these birds. Raptors was what they were called. She liked the way talons clutched the furred things, lifting them up against the sky to somewhere they could plunk them back on the dirt and eat. She liked the nature shows. Bears scooping salmon from the streams, stripping the skins off. The way the big cats stalked. The hammerhead shark and the way it used some kind of sonar to sniff out things to eat buried under the sand. They were smart. Every creature in the world was smart when it came to feeding time. That was one thing she'd learned from the nature shows.

Her daughter thought she was strange. But the old woman said it was just nature she loved, flowers and fangs and all. Now she looked up at the full moon. *You should see this*, she thought to her husband, who had died twelve years before. He probably saw the moon. He probably saw the whole world, giraffes in Africa, the northern lights in Finland, and he probably saw all that meanness too that went on in the cities. That went on everywhere. But then there were always babies laughing somewhere, and that made things easier to bear. She liked to think that was what death might be like. It would be like the moon that sees everything, that circles around and around this world, just watching, waxing, waning, circling back around to see it all.

She saw a rustling in the brush at the back of the yard, made it out to be the pair of deer that liked to come for the salt lick she'd laid down. She liked watching the deer but had to keep her garden fenced. One year they'd snapped off the buds of all her lilies just as they were about to bloom. She saw them out there watching her. She made a little chucking sound, the way she talked to babies. She didn't know deer language. They just stared at her for a minute and walked off. A breeze shook the trees. There had been such a drought lately. Here it was, late summer, and the leaves were already making a dry, brittle sound. She looked out at the field behind her house and ached for her husband, who used to plow that land, grew the sweetest corn in the county. She looked up, saw a shooting star, and made a wish for the safety of her daughter, who for some reason had decided to move up north.

She looked back at that field, remembered the lush corn that used to grow. And she felt a sorrow as if something very sad had just flown over. She wondered how many more years she'd have to walk this world, waiting to meet her husband in eternity somewhere. She was ready. She looked up, hoping to make another wish, but saw only a few blurred stars in a dull black sky. The humidity, she thought. Her daughter was always telling her to sell the farm and move to a place with milder weather. She sent a prayer to her husband, asked him to give her a sign to tell her whether she should give up the place and move or hang on and stay. *I'll know when it's time*, she thought. And then she thought maybe those were his words in her head. *Patience* was his favorite word. *You'll know when it's time*. That was exactly something he would say.

Love Calls Us to Things of This World

Billy woke in the dark, a jolt in the spine and a wide-eyed stare at the ceiling. Day three and she wasn't back yet. He sat up, looked at the clock: 3:30 A.M. As usual. Somewhere between 3:30 and 4:30, he would wake. She was always home by then, even when she worked late at the bar, partied with the wait staff. He stared into the dark. Not a sound in the house. Most nights he'd hear the clicking of ice as she brought her glass of ice water to bed. When she worked late, she always came in quietly, took a shower, brushed her teeth, and he never heard a thing but the clicking of her ice water as she set it on the side table, slipped so quiet, soft, and damp into their bed.

Three thirty A.M. What does a man do at 3:30 A.M.? Five thirty is a civil time to rise. That was what Katy said: "Five thirty is a civil time to rise." Farmers did it. Fishermen. Even those yuppies with some 6:00 spinning class at the gym. She said that getting up before 5:30 meant you were anxious or a nut of some kind or a workaholic. Katy liked sleeping in. In her ideal life, she said she'd like to be able to rise clean and clear-headed with the sun so she could watch the night turn to day. She said that as if she believed it. But Katy never got up early unless she had to. She wanted to be the kind of person who got up early, greeted the day just for the beauty of it, but people did that only in the books she liked to read.

If she were there, she'd reach, stroke his back softly with her nails. She'd pull him to her where he could smell coconut, amber, some sweet-smelling cream she used. He'd nuzzle at her neck while she softly rubbed her fingers across the back of his head. "Come to bed," she'd whisper, even when he was already there. He'd just nuzzle closer, breathing her sweetness.

He flicked on the light, threw a t-shirt over the lampshade to soften the glare. Katy hated when he did that, said he'd forget the shirt one day and burn the place down. Right now he didn't care. He looked around the room as if looking would reveal some sign of her, as if all that time he was looking she was right there, the way you looked for a drill bit you needed in a toolbox. You looked and sifted and looked, and you gave up, made some other drill bit work. You went to put it back, and there it was—the drill bit you needed was sitting right there.

He ran his hands over the tangle of sheets. Katy would have had them smooth, tight, and clean. He could see a stain. She hated stains on a sheet, kept saying she wanted new sheets. And so he'd bought these eight-hundred-thread-count sheets she'd wanted. He was saving them for a wedding present. Their first night married, they'd sleep on those ivory-colored eight-hundred-count sheets. "Katy," he said, "I got you those great sheets you've been wanting. Come home."

The cops had said it was probably prewedding jitters. He was worried she had run back to Frank, the asshole who never remembered her birthday or Valentine's Day. Frank, who seemed to want her just enough to hurt her. Some guys were like that, and some girls just couldn't leave it alone. And now there was this other guy called Randy. Who the hell was Randy? Katy's mother suspected

Frank. But even Olivia—he could hear it in her voice—was scared. Olivia didn't know about some guy named Randy. Billy didn't want anybody to know about Randy. He'd read about him in the journal, the journal he'd promised not to read. She'd written, "Randy the randy man. Yikes! Ha ha!" What kind of grown woman wrote things like that? No hearts around Randy's name the way she did with Frank, just little doodles of firecrackers and stars

He glanced at his bedside table, the half-empty bottle of Jim Beam, the bag of pot. Nothing worked. He sat, nerves jangly at 3:35 A.M. If he finished the bottle, took a couple hits of weed, he could sleep again and maybe wake again when it was a civil time to rise. But his mouth was thick and dry as cotton, so he drank the glass of water instead, what should be Katy's glass of water, and there it was, in case she came in, on his side of the bed.

He grabbed his phone, punched in Frank's number—of course he remembered Frank's number. He'd gotten it off her phone when they'd first gotten together. She knew he'd done it. After that the phone stayed locked. It was a sign of guilt that she had to keep her phone locked. She just sighed and shook her head when he asked about Frank. "We're friends, Billy. Old history. Sometimes old lovers, the chemistry dries out. I'm marrying you, Billy." She said it like it was the biggest news of the world. Then she'd turn away, say something like "Sometimes old lovers can just be friends." Yeah, he knew that. But he knew she was lying. He'd seen the heat between them, the kind of heat that never fully went away. And now he had some guy named Randy to worry about too.

He listened as the phone rang a few times, wondered if Frank would bother to answer. Probably not. He'd be with some girl. Maybe Katy. The phone kept ringing. Well, it was 3:45 A.M. Hardly a civil time. It switched to voice mail, *blah blah*, Frank's voice, "Leave a message." He sat in the silence. What could he say at 3:45 A.M.? Frank had to be sick of him calling just to ask, "Is Katy there? Tell me the truth, is she there?"

Then there was a click and the deep, thick voice. Frank, with the kind of voice women liked, dark and smooth. A goddamned white Isaac Hayes. Shaft and you can dig it. The voice said, "Hello," but Billy could hear it really saying, *Yeah, what now?*

"It's me," Billy said.

"Billy," Frank said, "I've got caller ID." Billy could hear him sitting up, maybe readjusting the pillows. "She's not here, Billy. I swear I've got no idea where she is."

"Yeah," Billy said. "I'm sorry, man. I know you said that. But you'd tell me if she's there? 'Cause I'm going crazy not knowing. I mean I've called her mom. Nobody knows where she is, and I just keep thinking if it's anybody, it's you. 'Cause, oh, hell." He sucked back a breath. "Hell, everybody knew she still loved you. I was just the safe guy. You're the danger guy, and the girls, they like the danger guy."

"Billy," Frank said, calm like a doctor, like his daddy, who had this preacher's soft way of saying just about everything.

"What?"

"She's not here, Billy. I haven't seen her since y'all came back here for the engagement party."

"Are you alone?" Billy said. There was a pause. "You're not alone, are you, Frank? Shit, guys like you never sleep alone."

"I'm gonna hang up in one minute, Billy. I'm just trying to be decent here. I'm trying to help, but I got no idea where she is. Hell, I wish she was here, and I don't mean for me but for you. I know it's been three days, and I know this ain't like Katy."

"Her mom's coming," Billy said. "Her mom's so worried, she's coming down." Billy didn't know why, but it soothed him just to have her mom come down.

Billy heard Frank saying something, then the mumbling of a girl's voice in the background. She sounded sleepy. She sounded pissed. It wasn't Katy. "I'm sorry, man," Frank said. "It's just three days. Sometimes girls run off longer than that."

"Maybe the kind of girls you go out with. Girls I go out with don't run off. They want to marry me. She wants to marry me." Billy felt the crying in his voice. He leaned toward the ashtray, picked up the half-smoked joint. Relit it. Held it. Breathed. Billy held the joint away from the phone as if that could hide what he was doing.

"Get some sleep, man," Frank said. "We'll all feel better if we can get some sleep."

"Yeah." Billy rubbed the joint out, looked at the bottle of Jim Beam.

"Look," Frank said, "call me if you hear something."

"Sure," Billy said. "Sorry, man." He flicked the phone shut, opened the bottle, but when he went for a swig, a heaving rose in his gut, and he ran to the john to throw up.

He retched and heaved until his whole body was shaking and tears ran down his face. He leaned back against the cold tub, grabbed a towel off the rack, and wrapped it around his shoulders. He pulled the bath mat under him for a little cushion and leaned back against the tub.

He reached up to the sink, ran the water cold, filled a glass, leaned back and sipped. *Easy, now*, he thought. *Small sips*. He leaned back, closed his eyes, felt the pounding in his chest ease. Olivia had said it would be all right. Olivia had said that there was an explanation for these things, that her daughter would never run off, but sometimes a girl just needed girl time. Maybe Katy was off with her girlfriends. Olivia didn't know about some guy called Randy, and Billy couldn't bring himself to tell her about the name in Katy's last journal, the one Billy had sworn he'd never read. So let Olivia think Katy was off with girlfriends; let her try to believe that. But Billy had heard the shaking in her voice. She wouldn't have booked a plane if she thought it was all right. And even if Katy had run off with some guy named Randy, it wasn't like her not to call and tell him where she was. She'd at least text if she didn't want to talk on the phone. Unless she'd really left him for good.

Billy walked to the living room, saw the photos of Katy spread on the coffee table. The REV lady had said she'd need a photograph if he wanted her to make a flyer. Billy stood there, afraid to go closer to the photographs. He couldn't believe this was really happening. The REV lady was coming tomorrow. You didn't get calls from searchers if everything was all right. He'd seen her on the news. Shelby Waters. She helped cops find bodies, although that wasn't how she'd put it. "No, I don't go searching for bodies, Mr. Jenkins. I support people who have lost . . ." She went on, but that was all he heard. *People who have lost.*

He went back to the bathroom for another glass of water. He looked down at the grime caked at the base of the tub. It was his turn to clean the bathroom. He grabbed a piece of toilet paper, scrubbed at a black spot in the caulk where dust and dirt and moisture made that black mildew not even bleach could get out. He spit on the toilet paper, wiped at the spot. The toilet paper fell apart. He tossed it into the toilet, slammed the lid down, sat up. The cops had asked, "Are you sure nothing's missing? Toothbrush, birth-control pills, perfume?"

He looked around. She'd left her cell phone. But she was always forgetting her cell phone. And all her favorite things were here. The birth-control case. Her Vitabath soap, the stuff she loved and they couldn't afford so her mom always got it her for Christmas and her birthday. And there were her other things: Amber Shea Butter, bath salts, her makeup and cleansers and lotions overfilling the two drawers, cluttering the shower. It was no wonder he always put off cleaning the bathroom when he had to go to all that trouble to move her things. She could always tell when he hurried and wiped the rag around whatever was on the shelf, said, "Do it right, Billy." But it wasn't like she was perfect. Her truck was a garbage can on wheels. He hated to ride in that truck of her daddy's, but the truck was one good thing he'd left her, so she kept it running, new engine, transmission, but something was always going wrong. She said she'd drive it into the ground, and she drove it hard, filling the floorboards with Coke cans, beer cans, chip bags, candy wrappers, and rocks and leaves and branches she'd found from walking around the lake. She was always filling the truck bed with driftwood and broken chairs and lamps she'd pull from the garbage on the side of the streets. "We all have our sloppy spots," she liked to say. "We're all entitled to our sloppy spots, and Daddy's truck is mine." He figured it was hers to do what she wanted with.

At least she liked the house clean, and Billy was grateful for that. No matter how messy his mind felt after a day on the job, when he came home to see the prettiness, the brightness, the clean sheets and shelves she'd brought to his house when they'd made it their house, it was all peace. She took one shabby brick house and made it something wonderful just out of scraps of things she'd find, stitch up, repair, and paint. Only one month after she moved in with him, he asked her to marry him, please. She gave one little blink and looked around as if the answer hovered around her head like a little bugging mosquito she needed to catch. She looked at him as if there were a sudden solution to something she had been puzzling over for years.

"Yes," she said. "Billy Jenkins, I'll marry you. I'll even change my name for you if you want." But later they'd talked about that. She didn't see why a woman would give up the name she'd been born and raised with when she married some guy and odds were they'd end up divorced, and then she'd be carrying around some name like gum stuck to her shoe.

He just nodded like he agreed and said okay because there was no use arguing. He just kissed her and asked if she'd mind wearing his grandmother's ring. And she kissed him and said it would be great. Or maybe he said that, or maybe he just thought that. But anyway, she was wearing it. He hoped she was wearing it. Wherever she was.

He looked around the bathroom that she'd wallpapered with sentimental-looking little blue cornflowers on a white pattern, girly but not too girly, a clean little print, so fine and crisp you had to look close to know it was a cornflower. She'd pointed that out—he hadn't even known what a cornflower was. She'd been so proud of hanging that wallpaper, he hadn't bothered to point out the places where the design didn't line up. There'd be a row of half flowers jutting up against white space where the row of other half flowers was supposed to be. But that was all right. It was Katy. She always meant to get things perfect, and that was one of the things he loved about her, but sometimes he thought he loved her more because she didn't get things perfect. It was the trying to get perfect, a sweetness in the trying, that he really liked.

And there on the racks were what she liked to call her "delicates"— had to be a word her mom had taught her, some proper term for panties and bras. She liked good underwear, was always cruising T. J. Maxx for cheap prices. She liked lace, black, white, green. Nothing too trampy, and little thongs, and her little bras that never matched. Now he sat there looking at her delicates, waiting for her hands, her fingers to take them down, fold them, place them in her drawer the way she liked.

She liked everything just so. She'd studied poetry and philosophy and all kinds of stuff in college. And she always had this simple, smart way of talking about things that he liked to hear but didn't understand. Like the poem she loved: "Love Calls Us to the Things of This World." It was a line she liked to say. She couldn't remember who wrote the poem, or much of the rest of the poem. All she remembered about it was something about laundry.

He couldn't believe some guy had gotten famous for writing something like that. It was kind of obvious to him that if you liked the world, you liked the things in it, but she said it was all more mysterious, or did she say it was more complicated, than that. He didn't know, but she liked the line so much she wrote it out in calligraphy letters and framed it. All Billy knew was that the poem was about laundry. Billy didn't get that either, that some guy could get famous for writing about laundry. But here it was: "Love Calls Us to the Things of This World." And there near the bottom corner of the frame was a little drawing she'd done: his shirt and her blouse on a clothesline. She'd said it was their clothes, and the clothes hanging there were a metaphor. He loved it when she talked like that. He loved all the pretty, useless things she made and put all over his house. Their house. But he couldn't remember what love had to do with laundry.

"Katy," he whispered, and felt that little rush of anger like when she came home too late from work. But then he felt that knot in his throat. She wasn't with Frank. So maybe it was this Randy guy. But she would have called by now. She wasn't that cruel. He thought maybe he should just take her things down, stick them in her drawer like everything was normal. He started to reach, but he couldn't touch them. Her things would wait for her hands to put them away. "Please don't touch her things," he'd said when he'd seen the cop reaching for them. He was glad he'd said "please" because his voice had snapped, and the cop had flinched a little, had given him a look like *One more word out of you and I'll bust you just for getting in my way*.

The cop had taken a box of her hair dye from the bathroom trash, studied it carefully, held it at a distance with his latex-gloved hand. "So she dyed her hair before she left," he said as he dropped the box into an evidence bag. "She was touching it up," Billy said. And the cop said, "She wasn't a natural blond, was she?" Billy walked out of the room because he knew there was pot in the coffee can in the freezer, and he knew the cop was just looking for a reason to put cuffs on him, take him in.

He stood and looked in the mirror. He looked like a drunk. Red eyes, crazy hair, the puffed, sagging jowls of a drunk. No wonder the cop was itching for a bust. He looked like the kind of guy who hung around job sites scoping them out for scrap metal, tools, a cooler with some food in it. He heard the twittering of the predawn birds. Another day was coming, another day she was gone. Another day he'd skip work, just go crazy. He washed his face hard with a rag and soap, hot water, then cold, and more cold. Cold water helped hangover skin. Katy had told him that. But he still looked like a drunk. And it was because he *was* a drunk. He'd been drinking solidly since the night Katy hadn't come home. And he wasn't even really a drinker. Katy was the drinker—not a big drinker but a drinker. He liked pot. Pot worked to smooth the edges out of any long workday. But whiskey did something more. This guy named Gator who hung at the bar where Katy worked, he believed in the power of whiskey, said, "Pot softens things, but whiskey just blots it all out like a total solar eclipse, man. It all gets still and dark. Just don't look too long straight at it. You go blind, man." Gator had this way of laughing like there was nothing better in the world than going blind. Billy thought he was nuts, but Katy liked him. Katy felt sorry for him. But Katy was always feeling sorry for things most people didn't notice. Maybe that was all this Randy person was, some other guy she'd taken in.

He looked back at her drawing, his blue cotton shirt, her pink ruffled blouse, like the kind of blouse she liked to wear on days she was feeling "girly." The last thing he thought of her was girly. But there they were in the frame: his shirt, her pink blouse, framed like they'd be sharing the bathroom and laundry forever. Then he remembered: "Let there be laundry for the backs of thieves." The other line from the poem. She'd shout it sometimes: "Let there be laundry for the backs of thieves," and laugh the way some people did when they hollered, "Merry Christmas."

He didn't get it. He'd read the poem. It said "clean linen," not "laundry," but he still didn't get it. And he didn't correct her when she shouted it out wrong. It made her happy. She had told him the poem was about forgiveness, that to love the world was to forgive it. But he'd never gotten what all that had to do with laundry and thieves.

But he figured it had something to do with the fact that she'd volunteered to do laundry for this homeless guy named Gator. He was a Vietnam vet, and he lived in the marshlands across the river. He made what money he could by working as a river guide for tourists and fishermen. He was a good guy, all tanned and blue eyes, not bad-looking when he smiled. But he was just a little bit crazy in that he preferred living his life out there with the gators and snakes rather than with people. Billy just figured that was what war could do.

And Gator was looking a whole lot better with Katy's care. She cut his hair once a month, and she did his laundry every week. Brought it home in a trash bag from the bar and took it back all folded and neat in another trash bag, a clean one.

Billy thought maybe Gator had some idea where Katy was. He'd been a scout in the army . . . maybe he knew something. Maybe he could help. After three days of solid drinking and steady smoking,

Billy wasn't blind yet. He could see enough to know he looked like a drunk in the mirror. He could see her panties on the towel rack, the empty wastebasket, the grime around the tub. He took the framed picture off the wall, hugged it to his chest. "Hold on," he said as he walked to the kitchen. He saw that it was bright with daylight and a wreck of Chinese takeout and uneaten pizza. Flies buzzed all over. "Shit," he said. "I'm sorry, Katy." He swatted at flies around the sink and stuck the dishes in the dishwasher. He poured the powder, slammed the door closed, and jammed the button to click the machine on. He opened the back door, used a newspaper to swat flies out. Then he dug under the sink for the last trash bag. That was on Katy's list. She was going to pick up trash bags at the Rite Aid when she got her prescription. There were other things they needed that she'd been supposed to pick up that day. He stood gripping the sink, enjoying the steady vibration of the dishwasher. As long as he gripped that countertop, he was pretty certain he wouldn't fall to the floor and be a puddle of hungover mess when that REV lady showed up. He remembered she was coming tomorrow. But tomorrow was today.

"Shit," he said, and he pitched beer cans, containers, and boxes into the bag. They had company coming, and Katy would want it clean. He sprayed air freshener all around the kitchen. "It will be fine, Katy," he said, talking to the framed words of the poem. He grabbed a broom. "We've just got to go through the motions of looking for you. It's like that drill bit I thought I lost one time. I was looking and looking, and when I reached in my pocket for some quarters, I found it. It was right there next to me the whole time. I'm gonna look and look for you. And then I'm gonna turn and see you are right here. Where you belong. With me."

The Luckiest Girl
in the World

Molly Flynn panted hard in the last stretch of her five-mile run. Her house was in sight. Time to sprint the last quarter mile. Then she saw the guy with the dog at the end of the street. She stopped, slowed to a walk. If she sprinted, she'd meet up with him, but if she went real slow, he'd have to keep moving and be on the side street if he really was out just to walk that dog. He lived just a little ways over, and of all the trails and streets he could take, he always seemed to pick her street. She didn't like the way his eyes traveled up and down her legs, over her arms, her chest. He never really did anything she could say was wrong, but it was like he was making fun of her somehow. She knew without speaking to him that he was a jerk.

She saw him look her way as if he might wait for her. She pretended not to notice and crouched down to retie her shoes. For God's sake, it was a nice neighborhood. A girl should be able to run in shorts and a sports bra without feeling like the neighbors would jump her bones first chance they got. She looked up, saw him bend and pat the dog like he was speaking to it. Then, without another look her way, he moved on. Thank God. He was so not her type, cute but a little too lean with these tight muscles, like all he was made of was muscle and bone. He looked like some kind of guitar player, wannabe rock star. He had the looks, all right. "But not my type," she said out loud as she walked toward her house. She hoped he'd gotten that message by now. She ignored him whenever she drove by him while he was walking that damned dog on the sidewalk. He'd let the dog shit anywhere, never once picked it up. He might live in the neighborhood, but it was clear to most everybody that he didn't belong.

By the time she reached her house, he was out of sight, so she didn't pretend to fiddle with the lock; she just pushed the front door open and walked in. Her mother had fussed at her for not locking the doors. But a five-mile run with a house key dangling from your wrist, who needed that? She was sweaty, and the sudden rush of air conditioning gave her a chill. She grabbed her hoodie from where she liked to leave it on a chair by the door—her mother didn't like that either, said the living room was a place for greeting people, not a place for throwing down your clothes wherever convenient. She pulled the hoodie on as she headed to the kitchen for a bottle of water. Hydrate, hydrate, hydrate, her coach always told her, so when she wasn't running or drinking water, she was usually needing to pee.

She went to the bathroom, washed her hands, studied her face in the mirror. She'd forgotten to put on sunscreen, and her skin was so delicate. It was something her mother had told her: "Freckles are cute on a girl, but not on a woman. They start to look like age spots after a while, and you're too pretty for that."

Molly Flynn had the face of a Botticelli angel. People often told her this. She was striking in a way that could make strangers walk up and say things like, "You have the face of a Botticelli angel." It always made her blush, but she'd learned to just shrug, say "Thanks," and turn away. She had looked up Botticelli's art at the library one day and had to admit there were similarities: the fair skin, round face, delicate lips, long hair that kind of rippled down the shoulders, and big, dreamy eyes. Yeah, she was kind of like that. But she wasn't impressed. It was just a lucky mix of her mother's Italian and her daddy's Irish genes. And these days, looking like a Botticelli angel wasn't exactly the hottest thing. She'd studied the magazines for what was hot, and she was not. Her thighs were too thick from all the running and gymnastics, her ass just a little too, well, round. They'd never pick her for the J. Crew catalog. She was glad Matt loved her just the way she was. He said women in the fashion magazines looked scary, while she looked real and hot and sweet.

So she looked like some old Italian painter's idea of an angel, the same painter who would've painted Jesus with blond hair and blue eyes. What did art know about anything anyway? It was all just somebody's idea of things.

Molly wasn't big on angels, like many of her friends. They'd buy little statues of angels to keep on their bedside tables, little angel bookmarks, posters; one of her friends even had an angel tattoo on her belly, a sexy little angel. "Great place for a guardian angel," Molly had said with a laugh. "Think that will keep the boys out of your pants?" But her friend had just given her a sly look, said, "Oh, no, it'll make 'em want to come a little closer for a good look at what I have."

Molly thought that was trashy, but she didn't say so. She knew the way to keep her friends was to keep half her thoughts to herself. Like church. Most of her friends went to church. Mostly Baptist, and they were always trying to bring her along. But she got out of it by saying she was Catholic; she had her own faith. Right. They used to be Catholic, which meant her dad could run around all he wanted as long as he confessed, said a few Hail Marys. All that faith in God hadn't done her mother any good with the breast cancer. No, it was a good doctor and a plastic surgeon who'd saved her from that. Her mother had learned a few things from how the church and a husband could fail you. She went to a women's support group every Wednesday night—an excuse to drink wine and gossip, but it made her mom strong. She'd learned a few things there and kept repeating them to Molly: "Believe in this world, not the next, Molly. Keep your body fit, your mind sharp, and your money invested. If your wits don't save you, nobody will." With her mother's words in mind, she remembered what day it was and hurried down the hall to her room. Molly sat at her computer to log on to the college website to see if the class she wanted had any openings yet.

Down the street, Jesse unhooked the leash from his dog and let him run through the woods alongside the trail. He needed to run. He thought about the girl. Yeah, she'd seen him. And what was with that stopping and bending down to tie her shoes? He let the dog run and sniff and pee on just about every tree in those woods. Dogs did that. Marked turf. He loved that dog, his muscled chest, the way his fur glimmered in the light, loved watching him run through those woods like the wild thing he ought to be.

His cell phone buzzed. His mother. She'd been completely on his ass since he'd stayed at Mike's that night. He answered. "I'm walking Luke; I'll be right home. Yes, ma'am," he said. He clicked off the phone. He'd forgotten to edge the sidewalk after he'd mown the grass. Everyone else in the neighborhood had a lawn service. But oh, no, his parents had him, not a good boy but the bad boy, the one they'd bought on sale and couldn't take back to the store. He called his dog, and he came running and stood at Jesse's side while he clipped the leash on. He crouched, patting the dog's side with firm, loving smacks. He ruffled the dog's ears, bent close, whispered, "We've got a job to do, Luke. Let's go."

. . .

Molly looked at the clock. Just after 5:00. *Perfect timing*, she thought. It was the last day for students to pay their tuition; as of 5:00, those who hadn't paid would be purged. *Purged*, she thought. It was an ugly word, as if the great computer system vomited out the poor ones who didn't have the money, whose financial aid hadn't come. So they were purged from the classes they'd registered in—no money, no class. *The world isn't fair*, she thought, and that really did strike her as a sad thing for a moment. It wasn't fair, but at least now there was a chance she could get into that afternoon section of the pedagogical theory class she needed. She was already in the night class, but she wanted her nights free to spend more time with Matt: dinners, movies, tennis at the club. She was trying to talk him into ballroom-dance classes, but he was resisting that. What she really wanted to tell him was that they needed dancing classes so they could dance at the wedding, really dance, not just wiggle and bounce around the way so many did. She wanted a real wedding with real dancing, even though Matt hadn't done anything like propose.

She clicked on the website for course options and started scrolling down the list of classes open and closed. She stared at the monitor as the list of sections rolled up on the screen: "Closed. Closed. Closed." In her introduction to psychology class, Molly had learned something about mind over matter, a theory that thoughts had energy, could actually change things in the physical world. *Visualize*, she thought, even though she didn't really believe in such things. Magical thinking, she called it. But what the hell, she'd try it. She sat back, sipped her water, and closed her eyes, saw names blinking off enrollment lists. Blink. Blink. Blink. Students were being purged, names blinking out one by one as the system's program sought out the ones who hadn't paid. "Amount due" meant blink, gone. *Sorry*, Molly thought, then sat up, watched the screen.

She glanced up at Matt's picture on her desk. He looked goofy with the snorkeling mask shoved on top of his head. But what a smile, a Brad Pitt kind of smile, just a little bit mischievous and sweet. She whispered to the picture, "I dare you to like ballroom dancing." It was a game they played, getting each other to try out new things. She had learned kickboxing, and he'd learned just a little bit of French, just enough to get by when they went to Paris one day. They took turns choosing things they'd never done before. Her mother worried sometimes about just how far Molly would go, had made her promise to always ask permission before she did anything too crazy like bungee jumping or leaping out of planes. Molly didn't know where she'd draw the line at too much risk. Molly had a belief, another thing she'd learned from her mother: *Never let fear keep you from what you want.* That was what she wanted to teach her students one day, fearlessness, faith in your own strength, curiosity— these were the things she wanted to teach the world, along with long division, and reading, and writing, and geography.

She stared at the computer screen, thought, *Come on, come on,* feeling like a gambler watching the balls whir around a roulette wheel. The unseen programmed intelligence was playing God now, choosing who was in and who was out while Molly sat in purgatory, eyes fixed on the screen, waiting for the word *Open* to appear. She stared at the line with the section she wanted: Tuesday/Thursday, 4:10 to 5:25. She stood, paced, waiting. She wanted dance lessons with Matt on Wednesday nights, not some pedagogical theory class. She wanted Matt to twirl her, dip her, lift her, her legs flying through the air. She wanted—that was her problem, her daddy had told her—sometimes she wanted too many things.

Molly stopped. She could feel it. She turned and looked toward the screen. "Open." She sat and signed into the course, then clicked for her registration list to see if the course was really there. Yep. Done. She stood as the printer clicked and hummed out proof of her new schedule. *Perfect*, she thought as she glanced out the window of her bedroom to the sunny day. Her mom would be happy. Since the divorce her mom had come to believe in grabbing pleasure. Now she was doing it with tennis lessons, yoga classes, book clubs. They lived together more like roommates than mother and daughter, but her mom still played the mom three nights a week, making supper for Molly, good-mom suppers like baked chicken and fried pork chops. Sometimes Molly felt she was the luckiest girl in the world.

Then she saw him, with that dog. Coming back down the sidewalk. She thought, *You don't even live on this street.* If she could get the double-paned windows open, she'd lean out and give him the finger. But instead she moved back from the window, stood to the side so he couldn't see her. He paused in front of her house, looked at her car. Lots of guys liked to look at her car—that was one reason she'd picked it. She knew she looked good in it, her red hair flying all around when she drove with the top down. He bent and spoke to his dog while he looked at the house, and Molly had a sudden urge to duck away from the window. She thought she really ought to listen more to her mother sometimes. Lock the door. Park the car inside the garage. Be a little more careful.

He gave the dog some quick, hard pats, then stood, walked on. Molly watched until he disappeared down the street. *Geez*, she thought, *lighten up. He's just another horny guy after your ass.* He was a neighbor, just a neighbor. She'd seen him help his daddy, working out in their yard. *Just a guy*, she thought. *Just a jerk.* But there was something in the way he studied her house. She felt a chill, pulled on her sweatpants over her shorts. The guy with the dog was gone, but something made her walk downstairs and lock the door. She glanced at the blinking lights of the security system she and her mother never used. Her mother was from rural Pennsylvania, where no one locked doors, where no one had anything worth stealing. Her daddy used to yell about their indifference to security: "I work my ass off to buy all these things, and you two don't care enough to lock them up." Her mother would just shrug and respond: "We live in a gated community. We have a security guard by the road who keeps an eye on every license plate that goes in and out of this place. What can happen here?"

Dubious Designs

Ominous, you might say, if you believed in things like portentous events, connections between random things. Let's say you pull into the post office parking lot to pick up a certified check, a donation in honor of a dead boy named Jimmy Reed. Okay, you're not likely to get a check in honor of a dead boy you found—this is my story. So let's say you get out of your car at the post office to do any of those mundane things you do and you step straight into a pile of bones. Rib bones, but bones nonetheless, baby-back pork ribs to be precise. So let's say you bend to look at them, gnawed, sucked clean, and you think—well, first you think *yuck* or *shit* or *what the fuck* or something like that. And then, especially if it's your first event of the day and you're still digesting your cup of coffee and toast, my guess is most of you couldn't help but think that stepping into a pile of bones first thing in the morning has to be a sign of something bad. It can't be good. And it wasn't good for me, with my foot pretty much bare in strappy flat sandals, my skin getting poked by the bones of some pig raised for slaughter. Nothing good in that, except maybe for the person who sat in that car at God knew what hour and ate those ribs, threw the bones to the pavement. I looked around, saw a paper plate and a wad of napkins blown against the chain-link fence along with leaves and all kinds of fast-food trash at the edge of the parking lot. And I was thinking if this were New Orleans, some old black woman might bend over to read those bones the way they read cards and palms and cat bones collected in a little leather pouch to be shaken loose to tell someone's fortune in the moonlight.

People believe in all kinds of things. Me, I see bones on pavement and I just think, *How rude*. I think about the indifference of appetite, especially when it comes to humans and pigs. I mean some animals eat with delicacy—raccoons, squirrels, gorillas, and birds; I love the birds. But humans, we're right there with the jackals and the crocodiles and the pigs. So I was standing in the hot morning sun, thinking about how someone ate the back meat of a pig, no doubt drizzled with hot sauce, then just dropped the remains out the window of a car. Then, satisfied, the careless carnivore drove off, leaving the bones for the ants, or flies, or rats, or me, the skin of my instep.

I told myself it was no sign of anything, but it didn't feel good, I can tell you that. I had Katy Connor pressing on my mind. I was meeting her mother the next morning, and I had to get ready for that. And then there were those two kids stolen from Ohio; their mom's boyfriend took them, and, being a fool, he was using her credit card to buy gas, so it was easy to track him. The mother said he was probably heading to Miami, and that would have him going down I-75, but they were tracking him on I-40 and heading south, which meant he could have been heading my way. So it was heads-up time to spot a blue van with Ohio plates. And that was just the top of my list for the moment—who knows what awful thing can rise up when my cell phone rings. There was a knot in my chest where a heart's supposed to be, and my things-to-do list sat ready on the dash. I was thinking post office, bank, then Whitey's Barbecue to get pulled-pork sandwiches for the staff. My crew deserved a treat after the case of

Jimmy Reed. He was a good boy, handsome, a star on his high school track team. I remembered the flyer:

MISSING
from Wilmington, North Carolina:
Jimmy Reed.
19, blond hair, brown eyes.
Last seen in a red Honda Civic with a spoiler,
red running lights, mag wheels.
If you have any information, please . . .

We had found the wheels at a used-parts place, asked questions, and searched. It took a couple of weeks, but we found him dumped in the woods behind an abandoned garage, head bashed in with a tire iron, car stripped of anything the dealers could sell. He owed them money, so they felt justified. We found Jimmy, and the cops busted an oxycodone ring. One detective put it this way on the evening news: "It's a tragedy but not a waste. Jimmy's death lead to the arrest of . . . his death will help prevent . . . blah blah blah." That was when I clicked off the TV. Cops love to grandstand on any dead body when the killer is caught. So REV made the news again, and we got this donation. But I didn't really want the donation because I didn't really want this business I'm in. I didn't want anything but Jimmy Reed alive. I wanted to see a lot of things, not pig bones licked clean and left on the pavement. I still think sometimes why don't I just go be a hairdresser like my momma wanted me to be? She said I'd always have a job doing hair. But you can also always have a job searching for the missing. Some days I'd give anything to have the peace of a hairdresser's dreams. And I was thinking after this one, I'd quit. One more grieving momma was still about all I could stand.

So I got back in the car. That would be your instinct too. You step into a pile of bones and it's only natural to think, *Do not go forward, step back, get that check another day.* I started the engine and sat thinking what to do next, and I decided I was in no mood for barbecue. I would take the staff Chinese. So I turned left at the light instead of right. Sometimes a left instead of a right can make all the difference in a day.

The traffic was backed up the way it always is on Oleander Boulevard. We were stopping and starting as the light let its little clumps of traffic through one bit at a time. I was in the right lane when I should have been in the left because just ahead I'd need to make that left, but no one would let me over because everyone always has someplace so important to go, and I looked over at the Calvary Cemetery there and thought of how a lot of bad shit goes in there once the sun goes down, and I'm not talking ghosts. Momma always said, "Don't worry about the spirits of the dead, Shelby; it's the living ones you've got to look out for." I've always had a fondness for graveyards. The peace and the green and all those silent markers of lives gone by. I looked over, and I was glad for the green of that cemetery in a part of town all littered with strip malls, wig stores, pawnshops, and carryouts. It seemed a good thing to me.

While we were all sitting in traffic, crowding up on bumpers and honking our horns, I thought we could use a reminder of where were going in the end. I looked ahead to try to guess how many cars were between me and the stoplight, tried to figure how many rounds of that light changing it would take before I could get through, and I saw what I thought was a pile of rags on the side of the road, right there on the sidewalk. Then, moving up, I saw it was a woman, a little old black woman sitting on the sidewalk, and the cars were just going by. I punched my hazard lights on, knowing what I'd do and how it would piss off everybody behind me.

I got close and saw that she was propped against a light post, and she was staring out as if there wasn't a thing she needed from this world. I got out, gave the finger to the car honking behind me. He went around me and yelled, but I just smiled and went to the woman sitting there. She was dark and gnarled as a tree blown down by a storm. I bent to her, said, "Ma'am, are you all right?"

She looked up at me with cloudy blue eyes, said, "Baby, I was praying you'd come back to me."

I crouched beside her, studied her face etched with deep lines, tried to remember if I knew her, how she knew me. She smelled like bread; she smelled like cotton sheets in hot sunlight. She smelled like heat and skin and leaves. She smelled like my mother. And for the first time in years the knot loosened in my chest and I wanted to cry. I remembered my tiny little mother, shrunken and weak with disease. She had said, "I'm leaving you this time, baby." I felt like I'd found her in a little black woman leaning on a light post near the oldest cemetery in town. Strangers stared from their cars, and the traffic crept by.

Sweat was rolling down my face, and I saw that she was dry as, yes, a bone. "How did you get here?" I asked. "I don't know, baby," she said. "I'm just visiting." I scanned through the "Missing" files in my brain. No one had reported an old black woman lost. I asked if she knew where she lived. And she gave me this surprised kind of look and said, "Why, baby, I live here." I looked around, saw nothing but the graveyard and the Kwik Mart across the street. "I mean your home," I said. "Your address, where you live." She nodded, said, "Five oh nine Wabash Street. That's where I live." When I asked if she wanted me to take her home, she said her boy was coming to get her, that he had gone to get some bread. I looked around, knowing you didn't buy bread in that part of town and you sure as hell didn't dump your momma on the street. So I asked her would she mind sitting in my truck while I tried to figure out how to get her back to where she lived. And she blessed me and blessed me, the way they do back home. She let me help her into my truck, and she clutched this old shopping bag to her chest. I was thinking she was homeless. She watched me get my map and said again, "Five oh nine Wabash; that's where I live."

I doubted it, but still I found the street. I gave her a bottle of water from the cooler in the backseat, and she blessed me again. I thought maybe this day would have a happy ending, with some woman disoriented, lost, and I would get her home. I like a story with an ending like that. But Wabash Street was a good eight miles away in the worst part of town. All crack houses. So I asked her name, and she sat up all ladylike, said, "Patricia England, and five oh nine Wabash is where I live." She reached in that plastic bag and gave me an old envelope that had her name and address written there in perfect handwriting, the way your grandmother writes, in the old-fashioned loops in all the right places kind of way.

I told her okay, and I was feeling hopeful as I opened it to see nothing inside. She looked in the backseat, smiled, said, "Oh, what pretty babies you have back there. Such good babies too." She said it so real that I glanced back. There was nothing but the cooler, an atlas, a black umbrella, and a Dunkin' Donuts coffee cup. She was smiling and waving so happy that I wondered for a second if she was real, maybe a spirit being I'd found at the cemetery. I figured she was just crazy—not bad crazy, just confused. So I thanked her for complimenting my babies, and I said yes, they were very good babies. She kept smiling at them while I drove. Then I heard her singing in this creaky soft voice, "Jesus loves the little children." She seemed too tired to finish the song. She straightened in her seat, leaned back, closed her eyes. I clicked my phone on silent so Patricia England could sleep.

When we got to 509 Wabash Street, there was a "Condemned" notice nailed to the door. The front porch was falling in. Paint blistered and peeling off the side of the house. A vase of pink plastic flowers sat in the window covered in yellow drapes. Whoever had lived there hadn't gotten a chance to pack the flowers, that vase that must have meant something at some time.

I reached and touched her arm. "Miss England," I said. "Miss England, you need to wake up now." It took her a while. Then her eyes popped open, and she said it again: "Bless you, baby, I've been waiting for you." I pointed to the house, asked if it was where she lived. She nodded, waved the envelope at me, said, "Five oh nine Wabash." Then she pointed to the numbers nailed to the banister of the porch. I looked at the envelope. There was no return address in the corner, just the smudged remains of where a label had been. Whoever had written the letter could afford address labels, wrote neatly. I asked who had sent her the letter, and she said it was a Mother's Day card from one of her babies, but all she had left was the envelope.

I asked if I could look in her bag to see if anything could help me get her home. She said firmly that this house was home, and I had to explain that it wasn't her home anymore, that it was condemned. She nodded and quoted, "'In my father's house are many mansions, if it were not so I would have told you. I go to prepare a place for you.'" She said I'd understand one day, and then I'd find peace.

When I looked in her bag I found a pink sweater, a clean dish towel, a green satin–covered cardboard jewelry box with broken strings of beads, a brooch in the shape of a Christmas tree, and an embroidered handkerchief all knotted up to hide a dollar and some change. I asked if that was all she had. While she sat nodding, I took a twenty from my purse and put it with the dollar, knotted it all up tight, and told her to be careful with who she trusted to go through her things.

She said, "Bless you, baby," and turned back toward the house like she was happy just to sit there and look at it. I speed-dialed Bitsy the research queen, told her to look up Patricia England, anything and everything about the woman and the address. I clicked the phone off, looked in the rearview mirror, and saw a couple of thugs standing at the corner watching us, nothing but trouble on their minds. I put the car in gear and headed for the police station, hoping maybe she was in a system that could tell us where she was supposed to be. I told her I wanted to get her back to her own babies, and she just gave a little sigh, said her babies were with Jesus now.

I was thinking she was crazy with grief and age and just being worn out by the world, and I was thinking what a sad place this world can be. Then she laughed a soft sound and said, "I can see you are a troubled child. In the name of Jesus, baby, I'm blessing you. You will find what you're looking for in this world."

The light turned green. I told her thank you and drove. She asked if I was a believer, if I had found the Lord, and I told her I tried. When I saw the police station, I told her I had great faith that we'd get her home. She just nodded and said with great certainty that she was going home.

At the station she looked around the parking lot. She shook her head and said it wasn't the right place. I told her we had to find where she lived, and she gave a little shrug. She said, "You won't find what you think you're gonna find." She looked up as if hearing a voice. Then she smiled and said, "One day, baby, you'll know what I mean."

Helping her out of the truck, I saw her tuck her white blouse into her big floral skirt. She was clean. Once out of the truck, she went weak, and I saw that the weight of standing pained her. Her ankles were so swollen, it seemed as if her legs had been stuffed into her shoes. Her skin was ashy, flaky. I thought of sycamores, the way the bark lightens, sheds as it grows. She leaned on me, and I walked her toward the door.

We walked in, and the cop behind the counter rolled his eyes. He didn't see me, just saw a hard-looking little woman in tight jeans and a tank top, big hair gone wild from the humidity. He saw some useless old black woman. He didn't give a shit.

I settled her in a chair and headed straight to him. When I told him who I was, he gave me a look like I was a stray dog just peed on his floor, said he knew who I was, the one who thinks cops can't do their job. I told him I'd never said that, but I was thinking, *Little Cub Scout cop, you don't know a thing about me.* But I played polite and admitted that on occasion I'd criticized the police work in town, but I always came around to the fact that we all work best when we work together. That was when Patricia England leaned forward and looked up to the ceiling and quoted, "'And we know that all things work together for good to them that love the Lord, to them who are the called according to his purpose.'" Then she sat back and closed her eyes like she was resting for the next little speech.

He shrugged and said, "Where'd you find this?" I looked past him to a guy at a desk who was pretending to be reading something, but I could tell by the little tilt of his head that his mind was on me. I said, so he'd hear it, Patricia England's name and where I'd found her and where she was supposed to live.

The cop at the back desk came over, gave a little tap to Cub Scout cop's shoulder. "This is Shelby Waters," he said. "Give her whatever she needs." Then he gave me a grin, said, "My name's Jack Walker. I'll see to your friend over there."

I handed the envelope to the Cub Scout. He took it, made a what-the-hell face, turned to his monitor, fingers pecking at the keyboard. I looked over, saw Walker offering the old woman a Coke, asking when was the last time she'd had a meal.

She shook her head, said, "Whatever I take just runs right through me."

Cub Scout motioned to me to bend close and said, "Patricia England is dead." I looked at the old woman sipping her Coke, asked the cop, "Did she have a sister?"

He grinned all smart-ass at me, said, "It's not like I have a obit here. Want me to pull out my crystal ball?" He pushed back from the desk, walked away. I called Bitsy. She had it all: Yes, Patricia England was dead. She had a daughter who'd died as a kid. And a son. A thief. Did some time. Last known residence 509 Wabash Street. Patricia England was buried, yes, at Calvary on Oleander Boulevard. My guess was that this woman had been a family friend. Maybe had lived there a while. Maybe the son took this woman to visit his mother's grave and left her there.

Walker said to leave her and they'd call Social Services, and I knew what that meant. Nothing would happen for hours. It meant they would just dump her at the Magnolia Street shelter and leave her sitting around until someone figured something out.

I told him to work on getting her a bed somewhere and I'd take care of Patricia England. I told him I had a doctor friend who'd look her over, get her what she needed.

"That's not procedure, and you know it," he said, but he was grinning. He knew my ways, and he was enjoying the view down my tank top. I gave him my card and said, "Call me."

"You bet," he said, and he opened the door, followed us out to the truck. He helped the old woman up into the seat, steadied the crackers in her lap and the Coke in her hand. I gave him a little salute and got going.

I called my friend Dr. Bev to set up the exam for the old woman, and she of course said to come on. Bev is good that way; she'll be on call around the clock and never charge a dime. I just had to make it up to her office in Castle Hayne, a farm town north of the city. So I settled in for the long drive. I was supposed to be meeting Billy Jenkins about Katy, and I needed to be calling Roy because this Billy had said Katy liked to spend time at Lake Waccamaw. Roy is sheriff in that county, and I was thinking I should get him on the Katy case, and I was thinking I had to make more calls about those Ohio kids, and I was thinking there were a hundred things I needed to be doing. She sat there looking out the window and nibbling a cracker like a little bird. But what can you do when a broken little old woman appears by the side of the road?

My cell phone buzzed. It was Bitsy at REV. She said the Ohio man had just charged a bunch of breakfasts at a McDonald's up in Rocky Point, and I couldn't help grinning, knowing he was just north of where I was heading, and most likely he was coming my way. I figured he was heading for the coast. Myrtle Beach, most likely; it's a place where losers like to go. Or he was taking some kind of long way to Miami. I got Bitsy making calls to try to get volunteers at every rest stop and gas station between Rocky Point and Myrtle Beach. And I watched the highway ahead of me with what my daddy called hunter's eyes. You go still somewhere in your brain and look out, eyes open to everything but seeing what you need to see, some movement, a color, a little flash of what you want out there. I called Bitsy to call Billy Jenkins and remind him that I wanted to see Katy's momma when she hit town. The old woman was sleeping, her breath making a rattling sound, and I thought she had walking pneumonia or bronchitis. I pressed the engine harder to get her to Dr. Bev.

The phone buzzed, and I was happy to see it was Roy. Patricia England sat up and patted at the seat around her. "I'm sorry, so sorry," she said. "I've had an accident here." She tried to lift up and get away from the wetness on the seat but sank back into it and looked at me, all tearful.

"It's all right," I said. "We'll get you cleaned." Out on the highway I saw nothing but gas stations and diners. I remembered there was a Walmart at the next exit.

She was bent over, making these little crying sounds. I kept telling her it'd be all right, that I'd get her clean things at the Walmart. Then she just kind of gave up and leaned against the door and tried to sit on the edge of the seat.

I parked at the far edge of the lot and told her I had baby wipes and dry towels in the back. She sat up, quiet, but I could see the tears running from her eyes. I was looking for my box of latex gloves in the back. I found the gloves, then heard her say with something like wonder, "Would you look at that? Look at those poor little babies, look at 'em crying like that. No babies should be as broken-hearted as that." I figured she was talking about the invisible babies. I headed around front and opened the door to try to put some towels under her. She wasn't looking in my backseat. She was staring straight ahead. "Look at 'em," she said. "You need to go take care of those babies in the van over there."

I looked, and there just in the next aisle was a blue van, Ohio plates, two kids staring from the back window.

I hurried around the truck to grab my Taser and my phone. The kids tracked me with their eyes. They matched the description: little brown-haired boy, about four, two-year-old girl. I figured they'd been warned not to call out for help. I dialed Bitsy. The driver was gone, doors locked. What the hell was he doing at Walmart? Bitsy read me the plate numbers on the missing van.

I said softly, "Sweet Jesus!" And the old woman said, "Amen." I gave our location to Bitsy, knew she'd take care of the rest.

I went to the van. The kids backed away, crying. I stepped closer, peered in, saw a cooler, a sleeping bag, bags of clothes. "It's all right," I said. "We'll get you back to home." A guy walking by stopped, then a mother and her teenaged girl. I turned. "It's all right," I said. "Just some kids locked in. Cops are on the way." They backed off, but not too far. I moved toward my truck. I looked to the old woman. She was sitting deeper in the seat. I figured she was asleep.

Then the man came out the doors and headed across the parking lot, just like he was supposed to: six foot, one seventy pounds or so. Skinny. Dark, curly hair, even wearing the same Guns n' Roses t-shirt he'd been wearing when he'd left with the kids. He spotted me, stopped. "Cops are on the way," I said. He dropped the bags and ran. But a running man can get only so far in a Walmart parking lot. Some big guy climbing out of a truck saw him taking off, gave me a look, made a lunge and a tackle, and the skinny dude was down. The big guy stood, his work boot planted on the man's back, not pressing, just holding. He looked at me. "He do something to you?"

I told him no, that the man had stolen two kids in Ohio. He gave the guy a little kick in the side, said, "Keys, asshole." The guy hollered, "I didn't do nothing to those kids." Big guy rolled him over, slapped him the way a man slaps a woman, and yelled again for the keys.

The guy on the ground was crying, shaking his head. He dug in his pocket, offered up the keys. He looked at me, said, "You don't know their mom." And that got me to thinking how behind every horror story there's another horror story. I took the keys from big guy, who put his boot on the man's chest. People were standing around, some applauding and some yelling to beat the hell out of the son of a bitch. And not a damn one of us knew what was really going on. Some followed me to the van. I unlocked it. The kids stayed hunched in the back.

I asked if they were all right, heard sirens coming our way. The boy came forward, and the baby girl sat making that dry sobbing sound like she was all out of tears. I asked the boy if he was Tim.

He nodded, pointed back to his sister, said, "That's Jenny." When I told him who I was, he asked if they were going to jail.

"Heavens, no," I said. "Did that man hurt you or your sister?" He shook his head. I asked if he knew where they were going. He shrugged and stared out the door of the van to where the cops had the man cuffed, shoved against a car, and asked, "Is he a bad man?"

"I don't know," I said. "Do you know this man who took you?" The boy nodded, said the man was his momma's friend, that his momma gave them to him and told the man to sell them in another state. His face squinched up with tears. And he sat on the floor of the van. The sister crawled over and squeezed into him.

"Sell you," I said like this was a normal thing.

The boy said, "She didn't mean it. She was just sad." Tears were running down his face. He wiped his nose with the back of his hand.

I looked back at the man. They all circled around him, barking questions the way cops do when they really want to knock hell out of you and all they've got is words. He looked like the bait dog with the pits moving in. He shook his head, kept saying, "You should see their mom."

"He didn't hurt us," the boy said. "He just said we had to keep quiet. If we didn't keep quiet, the cops would come put us in jail." I looked at the ring of sweat and dirt around his neck and asked if he and his sister would like to come out of the van. I told him I was with the policemen. He took his sister's hand and led her toward me.

Helping them out, I asked if they knew why the man had gone into the store.

The boy nodded and said they were running low on diapers and Dennis didn't want Jenny to get a rash. And he needed oil for the van.

Once they had the man in the back of a cruiser and the kids sipping juice boxes, a cop came to me, shook his head. "Ol' Dennis has got one hell of a story back there."

I nodded, my eyes on those ragged kids, said, "So does the boy."

The cop spit on the ground beside me—there ought to be a law against cops chewing and spitting on the job, but not in tobacco country, I guess. "He says that the mom told him to take the kids to Florida, and she gave him her credit card to use for gas." I looked at his spit on the ground, gave him a look that told him what I was thinking, and said, "This is hardly the most direct route between Cincinnati and Florida."

The cop shifted the chew in his mouth. "Dennis wasn't taking them to Florida. He was taking them to Myrtle Beach. He wanted his momma to watch the kids until he figured something out. He didn't want them in the system. He's been in the system. Foster home to foster home; he didn't want that for the kids." I had to ask, "So he was taking them to his momma?"

The cop shrugged. "We're checking it out. He says his mom got rehab, been clean for years now. Says he was only doing what he thought was best for the kids. And get this: The kids' momma, after a while she gets straight and realizes she's given him the kids and the credit card and thinks maybe that wasn't a good idea. So she calls it in. Says her drug-dealing boyfriend stole her kids."

I had no words for that. Heading back to the truck, I saw Patricia England, sunk deeper into the seat. When I got closer I saw that she was long past sleep. She was gone. I looked at her. She really did look peaceful, and there were much worse places she could have died. Like that sidewalk on Oleander Boulevard.

I got into the truck. Looked at the crowds gathered all around the cops. I saw the tow truck coming for the van. "You found them,"

I said to Miss England. "The babies. Thanks to you, they'll be all right." But she just sat there, her eyes closed as if in a deep sleep. In some religions they say the spirits of the dead hang around a while, that spirits hover around to see what will be done with what is left. They say the dead call out to the grieving, try to offer some kind of comfort to the ones left behind. They say it's very important to pray for their souls to move on to a good place so they won't get caught up with wandering here. I closed my eyes, gave thanks to Patricia England. I told her to go on to live with Jesus and her babies since that's what she believed. I heard the cars drive away, the people talking. I heard them walk by, felt them pause to look at me in my truck. Someone said something about the old woman, but they moved on. I guessed they figured we were praying. There was a rap on my window. I turned and saw him. Roy.

Tears stung my eyes. I rolled down the window. "Roy."

"Shelby," he said with that voice that says, *License and registration, please*. "Where do you think you're taking her?" He leaned close, and for a cold second he felt more like a cop than the man I knew.

"I couldn't just leave her here in a parking lot." He backed away from me, said, "You know the coroner's number." I told him not in that county. He shook his head and dialed a number on his phone, walked away, and squinted back at me like he was trying to get me in focus.

I looked over at Miss England, which is the name I'll always give her. I told her I'd take care of her, and I thought of countries where it is a loving thing, not a crime, to bury your own dead. I thought a woman who clung to the name of Patricia England deserved better than to be burned and packed, stored under some number. The way of all indigents. I hate that word. So there I was letting Roy do the work and talking to a dead woman, and the truck smelled of piss, and Roy was looking back at me like I'd really gone too far for the first time. My phone buzzed. I was happy to see it was Bitsy, who said what she always says when a search ends with the living and not the dead: "Look up and give thanks. It's a good day to be here." We say this at the center whenever there's something good. We say it the way some people jump up and say, "Look at that rainbow," or "There's a shooting star," something so natural and yet so amazing that your heart lifts and you just have to point and holler at the wonder and beauty of this world.

The Kindness
of Strangers

The plane trembled, engines revving up enough power to rip free
of the grip of gravity and lift them all above the miles of mountains
so blue-green and beautiful, east past the mountains to the flatlands
of the North Carolina coast, where solid ground gave way to swamp,
then finally fell away to the rolling tides, pushing, pulling, always
the line between what was solid and what was gone. Livy wondered
why Katy had had to go so far away just to prove who she was,
whoever she was these days. Livy knew she didn't really know her
daughter. A mother only liked to think she knew her child, but there
was always a hidden side. She knew there was a Frank-Katy and a
Billy-Katy—the wild and the safe. She liked to think the real Katy
was the safe Katy, the one who wanted a brick house and a husband
with a regular job. But she knew no one thing was true of anyone,
not Katy, not Billy, not even herself.

Livy held the armrests, closed her eyes, and told herself that
Katy was safe. She had just run off somewhere. She opened her eyes,
looked out the window, saw the rolling green of farms, mountains,
the shimmering blue of a lake. She wondered just where Katy was
down there on the ground beneath them. She felt a little shudder

of nausea at the thought of the words *Katy* and *ground*. "Stop it."
The lady across the aisle gave her a glance, edged a bit away as if she
might be sitting next to a crazy woman. Livy hadn't meant to say the
words out loud. She ran once again through the options of where
Katy could be: off with girlfriends, maybe another boyfriend, which
wouldn't be good, but at least she wasn't with Frank. Livy had
called him, but he hadn't heard anything from Katy.

Maybe Billy wasn't telling her everything. Maybe they'd had a big
fight. But if Katy had left Billy, she would have called. If Katy had left
Billy, the first thing she'd have done would have been to call Frank. Or
Livy. Or somebody. Three days. Livy thought about how bad things
come in threes. It had been three days, so today things would turn
good again. She had called Billy before she'd left for the airport, just to
be sure, still hoping Katy had come home. But no. Billy sounded high,
hungover, and drunk. He sounded lost. And he was crying. He was
counting on her to find Katy, make everything right.

"It will be all right," she said out loud.

The attendant walking by leaned, whispered, "There's no need
to worry. The pilot's flown this plane a hundred times. We'll be fine."

But you haven't made this journey, Livy thought. *You're just a boy.*
She looked down, thought of the earth spinning, sliding away from
them as they rose higher in the sky. Livy looked out and saw the
slight curve of the horizon. The earth was round. She thought if she
were dead, she'd circle and circle the earth, unable to let go, unable to
say good-bye to the people she loved. She'd keep circling back. She
wouldn't want to go to heaven, wherever heaven was. *If* heaven was.

She felt the air pressure shift, and she eased to the softening
sound of the engines. The planed rocked with turbulence, and she
grabbed the armrests. She hated flying, all the bumping and rattling
against the air, never knowing when the plane could drop thirty feet,
right itself, or keep on dropping. Lawrence had told her it was only

103

air currents. "Just like waves on the lake," he had said. "Think of it like a boat on a choppy lake, that's all." She tried to think of it like that, but still, what good was a life vest if you dropped from thirty thousand feet? The engines hummed softly now, no turbulence, just that comforting whir.

Livy knew takeoffs and landings were the most dangerous parts of a flight. Takeoffs were like breaking free from the bottom of a creek, like Suck Creek, which had that current that wanted to pull you down. You had to flap your arms hard to get momentum, kick, push, keep your eyes on the light above; you had to push until you broke free of the pull beneath you, and suddenly you shot to the surface, where you could relax and float on your back, and the water would hold you. She'd taught Katy how to float in Lake Chickamauga. She could see her skinny, long-legged Katy just learning to swim. She was nervous at first, wouldn't put her face in the water, so Livy started by teaching her how to float on her back, Katy's long legs and arms bobbing in the water while she kept her eyes on Livy's face. Livy would support her back, then say she would let go and Katy would drop a little. "If you relax, the water holds you," Livy promised. "Just lie on your back, wave your hands a bit, don't clench, and keep your head up; you just relax, you'll be fine."

Livy realized she was scratching at the polish on her nails—one chipped spot, and she was flicking and flicking at it. She did this when she was nervous, scratched and picked at things. When she was a girl, she liked to pull at the split ends of her hair. Sometimes she chewed her hair, her nails. When something was tearing her up inside, she had to tear at something on the outside as if that could let it out. She sighed, folded her hands in her lap, told herself again, *It will be all right; it will be all right*. But she knew the phrase was as hollow as those little Hail Marys she used to say in church, fingertips clutching rosary bead after bead as if she could pinch her way toward salvation. She'd never believed in that rosary thing.

She looked out the window and back toward the glare of a sun setting in the west. Lawrence was angry when she left, said she was overreacting. His voice still hung in the air around Livy even thirty thousand feet above the ground: "She's thirty years old, not some runaway child. Maybe she decided she didn't want to marry that guy. He's a bricklayer, a pothead who just happens to have a house. And she's a bartender, for God's sake. Maybe she just got drunk and took off for a party. You're gonna get down there and she'll be sitting in the living room with a hangover." Livy squeezed her hands together in her lap to keep from slapping him. "It happens," Lawrence said. "Women get a wild streak and run off. You see it on the news all the time."

"Not Katy," Livy said, even though she knew there'd been some pretty wild times with Frank. The woman across the aisle glanced at her, turned back to her *SkyMall* catalog. *Oh, God*, Livy thought, *I'm losing it, talking out loud*. She bit her lip, held it between her teeth to keep from talking. She stared at the blue upholstery of the seat in front of her. Lawrence hated it when Livy did anything that wasn't a part of his plan. They were supposed to have dinner that night, entertain some client and his wife. Fine food, good wine. Lawrence liked to take her out with clients. There were times it paid, he said, to have a glamour girl for a wife. Good-looking and knows numbers. Plays golf and cooks like a five-star chef. Livy hated it when he tallied up her virtues as if she were an investment. She felt like a dearly bought racehorse when he bragged and sat back with his friends watching her, proud of her grace and speed as she ran around the track.

Livy closed her eyes and prayed, *Please God, let her be all right*. Livy opened her eyes. The woman across the aisle was staring at her; then she looked away. Livy sighed and told herself that Billy had done something and Katy had run off. That was all. When Katy was a girl, she'd often run off when she was hurt, afraid, or ashamed. Livy always knew where to find her: up in the tree house her daddy had built. Sometimes Livy thought that was why Katy had moved to Wilmington, to hide from the girl she'd once been, as if striking out for a new land could make the old world disappear.

Livy's eyes teared. But she kept her gaze on the eastern horizon, knowing another day was passing and her daughter was gone. When Livy had called Billy from the airport just before stepping on the plane, he'd been crying. He had told her what she already knew, that this wasn't like Katy, that something was wrong. He'd called the cops, but they had said there were no leads and no signs of foul play. Livy's throat clenched as she swallowed back the nausea watering at the back of her mouth. She raised her hand for the attendant. He was a sweet-looking boy with dark hair, blue eyes. He looked at her with such tenderness, she could have been his weakened old aunt. Lord, she thought, did it show? Did she look as weak and broken as she felt?

"Yes, ma'am," he said. "Are you all right?"

"A Coke, please?" she asked. "I'm a little ill."

"Right away," he said.

Livy glanced out the window. Maybe Katy had crashed somewhere on the side of the road. Or maybe she'd gone to Lake Waccamaw by herself. She was always doing that, driving off to lonesome places to sip a beer, be alone. Maybe someone had grabbed her out there. It could happen. It happened all the time. She felt a sob breaking in her chest. Her mind fluttered over images of children on milk cartons, those "Missing" flyers flapping on phone poles, stuck on bulletin boards in grocery stores and Laundromats. Livy's mind turned over possibilities. Date rape? Drugs? Could Katy have stopped at a bar for a beer and someone—her mind skipped. She sucked in a breath, released it, and managed to say thank you as she reached for the cup of Coke from the attendant.

"You'll feel better in a minute," he said. "The plane has leveled off, and the captain predicts a smooth flight." His comforting words sent tears spilling from her eyes as she gulped down the Coke. The woman across the aisle glanced at her, then quickly turned away. Others looked and turned. No one wanted to see a woman collapsing on a plane. It was all so pathetic. Public grief. Lord, she should have ordered a beer. "My daughter is missing," she said out loud to no one.

The woman across the aisle, well dressed, like any middle-aged woman without fear on a plane, leaned toward her, reached as if to take Livy's hand. "I'm so sorry. I knew something was wrong." Livy kept her hands firmly clasped in her lap, so the woman pulled back. "Your daughter is missing?" she asked. "How old?"

"Thirty."

The woman looked away, indifference passing over her face. She was like Lawrence, believed thirty-year-old women disappeared only because they wanted to go.

"She would never run off," Livy said. "You don't know my daughter."

"She'll turn up," the woman said. "How long has she been missing?"

"Three days. But—"

"You don't need to worry," the woman said. "She's a grown woman. She's probably run off for a while the way people do. You see it on the news all the time." The woman's face looked so smooth, Livy wondered if she'd had a facelift. But her words were soothing, so Livy listened as if this strange woman with a too-smooth face were an authority on things. "You don't need to worry until they find something. Like if they found her car, her purse, something—what is it they call it? Evidence of foul play."

"This isn't *Law and Order*. This isn't TV. My daughter is missing!"

The attendant was rushing toward them. "Ma'am," he said, "please. You're creating a disturbance."

"I'm sorry," Livy said. "I'm sorry. It's just I'm afraid something awful has happened to my girl."

"She'll turn up," the woman said, her eyes fixed again on the *SkyMall* catalog.

Tears seeped up, and Livy didn't know if she could keep holding back a scream tearing at her throat. A voice spoke inside her, a quiet voice: *This isn't the time for wailing.* It was her saner self, the self that spoke to her, kept her calm.

The woman with the smooth face and blank eyes was still talking: "Think positive. She'll be there at the airport waiting. Then the two of you can go to Myrtle Beach—buy silly t-shirts, work on your tans."

Livy turned back toward her window and closed her eyes. She didn't want to see this day ending, another night coming without her girl. She wanted to think she would land and see Katy waiting at the gate. She wanted to think they'd drive together and sing along with a soft-rock station all the way home, and she'd see her girl smiling with some wild story of why she had disappeared. *She'll be there*, Livy told herself. Then she raised her hand to the attendant, asked if she could order a beer.

"What you need is a martini," the woman beside her said.

"I don't drink hard liquor," Livy said, but then she thought a cold shot of vodka could be nice. "Okay," she said, "a vodka martini. And bring one for this lady."

"My name's Marianne," the woman said, offering her hand. "And the drinks are on me."

Livy nodded. "I'm the one who should be buying."

"This is business class. They're buying." The lady gave a little laugh, and it was good to hear a happy sound. "And if you think you're getting a real martini, I've got news. It'll be a shot of vodka with an olive in it. But we'll call it a martini."

"I drank martinis with my daughter once," Livy said. "Her twenty-first birthday. That was between the marriages, when we were more like girlfriends." Livy looked at the woman watching her, saw the smile and then the concern in her eyes. The tears seeped up again. "I'm sorry. I'm not usually like this. It's just my daughter."

"I know," the woman said. "I have a daughter too. It's just that thinking the worst thing never helps." She offered her hand again, and this time Livy took it, held on. "Tell me something good about her," the woman said.

Livy thought, where to begin on the good things about Katy. "She likes to find broken things and fix them," she said.

"That's good," the woman said. "We could use more of her in the world." The attendant was coming with their drinks. "You can come over and sit with me if you like. I can move over to the window." She was already moving, so Livy scooted over, and they lowered their trays.

They clinked their glasses, and Livy felt happy for a moment. There was still the kindness of strangers out there, even at thirty thousand feet above the world.

With a Knick-Knack Paddy Whack

Jesse pulled into the gravel parking lot of the Over the Rainbow Day Care Center, put the car in park, and sat there with the engine running. He hated doing his mom's good deeds. It was like she thought making him do good things could make him be a good man. He thought, *Sorry, lady; too late for that.* But he would go in and be polite when the last thing he felt like doing was looking at a bunch of scraggly kids in a raggedy day care center in a neighborhood where there had to be a crack house on every other block.

Okay, so he'd do it for the old lady because doing for her was the only way he got rights to her car. So yeah, he'd do it. Jesse picked up a book from the box beside him. It was the pirate book; it had been his favorite. He was long past kids' books, so he'd thrown them all in the trash. But his mom had found them, carried them back into the house with tears in her eyes saying she couldn't believe he'd want to throw out the books she'd read to him every night when he was a kid, the books that were so important in teaching him he could be a loved little boy. He told her was sorry. He wasn't sorry for dumping the books, but he was sorry that once again he was making the woman cry. She sat at the kitchen table, ran her hands over the books as if they could appreciate her touch. "I'm sorry," he said. "What do you want me to do?"

She looked up at him and said. "I'd like you to do something kind, Jesse, something for someone beside yourself." He stood there thinking, her eyes on him. She looked at him with such hope always. It couldn't be anything but love. And he didn't get why she could love some messed-up kid who'd torn up just about anything they'd put in his hands. She'd talked his dad into getting him a puppy to make up for the one that had choked on the chicken bone. This mom had taught him to hold some things and not hurt. She was trying to keep him safe. She was trying to keep him from going to jail. He had to give her credit for that. She was the kind of woman who thought if you kept pouring clean water into a dirty creek, you could clean it. But sometimes the poison was in the dirt, and it just leached back into that creek. Some things weren't worth saving. But he wouldn't tell her that. So he told her he'd take the books to the day care center so some other kids could enjoy them. She liked that.

So there he was in his mom's white Beamer with a box of books, looking at the building that looked about to rot from the lack of paint. The sign seemed just thrown up on the roof, plywood with a painted rainbow and a couple kids and bluebirds floating above it. The kids looked kind of freaky with too-round faces and stuck-on smiles. His momma had said the place barely got by on its budget, so Jesse figured they couldn't get a real sign.

He got out of the car to smoke a cigarette. He heard the crunching of gravel, looked up, and saw a girl pulling in. She looked like she couldn't be eighteen, but there she was in her Arby's uniform, bending in the backseat to get her kid. *Nice ass*, he thought. She must have felt him looking because she turned and gave him a smile. But his eyes went to the boy, who had big dark eyes running with tears and snot running from his nose. He was sucking in little breaths like he was trying not to cry. "He all right?" Jesse said.

The girl nodded. "I just took him for his shots. You'd think I'd beat him half to death or something." The boy stared up at Jesse, calmer now.

Jesse crouched to him. "That's it. Don't you cry, now. And I'll give you something." He opened the car door and reached in for a book. It was the good one, the pirate pop-up book. The girl took it, bent to her kid, turned a page, and a ship jumped up from the page. The boy laughed and looked back to Jesse, as if he couldn't figure just who he was. "Now, that's for you to take home." He looked at the boy's mother. "You got that. That's for your boy." He touched the boy's head. "You be strong, dude. Like a pirate."

The girl leaned in. "Thank you," she said. "I gotta get him inside and go back to work." She gave him one of those please-ask-for-my number smiles, then looked past him to his mother's car. "Nice ride," she said.

"Yeah," he said.

The kid grabbed her leg, and she picked him up, went inside.

Yeah, he thought, *nice ride*. He mashed his cigarette on the ground and turned to the sound of kids yelling and squealing and running around the lot made up like a playground. He could feel it, the *I'm free* squealing feel of being released from a classroom, set loose to run and play. He walked toward them, watched them scrambling to be first on the swings, the seesaw, to see who'd be first up the slide, on top of the monkey bars. He stood at the chain-link fence and watched them run. "Go on, kids, have yourselves a good time while you can. You got no idea what might be coming at you." He closed his eyes, held on to the sound of their high, happy voices floating in the air.

"Okay," he said to the chain-link fence between them and went back to his mother's car. The girl was standing there, waiting for him. He nodded, reached into the backseat for the box of books, felt her eyes on him.

He turned, saw that smile again and her hand holding out a little piece of paper. "You want my phone number?"

"No." He saw the hurt in her eyes, the paper crumple up in her hand. "Just take care of your kid. That's all I want." He slammed the car door shut and walked away. He didn't look back, but he felt her staring as he went up the sidewalk. Going up the steps, he heard the sound of her starting her car, peeling out.

He gripped the box of books to his chest, looked down and saw *If You Give a Mouse a Cookie*. It was an old one, one of the first his new momma had read to him. He tried to remember the story, something about giving a mouse a cookie and it keeps wanting more of everything. Like the other one, *The Very Hungry Caterpillar*. It seemed in most kids' books everybody was wanting to eat. Goldilocks stealing porridge. Hansel and Gretel eating that lady's house. Then her trying to eat them. The big bad wolf. Everybody was hungry. He shifted the box, watched the books slide around. *The Runaway Bunny*, who kept saying he'd run away but then in the end decided to stay home and eat a carrot. He steadied the box against his side while he gave a rap on the front door, turned the knob. He pushed the door open and put on his best smile. The lady who ran the place would be sure to tell his mom how polite and well-behaved he was. "Good morning," he called to the big black woman behind the desk. She stood up and smiled, a real smile, the kind of smile that rose up from the belly and didn't just flicker across a face. He was glad she looked sweet. "I'm Jesse Hollowfield," he said. "My mother sent me—"

"I know who you are." She came toward him, moved like she might give him a hug, but he pushed the box of books at her. She stepped back a little. "Your momma just called to see if you'd dropped

113

by yet." She glanced at the books between them. "Put them on my desk there."

Jesse set the books down. "She worries," he said.

"Why, sure," the woman said. "Every lovin' momma worries about her boy, no matter how old he is."

"Yeah," Jesse said.

"You all right, honey?" she said. "You look a little green around the gills. Is it the heat? Want a glass of water?"

"No, ma'am."

She reached to shake his hand. "They call me Miss Moniece around here." She had soft hands, a good grip. "Tell your momma we sure are grateful for all the things she does. Last month she paid the light bill. She's a saint, that momma of yours."

"That's what they say." He watched her going through the books: *Curious George*, *Treasure Island*, *Where the Wild Things Are*. He wished he hadn't given away the pirate pop-up book.

She stopped rummaging, looked up at him. "These must have been your books, Jesse."

He was surprised she remembered his name. Most never caught a name on first greeting. Then again, his momma had probably told Miss Moniece all about him.

"Don't you want to hang on to some of these? Might want to share them with your own kids one day."

He kept his smile on, backed toward the door. "I don't plan on having kids."

She laughed. "Hardly nobody plans on it. Good-lookin' boy like you, you'll be making babies."

"No, ma'am, I'm dead set against it."

She looked at him, surprised. "What, you don't like kids?"

"Oh, I like kids." He watched her pull out *Goodnight Moon*.

She held it to her chest. "I always loved this one. Gave a copy to my grandbaby. He's six now, thinks he's too big for it, but I sure love reading it. Just calms you right down to look at the thing."

He leaned to look as she flipped through the pages. "That was my first book," he said. "The first one I remember."

She offered it to him. "You sure you don't want it back?"

He thought about it. He could give it to Zeke and Nicki Lynn's kid coming: Jesse James Daniels. But they'd probably tease him about giving a book to a baby. "I got a baby cousin on the way," he said. "They're naming him Jesse. For me."

She put the book on her desk. He knew she wanted to keep it for herself. "Isn't that something," she said. "Your momma didn't tell me there was a new baby on the way."

"Well, he's not really a cousin," Jesse said, picking up the book. "I got a friend with a baby coming. Kind of like a cousin." He pushed the book toward her. "You keep this one. You give it to someone good."

She leaned back, looked him over. "Well, ain't you a sweet one."

"Not really," Jesse said.

She turned toward the playroom and called, "Dee-Dee, come on out here and meet somebody. He brought us a box of books, good hardcover books for these kids."

He didn't want to bother meeting somebody and playing nice again. Then as soon as she came through the door and he saw that flaky bad skin and those dead eyes, he knew what she was. She nodded at him, looked at the books as if they were already a chore. All skinny arms and tight jeans and that kinky bleached-blond hair that looked like it'd break if you touched it. He stared at her until she looked back at him.

Miss Moniece nudged her. "Well, mind your manners and say hello, Dee-Dee."

She gave a half nod. "Hey." Their eyes stayed fixed on each other.

He knew what she was, and she knew he could see it. A damned crack addict trying to set up a fake life working with kids.

Miss Moniece picked up the box, pushed it toward the girl. She took it, gave a little sigh, and walked back to the playroom with that lazy I-don't-give-a-shit-if-I-get-across-the-room way addicts had.

He felt Moniece watching him watch the girl, but that was all right.

"You two know each other?"

"Nope," he said. But he pulled his lips in between his teeth, reached into his pocket for his mother's keys.

She frowned a little, looking at him. "Well, it just seemed . . ." She wasn't stupid.

Jesse shrugged. "She's familiar, I guess. There's a lot of girls out on the street like that."

"Yeah," Moniece said with a laugh. "We got a lot of skinny bleached blonds around here. Sometimes I swear all those white girls look alike to me." She gave him a quick look. "No offense meant."

"None taken," he said. "Sometimes they all look alike to me too." He looked toward the playroom, where the girl was shoving his books onto the shelf. "How long she been working here?"

Moniece sat as if happy to be off her feet. She was rifling through some papers, letting him know it was time to go. "'Bout six weeks. I don't think she'll last. Kids work her nerves a bit."

"That ain't all working her nerves," Jesse said.

She kept going through her papers. "You some kind of doctor, or a psychic?"

"Well, you know the look. Worn out at twenty-two. Hard-looking, real hard-looking. Don't y'all do drug tests on the girls working here?"

She rolled back in her chair, gave a *good God* kind of sigh, looked toward the girl and back to him. "I ain't no fool, Jesse Hollowfield.

I can tell when they using on the job. Ain't my business what any-body does on the weekend. I just make sure they do right by these kids when they here."

Jesse watched the girl shoving the books onto the shelves, not looking at the titles. "She got her own kids?"

Moniece stood, got in between him and the door to the play-room. "I don't think that's your business."

He gave her the I'm-just-a-guy-who-cares smile, a little shake of the head like he was disappointed with something sad in the world. Old ladies liked that. "It's just my momma sent those books. I gave those books to be read. So kids could see them, learn something maybe." He jerked his head toward the girl. "Shouldn't she be look-ing at the titles, thinking which kid might like what book? Shouldn't she be laying out a few books on the tables so when the kids came back inside from playing, they might get a little surprise?" He clenched his momma's keys.

Moniece blocked the doorway to the playroom. He gave a little shrug, stepped back. "I'm just saying . . ."

"That's very thoughtful of you," Moniece said. Her hands were moving into something like fists at her sides, but her face, it kept smiling. "I'll make sure I talk to Dee-Dee about that as soon as you leave. And I thank you. It's a rare thing to see a boy your age think so much of what might be best for the children."

She opened the front door, and he went to it, felt the heat of the day on his face. He turned to her. "I'm sure my mother has told you about me."

She nodded.

"I always think about kids. And I'm telling you to keep an eye on that Dee-Dee."

Then he left. Heading toward his mom's car, he heard the squeals of the kids again, not as loud as before, but happy sounds.

Then he heard the singsong rhythm of girls singing: "Pocket full of posies, ashes, ashes, we all fall down." He hated that song.

He leaned against his mother's car and lit a cigarette. Across the street, a couple thug types stood there, eyeing the car. "Just try it, fuckers," he whispered. They walked on. His cell phone buzzed. Mike. He flipped the phone open. "What."

Mike was freaked. Like he was always freaked when he couldn't get a handle on something going down. "That girl," Mike said in a voice that sounded like a whisper, had the feeling of a scream.

"What girl?"

"The blue-truck chick." Mike went on about how they found the girl's truck, traced the tags, and were doing searches all around Lake Waccamaw.

"So?" Jesse said. "That means they're looking for her, not you and me."

"Yeah, for now," Mike said. "But somebody's bound to say something. I mean it was my car. Anybody could remember a rusted-out red Datsun."

"Tell you what," Jesse said. "Go park your car at your granny's for a while. Let it sit, and get cool, dude."

"But the girl—"

"You're taking up my minutes, Mike. My mom monitors my minutes. You let me worry about the girl. When you get worried, you run your mouth off."

Mike said, "Okay, but—"

Jesse flipped the phone shut. Then he heard the kids again. Another song. He walked toward the playground, listened to them singing: "This old man, he played two, he played knick-knack on my shoe. . . ." He stood at the fence, saw that an old lady had a bunch of kids sitting in a circle on the shaded patio. They were all smiling.

"He played knick-knack on my knee, with a knick-knack paddy

whack, give a dog a bone." His mother could never get him through that song. It scared him. He didn't like the old man. But these kids were laughing and singing like it was "Jingle Bells." And the other kids were all playing, a little girl in a pink shirt pumping hard to get as high as she could on that swing. A boy and a girl on the seesaw going up and down. And there was a boy standing at the top of the slide, the other kids piled up on the ladder behind him, chanting, "Go on, sissy, go on." The boy didn't look scared. He was just standing there, taking in the view. "That's right, dude. You're king of the world right now. You go when you're ready."

He heard the lyrics: "This old man, he played four, he played knick-knack on my door, with a knick-knack paddy whack . . ." He looked back to the girl. She was watching him, slowing down by dragging the toes of her sneakers across the ground. The sole of her shoe was flipping back, all loose. She needed shoes. He'd have to tell his momma about that. He knew he needed to get home. His momma would be calling, but he wanted to hear the rest of the song. He'd forgotten what rhymed with five and nine.

He saw the crack bitch Dee-Dee come out the back door, stand on the edge of the playground, and light a cigarette. She was just like his blood mom. It wasn't the cigarettes that put those burns on her hands. If he could get hold of her, he'd do a good knick-knack paddy whack on her.

The song droned on: "He played knick-knack up in heaven."

The crack bitch was staring straight at him. She knew what he was. Yeah, she'd seen some shit, he was sure of that. He pointed his finger at her, gave a nod, said, "You." She might not have heard it, but she felt it. She threw down her cigarette, went over and said something to old Mother Goose lady, something like "There's a pervert over there by the fence." The old woman looked at him now, said something to Dee-Dee, who ran back inside. Yeah, she was scared. He could get her. It'd be easy to follow her home. They were coming toward him now. Mother Goose old lady with Moniece leading the way. "Jesse Hollowfield!"

He let go of his grip on the fence, didn't know he'd been squeezing so hard. His fingers burned. He smiled. "Yes, ma'am?"

She was right up on him. "What are you still doing here?"

"I was just watching the kids a little before I went home. It was nice to listen to them singing."

"I called your mother," Moniece said.

All the kids were staring at him. They'd been warned about strangers.

He looked to them, gave a nod to the girl in the pink t-shirt with the busted sneaker. She was standing close to Mother Goose lady. A few minutes ago he'd just been a guy standing there. Now all of a sudden he was bad. "It's all right, kids," he said. "I'm Jesse Hollowfield, and I just brought y'all a bunch of books. They're inside. Tell them, Miss Moniece. I'm not a bad guy."

She leaned close. "You've got no more business here. Don't you make me call the cops."

He backed away, palms up. "Whoa, now. I was just watching the kids. I saw that one there needs new shoes, and I'm gonna talk to my momma about getting these kids some new shoes." The little girl crouched down, tried to hide her torn shoe.

"It's all right," he said. "Ain't no shame in needing new shoes. I'm gonna see to it that you get some new shoes."

She stared up at him, not believing, not disbelieving, just waiting to see what would happen next.

"You get on home. Now!" Moniece turned her back on him, waved her hands to gather up the children, herd them back inside. "Play time's over," she said softly. She wouldn't give him another look. But Mother Goose did, a squinty-eyed sneer. He just looked right back until she turned away.

He walked to the car, thinking how he'd tell his mom he'd been polite, he'd just stopped to listen to the kids sing. He wouldn't tell her about the crack whore. He wouldn't tell her a lot of things he was thinking. He'd keep it all positive. His mom liked that. He grinned, thinking he'd get that Dee-Dee in time. He got in the car, singing, "With a knick-knack paddy whack, give a dog a bone, this old man is going home."

So Much for Grace

Billy pulled the truck to the curb, braked, cut the engine, stared at his hands on the wheel. He had hardly spoken on the ride from the airport. Had just given Livy a shake of his head. *Not a word yet. Nothing.* That was all Livy could recall of his responses to her questions. Finally she'd given up trying to learn anything about Katy and just sat back in her seat, let him drive.

She leaned forward to see any sign of Katy. The house glowed in the darkness, blazed a warm yellow light. "The lights are on," Livy said. "Could she be home?"

"I can't turn the lights off," Billy said. "Can't stand the dark." He got out of the truck, went to the back for her suitcase. Livy didn't want to get out, didn't want to walk down that sidewalk, up those steps to an empty house. The front porch was covered with Katy's plants arranged on tables and pieces of furniture someone had thrown in the trash, junk that Katy rescued, sanded, painted, revived. "Katy likes to rescue things," Livy said.

Billy stopped, turned toward her. "What?"

"Nothing bad could happen to her. Right, Billy?"

Billy hefted the suitcase up the sidewalk. Livy stared at the house, waiting, as if any minute Katy would rush out with her hands dirty from digging in the yard, or smeared with paint. But the house just sat there.

"Katy always wanted a brick house," Livy said, "ever since she was a girl."

"I know," Billy said. "We have a joke. Our nice brick house can keep the wolf out." Billy opened the door. "We ought to get inside. Maybe there's a message."

Livy followed him across the porch, lush with hanging baskets of ferns, pots of all kinds of plants that Livy should have known but couldn't name. Billy stepped inside while Livy stood at the threshold, breathing the scent of Katy in the air. No perfume, just Katy, the scent of her life: candles, old books, stripped wood, and paint. Livy walked into the living room. The walls were painted green. Tobago Green, Katy had told her when she chose the paint. Like the Caribbean. "Artsy," Livy had called it. Bare floors, green walls, plain white muslin over the windows, and objects most would call junk scattered around the room. A blue mason jar filled with wildflowers going limp. Rocks and odd pieces of wood on the mantel. An old tricycle in the corner.

The room felt abandoned, like a set where a drama would begin as soon as the actors arrived. Livy sank into a chair. Billy stood over the answering machine, his face blank, body frozen as if waiting for a cue. But there were no messages.

"There has to be something," Livy said, standing, heading toward the bedroom. "She didn't pack anything? No note?"

"Just this: 'Be back when I can.'" Billy pulled the crumpled piece of paper from his pocket.

Livy read the note, eyes moving over every curve of the letters. "So she'll be back," Livy said. "She just had other things do to. Wasn't sure how long it would take."

123

Billy studied the note. "Most times she writes, 'Be back soon.'"

Livy felt a hardening in her chest, as if the breath that went in stayed there, solidified. If she exhaled, she would collapse. "Katy never lies," Livy said.

"Sure she does." Billy took the note, spread it out on the coffee table. He studied it as if maybe he'd overlooked something. "We all lie sometimes." Billy glanced up at her. "I mean—" He shook his head. "Oh, hell, I don't know. Just because you leave a note—"

She turned away. "I'm going to look through her things in her bedroom." She paused, looked back at him. "I mean your bedroom. Do you mind?"

Billy sighed, sat on the floor, his back resting against the couch. "Have at it, Livy. I've gone through everything. Even looked in the trash. She dyed her hair before she left. There was a box of dye in the bathroom, those plastic gloves. But she left all her lotions and creams. She wouldn't go anywhere without those lotions and creams. You know how she is."

"I know my daughter." She couldn't control the fury in her voice. "I'm sorry, Billy," she said softly as she headed for the hallway.

Livy stood in the doorway and looked over the bedroom. She saw no signs of a fight. This was Katy's room. Books, candles, perfumes, and creams. Jeans and t-shirts piled up on a chair. The bedroom reflected the private Katy. The messy Katy, the one who shoved coupons in books as bookmarks, the one who kicked socks and shoes under the bed, tossed her clothes into drawers, mashed them down to get the drawer shut. There were two Katys at least. The smiling Katy who won homecoming queen. And the other Katy, the troubled Katy who Livy tried to pretend she didn't see. The Katy whose habit of thoughts always turned to sorrow, the Katy who was always wishing for her daddy's love, for everyone's love. The Katy who craved a strong brick house to keep her safe from the wolf.

Livy's gaze moved over the crystals hung in the windows, the guardian-angel print over the bed, a silly thing Katy had kept from her childhood, the shamrock plant growing by the window, the little gold cross hanging on a chain over the vanity mirror. Katy collected good-luck charms: a cross, a shamrock, a crystal, even an eye of Fatima—something she'd gotten from a Muslim friend. It was meant to be a necklace, but Katy kept it on a piece of fishing twine and hung it on the wall. The eye of Fatima was supposed to ward off evil. Livy looked at the eye staring out from a setting of blue stone and silver filigree. The eye just looked back. It seemed to her they should at least put some kind of expression of love in the thing. Livy fingered the cross hanging on her neck; she'd slipped it on just before she'd left for the airport. For luck, she had thought at the time. She told herself that before the night was over, she should at least try to pray.

Livy walked past the clothes, the shoes, the books scattered on the floor. Livy sat on the bed and saw the journal on the bedside table. Katy had kept journals since she was a teenager. Livy had sneaked a peek once, regretted it. She had read about her daughter having sex with her boyfriend, saw that her daughter didn't really like the sex but liked the smell and strength of the guy. She could see the soft, curving letters in that diary, the kind of writing used on valentines. Her daughter had wanted a man like a woman and written like a little girl. Livy clutched the journal to her chest. She closed her eyes, sank into the loss she felt coming, then fought it with the words almost shouting inside: *Don't think the worst things. Katy will come home!* She straightened, opened her eyes, and saw her own reflection in the mirror across the room. She could see Katy there. Livy opened the journal, flipped through pages, saw Katy's scrawl, still the handwriting of a girl.

She wasn't ready to take in words yet. She let her gaze slide over

125

the letters, fragments, doodles of hearts, questions marks, flowers and vines curling between patches of words. Some pages were filled solid, as if Katy couldn't keep up with the flow of thoughts spilling faster that her hands could catch.

Billy stood in the doorway. "That's not her journal, if that's what you're looking for."

"I'm sorry," Livy said. "I was just seeing if there was a clue."

"She called that one her scrapbook. It's a collection of words, lines, stuff she liked and wanted to remember." He sat beside her, took the book, flipped to a page, read, " 'Be not afeard, the isle is full of noises sounds and sweet airs that give delight and hurt not.' That's Shakespeare. It sounds prettier when she reads it."

Livy reached to open the bedside drawer. "Well, there must be a journal around here somewhere. She's always kept one."

Billy took a firm but gentle hold on her wrist. "That's private."

"I'm sorry." She sat with her hands folded in her lap. She probably didn't want to see what was in the drawer of the bedside table. She stood. "So you didn't find a journal." He shook his head. She could tell by the way he dropped his head that he was lying. "There's something you're not telling me."

He sighed. "Yeah, there was a journal. But it's private, and you've got to give her that."

"Okay," she said.

He kept his eye on the rug. "It's nothing you'd find helpful. Lots of doodles, and leaves, and hearts, and tears. And Frank. Lots of stuff about Frank. I know she wants me because I have a house and a job. And, well, she knows the way I feel. I'll love her no matter what she does. Wish it didn't work like that some times." He shrugged and sat at the foot of the bed. "We all know she has a weakness for the bad boys."

Livy patted his arm, but he moved away. "I'm sorry," she said.

Billy stared at the floor. "I'm not mentioned at all. Just Frank. A few things about Dan, that decorator she worked for. And Gator, this homeless guy she liked to take care of. Personal stuff." He sighed. "There was a name I didn't know. Randy. You know anything about Randy?"

Livy could see him squeezing back tears. "No. But you know how she makes friends wherever he goes."

"She was sad a lot, Livy. Do people just write in journals when they're feeling sad? Because there wasn't a word about being happy. Just sad and hurt all the time. I thought I'd be the one to make her happy." He glanced up. She saw the pain in his face, reached for his hand. He stood and went to the closet and stared at the clothes hanging there. He shook his head. "I couldn't read all of it. It's Katy's thoughts, just her thoughts, you know. If people knew our private thoughts, we'd all be locked in the nuthouse or jail."

"She always had a problem with depression. I told her the best way out of depression was to do something for someone else. And their happiness, it rubs off."

He looked back at her, went toward the window, looked out. "She does help people. And that helps some." Billy shook his head. "I can't make her happy."

"No one can make anyone happy. I've tried." Livy stepped past Billy and headed for the kitchen. "Happy? We have to do that on our own."

She felt Billy following her down the hall like a stray pup. "Katy was always thinking too much, and if you think too much, it's hard to be happy. I told her that." She turned to Billy. "Tell me about Dan?"

Billy opened the back door, lit another cigarette. "Her boss. He likes her."

"Everyone likes Katy. I thought her boss's name was Pete."

"That's at the bar. Dan's the decorator. Katy was working for him, painting, hanging wallpaper. You knew about that."

"What's she say about him?"

"Something about a door." Billy nodded. "She was working at this house. Left with the back door open. Wide open. You know how Katy could be. Forgetful sometimes. Well, the lady who owned the house got real pissed, said she didn't want Katy in the house again." Billy stepped onto the back porch, blew smoke to the darkness. "So she messed up. Big deal." Billy moved into the backyard, sat in a glider, rocked with his feet, and looked up through the trees. "Lately, I don't know. She's been distracted. Leaves the coffee pot on. Lets the truck run out of gas. Goes off to do something and comes back wondering what it was she was supposed to do."

Livy sat beside him. "Billy, maybe she ran out of gas. That gas gauge hasn't worked for years. Did you report her truck missing?"

"Of course I did. I talked to the cops." He looked up into the night. "But there's a lot of country out there. And you know how she likes to drive. She calls me when she runs out of gas."

"But she hasn't called." Livy's voice rose to a childish whine.

"That's because she left her cell phone on the porch. I thought I told you that. I found it on that table where she keeps all those plants." Billy squinted at the burning tip of his cigarette. "Come on, now, Livy. You're thinking the worst possible thing. Gotta be positive." He gave a hard laugh. "Like maybe she just ran off with some man. Not Frank, though. Maybe there was some new man. Randy."

"She's going to marry you in a month," Livy said. "Who's Randy?"

"Nobody." Billy shrugged. "Girls do all kinds of things," Billy said, standing. "I'm going inside for a beer. You want one?'

"No," Livy said, then, "Yes, a beer, Billy. I'll have a beer."

He nodded, headed in the back door.

Livy sat for a moment surrounded by the night, the wind in the trees, and the heaps of brick. Her eyes locked on the yellow light from a neighbor's kitchen window. As she stared, it seemed to be receding, darkness seeping into the distance between her and the house, between her and Katy, between her and everything she knew. She jumped up and ran for the back door, wanting the light of the kitchen, wanting anything but to be left out there alone.

Inside, she saw Billy leaning against the counter holding an empty picture frame.

"Where the picture?" Livy said. Billy tossed the frame onto the counter, reached into the refrigerator, and grabbed two beers. "I gave it to the lady at REV." He handed a beer to Livy, took the other, and stood by the window.

"REV?" Livy said.

"Rescue Effort Volunteers. They help people. When the cops were being dicks, I called REV." Billy gazed out the window. "They do things cops don't. Start work on the search while cops are still sitting back thinking about it, eating doughnuts and staring at computer screens." Billy shrugged. "Shelby said somebody goes missing, you gotta get right to work on the search. Every minute, every hour counts."

"Stop," Livy said. She didn't want to think about minutes, hours, days, what might be happening to her girl. She grabbed the beer he set out for her. Blue Moon. Katy liked it with an orange slice. She took some hard swallows, wanted to chug the whole thing the way she'd seen boys do. "Who's Shelby?"

"This lady—she runs REV. Some kick-ass woman. I heard about her at the bar. Used to be a bartender out at Wrightsville Beach. She's little but tough. Looks like some kind of biker chick. I wouldn't mess with her." Billy reached into his pocket, gave Livy the business card. She studied the words: *Rescue Effort Volunteers* and a cartoon kind of logo with a muscular arm flexed around a heart. Livy gave him back the card.

Billy studied it as if it held an answer. "They take missing people seriously. This Shelby, she showed up the day I called. Walks right in, asks for pictures, any information I had."

"Did you give her the journal?"

"Yeah," he said.

She studied him for a lie, couldn't be sure.

"Shelby wanted a really good picture for the flyer. She wanted something that would make people really want to keep an eye out. She looked at about everything we have before she picked that one to make a flyer." Billy pointed his beer bottle at the empty frame. "She said that was the best one."

Livy sipped her beer. "I don't want to see Katy's face on a missing-person sign."

"Me neither." Billy finished his beer. "But you gotta do it. Shelby said no effort toward saving someone is wasted." He shrugged and headed to the living room.

"Please don't do that, Billy."

"What?"

"That." Livy gave a quick raise and drop of her shoulders. "It's so, so . . ." She couldn't find the words. He turned for the living room, and she followed. He paced the room like a cat in a cage, and she, suddenly exhausted, dropped to the couch. There was the sound of a car door slamming shut outside.

Billy pulled back the curtains of the window, looked out. "Cop," he said.

Livy put her beer on the floor and braced herself as Billy opened the door. "Have you found her?"

A man in a sports jacket gave them a blank stare.

"Have you found her?" Livy asked. She stood, went to him,

could read nothing in his little gray eyes, but she did see the badge fixed on his belt. "If you have some kind of information, I'd like to know." Livy hardened herself. She didn't like this man. She stepped back. The words came weakly. "Come in."

He stepped inside, scanned the room, eyes snagging on Billy, who sank onto a chair.

"Billy Jenkins?"

Billy nodded. "I made the report."

"I'm her mother," Livy said "Have you found her?"

Standing there in the large room, the man looked small under the high ceiling, a little boy–man dressed up, playing cop. He stood there holding a plastic shopping bag and a cheap portfolio. His shoes were scuffed and his face shiny.

Livy saw his shoulder holster as he propped his hands on his hips, moved closer to Billy, who wouldn't look up. Billy always looked guilty. She had never trusted Billy, pot-smoking, brick-laying Billy. He hardly talked unless you asked him a question. Katy had said he was just shy around strangers.

Livy moved toward the cop. "You're here about Katy. My daughter." She sucked in a breath, straightened, crossed her arms over her chest, hands clenched tight to stop the shaking. "You can tell me," she said.

The cop looked again toward Billy.

Livy grabbed his arm. "What?"

He took a seat, set the bag and the portfolio on the coffee table, reached into his pocket for a pad. "I've got good news," he said.

No, he didn't. Livy stared at the man in the suit with the gray little eyes and the bloated face that looked like he drank too much. He flipped the notepad open, eyes on the pages as if he'd forgotten what he'd come to say.

"We found your daughter's truck."

She studied the bald spot on the top of his head. "And was Katy with it?"

"No, ma'am."

"Then you don't have good news for me."

He glanced up at her and shrugged. Fury surged through her, and she clenched her fists, fingernails digging into her palms. She swallowed the words *you bastard* and said, "You won't have good news for me until my daughter is home."

"I'm doing you a favor coming here like this. Doing more than my job."

"I suppose I should thank you." Livy walked to the window, looked out at the dimly lit street, saw a neighbor setting garbage out. She glanced back.

The detective set his notepad on the coffee table and watched Billy. "We'll need you to come down to the station and answer some questions."

"Am I being arrested?" Billy patted the front of his shirt for his cigarettes.

"No. Just come by tomorrow morning. You ever take a lie-detector test?"

Billy paled. "No."

"You willing?"

Billy sighed. "Yes, hell, yes. I'll take the test."

Livy felt her head was expanding from pressure building inside. She looked at her hands, felt her face, everything was normal, feet on the floor, arms at her sides, ears trying to hear what this stranger was saying, but she couldn't connect.

"I've got an idea about your daughter."

"An idea?" Livy said. "Based on whatever you've got in that little notebook of yours?" Livy paced. "This is Katy's house. She painted these walls, refinished those floors. See that coffee table? She found it by the side of the road; she stained and inlaid all those little pieces of wood. See those shelves? She built them. Katy could find any piece of junk by the side of the road and make it something good."

"I know you're upset. But these things aren't relevant to the case."

"'Case'?" Her voice shrieked. "We are talking about my daughter."

The man held her in his gaze as if he were straining to be patient with a nut. "Ma'am, you are gonna have to calm down and listen to me."

She crossed the room, sat next to Billy. "Calm? You want me to be calm?"

He nodded. "We called in dogs, searched the truck. There was no sign of foul play. Keys in the ignition, no sign of a struggle. We found this shopping bag." He nudged it toward Billy. "When you reported her missing, you didn't say anything about a shopping trip. You know anything about this?"

Billy shook his head.

Livy grabbed the bag, found the skirt, the top, the underwear, and the receipt. "It's dated three days ago. The day she disappeared. 6:22 P.M." Livy leaned toward the detective, clutched the receipt with both hands. "Dollar Daze. She bought these things the day she disappeared. Have you asked anyone at the store if they remember her?"

The detective made a note in his pad. "We'll check it out."

Livy threw the receipt at him. "You didn't even bother looking at the receipt, did you?"

He tucked the flimsy piece of paper into the portfolio. "I told you we'd check it out."

Billy reached for the matching underwear, beige with black lace. "She never buys stuff like this."

"Sure, she does," Livy said, grabbing the underwear, shoving it into the bag.

"Not for me," Billy said. He sat, looked toward the door and shook his head. "Not for me," he said again.

The detective pointed his pen at Billy. "Any ideas who she bought that underwear for? You the jealous type?"

"No." Billy stood. "Do I need a lawyer?"

"Not at the moment." The detective shoved the clothes back into the plastic bag. "Evidence," he said as he watched Billy leave the room.

Livy grabbed the bag from his hands. "You could at least fold her clothes. My daughter bought these things. My daughter." Livy sat and concentrated on getting the seams straight on the skirt, folding the top carefully so no crease would show in the front. She glanced at the detective. "Something awful has happened. She's in some kind of trouble somewhere. She's . . ." Livy stacked the clothes neatly on her lap, hid the underwear under the skirt, smoothed the fabric.

"I'll need those," he said as he took the clothes from her, placed them in the bag. "Ma'am, we've profiled her."

"What?" She'd heard the words but couldn't take her attention away from Katy's things disappearing into the plastic bag.

"Profile. We gather facts, habits, age, race, income, where she liked to go." He paused. "What she liked to drink."

"I know what a profile is."

He went back to flipping through his pad. "There were beer cans, lots of beer cans under the seats of her truck. Did your daughter have a drinking problem? Was it her habit to drink and drive?"

Livy stood and faced him. "My daughter is not the criminal here."

"Ma'am, we dusted the truck for prints—but now I have to tell you, the truck, it was filthy. Full of trash and dirt and leaves."

"She liked to collect plants from the woods," Billy said. He stood in the doorway now. "She liked to collect leaves and rocks and sticks and things. Is that a crime? She worked two jobs, was always running somewhere. So sometimes things slipped her mind. She was not a drunk." Billy crossed the room, mashed his cigarette out in an ashtray on the table. "You profiled her? Your profile say she keeps a perfect house? It say anything about that garden in the backyard? Does it say Katy is the kind of woman would give her last dollar to a stranger if he had the need?"

The detective cleared his throat. "We found evidence of marijuana."

Billy laughed. "'Evidence of marijuana.' Want to tell me just what that means?"

"We found marijuana."

Livy yelled, "My daughter is not a drug addict!"

"How much marijuana?" Billy said.

The detective looked to his notes. "On the seats, in the glove box, not a lot, but enough to know she smoked dope."

Billy turned away. "So you found some pot. Did you find enough pot to make a bust? You got that there in your notes?"

The detective snapped the notebook closed and stood. "She had pot in her possession. So maybe she was partying when she, ah, disappeared."

Livy sank back into the chair. Grace and dignity. She'd taught Katy that. *No matter how bad things are, if you get through each day with grace and dignity, you're doing all right.* She gripped the arms of her chair. "Her truck," she said. "Where did you find her truck?"

"Lake Waccamaw." He looked at Billy. "You gave us that clue."

"She liked to drive there," Livy said. "We all knew that. She liked to drive out there because she liked nature. She liked to sit out there and write."

135

"And drink, most likely," the cop said.

"Would you please quit slandering my daughter?"

The cop shrugged and looked at his notes.

She turned to Billy. "Maybe she went for a hike out there, wandered off out there. Maybe she just got lost." She turned back to the cop.

The detective softened then. "Our dogs got no scent of her."

Livy stood. "Your dogs. How would they know what she smells like?"

Billy leaned forward. "I gave them a shirt. The one she sleeps in. I gave them something in case they needed to track her."

"Track her?"

"Shelby said it could be useful." Billy stood and went back into the kitchen.

Livy turned to the detective. "Mr. . . . ." She paused. "I don't even know your name, and you talk about tracking my daughter with dogs."

"Block. Detective Block," he said. "And this would all go easier if you wouldn't resist."

"Resist?" She turned back to the bookshelf, read the titles: *Walden, The Road Less Traveled, The Wizard of Oz*. She could still feel him there behind her. "Would you please leave?"

"I'm sorry. No parent wants to hear these things."

She faced him. "What things?"

He opened a larger notebook now. Livy caught a glimpse of a computer printout. "The profile. Mr. Jenkins gave us some information, and some we gathered ourselves. Facts, random facts, we put them together, draw conclusions. Most times we're right, Mrs. Connor."

"My name is Mrs. Baines. Connor was her daddy's name. I remarried. Add that to your list of facts. Married twice, and yes, I like a cold beer now and then. We were just having one. What do you conclude from that, Mr. Block?"

He sat. "You really should listen to this. We're almost always right."

"'Almost always' doesn't mean a thing to me."

He studied his papers. "As I said. Beer cans, marijuana."

Livy stared into his puffy, pinkish face as he read from his list of facts. "She's a bartender. And a decorator," Livy said.

He went on. "One arrest for driving under the influence." He nodded toward Livy. "She's an attractive woman. If you don't mind my saying, she seems to have a record for closing bars in this town."

"My daughter is not a tramp!"

He kept his eyes down. "I'm just noting the information we've gathered on her—I made no conclusions about her morals, ma'am."

"Yes, you did."

He read on. "Katy Connor recently received five hundred dollars for a wallpapering job, according to Mr. Jenkins, on the day before she disappeared."

"She never deposited that check," Billy said. "She left it in a cookbook she was reading."

"Distracted," the detective said. "And she dyed her hair."

"She dyed her hair?" Livy said. "I dye my hair. Are you calling that evidence of something?"

The detective looked at her directly now. "According to our profile, most likely Katy Connor gets a case of the prewedding jitters, she dyes her hair blond, runs off to Fort Lauderdale with friends she met at a bar, one last bash out of town. She'll run out of cash in time, decide she needs to come home and face the music."

"If my daughter were going to run off, she'd run home. She'd run to me."

"We don't always know our daughters, ma'am. My own daughter, she did the same thing once. Ran off to Fort Lauderdale for two weeks, did things I don't even want to think about. Came to her senses and called home."

Livy spoke calmly: "And how old was your daughter?"

"Eighteen."

She rushed across the room, got so close that spit flew at his face as she spoke. "My daughter is a thirty-year-old woman. She's not some tramp who ran away."

He took it calmly, no doubt used to crazed mothers and worse. "Like I said, sometimes we don't know our daughters."

She slapped him. Heard the sound, saw the shock on his face before she even had the thought to do it. Her hand, it just flew, and now it burned. She stepped back, shocked. They faced each other, breath rising and falling between them.

"Livy, are you all right?" Billy was beside her, holding her arm.

She jerked free. "No, I am not all right."

The detective grabbed up the plastic shopping bag, tucked it under his arm with the purse. "I'll just write that up as extreme distress." He headed for the door. "Ma'am, you better just go on back to Tennessee and leave the business of investigation to us. But you'll owe me an apology when your daughter comes home."

She went after him again, but Billy held her, whispering, "Shh, Livy, let it go." The detective walked out, slammed the door.

She turned to Billy. "You really have no idea where she is?"

"I told you, Livy. I've checked everywhere. She didn't dye her hair blond, just those highlights things. And she sure as hell didn't run off to Florida."

Livy walked across the room, stood at the window, and stroked the fabric of the curtains her daughter had made. She had hemmed all the edges by hand. Livy studied the uneven stitches, kissed them, turned and looked around the room. The gleaming floors, the scattered rugs Katy had picked up from yard sales. She felt Billy watching her. "I'm doing all I can, Billy. I don't know what else to do."

He lit a cigarette. "Maybe they'll find something when they trace the numbers on her cell phone. Probably something there we don't know about."

Livy squeezed the fabric of the curtain, told herself to relax or she'd pull the whole thing down. She looked toward Billy, blowing a cloud of smoke between them. She wished she smoked. "I could use another beer."

He nodded, and she followed him into the kitchen, her eyes burning in the harsher light. She flicked off the switch as he opened the refrigerator door. "I need the darkness," she said. "Just for a little while." Billy cracked open the beer, slipped the bottle into her hand. They sat at the table, drank, listened as the old refrigerator cranked up, rumbling, whirring, the machinery struggling to keep things cool.

Billy swigged his beer, leaned back, and started laughing.

"What?" Livy clutched her beer with both hands.

"You slapped him!" Billy said. "You popped a cop in the face."

Livy felt the laughter well up, shake inside her. "I did. I slapped a cop in the face. Wait until Katy hears this. Her mother slapped a cop." She thought of Lawrence. He'd be horrified. Just the thought of the shock on his face made her rock with a new swell of laughter. "Livy Connor Baines assaulted a police officer." They both sat in the dark, laughing. "So much for grace." She reached for Billy's hand. "Katy's gonna love this." They looked across the table at each other, holding hands tighter, tighter as the clanking of the refrigerator shut down and left them sitting in the dark with the slant of yellow light from the living room and a quiet hum of hidden machinery whirring on.

As if the Words Could Make It True

The sound of the wood chipper grinding branches made Jesse's teeth hurt. He stopped raking the matted leaves and sticks onto the tarp and looked back at his dad. Jesse could see the grinning pleasure of destruction in the man with the hat and goggles hiding most of his face. He glanced up at Jesse, turned the machine off with only about half the branch chewed. "You get those leaves under the live oak?"

Jesse nodded, kept raking. Jesse had gotten the ground clean enough for the workers to come in and start digging the foundation for the cabin his dad wanted built. His dad called it their "getaway place." Jesse heard the bullshit: his dad standing at the backyard grill, looking at the other houses all around them and telling his wife he was feeling closed in by too many neighbors. Jesse knew his dad's real plan. He wanted to build a place so he and his girlfriend could take the boat out, run up here, and screw their brains out all weekend while Jesse's mom believed his dad was away doing manly things in the woods with other men—things like fishing, chopping wood, playing cards. His poor mom. She'd believe anything.

Jesse had seen his dad at the marina. Jesse had gone there to bring Jenny some pot, get a little massage. They'd screw on her daddy's houseboat. Jesse knew all about boats and men and screwing around. He and Jenny were just getting ready to head back to the marina so she could get to her shift waiting tables. Jesse looked out the window and saw them: his dad in khaki shorts and that pink polo shirt and those deck shoes he'd buy new each summer just because, as he said, he liked things clean. And this chick, not much older than Jesse, blond hair all caught up in a high ponytail, a halter top, and short shorts that looked something like a skirt. Long, muscled legs and spiky shoes. Everything about her kind of jiggled and swayed, from the bouncy ponytail to the boobs and the ass. Jesse had to sit back and laugh. Jenny had a way of making him go easy about things with the way she could loosen the muscles in his back. Jenny asked what was funny, and he pointed to his dad. "That old man," he said. "That chick, what you think, she a stripper or a whore?"

Jenny grinned, took a hit from the one-hitter. "'Entertainment,'" she said. "That's what management calls her. Stripper is what she is. Works private parties in the back room."

Jesse watched his dad put his hand on the girl's back like it was used to being there. "Bitch," he said.

Jenny laughed. "She's actually not so bad. Just making a living."

Jesse watched his dad, a perfect gentleman as he unlocked the gate that led to the private docks, let the girl walk through, then turned to make sure the door locked behind him. He offered his arm to steady the girl so she wouldn't trip walking around in those shoes. Jesse thought of his mother, picking up the old man's laundry, making his low-carb meals.

Jenny offered him a hit.

"Nah, I don't need that," Jesse said. He kept his eyes on the boat. His dad leaned close to the girl, said something that made her laugh. He could hear the high, ringing sound. He'd never heard his mom laugh like that. He watched them disappear inside the boat.

He turned to Jenny. "Could you rub my neck a little?" She pressed her fingers into his neck. He closed his eyes, tried to ease up under the touch of Jenny's hands. But he couldn't shake the sight of his blood momma taking men back into her room with a crack pipe and a laugh.

He flinched, felt the cold touch of a bottle of Coke against his arm, and saw his dad standing there. "You look like you need a break, Jesse." Jesse took the Coke, chugged half of it down. "Let's just sit and cool down a while." His dad sat on a stump, motioned to Jesse to sit on another one. But Jesse just stood there. He wasn't in the mood for this old father-son bullshit. "Come on, Jesse, stop and take a look at this place." His dad waved his hand toward the river. "I'm seeing the boat dock right there. Build it a good fifty feet." He pointed up the bank a ways. "A boathouse there. Get a couple canoes. Kayaks, maybe." He got up and took a couple of steps toward Jesse, that smile beaming. "You and me, we can fish off that dock." He squeezed Jesse's shoulder. Jesse stepped away.

"You all right, Jesse?"

"Just hot." Jesse pulled his cap off, wanted to yell, *You're such a liar*. But his dad was the man who paid the lawyers, and the right lawyer made all the difference in front of a judge. Jesse fanned himself. "It's a damned hot day to be burning leaves."

"Yeah, but it's humid. Less likely to start a fire we can't keep under control." He looked Jesse up and down. "You can always cool off in the river."

"I'm all right." He finished the Coke, put his cap back on, and tossed the bottle on the ground. He picked up the edges of the tarp and pulled it down toward the fire pit by the river.

His dad moved toward him. "Need help?"

"I got it," Jesse said. His dad watched as he dragged the tarp to the pit. He tossed the branches on and, with a couple of hard shakes, dumped the leaves and branches on the heap.

He walked down to the river's edge and looked into the shadows in the water, the black mud beneath. He heard his dad go to the truck and rummage in the cooler. He crouched for a closer look at the water, figured if he sat real still, he'd see some minnows darting around in the light spots. He waited for some kind of movement. Nothing. All the noise had scared them off, and they'd take their time coming back. Fish. They had a simple life, just floating, darting up and down and around. They'd take their own sweet time before they swam from the shadows. They had such patience, such caution that Jesse wondered how a fish could be so stupid as to get caught by some fake lure. "Always hungry," he said out loud. He heard his dad coming up behind him.

"I knew you were hungry. And I know how that temper can stir up when you don't have something in your belly to hold it down."

Jesse dropped from his crouch and sat on the dirt, kept his eyes on the water. "That's what Mom says."

"She's a smart woman," his dad said. "A good woman." He offered Jesse another Coke and a tube of Ritz crackers. He knew what Jesse liked. Jesse ripped the wax paper open, took a few crackers, offered the rest to his dad, who waved them away. "I packed those for you. Too much salt and fat for this old man."

"Since when did you start worrying about salt and fat?" Jesse kept his eyes on the water, stuffed a couple of crackers into his mouth.

"Can't stay young forever, Jesse. It's all about maintenance. Won't be long before you'll come to understand the need for a plan to make your life what you want."

"I know all about plans," Jesse said. He could feel it coming, one of those long talks about his future. If the man asked him one more time, *Where do you see yourself in five years?*, Jesse would tell him prison, maybe death row. Or hell. That was where he really knew he'd be in the end.

He glanced at his dad, a man so busy chugging his bottled water that he couldn't have a clue as to the kinds of plans that were stirring up in Jesse's head. When his dad finished the water and looked out at the river, Jesse saw a sagging under the jawbone. He was looking old. Jesse's mom was still looking smooth and fine. Probably because she didn't drink. And she didn't wear herself down with the worry of lying and scheming like the old man. His mom, she liked to keep her mind on higher things. "You ought to be nicer to mom," Jesse said.

His dad stood went to the river, straightened his shoulders, and took a breath. *Here we go*, Jesse thought, *the old tactic: Change the topic fast, get the ball in your court.*

"Your mother told me about the incident at the day care center."

Jesse stood, walked over, and looked into his dad's eyes. He was taller than his dad now. "'Incident'?"

"You hanging around outside that fence, staring at the children. Hell, Jesse, any grown man knows better than to stand around and stare at kids."

Jesse smiled the smile that he liked to think could charm a pit bull into backing down. He looked down at his workboots and thought of Zeke and that Rottweiler.

"I'm talking to you, Jesse."

Jesse smiled again and shook his head. "I took the books Mom used to read to me when I was a kid. I liked seeing them happy out there. So when did it get wrong to watch kids playing? What the hell is wrong with this world?"

His dad shook his head. "You've got a point there."

"I know I've done a lot of shit, but I never was a perv."

"I know. It's just, there are rules." He crouched down, studied the ground at the shoreline. He fingered the rocks. Jesse knew he was looking for the smooth, round, flat ones. He watched as his dad found one, stood, and leaned a little to get good aim. They stood in silence, watched the stone skip four times, then sink. His dad smiled back at Jesse. "Remember when I taught you that?"

Jesse nodded. His dad picked up more stones, offered them to Jesse. Jesse studied them and in one quick move picked one and sent it out. He smiled, watching it skip, one, two, and finally six times before it dropped.

"That's my boy," his dad said. "I can teach you something, and you take it and run with it. It's nothing for you to outdo your old man."

Jesse kept his eye on the spot in the water where the rock had sunk. He heard his dad sigh. The old speech was coming.

"You know you can be anything you want to be, Jesse."

"I know."

"You know you've got our support to the ends of the earth."

Jesse nodded.

"Jesse." His dad squeezed his shoulder. Jesse flinched. His dad took a step back.

"Sorry, I was just thinking." Jesse patted the old man's shoulder. "You know how jumpy I can be."

"What's on your mind, Jesse?"

Jesse shook his head, looked out at the river. "You ever feel like you were too big for a town?"

His dad nodded, gave a little laugh. "That's called ambition. You know the answer to that question. When I was a ten-year-old boy, I told my momma back in Pembroke, Georgia, 'I'm gonna grow up and be too rich for this town. They don't have a house big enough for what I want here.' And you know what she said?"

Jesse nodded. "She laughed."

"Damn right." His dad stepped closer, put his hand on Jesse's shoulder. "Believe in yourself, Jesse. That's how you start. You just gotta believe."

"Oh, believe," Jesse said. He made his muscles stay easy under the little squeeze of the man's hand. "Right now I believe it's time to burn this shit."

"Sounds right to me." His dad went to the truck, brought back a can of charcoal-lighter fluid. He started to pour it on the heap of sticks and leaves, but Jesse stepped forward and took the can. "Come on, let me do it. I did the work of dragging it all down here. You know how I like to burn things."

His dad stepped back, gave a little laugh, and Jesse could hear the nervousness in it. Jesse poured the fluid on the pile, breathing in the sweet, hot smell. He capped the can and offered it back to his dad. "It's a guy thing, I guess." His dad nodded and gave him the matches from his pocket. "You let me take care of this and get on back to your wood chipper. I could see you were into that. It's a guy thing. We get a kick out of building things up, tearing them down." Jesse shook the matchbox in his hand. "We all like our different ways of destroying things."

A flicker of something moved across the man's face. Jesse hoped it was guilt. "There's a right way and a wrong way to destroy things, Jesse."

"Yeah and Mom's probably the only one of us who really cares about right and wrong." Jesse gave his dad a sneaky smile. "But she don't know everything, does she?"

His dad dropped his head. "Damn it, Jesse, just when I think I've made some connection with you."

Jesse laughed. "Come on, Dad, I'm just yanking your chain. We know sometimes a man's just got to do what a man's got to do."

His dad shook his head and looked out at the river.

Jesse stepped nearer to him. "I'm not some kid anymore. I know there's no man perfect." Jesse felt the stillness in the air. "I'm just calling what I see."

"And what do you see?'

Jesse looked at him. "You want me to tell the truth?"

His dad sighed. "Yeah, let's try the truth."

Jesse reopened the can and sprayed more fuel on the heap of branches. Capped the can again and gave it to his dad, then bent, struck a match, and lit a clump of leaves. He moved to the other side of the brush, lit another clump of leaves. He stood and watched the burning spread. "Truth is, I see a world where there ain't no right and wrong, really. That line is always shifting. It all depends on things. You ask me, it's all about consequences. You want to do something, weigh the consequences. Do what you gotta do, but take what comes of it like a man."

"Yep." His dad kept his eyes on the fire. "Don't go at it blind, I guess, and you'll be all right."

"Right," Jesse said. He squeezed the old man's shoulder. "Now, you get on back to the wood chipper. You tear up shit your way, and I'll do it mine."

"I'm making mulch for the lawn, Jesse. It's not always about tearing shit up."

"Right," Jesse said, keeping his eyes on the growing flames. His dad stood there as if he might say something, then just headed back to keep building that pile of mulch under the trees.

Heaven Beguiles the Tired

Livy sat at Katy's table, with her coffee going cold in Katy's favorite cup. It was Royal Doulton bone china from England. *Probably older than I am*, Livy thought as she ran her fingertip along the rim, where the gold was fading, then traced the outline of the hand-painted clutch of violets. Katy had found the cup at a yard sale, no saucer, but she made it work with a green saucer. Livy tried to imagine how Katy was waking now. Katy had run off before, but she'd always called the next day. She was eighteen, and in those bad years with Frank you could never be sure where she was and when she might come home. But she was older now. Steady. At least that's what Livy thought. She reached for Katy's scrapbook and flipped through the pages. She'd already gone through it a dozen times. Katy had always loved scrapbooks, saved birthday cards, postcards, pressed flowers, concert tickets, and Valentines. This one was more like a journal, with some of the poetry she liked, sketches, doodles, quotes from scripture, and little bits of writing in her own words. Livy had read and reread those pages. Billy wouldn't let Livy see the journal. Livy knew the worst of Katy would be in those pages. Katy only wrote when she was feeling lost, confused.

Livy stood, rinsed out her cup. She had a jangly feeling. The feeling had started with Billy's phone call that awful night he'd told her Katy was gone. Sometimes the jangling would fade, like when she was doing something: making phone calls, doing laundry, washing dishes, but it never really went away. It just faded the way the sound of a barking dog seems to fade when you turn up the music a little louder.

Livy was feeling less like flesh and blood and more like mismatched silverware banging around in a box, waiting for someone to come clean her up, sort her out. In truth, there was no real peace of mind, just the "distracted from distraction by distraction" feeling. Livy had read those words in Katy's scrapbook. T. S. Elliot's words. Katy had written his name in tiny letters under the quotation. Katy wanted to write one day, but all she managed to do was collect other people's words. Livy figured there had to be some value in that.

Livy put her cup and saucer in the drainer and looked around the kitchen, felt the ceiling coming down, making it hard to breathe. She'd been up since dawn, had awakened with the sound of the birds that had made a nest in the gutter outside the guest-room window. Normally she liked the feeling of waking to the sound of life twittering. But now it seemed that every waking moment hurt. She was beginning to understand why people did drugs. Ambien wasn't enough. A beer before bed wasn't enough. And she knew to avoid the habit of vodka. So she had lain there in the dark, trying not to think of all the awful places Katy might be.

Livy went to the back porch, where she could admire the garden. It was overgrown with weeds, the herbs going to seed. Katy had always been a girl of good intentions. She'd have to tell the REV woman that. Katy wasn't a tramp, and she wasn't a drunk. She had a few flaws, like anyone, but she always tried to do the best she could. Livy looked at her watch. It was 8:45. Shelby Waters was supposed to be there at 9:00. Livy went back inside, picked up the scrapbook, and held it close to her chest, trying to feel Katy there. She put the scrapbook on the coffee table and went into the bathroom to check her makeup. She wondered if the capris and sandals were too casual. She had gotten dressed quickly because she had waited for Billy to be up and out of the house before she started moving around. She'd lain there in the predawn darkness, listened to the sounds of Billy in the bathroom, in the kitchen, then back in the bedroom for something. She'd listened to the back-and-forth of his steps in the hall.

Now Livy studied her face in the mirror. She saw Katy's face looking back, an older, thicker version of her girl. She closed her eyes, said, "Where are you, Katy?" She heard only the twittering of birds outside. She opened her eyes and headed for the kitchen.

Billy had said Shelby Waters was from Tennessee, said she was one of those backwoods country types. Livy had let him talk, wondering how much Katy had told him about her own past. Livy had trained her country manners out of herself and had brought Katy up with the ways and tastes of an educated, middle-class young woman. And sometimes Livy was sorry about that, thought maybe Katy had missed out on something.

Billy said this Shelby Waters was scrappy—like those mountain people. Livy didn't like the word *scrappy* applied to anyone. It made a person sound like some kind of stray dog with fleas. "And what do you mean by 'mountain people'?" she asked. "Katy and I are mountain people." He looked at her, grinned, and said, "But you're top-of-the-mountain people. There's top of the mountain and there's those from back in the hollers. This Shelby Waters, she's a back-in-the holler kind of girl." Livy decided then that she'd probably like Shelby Waters. "So this Shelby, she's from back home, but not like me and Katy." Billy shook his head. "Nah, she's kick-ass. You know, like those rednecks who can look you straight in the eye and grin, and you know they're just figuring how they could take you when you turn your back. You know the type."

She said, "You don't know squat about mountain people, Billy."

"I saw *Deliverance*," he said. Then he laughed and lit a cigarette.

She turned to do the dishes to keep from saying things she'd like to say. Billy said, "I bet you've never even seen *Deliverance*. 'I'm gonna make you squeal like a pig.' Bet you don't know that." She turned, wanted to throw the beer bottle at him, but she set it down carefully in the drain, wiped her hands on a towel, said, "You're stoned again, Billy. And I've got no use talking to you stoned." She went straight to Katy's guest room and waited there, listened to the sound of Billy opening the refrigerator and getting another beer. She couldn't stand the way she could hear every little sound in the house. She sat on her bed, hating him for no clear reason. Then after a while she caught the scent of another joint lit. She thought of going to yell at him, but it was his house, Katy's house, not her house. Then, as if Lawrence could hear her thinking, her cell phone buzzed. She decided she hated him too and clicked the phone off. She sat there on the narrow little futon bed that was awful for her back, thinking there wasn't anyone in the world she could stand. Except Katy.

So she took her Ambien and wished she had another one of those martinis, or two, or ten, or whatever it would take to turn her brain off. She finally slipped out of her clothes and into her gown and got under the thin blanket. She had told herself she could wait until Billy went to bed before she went out there to brush her teeth.

Now, awake to another day with Katy gone, Livy walked through the living room and wished this Shelby Waters would hurry up and appear. *Positive*, she thought. *Think positive*. She'd tried teaching Katy that. And Katy acted like she believed in positive things like lucky charms and that special license plate. She was always ready to treat anyone more like a friend than a stranger.

Heaven beguiles the tired, Livy thought. Katy's words, well, someone else's words in Katy's scrapbook. It was written several times in the scrapbook. Livy hated to think of Katy being so sad. She picked up the scrapbook, went to the page where Katy had written more of the poem as if it was a treasure she'd found. It was only the last line of the stanza that kept reappearing on other pages. Livy read the words:

As Watchers hang upon the East,
As Beggars revel at a feast
By savory Fancy spread—
As brooks in deserts babble sweet
On ear too far for the delight,
Heaven beguiles the tired.

Livy ran her fingertip over the last line, considered whether *beguile* meant *beckons* or *teases* or *deceives*. She decided it meant all those things, and that only made her sad. She closed the book, went to the screen door, and looked out. A black Durango pulled up slowly and stopped in front of the house. It was one of those oversized things boys like to drive, and it had tinted windows, fancy rims, and lots of chrome. Definitely a man's truck. Some friend of Billy's, Livy thought, bracing herself. Then she saw a woman step out, a little woman with big reddish-blond hair. She had thin, muscled arms. Billy was right; she did look like one of those tough women from back home. Livy pushed open the screen door and stepped out. The woman stopped, looked up at Livy, and smiled.

Livy moved forward, offering her hand, "You must be Shelby Waters."

The woman came up the steps and shook her hand with both hands, warmly, softly, the way a preacher does. "I'm happy to meet you."

"No one's really happy to meet me. But I do my best to remedy that." She gave Livy that smile again, still holding her hand. She had the sharpest, greenest eyes Livy had ever seen.

"Billy didn't say you were so pretty."

Shelby laughed. "That's sweet of you to say, Mrs. Baines." Livy invited her into the house. "Thank you for getting my name right. Katy carries her daddy's name."

"Billy told me." Shelby stood in the living room, looked around.

Livy studied her. She looked so small but was muscled as if she were used to moving the world stone by stone to wherever she needed it to go. "Would you like some coffee? Water?"

"No, ma'am," she said, her eyes going to the stack of books on the table.

"Sit, then," Livy said. "You can call me Livy. My name is Olivia, but my friends call me Livy, and I'm counting on you to be the best friend I can have."

"I'll try," Shelby said.

Livy picked up Katy's scrapbook, thought to offer it to Shelby, but then just sat and said, "It's a nightmare."

"It always is," Shelby said. Livy watched Shelby look around the room as if there were something she needed to see. "Where's Billy?" she asked.

"Work. We're trying to keep things normal. He has to work. The police want him to come take a lie-detector test. Do you think he had something to do with this?"

"No," Shelby said, her hands moving over the books on the table. "He's as lost as you are." She looked up. "We're going to find her. I've got a sheriff friend out at Lake Waccamaw. He's the one who found her truck. As soon as Billy told me Katy liked to drive out there, I got Roy looking. And they're checking out her phone records. We'll find something soon."

Livy handed her the scrapbook. "I wanted you to see this. The detective seemed to think my daughter was some kind of tramp. I wanted you to see the kinds of things Katy kept, words she hung on to. Scripture, poetry. She's thoughtful. Not the kind of woman who just gets drunk and runs off."

"I know that." Shelby said. She went through the book, running her fingers over the words.

Livy noticed her long lashes, the fine angle to her cheekbones. "You're too pretty a girl for such an ugly business," she said.

Shelby looked up, smiled. "Thank you." She closed the book. "It isn't always ugly. I found two kids the other day. Alive. They were fine in spite of their mother. She reported them stolen by her boyfriend, but she was trying to sell them off."

"And that isn't ugly?"

Shelby stood, paced around the room a bit, stopped at a bookshelf. "The thing is, we found them. It had a happy ending. There are happy endings sometimes, Mrs. Baines. You have to have faith in that." She went to the screen door, looked out. "It's a long road," she said. "It's a very long road you're about to go down."

"I'm not going back home without my daughter," Livy said.

Shelby nodded. "I figured you for staying. I guess that means you'll be wanting something to do. It helps to stay active."

"I'll do anything it takes."

Shelby kept her eyes on the truck gleaming in the sunlight. "Well, there's search crews. I've already got them going out by the lake. It's hot work, and it's dirty."

Livy pushed away the thoughts of Katy in the weeds out by the lake, Katy in one of those canals. She swallowed hard, blinked her eyes, said, "What else could I do?"

"There's posting flyers. And meeting with the media." Shelby turned, looked at her. "You'll do well on camera. When they see your face, they'll see your daughter's face. They'll start to remember things. Everybody tries to remember something that could help." Shelby turned to look out the door as if she knew Livy needed time to get her face back from the crying inside. "Billy gave me a list of her friends, the acquaintances he knew of. It might be helpful to meet with them, ask questions. You might learn some things about your daughter you don't want to know."

Livy couldn't stop the tears running down her face.

Shelby turned to her, squeezed her shoulder, paced around the room. "We'll also need to do a few things to help you relax. Are you eating?"

Livy couldn't remember. "I think so."

"That's not good enough." Shelby pulled out her cell phone, speed-dialed someone. Livy listened to the greeting at the other end. A man's voice, deep and soft, a South Carolina sound. "Roy," Shelby said, "I know you've got court all day, but when you can spare some time, I'd like you to meet Katy Connor's momma. Give me a holler when you can."

Her voice was warmer, softer, when she left the message for this man. *She likes him*, Livy thought; *she lets her real accent come out. She lets this man know who she really is.* Livy waited until she clicked the phone shut, put it away.

"Billy told me you're from Tennessee." Livy studied Shelby's face, that fair coloring to her skin, her hair. She knew that face, those eyes. "You wouldn't happen to be from the Waters family in Suck Creek, would you?"

Shelby nodded, pulled out a notebook, started writing things down. "That'd be where I came from, but I left it behind years ago."

"I can still hear it in your voice. I left Suck Creek too. Went to college, took speech classes to lose the accent, changed religion, married two husbands, and moved to the top of Lookout Mountain, but I still can't shake that place loose."

Shelby hugged her quickly. "Shoot, what's your family name? We might be related."

"McLain."

She nodded, her gaze fixed on Livy. "The tame ones or the wild ones?"

"The tame ones. My family established the Suck Creek Baptist Church."

Shelby laughed. It felt good to hear a laughing sound. "Well, there's just one question I've got to ask. What kind of church board members get together and decide to name a place of worship Suck Creek Church?"

Livy smiled. "Suck Creek just meant a creek back then. Nothing dirty to it. More innocent times, I guess."

Shelby looked out through the screen toward her truck. "Definitely." She sighed again. "That truck of mine's been down some sorrowful roads, Livy. I'd give everything and anything to get back to more innocent times. But the road to there just doesn't seem to be on any map I can find."

"I don't know the way back either." She wanted to touch Shelby somehow but held back. "You've read Katy's journal. Her last journal. Billy said he gave it to you."

Shelby nodded.

"Was there any kind of clue there? Anything?"

Shelby pressed her lips tight as if sealing in what shouldn't be said. "She's troubled. Like all of us. No deep, dark secrets. She has doubts about things. But who doesn't?" She looked at Livy. "I promised I'd keep what I read to myself. That was the only way I could get the journal from Billy."

Livy nodded. "I know she doesn't really want to get married. I know she still has a thing for Frank. And Billy said she'd written some other guy's name. Randy. Was there anything more about him?"

Shelby shook her head. "Just a name."

Livy wanted more than a name. She wanted some kind of hope that Katy might have run off with Randy. That would be bad, but she could live with another disappointment from Katy. "I know I was pushing too hard for her to get married." Tears came stinging her eyes again, but she would not cry. "I just want her to settle down."

"I don't know why anybody gets married," Shelby said. "I mean really. No one has to get married these days." She turned to Livy, gave a tight grin, and shook her head. "We need to do something. Do you have any plans for today?"

"You are my only plan, Shelby Waters. I've been awake since dawn, doing nothing but waiting for you."

"Let's go to the beach. I've got my crew and Roy working on finding Katy. You and me, we need to go walk Kure Beach and let that ocean breeze blow this worry out of our skins. Then we'll go to this place I know that has the best shrimp and grits in town."

"You sure? We can start out by taking a day off?"

"Today we'll call it getting ready. What you need is rest and recovery and shrimp and grits. Trust me on these things." She looked around the house, then back to Livy. "You like staying here or you want to be someplace else? I can arrange an apartment."

"I like to be near Katy's things," Livy said. "But it's sad. And Billy. Well, there is Billy."

Shelby nodded. "I know Billy. A boy-man. Lots of boy-men in the world. Very few grown ones."

"Well said. You're a wise woman, Shelby Waters."

"We'll look into finding you a different place to stay. Someplace by the water, a place where you can get out, walk, and breathe. When you're going through times like this, you forget to breathe." She took a slow breath in and out. She patted Livy's arm. "So we're going to start today by breathing good air and eating good food." She looked down at Livy's feet.

Livy followed her gaze. "Too dressy?"

"Those sandals might be too good for the beach."

"I can slip them off," Livy said. "You know the only way to walk a beach is barefoot."

"Damn right."

Livy reached for her purse, paused. "There's one thing," she said. Actually there were a million things she wanted to say, like *Where is Katy?* and *What was really written in her last journal?*

"What?" Shelby paused halfway out the door.

"I don't mean to sound too . . ." She paused, wondering how she might sound, but pushed on. "I don't mean to sound too righteous, but I'm not fond of cursing."

"Yes, ma'am," Shelby said. "I apologize. I do get a little foul-mouthed sometimes. I'll try to be more mindful of my language."

"Thank you." Livy headed toward the door, checked for her keys, stopped again. "I ought to get some sunscreen."

Shelby kept going. "Not a problem. I have everything you need in my truck."

Livy followed her out onto the porch, locked the door, and headed down the sidewalk. "You'll come to know and love my daughter," she said.

Shelby beeped the truck unlocked and glanced back. "I already do. Now, you climb in, sit back, and relax."

Livy sat back in the plush leather seat and sighed. "Can I just close my eyes a while? They feel like they've been open forever."

"You do anything you want. I've got liquid tears and Visine in the glove box if you need them."

"I just need to close my eyes." Livy squeezed Shelby's arm. "You'll find my Katy, won't you?"

"Yes, ma'am, I'll find her." Livy looked into her eyes, saw some sorrow there, knew Shelby kept her own crying inside.

They passed a corner with a rundown house, and on the sidewalk there were guys in hoodies and pants slung halfway down their butts. "What kind of neighborhood is this?" Livy asked, already knowing. "Katy told me she lives in the historical district."

"It's transitional," Shelby said. "Varies from block to block."

Livy shook her head. "I know what *transitional* means."

"Katy lives on a nice block," Shelby said "To get to the highway that takes us out of town, we have to go through a bad part."

"Every town has its bad part."

Shelby nodded, forced a smile. "Tell me something good about Katy."

Livy and settled back in the seat. "Katy loves to watch a sunset. She says there's something magical about transitional light. It's something she learned in an art class."

Shelby nodded. "Tell me something else."

"She loves to watch the sky. Back home on the mountain you can see the sun rise and the sun set. Katy likes that. And from our deck at night you can see the stars spread out so white and thick, if you squint your eyes and let go and imagine a little, it's hard to tell the stars in the sky from the lights in the city below. And it's quiet up there. Katy likes to stay out and watch the stars. Sometimes she'll fall asleep in the lounge chair, and I'll go out and cover her with a

159

blanket and let her stay, and in the morning I have the coffee ready." She grabbed her purse and dug for her emery board. She had to do something with her hands. She felt Shelby watching her but kept her eye on the file smoothing her nail. "Katy loves my coffee. I grind my own beans, use a French-press pot. Katy likes that. She sits at the table and drinks it, and she looks so pretty. Katy has the kind of face that fresh out of bed and no makeup at all is pretty."

"She looks like you," Shelby said.

"Thank you," Livy said. "There was a time people thought we could be sisters, but that was a long time ago."

"Tell me something else," Shelby said.

"She could have finished college if she'd just stayed one more semester. She could be anything, but she says she's happy being a bartender. Lately she's been painting for a decorator, hanging wallpaper. She told me once she was tired of thinking, didn't want to spend her life analyzing things." Livy looked at her hands, wondered when they had started looking so old. "I guess I can see the point in not wanting to think. But why'd she have to leave home to tend some bar?"

"Everybody has to leave home sometime," Shelby said. "That's how we grow."

"I never left." She clenched her fist, rapped her thigh. "And I did just fine."

"You left Suck Creek."

Livy smiled. "Yeah. Thank the Lord. It's just a few miles from Suck Creek to Lookout Mountain, but I might as well have moved to the other side of the world. What a difference one turn down a road can make."

They were in another bad part of town. Fat girls in tight tube skirts and guys in hoodies were standing around a strip mall with a Value City, a Salvation Army, and a Rite Aid. She checked the lock on her door. "I've been coming to this city for years, and I've never seen such places as you're taking me through."

"They like to protect the tourists," Shelby said "They keep you on the clean path to the beaches and the highway to downtown. Kind of like a yellow-brick road."

"I know Wilmington quite well," Livy said. "We've often rented a condo on the beach. We'd drive into town for dinner. It was always lovely, just lovely. That's why Katy moved here. We introduced her to the place. Then she met Billy at some bar at the beach. Nothing more romantic than meeting some new love on a beach."

"Shorelines," Shelby said. "There's something that draws people to shorelines, something promising about living where something as simple as the tides can make a shoreline change. I remember walking the beach the first time and thinking the ocean air, the saltwater could clean all the hurt out. When you are on the shore, no matter what kind of day you've had you just breathe and you're clean."

"But hurricanes hit shorelines all the time," Livy said. "That's why we'd never buy a condo here. Hurricanes can take it all away in one smack. Remember Katrina? You tell those people in New Orleans and Biloxi how great a shoreline is."

"Resilience is a virtue," Shelby said. "Right there next to patience."

"Oh, God," Livy said. "I know all about resilience."

"The idea is for you to relax today. Leave anything like worrying to me."

Livy nodded, felt the tears seeping up in her eyes. She wiped at them with her finger, then leaned back, shut her eyes. "Okay, I'll just rest a little now."

"Good," Shelby said. "Go on."

Livy settled deeper in the seat and hoped she'd slip into something like sleep as she closed her eyes and gave in.

The Other Side
of Living

When Molly pulled into her driveway that night, she didn't know
Jesse Hollowfield was waiting inside. She was thinking about all
the other things she'd rather be doing than going home alone. The
ballroom-dance classes she'd wanted to take with Matt had been
canceled—not enough enrolled to make the class. Matt was playing
Texas hold 'em with his boys at the frat house. And her mom had
declared Wednesday nights tennis nights, so Molly was alone with
her homework and Chinese takeout. She didn't know Katy Connor's
image was fluttering on flyers tacked on phone poles in Wilmington streets, her face beaming from the black-and-white photograph.
Molly didn't see the curtain move at her living room window. She
beeped the garage door open, pulled in, then got out of her car,
dreading the night alone.

   Jesse stood at the window and took a long pull from the bottle of
scotch. The good stuff. Peaty. Single malt. He grinned as he moved
toward the kitchen. She thought she was playing it safe, parking in
the garage. He knew she'd walk in thinking she knew what was
ahead, a night of homework. Jesse knew her schedule, her mother's
schedule. He knew that for the next few hours she would be alone.

Molly gathered her books, her purse, her Chinese takeout, clicked the garage door to close, and turned toward the kitchen door. Her mother was never home on Wednesdays; still, Molly hoped for light and something cooking in the kitchen. Even though she was twenty-two, she hated to walk into the house alone.

As she stepped inside, her belly trembled and a prickling ran down her back. She listened for the sound of someone in the house. She told herself she was silly, had watched too many slasher movies with her friends. *The media trains us to live in fear: random killers, robbers, flat tires, bad breath. Help me, I've fallen and I can't get up. And then they try to sell you something. We are a culture that profits from fear.* A communications professor had taught her that. She would not live in fear. That was why she'd taken kickboxing; she would not let fear run her life.

Molly shut the door and reached for the light, but there was tape on the switch. She ran her fingers over the strip of duct tape, wondered why her mother would tape the switch. She dropped her things on the counter and reached for the light over the sink. More tape. *Get out*, a feeling whispered, but Molly didn't listen to the nervous voice inside. She remembered that there was a flashlight under the sink. She crouched and opened the cupboard, felt in the darkness past the dish detergent and Brillo pads.

Jesse pulled the ski mask over his face, pulled on the baseball cap that had two knives dangling from the sides. He'd tied them on with his mother's cooking twine. They bounced lightly against his chest as he moved through the dining room, headed toward her. He was like Blackbeard the pirate, who terrorized his victims when he leaped onto their ship, waving weapons in both hands while flaming torches blazed in the long braids of his beard. The idea was to look like a devil, startle the sailors into thinking a true demon had jumped on board. Jesse liked the idea of running a ship along the Outer

Banks, watching for sailors who thought following the beams of a lighthouse would keep them safe from reefs that could gut and sink a ship in minutes. Jesse liked the idea of reefs under dark water, hard coral fluttering with sea anemones and hungry little fish. Sometimes Jesse felt like one of those reefs, waiting to rip boards and beams, filling hulls with a sudden rush of dark water. Jesse didn't like it when people felt safe. There were coral reefs and rocks and pirates out there, even on the most perfect bright, sunny days.

Jesse liked to think of himself as a reminder. That was his mission: to remind the innocent who believed in things like cops and locked doors and home safety systems and Jesus. He was here to remind them it could all flip in an instant. A boy could be pushing his little red Hot Wheels car down the wooden floorboard of the hallway, happy, *vroom vroom*, and a man would scream and kick the boy for no reason but to see how one swift kick could send a boy flying into another room. Some days were sweet with barbecue sandwiches and new toys and a big glass of Coke, but a boy never knew when the hand would smack, knock the bite from his mouth, and leave blood running from his lip down his throat to his shirt. Jesse was a reminder that you couldn't count on anything in this world.

He stood in the doorway and listened to the girl breathe as she fumbled under the sink. He watched as his heart pounded and a heat pulsed up from his gut, churning his blood. Sometimes the heat burst inside his head so thick and dark he believed he had hell inside. They had told him love could save him. But they had lied.

That girl fumbling under the sink didn't know he had taped the switches and pulled the lamp cords to keep her in darkness. He'd be the one to determine when and where the light would be. She didn't know he had cut all the phone lines. It was her fate. She still fumbled under the sink, found the flashlight, stood and turned with the circle of light illuminating the kitchen. She saw him filling the doorway.

He grinned, came toward her, knives dangling from his cap. She sucked in a breath to scream, but his hand clamped over her mouth. He shoved the gun in his waistband, pulled her arms behind her back, pushed her toward the living room, and knocked her to the floor. He stood back, held her in the flashlight's wavering beam while she rolled to her side, whimpering. "Don't hurt me," she said.

He laughed. "Yeah, right."

"What do you want?"

He aimed the beam of light at her crotch, then back to her face. "I'm gonna do it right this time. The last one, she was gone before I got the chance to fuck her. But you, you're right here."

She lay there panting, eyes scanning the room for something like a weapon. He moved the flashlight beam over her. She thought to try to stand and run, then a voice said, *Get him to tell you the story. He likes to talk. Get him to tell you the story.* She said the words: "Tell me the story."

He crouched next to her, laughed. "The story. What story?"

"The other story," she said. "The other girl. The one that got away."

"'Got away,'" he said and laughed, not a happy sound, something more like a growl. "You want to know the story." He flipped her over, face down, put his hand on the center of her back, squeezed her ass.

Keep him talking, the voice said. *As long as he's talking, he isn't hurting you.*

Molly took a breath, asked, "What was she like?"

He laughed. "Oh, you're curious. Like what I planned to do to her could get you ready for what I'm going to do to you."

Molly struggled to say the words: "I want to know the story."

"She was skinny, wasn't built like you. We saw her park that truck between the Dumpster and the ATM. Tennessee plates. And

I thought, *Perfect*." His hands moved between her legs. She stiffened, and he laughed. "She walked in that store and back out to that truck. Oblivious." He stood, put his foot on her back. "Like you."

The voice inside said, *Fight; don't go down like a lamb*. She swung back at his leg and tried to crawl away. But he crouched, grabbed her ankles. She lay there crying. "This is *my* house," she yelled.

"Yeah, and that skinny bitch thought it was her own blue truck she drove, but once I laid my eyes on it, I said, *Mine*." He squeezed her ass. "Like you."

"I want my mom," she cried.

He laughed. "That last one, she kept talking about her momma too."

She tried again to crawl away, but he rolled her over, straddled her, used one hand to hold her wrists above her head and to the floor. "The more you fight, the more it's gonna hurt."

She wanted to scream, but the voice said, *Shhh*. She wondered if it was an angel, or God, or if she was just going crazy. She lay still. He squeezed hard between her legs. Not like sex, just a punch. He leaned, the knives dangling over her chest. She tried to see his face but could only see that shape of him against the light glaring in her eyes.

The voice whispered, *Let him take his time. It will give you time to live*.

She could smell his jacket, the smell of burned leaves, the thick, bitter scent of smoke. She could feel the moisture of his breath, could smell the scotch. He'd been into her mother's scotch. "The last one, she did what I said. Drove me right over that river."

"You don't have to hurt me. Just take what you want."

He smacked her with the back of his hand, not as hard as he could have, just enough to hurt. "Oh, but the thing is, I've already taken what I want from this place—it's over there in my backpack. Only thing left I want is you." He gripped her arms, leaned closer.

The knives dangling from his cap clanked on her chest. She squeezed her eyes shut, smelled his breath. If he was drunk, he might get sloppy, but he didn't seem drunk. He seemed sure of every movement. She prayed, *God help me, Mom help me. Dad.*

She felt him move back, sit beside her. She tried to see him. He had taken his cap off, was fiddling with the string that held a knife. She could see nothing but something like a monster through the little holes in the ski mask. He cut the knives loose, held one. She could see that the blade was dull. He'd have a hard time cutting her if she kept moving. But he could kill her with a stab. *Keep moving,* the voice whispered again. *Keep him talking; he likes to talk, and as long as he's talking . . .* The voice seemed right there in the room, not just her head. She looked around for someone but saw only darkness beyond the glow of his flashlight. *Get him to tell you the story.* She closed her eyes, told herself she was going crazy. It was her brain separating, the distance of anxiety—she'd read about this in a psychology class. The voice came again, more insistent: *Get him to tell you the story!* She found a calm voice, the strong, steady voice she'd used in high school debates. "So what happened with the last one?"

He pulled back, put the flashlight closer to her face, gave a little snort of laughter. "You want to sit here and have a conversation?"

She closed her eyes. "It seemed like you wanted to tell me."

He put the cap back on. It'd be harder for her to pull the mask off with the cap on like that.

She thought it'd be less scary if she could see his face. If she could see his face, she could identify him. If she lived. She felt the tears rise up. *Do not cry.* She lay there, breathing, wondering how many breaths she had left.

He put the knives on the floor, moved toward her. "I've done some shit to lots of bitches. Put one in a coma."

"Why do you want to hurt me?" Molly asked in the most logical voice she could find. They did that in movies. Detectives, they talked so strong and calm to the man with the gun.

"Don't you believe in destiny?" He was waiting for her answer. She would not cry. "I been waiting for you," he said. "You know, a grizzly bear, he can stalk his prey for days? I read all about predators." He waved the beam of the flashlight around the room. "World's full of predators. Mountain lions, wolves." He flashed the light in her face. "Me."

She'd learned somewhere not to look an aggressive animal in the eyes. They took it as a challenge. She kept her eyes on the ceiling, which seemed to sink and rise with each breath. "You don't have to hurt me."

"Oh, yes, I do. This would make a great story. If you lived." He covered the beam of light with his hand.

The voice came again: *Get him to tell you the story*. Molly strained to see in the darkness. Either she was losing her mind or someone else was there in the room. "So what happened?"

"Okay," he said. "You want me to take my time. We've got plenty of time." Jesse got up, settled back on the sofa, reached for the scotch bottle he had left on the table.

"You're drinking my mom's scotch," she said.

"Yeah," he said. "It's the good stuff." He took a swig, sat back, stretched out his legs, and set the flashlight upright on its base, washing the room in a dim yellow light.

Molly pushed herself from the floor and sat up, looked around. She saw that the Lalique vase that usually sat on the table by the window was gone. And there on the coffee table between them was a tangled heap of her mother's jewelry, not the good stuff. She figured the good stuff was in the backpack. "You're a thief," she said.

He nodded. "I'm a lot of things."

Molly leaped up, tried to run across the room, but he lunged, grabbed her ankle, and brought her back down hard against the floor. She lay there, her jaw throbbing from the fall, waited for his hit, the smack, the knife. But nothing came. She could hear his breath. She could feel her heart pounding as she lay against the floor. She thought of how birds went still, played dead while the cat sat, watching for the flicker of life. She knew he was staring, could feel his gaze. She wished she hadn't worn the tight black jeans. She tried to remember if you were supposed to fight or submit if you wanted to survive these kinds of things. *Keep him talking. Let him know you are a woman, not a bird, not a mouse, not a bug.* That voice. Under stress the mind scatters, scrambles for safety in other voices, other selves. Under stress, breakdown of personality begins. She had studied this. *He is trying to break you down. Don't.*

She turned her face toward him. "My father will be home soon."

He shone the flashlight into her eyes. "You don't have a father."

"I do," she said. She heard the crying in her voice, tried to swallow it back.

He reached, grabbed her belt, turned her over.

"Well, he doesn't live here anymore." He looked straight into her face. Those eyes were familiar. He lifted her shirt, pulled at her belt buckle, unzipped her jeans.

She wondered how a man could look into your eyes when he was doing such things. It was supposed to be impersonal. She had read about that. Predators had to take the personality away from their victims before they caused pain. A sob broke from her throat as she realized this was really happening. "My mother . . . my mother."

"What is it with you girls and your mothers?" Jesse pressed one hand on her thigh and with the other reached and yanked off her shoe.

Molly dug her fingers into the carpet to keep back the awful feeling that she was disappearing. "How long have you been watching me?" She thought of the guy with the dog. But he wouldn't smell like leaves. They couldn't burn leaves in this part of town.

"Don't think you're so special," he said, "I watch everyone." He lifted her shirt, poked at her ribs. "Damn, you're skinnier than I thought. I bet if I cut you, you wouldn't hardly bleed." He cut her bra, tore it loose.

Tears streamed down her face. She sucked in a breath, a hard breath, wondered how many more breaths she had.

He laughed. "You want to go back in the kitchen, eat some of that Chinese takeout you brought home?"

She shook her head.

"You ain't hungry?"

The guy who walked the dog wouldn't say *ain't*, but he felt so familiar. He kicked at her hip. "I said, 'Ain't you hungry?' You're supposed to answer me."

"No, I'm not hungry," she said. Molly couldn't look into that masked face, seeing only those eyes gleaming like something in a movie, but this wasn't a movie. She kept her eyes on the ceiling. "Why did you pick me?"

He smacked her. "Because I wondered how it would be to watch a princess bleed."

She turned away, stared at the legs of the coffee table, wondering if that would be the last thing she would see. She kept her head turned to keep him from seeing the tears. *Don't cry; don't cry. It's what he wants, Molly. He wants you to cry.*

He grabbed her jaw, turned her to face him. "How's it feel to hurt? I didn't get a chance to ask the last one."

She shook her head and clenched her eyes shut to keep from seeing his eyes. She knew behind the mask, he was smiling.

He yanked the shoe from her other foot and threw it at the fireplace. Molly flinched, expecting the glass door to crash. But the shoe just bounced and hit the carpet with the smallest soft thud. He turned to her and grinned. His hand shot out, grabbed the waistband of her jeans, pulled them down, tore the jeans and panties off, and he slammed her back to the floor.

She tried to back away, but he grabbed her leg, straddled her. She froze, her head humming.

He leaned back to unzip his jeans, and she kicked at him, caught his hip. He rocked back. She kicked again, but he caught her leg, smacked her hard. She lay there panting. He leaned up, calm again. "You really want to fight me?"

She shook her head. But the voice whispered, *Fight; fight him like a man. Don't go down like a lamb.*

"That's it," he said. He tore off her shirt.

She bucked up, kicked, tried to fight. He punched her in the face. She fell back, tasting her blood. "Want to fight some more, bitch? You won't win." He grabbed her chin, squeezed. She lay still with her eyes closed, her breath panting. *Gather strength.* Gather strength? How could she gather strength? She heard him tear a condom open. And all she could think was that he was careful as he yanked her legs apart. He was even wearing some kind of gloves. There'd be no fingerprints.

Her hands clutched at the carpet as if the floor could save her from falling. He pounded, and she cried as she felt her life flying by. *He's not as powerful as he seems*, the voice whispered. *You've got power, Molly. Draw on that strength; don't give it away. The power of the world is stronger than this man.* She tried to imagine the power of the world, its turning through space, the force of the oceans rolling and rising, strong enough to move islands that only seemed to be solid things. She told herself she was just receding for a moment. She told herself she would come back with power. *Stay focused; don't fear*, the voice said. *The Lord didn't give us a spirit of fear, but one of power and love and soundness of mind. Hold on, Molly. Hold on.* The Lord didn't give us a spirit of fear. She'd hold on to that. If she didn't fear him, she could fight him. If she didn't fear him, she could take the pain, the way she'd taken the pain when she'd fallen once and broken her wrist. *It's only pain*, she thought. And she lay there, her eyes on the ceiling. *It's only pain.* The he stopped, leaned up. "You ain't hurting enough." He leaned back. She bucked up, kicking and swinging, and he kept laughing and punching, pinning her back to the floor.

"There you go," he said. "Holler, little princess. Nobody gonna save you now."

Next door the neighbors turned up the volume of the news. Marty Shorling shook his head at the screen and forked a bite of steak into his mouth. The president, that rascal, was at it again. Politicians thought they were invincible just because—well, they did have a way of getting away with things. Marty was a lawyer. He'd sat through enough dockets to see the repeat offenders. Sure, some slipped through the system, but if a man kept doing a thing, someone somehow would call him up, lock him down, make him accountable. That was the problem with this country, Marty thought. No one was accountable. Marty liked to keep count of the good things and the bad things in the world. The crimes that were punished; the crimes that got away. He glanced over at his wife. She was a good thing. Made him a steak dinner and didn't mind at all if he wanted to take it to the den, eat in front of TV. She felt his gaze, turned to him, smiled, and said, "When did politics become a nighttime soap opera?" He shrugged and said, "There's always been a drama, Sally. The Kennedys? Things we never know about, they happen all the time. Always did. It's just these days, everything and anything is public domain." He looked at the president's handsome face as he stood tall, shaking his head, making that little gesture of authority with his hand.

Sally sighed as she left the room. "Well, at least it's got everyone watching the news." She didn't like the news but felt obliged to know what was going on. She walked out onto the porch, sat in a wicker rocking chair, and closed her eyes. She liked the sound of cicadas in the trees. She liked the sounds of night. A dog barking in the distance. Another dog calling back. They were all talking. All sorts of things going on in the world, and the human ear lacked the range to understand. She glanced at her neighbors' house. All in darkness. *Odd*, she thought. Usually when Molly came home, she turned on every light in the house. Sally thought she had just heard Molly's car pull in. She stood, studied the house. Felt something was wrong. She thought about going over but couldn't think of a reason. She turned to go inside, figuring if Molly needed something, she'd call.

Molly lay curled against the carpet, naked, shivering, listening for the sounds of him in the kitchen. She prayed something, anything could happen that would prevent his return. An earthquake, a heart attack, the house burning down. She prayed to God, but it was the voice that answered. *Get him to tell you the story.* Maybe she was just going crazy. Maybe she should just give in, let voices go unraveling in her head, let him squash her and get it done with. But the clock chimed over the fireplace, and she remembered that her mother would be home soon. Her mother. It had to stop. She had to find a way to save herself, to save her mother, to save all the other women this man might hurt. She remembered his words: *This would make a great story if you lived.*

She was naked, and her hands and feet were duct-taped. She prayed that her mother wouldn't come home, then prayed that her mother would come home and save her. She opened her eyes, not knowing what to pray for.

She heard his steps coming toward her and squeezed herself into a tighter ball, as if she could disappear like one of those roly-poly bugs she used to find under bricks in the backyard. The little bugs would squeeze themselves into tiny gray balls in the palm of her hand as if by curling tightly in on themselves, hiding their blind little eyes, they could make the hand that held them disappear. She never hurt them. She just rolled them around in her palm a while, then dropped them back to uncurl and crawl away in the dirt. Dirt. She could see dirt. Taste it. She was a woman dying into the leaves. But she wasn't dead yet. *You are stronger than he is*, the inner voice whispered. *Get up!*

She pulled herself up to face him where he stood in the doorway. *Keep him talking.* She would keep him talking until she found a way to run.

"Don't you have any Coke in this house?"

Be polite. Be patient. She swallowed the crazy giggle rising in her throat. *Be patient?*

She looked up at him, fully clothed and so relaxed. He was eating her shrimp lo mein, finishing it off as far as she could tell. "In the garage," she said. "There's a refrigerator where we keep party supplies. Beer, Coke, all kinds of stuff in the freezer. I could get up and make you something if you liked." Where were these words coming from? She sounded so normal, offering snacks while she was duct-taped and naked, sitting on the floor.

He walked away. "If I want you to do something, I'll tell you."

He likes to talk. Get him to tell you the story. Molly tried to remember just when her mind had started unraveling. He'd raped her. She had seen that from a distance. She had been at the end of a long tunnel, had seen it in a tiny circle of light in the distance, a naked girl being mauled by a dog. *But you're not dead. Keep fighting. Keep your head, Molly.* He had taken a break at one point to eat her takeout, come back, and done it again as if she were no more than a workout. And now he was in the kitchen eating again. *He plans to kill you.* It was someone else's voice. Not her own voice. She wondered if there really were spirits out there.

Panic swept through her. She was dying, crossing that line into the world where spirits came forward, offered their hands. No. She strained against the tape at her hands. She didn't believe in spirits. She was losing her mind. She told herself, *Stay in this world, this world.* She pressed her feet into the carpet as if the very soles of her feet could help her hang on.

He came back, plugged in a lamp, and sat on the couch. "I like Coke," he said, taking a sip from the can. "Settles my stomach. You got me all churned up inside, princess." Then she saw it, a stuffed floppy-eared beagle she'd had as a child. She still kept it on her pillows when she made her bed. He had been in her room. He had probably put his hands in every corner of the house. What could he want with her stuffed toy beagle? He poked a potato chip in his mouth, chewed, looked at her. "Are you scared?" He looked like some kind of monster, poking food through the hole in the mask. She could see his mouth, his teeth.

"Is that what you want?" she said. *The Lord didn't give us a spirit of fear. . . .* She cowered, wishing she could hide. But he didn't even see her. He rubbed at his belly, leaned back, and looked up at the ceiling. He took a long, slow breath, inhale, exhale. She hoped one of her kicks had hurt him somewhere.

He must have felt her watching. "What you looking at? Want some more?" *He'll smash you like a fly if you let him.* She could see herself as an insect now, trapped and dying on a windowsill while people moved in other houses, the sun set, the moon rose, the wind lifted, and the world turned away.

He stood, rubbed his belly. He walked to the window. "I am the devil, you know. Hurt a lot of women. I kind of have to. "

"But you don't—"

"Sometimes you have to." He leaned into the window, looked past the drapes, scanned the streets for traffic.

"What did you do to the other one?" She couldn't believe her voice, speaking as if this were a normal conversation.

"Which one?" He came back to the couch, smiling. He sipped his Coke.

She didn't know why the words came. "The blue-truck one."

"Miss Positiv on her license plate? She kept trying to talk to me like I was some kind of friend. Thought she could talk her way out of things." He laughed a little and went back to his Coke. He looked at her. "I see you trying to do the same thing. Talk to me. Keep me talking."

The words rose: *This will make a great story if you live.* "I know what you're going to do. I'm just curious," she said. She wasn't making any sense.

Jesse shook his head. "She had this old blue pickup—you know, that old kind, robin's-egg blue. Mike called it sky blue, but I know robin's-egg blue when I see it. No automatic locks. Went down easy. Didn't bother to lock her door. Like you. You think you're safe in this gated community. Why the hell they name a place like this Land Fall? Who wants to live in a place called Land Fall?"

"Was she rich?" Molly said.

"Who?"

"The last one," Molly said.

"Nah, bought her clothes at Dollar Daze. Nothing like you,

princess. But this one, man, she trusted me. Miss Positive Vibration, plays it cool when a guy jumps in her car. I could see her checking out my clothes. I was wearing good shit. She thought I might be a regular guy."

"What did you do to her?" She trembled at the sound of the question in the air. She hadn't even thought, and the words had popped out. Jesus, he could kill her just for asking that. But then, he would kill her if she stayed silent, if she talked; no matter what she did, he would kill her. *No. You won't let him.* The voice whispered calmly now.

He leaned back, looked at her, swallowed. "You want to know what I did. Like you some reporter for the news." He snickered, took a swig of beer. "We made her drive over the river and through the woods. God's country, they call it, but when you get out that far, it's the devil's land. Nobody hears you scream. But she never screamed. Fucking brave all the way."

Molly wondered if she could be brave, wondered how she would die. The voice cried inside, *No, you will not die.*

He sat back, scooped up the stuffed dog, looked at her and said, "This yours?" He squeezed the neck so hard it shuddered in the air. Then he dropped it. A silent, quick fall to the couch. "No pleasure in it when it goes so fast. That's why I'm taking my time with you." Molly sat shivering. *No pleasure in it when it goes so fast.* She realized he was waiting for her mother. He'd rape her mother. Kill them both.

He sat on the couch and tossed the stuffed dog from hand to hand. He stopped. He held the dog and patted it so hard that its head flattened against his chest. "I like dogs," he said. He laughed and stuffed the toy into his backpack. "I'm keeping it. It's a present for a friend. Don't look so shocked. I do have friends. Nicki Lynn, she's cool. Not like you, spoiled little princess. Nicki Lynn, she came up rough, and she knows how to love a man. You gotta be some woman

177

if Zeke lets you stick around. And you know what?" He looked cheerful, but she could hear the meanness in the words. "She just had this baby today. A baby boy. Named him Jesse. Like me. She tells me they're naming him for Jesse James. Could at least give me the satisfaction of saying the kid's named for me." He leaned close to her. "You bitches, man, can't count on you for a damn thing. Jesse James. I don't give a shit. So I'm taking her boy your stuffed dog here. Gonna get him to love it, and when he loves it so much he won't let go, I'm gonna tell her where that little old stuffed dog came from." He laughed. "She's gonna flip, and hell, you won't be needing it." He sat snapping the flashlight on, off, on again.

"What'd you do with the girl and her truck?"

"The truck?"

"The girl in the blue truck."

"Ain't your fuckin' business." He threw a pillow hard at her, hit her in the face. He stood.

He means to kill you. She could see her mother crying, her things being boxed and given away. She closed her eyes, felt herself sinking through the carpet, the floor, the basement to be buried in dirt, covered in leaves. She couldn't shake the thought of wind rippling through trees overhead. Black birds soaring in a dark blue sky. There was a world out there.

He stood suddenly, and she braced herself for him, but he bent over, then straightened, rubbed his belly. He bent, checked the duct tape at her ankles, saw where she'd kicked it loose, just a little but a start. "You are a fighter, ain't you?" He cut the duct tape from her feet, pulled her up, pushed her into the dining room, forced her to sit, and duct-taped her ankles to the chair legs. He checked the tape on her wrists and ankles. "I can't have you running away in case I need to leave the room." He paused, studied her in the beam of the flashlight. "Look at that skin. So white, so soft, little-girl skin. Bet you ain't got a scar on you." He ran his fingertip across her chest, up to her neck. "I didn't make you bleed yet." He waved the knife in front of her, jabbed it at her, but she raised her hands, swung against his jabs, the blade stabbing where it hit. Her grabbed her wrists, held them, and took a jab at her neck. She swung away, but the blade caught her shoulder, and she gasped, nearly passed out from the pain. *Don't panic*, the voice said. *Stay calm.* A crazy giggle rose up in her chest, and she couldn't stop the laughing. Yes, this was madness, a voice saying, *Stay calm. The Lord didn't give us a spirit of fear.* She looked up at him, grinning, felt the blood trickling down her chest. He patted her head. "You sit tight. I need another Coke."

Molly tried to pray. *Please save me.*

Save yourself, the voice said. She couldn't tell if the thought was her own thought or that voice unraveling in her head. *Focus. Fight like a man. Fight.* Molly sat in the darkness, listening for sounds of him in the kitchen. She heard him open the back door. It wasn't over yet. He was just taking a break. She didn't have to see out the window to know that one by one, lights were going out. Her neighbors were brushing their teeth, setting alarm clocks, preparing for bed. Oblivious. Her legs strained at the duct tape binding her legs to the chair. Duct tape. It could hold bumpers onto cars. It could hold anything. *Unless you start a little rip with your nails.* Her hands burned from the cuts, the binding of the tape, but she bent over, fought the dizziness, the pain, and strained to dig at the edges of the tape with her nails. She moved from the right leg to the left, shifting when pain seared. She heard his steps, sat up.

He stood in the doorway. "What you doing?"

She dropped her hands to her lap. "Praying," she lied. "I was praying."

He laughed. "Well, you go on and pray if you think that's gonna do you any good." He rubbed his belly, bent over, whispered, "Goddamn it." He straightened, took a breath. Molly could see something was wearing him down. Maybe she had broken a rib.

Molly leaned back, closed her eyes, whispered, "Goddamn you."

"I was damned a long time ago." He pulled the curtain back from the window, stared out at the darkness. "You ever seen anything die?"

Molly shook her head, wondered if a dead squirrel on the side of the road counted. *Talk to him*, she thought. "I've seen dead squirrels," she said. "A baby bird."

He let the curtain fall back into place. "I shouldn't have drunk your momma's scotch. That and Chinese." He shook his head. "They don't mix." He took a flattened joint from his pocket. He lit up and threw the match on the floor, mashed it out. As he drew the smoke into his lungs, he looked down the hall. "I had a dog once. Watched it bleed to death. My momma, she wasn't around to hear me crying. Bitch was never around. I had a pup once. Can you see that? Me? Little kid with a dog?"

She nodded. "Tell me about when you were a boy."

"To hell with that. Let's talk about you." He grabbed the knife, stabbed it into the table, leaned to study the cut on her shoulder. "You haven't bled enough." He grabbed the knife and stabbed at her. She flung her arms up, fought the knife away from her face with her hands, felt the stabs sting again and again at her hands, her arms, her neck. She kicked and kicked at the tape, felt it loosen at her ankles. She struggled up, legs almost free. She fell back with the chair, and he was on top of her, slinging the knife wherever he could reach. She would not die. She kept fighting with her bound hands.

His hand squeezed lightly at her throat. She could see him watching the blood ooze from her wounds.

She heard her own breath panting, could feel how with each pounding beat of her heart, blood trickled out. But she didn't feel a weakening. Not yet. He mashed one hand down on her chest and with the other hand swiped the knife across her chest, the pain sucking the breath out of her.

He stepped back. "There. Not deep but good enough to bleed." He winced again, bent over, straightened. "We gotta get this over now. 'Bye, princess." He squeezed at her neck, and she fought him, thrashed and turned so hard and fast he couldn't get a good grip. But her mind stayed quiet somehow. *My mother*, she thought, *my father, my life*. All the things she could be shimmered out on the horizon. She could see the shadows of herself, her mother, her father, her life. He squeezed at her throat, but she pushed against the floor with her feet, thrashed, fought. He kept grasping but couldn't get hold of the place he wanted. She got one leg free, tried to kick but tipped the chair, and the side of her head slammed hard against the floor. The pain took her breath, sent sparks behind her eyes. Then she could see him standing there. He was trying to stand tall, but he bent, one hand rubbing his belly as if to hold something there.

"Damn, girl, where'd you learn to fight? Like you got some super-power shit, man." He looked her over. "You like a damned cat. How many lives you got left in you?" He nudged at her, but she didn't have the strength to move. "You ain't got nothing left now, do you?" He straightened, clenched his jaw, went stiff all over, then breathed. Something was wrong with him. "I'm gonna do this right," he said. "But I gotta go do something else first. I'm gonna find something in the basement to finish you off."

He hurried to the hall, went down the stairs to the basement.

Molly lay there sucking in breath. Why wasn't she dead yet? *Run. You have to get up. Run.* But she didn't know how she could run. Standing would be impossible. On her side and with her ear pressed to the floor, she could hear him banging things in the basement. What would he find there? A screwdriver, a hammer, a saw. *It's your last chance*, the voice whispered. *Please.*

She rolled herself up, saw the knife on the floor. She grabbed it, sawed and poked at the tape on her ankles. She listened, heard the thud of something in the basement. In a few minutes he would kill her. She tore at the tape, kept pushing, pulling against it. If she died, she'd never marry. She'd never have babies. She'd never really get her chance to live. She hadn't known she wanted marriage, babies. But she wanted it all. She'd have to try anything, pick and pick at the tape, hoping, hoping and praying if she picked at it long enough . . . then she felt it. The tape ripped.

She heard the sound of the toilet flushing in the basement. She clawed the tape loose, stood, and ran to the living room. With her hands on the doorknob, she paused, heard him coming up the stairs. She said the words without thinking: "I'm gonna live," and she ran naked into the night toward her neighbors' house. She saw the light on, ran toward it, a small smudge of yellow light. It would save her. She ran up onto the porch, crouched at the door, reached, rang the bell, then pounded.

She looked back for him, saw only the streetlight, shadows, and trees. She pounded again, crouched lower. "Help me, please," she whispered. She shivered against the concrete of the porch. She was naked and bleeding and holding to the brick of the house with her palms. She was dying. She could feel it, her soul slipping with each pulse pumping her blood out to the air. The door opened. She closed her eyes and fell into the sound of a woman's scream.

A Man Ought to Be Accountable for His Own Bad Aim

The old woman looked off her back porch, gauged the sunlight left. There would be just enough time to dry her sheets on the clothesline. Sheets dried quick and crisp in the heat. She lifted the clothesbasket on her hip, pushed the screen door open, and headed toward the line. She caught the acrid scent of rot. She scanned her yard to the meadow line. Nothing there. The summer before, a possum had crawled under her porch and died. She lifted her nose to the little bit of breeze and tracked the scent to the line of trees, the patch of woods that stood between the back of her yard and the old farm that was still up for sale and gone fallow. Another wild pig badly shot and left to rot, no doubt. She remembered that smell. Hunters were often in the woods to the west, going for quail, pigs, deer, she didn't know what all; she'd gotten used to the sounds of guns going off. It wasn't the season for shooting wild pigs, but no one really paid much mind to the rules. It was poor farm country all around. And she figured a family had to eat. She couldn't blame a man for shooting a pig out of season if a family had to eat. She stood there, debating about hanging those sheets on the line or throwing them in the dryer. She wondered how many nickels it took to dry a load of sheets. Her husband had taught her this, to think of nickels falling down a drain every time she left the light on in a room, every time she was too quick to crank on an electric heater when she felt a chill, every time she chose to dry her clothes inside instead of hanging them on a line. He wasn't stingy, just frugal: *You'll thank me one day, when I've passed on and you'll get to keep this house with all those nickels I've saved.*

She looked up at the blue sky, could feel him watching. "All right, Melvin," she said as she headed toward the clothesline. She stopped at the wall of stench in the air, a thick reek of rot. A wave of nausea moved through her, making the back of her throat water, leaving a chill up her arms. *There ought to be a law*, she thought, *about leaving a badly shot pig. A man should be accountable for his own bad aim.* But she'd heard stories. One man lost a leg when he went into the brush for a wounded pig. It came tearing out, nearly killed him.

She reached into the pocket of her dress, where she always tucked a clean handkerchief to wipe away sweat and dab at the tears that slipped from her eyes on days when the pollen was bad. She tied the handkerchief around her head, covering her nose and mouth so she could get on with the business of drying her sheets the way she liked. They'd be crisp and would smell like sun and heat in the evening in spite of that rotten smell that hung in the air.

Some Kind
of Comfort

Billy sat at the bar, his eyes fixed on the "Missing" flyer taped on the mirror, Katy's face smiling above all those bottles of booze. There was another flyer in the men's room, and he figured in the ladies' room too. And there were others at the front entrance, inside and out. If anybody who came to the bar knew anything about Katy, he would have found her by now.

He heard Pete on his cell phone making plans for a fund-raiser. Shelby must have known how to say all the right things to get the old man to post flyers, set out donation jars, and even open the bar on a Sunday to raise money for REV. The event for Katy would be a night of Irish music, everybody drinking and smiling and slapping Billy on the shoulder, saying everything would be all right and then *I'm sorry; I'm so sorry, Billy*. Now he was thinking he'd just stay home.

"Not there," Pete said, louder now and coming up to the bar. He pointed at the REV donation jar under Katy's picture. "Move it out here on the bar, where folks can get at it."

The bartender—Allison was her name—looked pissed, but when she caught Billy's gaze, she smiled. She was always smiling as if she knew him in that secret way women had. She knew damn well the only woman he wanted was Katy. She set the jar in front of Billy, gave him a little shrug, then looked at Mike. "Don't you think somebody might just reach in and steal money just sitting in a jar?"

Pete reached and turned the jar around to show another picture of Katy. "You're just worried about losing tips. Nobody is going to steal from that jar—nobody, not with Katy smiling like that. Half the men come in here are in love with that girl." He turned to Billy. "Sorry, Billy, but you know it's true."

Billy raised his beer bottle. "I know." He took a sip. "But I'm the one she's gonna marry." He looked at Allison when he said this. She went to the other end of the bar, where a guy was standing, raising an empty glass. He wouldn't say anything about the man named Randy. They'd traced the number. A Miami number, but the man named Randy Stiller had a place out by Lake Waccamaw. The man named Randy Stiller was gone, no sign of him having been home for weeks. Billy counted the days. Katy had been gone for weeks. They couldn't say exactly how long the man named Randy had been gone. The man named Randy had canceled his cell. It sucked when your only hope was that your girl had disappeared with a man named Randy. *But she wouldn't do that*, Livy had said. *She would call.* Livy was right. Katy could do some wild things, but she always called. This was more than some new guy. Billy wouldn't say it, didn't need to say it. Something was terribly, unbearably wrong.

Pete moved the jar to a spot where Billy wouldn't have to look at it. He saw the tears starting to rise up in Pete's eyes. Billy knew Pete loved Katy too, even though he was old enough to be her dad. Any man could love Katy. Billy figured if something awful happened to Katy, it couldn't be anyone she knew. He glanced at her face in the photograph and thought of Frank. As far as Billy knew, Frank was the only man who had hurt Katy, but he hadn't meant to. Frank was Frank, and Katy wanted him to be something else. She kept slamming herself into him when he'd told her from the start he wasn't the type to settle, told her she should walk away. Billy wondered if she was still wearing his grandmother's ring. The detectives had checked the pawnshops. It was as if someone had grabbed her. No signs of a struggle, the cop said. It was like she'd just stepped out of the truck for a minute and disappeared.

He heard Pete say, "She's a hellion, that one." Billy realized that Pete had been talking for some time and he hadn't heard the words. Pete was behind the bar now, pouring a glass of sweet tea. "You can see it in her eyes."

"Who?" Billy said.

Pete raised his glass. "Shelby Waters. I've never seen anything like her."

Billy sipped his beer. "Yeah, she's a git-'er-done kind of gal."

He heard the guy at the end of the bar say, "Nah, that's for you, hon. You just remember that when I come back in this weekend."

Allison said something flirty, he figured, because the guy was grinning that dopey drunk grin when he walked back to his table. Billy didn't see how Katy could stand this job, having to smile at assholes all night. Allison came over, dropped a five and some change into the REV jar. She gave Billy a wink. Billy acted like he hadn't seen it. Pete came out from behind the bar to sit next to him. He was still smiling. Billy nudged him. "I can get you putting up the flyers and the jar and all. But how did she talk you into giving up the condo?"

Pete shrugged. "It sits empty most of the time." He shook the ice in his tea. "And you know I'd do about anything for Katy. Shelby said Katy's mom had a need for it, that she could use a change of scene." He shook the ice again, studied it as if he were trying to get it just so. Billy knew what he was thinking; he was thinking Livy probably couldn't stand to be around Billy. But he said, "It'd be hell to sit in your own daughter's house, looking at all her stuff, wondering if she's all right, wondering where she is."

Billy looked at Katy's face on the flyer. He'd taken that picture. They had been at Tybee Island. They had ridden bikes on the beach that day. He took some quick swallows of his beer. He looked at Pete. "It's hell, all right." He felt Pete looking at him. "Don't, Pete," he said. "If I hear one more fucking 'I'm sorry' . . ."

"I was just gonna ask about her mom. Shelby Waters is gonna bring her in here any minute to meet me."

Billy grinned. "She's married, Pete."

"I know she's married. I'm just curious."

"Is that what you call it?"

Pete smiled. "So I like to admire the ladies. Doesn't mean I paw at them like some old dog in need of a scratch." He looked at the flyer on the mirror. And Billy saw the little wince in his face. "Katy always had nothing but good things to say about her mom. But it must be strange having her in the house. You two get along all right?"

"It's all right," Billy said. "She doesn't like me smoking pot. So I told her that until we find Katy, I'll stick to beer. Katy would want it that way." He nudged Pete's shoulder. "And I'm guessing Katy would think it's cool, you letting her mom stay at your condo for a while."

Pete turned to Katy's flyer and looked at it as if waiting for her approval. "Yeah, it's like Katy says, it's never a wasted thing to do a good thing."

Billy wondered if people were always quoting Katy or he was just noticing it lately.

Pete sipped his tea. "I figure this is a good thing that will ease her mom. She probably needs to get out of that house."

Billy wasn't ready for Livy to leave. He didn't want to be alone. He wanted to tell Livy that he didn't want her going, but he'd sound like some scared little boy. "I guess she will be more comfortable out there."

The front door opened, and it seemed the whole place stopped to see who was coming in. Billy wondered if Pete had told people that Katy's mom was coming. Maybe that was why it was so empty. Nobody would want to see Katy's mom; it just hurt. Gator walked in with that quiet way he had. He was in his sixties but walked tall and smooth. Katy had said only dancers walked like that, but Gator had never been a dancer. He might have been a lot of things, but the only thing he claimed was being a two-tours-of-Vietnam vet, and a drunk and a stoner. Now he was a river guide, could take tourists way back into the canals where only alligators and birds cared to go.

"Hey, man," Billy said. Gator came over without a word. "I brought your laundry. Katy had it all folded on the dryer."

Gator leaned in, gave him a hug that could have cracked a weaker man's ribs. "Where's our girl, man?" He looked at Pete, back to Billy. Then he caught sight of the flyer. He sat. "This is fucked. Totally fucked."

Billy signaled Allison to bring Gator a beer. Billy could smell the river coming off Gator's clothes, his hair, his skin. He had shiny black hair almost to his shoulders, skin the color of maple wood. Katy said he was part Seminole, and that was why he had such a talent for getting in and out of the canals and marshlands. Katy said when Gator was younger, he must have been a handsome man. Billy couldn't see it. He just saw the creases around his eyes and mouth, the sagging of skin at his throat. Gator looked at the foam thinning at the top of his glass. "Nothing, huh?"

"Nothing." They both sipped their beers. Billy could feel the others in the room watching them. Somehow they all knew the story, and not one would come sit at the bar. Just Gator. But he was like Katy's little brother even though he was an old man.

"Your laundry is behind the bar in a duffel bag. Katy even bought you a couple packs of new boxers. She said no man as sweet as you should have to wear rags like the ones you had."

Gator smiled. "The only woman in the world who's ever called me sweet."

Pete was already digging around behind the bar. He plopped the duffel bag in front of Gator. Gator reached, unzipped it, and pulled out the packs of boxers. "Blue. She remembered my favorite color." He leaned into the open bag, breathed the fresh smell. "Clean," he said. "She always sends it back smelling so clean."

Billy raised his beer. "'Let there be laundry for the backs of thieves.'"

Pete gave him a little pissed-off look and walked away.

Gator turned to him. "What you talking about, man? I ain't no thief."

"It's just that line from a poem Katy liked," Billy said. "It's something she called a metaphor, I think." He remembered it was supposed to be "fresh linen," but it was laundry sitting there on the bar.

Gator tucked the boxers into the bag, zipped it closed. He grinned at Billy. "Guess I'll have to say it's been quite a few years since I was a thief. Just little shit when I needed it. Like a couple steaks at the Bi-Lo. Spent a night locked up for those steaks. Could've kicked myself in the ass all night long. I spent too much time in 'Nam to get stuck one more night in a place I didn't want to be."

"I hear you," Billy said. He thought of his mother's trailer in a park just outside Daytona Beach. When he was a boy, she'd said they were moving from Shithole, Florida, to Daytona Beach, and he'd thought how good it would be to live on a beach. But when you live in a trailer park, you don't get much chance to go to the beach. About the only sand he saw was in the trailer-park driveways, and it was nasty with car oil and cigarette butts and beer-can tabs. He told himself he would get out of that trailer park as soon as he was old enough to know there was such a thing as getting out. He got a job as a laborer with a bricklayer, and bucket by bucket and then brick by brick, he paved his way free. And now his mom was still sitting in that trailer, smoking her Dorals and sipping Natty Lites and pissed off at the world for not giving her what she thought she deserved. She didn't want out. She'd rather stay in that trailer park and complain about how Billy's daddy wasn't ever a daddy, and now her own son couldn't be a son when she'd spent so much time . . . *Doing what?* Billy thought. *Nothing.* He looked at his beer. *Doing shit*, he thought; *you never did more than the minimum for me.*

Gator leaned toward him. "You all right, dude?"

"No. Hell, no," Billy said.

"Want to go around to the alley and fire one up?"

"No," Billy said. "No, thank you, Gator. I'm giving that up for a while."

Gator nodded. "That's cool. Whatever you need." He drained his mug. "Thanks for the beer. I'm gonna meet up with some dudes. I'll be back for that laundry." He patted Billy's shoulder, slipped off the bar stool. Just when he got to the door, Shelby walked in. Tight jeans and a tank top. Pete was right. She did look like a hellion. He hadn't noticed that before. She was definitely the kind of woman you wanted on your team. She gave Billy a nod as she held the door open for Livy. Gator stood there looking at Livy. His mouth dropped a little as he stared. Billy knew what he was looking at: Katy, what Katy would be in twenty-five years. Billy saw it. And when he glanced at Pete behind the bar, he knew Pete saw it too. Everybody in the place was staring. Pretty much everyone in town knew who Shelby Waters was these days, and probably everyone in the bar had seen Livy on the news. Gator glanced back to Billy and shook his head. He gave Shelby a little nod and looked to Livy. He said, "I'm sorry for your troubles, ma'am," and he was out the door.

Billy caught Livy's eyes. She looked terrified. He got off his stool to go to her. He realized she'd never been to the bar, had probably never even been to this part of town. Wilmington was a whole different place at night, especially this part of town. The bar was set back a few blocks from where tourists liked to go. There was a porn shop down the street. And she'd probably seen the little park where the homeless liked to hang at night. Billy stood looking at her: Katy in twenty-five years. Shelby was leading her over, and Pete was already out from behind the bar and heading her way. Billy sat back down and leaned his head down, trying to find his breath. This was happening. It was really happening. Katy was gone, and her mother was there.

"You doing all right, Billy?" Allison touched the back of his hand. He flinched, and his arm flew up so hard he would have hit her in the face if she hadn't jumped back.

"Am I all right?" he said. He said it quietly. He had to keep his voice quiet or he would yell. "No, I am not all right. That's my fiancée on that flyer there. She's missing. Remember Katy?"

She nodded. "I'm just saying I'm sorry, Billy." He didn't even like her saying his name. She was only flirting again, making it look like concern because Katy had disappeared. He looked at her face, too round, that straight blond hair, her fake tits rising up in her shirt like a couple of things trapped there and trying to get out. He heard Pete getting Shelby and Livy settled at a table. He knew he should get over there. She touched his hand again. "You need another beer, Billy?"

"No," he said. She kept her hand on his, kept looking at him in that pitying way. He pulled his hand away and leaned close to her like he was going to tell her a secret. "I saw hundreds of girls just like you back in Daytona Beach. Beach bunnies. Fake tits, fake smiles, fake hair. All so blond. I think of girls like you as something like corn. Everybody likes corn. Tasty. Goes with anything. There's rows and rows of girls like you. I don't like corn. I ate too much of it out of a can when I was a kid. Please don't touch me anymore."

She jumped back and stood there. He could see tears starting at her eyes, knew he should say he was sorry, wanted to say he was sorry, but he wasn't. She glanced toward the table where Pete was rambling on about how happy he was to meet Livy, how Katy had said so many nice things about Livy, how he was sure she'd be back soon, saying all the happy-host shit. Shelby was sitting still as a stone, her eyes locked on Billy. She'd heard him. Billy found the words, turned toward Allison but wouldn't look at her. He said the word, but he barely made a sound: "Sorry."

She leaned over the bar. "I didn't know you were an asshole."

He nodded. He would accept that. He turned and went toward the table where Livy was looking around the room with that polite smile on her face. "How pleasant this place is. It's Irish. Katy never told me it was Irish. It's more like a pub than a bar."

Billy nodded and sat with them, thinking, *Poor Livy*. Katy had told him how she always strained to put the best picture on things. And now she was sitting there with Katy gone for over three weeks now, and all she could do was make what was just another bar into a place where she wouldn't mind her daughter working. A pub. Only happy drunks went to pubs, right? At a pub the worst thing that could happen was maybe an argument over a soccer game.

Pete leaned toward her, charmed. Billy watched the way he reached across the table and patted the back of her hand. He saw Shelby watching this too. "So glad you like my place," he said. "But I've gotta admit, it's fake Irish. I'm Polish, actually, but Irish sells.

Everybody wants to be a little Irish these days. Justifies drinking as a national pastime."

Livy kept that smile on. "But I'm Irish," she said, "and I hardly drink at all."

"Just joking," Pete said. "How about a round of Guinness? I keep the temperature the way it's supposed to be."

She looked over to the bar, saw rows of bottles. Billy could see it; her gaze was snagged by that picture of Katy. She turned to Pete. "To tell you the truth, I think I'd like a whiskey. An Irish whiskey, please."

"Attagirl," Shelby said. "Sounds good to me."

Pete patted Livy's hand. "I see you're Katy's mom all right. She likes a shot of Jameson at closing time." He turned toward the bar and called to Allison to bring a round of whiskeys. Told her to bring a round of water too. He was good, Billy thought. He knew most women liked to sip water alongside their drinks. And his hand, it stayed there on the table, close to Livy's, as if they were long-lost friends who had just happened to meet in a bar. Yep, Pete was charmed all right. Billy wondered if there was something about grief that was sexy to some people. Was it the weakness that made people think you wanted touching? Since Katy had disappeared, women were doing everything but inviting themselves to stay at his house. Kept showing up with casseroles, ribs, baked chickens. And Billy had seen the men doing it to Livy, standing too close to her as if they were at the ready in case she weakened, had some kind of fainting spell. He felt Shelby watching him. He looked up at her, shrugged, shook his head. She shook her head too, gave a little grin. God knew she'd seen plenty of this kind of thing, worry and fear making people flat-out goofy. Or mean.

He saw Allison coming toward them with the tray of drinks, her face tight. When she set the drinks on the table, he could smell her perfume, like some kind of candy. He held his breath not to breathe it. Katy hardly ever wore perfume. She just always smelled like Katy, a smell like bread and something clean. He felt tears pressing somewhere in the back of his eyes. He grabbed his whiskey, wanted to chug it down, but he sipped it, put the glass down, tried to listen to the conversation at the table. Livy was saying something about how generous it was for Pete to offer his condo. And Pete was saying something about how he really only used it when his daughter was in town with his grandkids for a visit. He went on about how with the way he worked, it was more convenient to stay in his apartment in town.

They were all being so polite, no mention of Katy, no talk of why they were all really sitting at that table in a bar where Katy should be laughing, serving the drinks. He remembered how when his granny died, people gathered in the front parlor of the funeral home. They talked of the quilts she made, her peach pies and pepper plants. They talked about the weather, and there was always a coming back around to something like how his granny would have wanted something that way. But Katy wouldn't want it this way. Katy would want them out there looking for her. Katy would want to be tending her own tomato and basil plants that were going to hell in the backyard because he couldn't stand it and doing anything in that garden made Livy have to sit in a lawn chair and cry. They were saying something about time. Oh, God, Livy was saying something about *in the Lord's own time*. She was trying to climb back into her religion, like religion was a tree you could climb into to keep you safe from a flood. Billy couldn't stand any more of anyone's words that kept trying to say everything was going to be all right.

Pete was touching Livy's hand again, patting it. He was saying something about how they'd take care of her, something about how he'd show her the best place to buy groceries out there on the beach

195

so she wouldn't have to pay tourist prices. Billy focused on the words when Pete said, "We can get you in there tomorrow, if you like."

He leaned forward, felt them all looking at him. He looked at Shelby, the only sign of real comfort in the place. He tried to make the words sound light. "She in that big a hurry to get away from me?"

"No," Livy said. He saw the strain in her face. Katy got that same look—he'd seen that effort of searching for words that sounded safe, that sounded honest and harmless, whenever he asked her about Frank. Livy touched his arm. "I just thought you'd be wanting some privacy." She looked to Shelby for help. He wondered if Shelby Waters ever got sick and tired of people looking to her for some kind of relief.

Shelby nodded, knew better than to touch him. "It's just that this could take some time, Billy." The room went still. Nothing like a pub or a bar. It was more like a funeral home, where everybody sits in the front parlor and hangs on to talking about anything but the dead thing in the casket in the other room.

He picked up his whiskey, said, "I know this is going to take time, but it's already taken too much time. And we walk around and try to talk like it's something normal, like it's just some kind of bad storm. It's not a storm." He was thinking it was the end of the world, but he wouldn't say that. It felt too true. He drained his whiskey and looked at them staring up. Livy was already crying, and Shelby was looking pissed, so he looked at Pete, who just looked like *What the hell you doing now?* "What's wrong with you?" Billy said. "Everybody acting like something normal when we know it's fucked. Whatever this is, whatever it's gonna be, I want it to be over." He slammed his glass to the table and headed out the door.

Outside, he sucked in the humid air. It was warm and thick, and it calmed him. He saw Gator crouching on the sidewalk, his back leaning against the building as if he could sit all night like that.

196

He sat smoking a cigarette, just watching the street, waiting for nothing while now and then a car rolled by. Billy stood there. He wanted to go around back and get high, but he couldn't say that. Not with Livy back in the bar, and probably crying. Because of him. Well, really because of Katy. But at this moment she was probably crying because of him. He couldn't say, *Let's go fire one up now, Gator*, because it would sound too much like he wanted to kick back and party when all he really wanted was something to turn the pain down in his head, just a notch or two, just enough so that being awake was something he could stand.

Gator shook his head, just kept staring out at the pavement. "This is worse than Khe Sanh, man."

"That bad," Billy said. It wasn't a question. Gator never talked about Vietnam. Never wanted to. Just said he had done two tours. He'd asked for it. At least 'Nam had given him something to do.

Gator stood, his movement quiet and smooth as a cat. Billy had never seen an old man who could move like Gator. Gator looked straight into him, as if he could read Billy with his eyes. Billy just looked back at him, seeing that Gator's eyes looked flat and gray in the darkness, set in a face like leather, it was so creased and etched with lines. Like an alligator, Billy thought, like something strong and silent and brutal, like something wild from nature on that city street. "I'm glad you're my friend," Billy said.

"Let's go fire one up," Gator said. "Booze ain't gonna touch what you're feeling."

Billy nodded and followed Gator around the corner to the alley. It felt good. It already felt something like a comfort to let Gator lead the way.

There's Often Much Comfort in Useless Things

Some nights I crave the darkness. Some nights I ache to push every-one away. Just being with myself can be crowded. Some nights I hear all the voices of those missing ones calling, and I want to tear all those pictures of their faces off the wall, yank out the phones, burn all the files, and just have my house, and me, not a woman like a refugee camped out in the REV center. Some nights I just want my mind clear of all the awful. I want my home to be my home. So that night I sent Bitsy home early, locked the doors, clicked off the land-line ringer, turned off all the lights. I sat in the wicker rocker on the back porch and pushed my foot against the rail to get the soothing movement I needed, but even something as simple as rocking felt like too much work. So I sat still, leaned back, and closed my eyes, thinking about Livy Baines and wishing I could reach down into a well and bring up the solutions to what everybody wanted. I was wondering where we'd ever gotten the idea that wishes came from wishing wells and shooting stars, or that a caught fish could grant a wish if you just released it back into water. I was wondering where we'd ever gotten the idea of lucky things. Humans had to be the only creatures on the planet that thought about things like luck. I caught the scent of my honeysuckle on the night breeze, and everything started to seem a little all right. It's not the mind so much as nature that ever really brings me peace.

I was glad I'd gone to the trouble of bringing that honeysuckle bush from back home. People thought I was a fool for going to the bother, all that sweat and heat just to dig up honeysuckle that grew all thick and tangled with the fence, vines gone crazy the way vines do, able to take over any fence or hedge or even a car if you let it sit still long enough. They laughed back home, saying, *Who transplants honeysuckle that spreads like kudzu? All you have to do is give it a thought to make it grow*. But I wanted that honeysuckle, my family's honeysuckle vines that reached back to my grandmother's time and probably even further back. It's a comfort to know how a green and growing thing can outlast generations of family that think they can really own anything in this world. The blooms were thicker, sweeter than anything you could find at a greenhouse. Pondering the reaches of green and growing things, that was about all I was up for that night. I leaned back, closed my eyes, and breathed that thick, sweet scent of the air. That honeysuckle is pretty much all I have left from back home. I let the land go wild after momma died, and some kids burned down the house. I couldn't sell it, and I couldn't live there because just looking at the thick woods all around makes me ache for Darly. So there it sits, meaning nothing to me but the taxes I pay every year. I took all I wanted after Momma died: her bedroom set and the antique pie safe. I can still remember the pies sitting in there. Muscadine, pecan, blackberry, and peach. Simple times. I also took my momma's Fiestaware. That was her wedding present. She didn't want fancy china. What was the use of good china for serving fried chicken and biscuits and beans in Suck Creek? My momma, she kept pretty plain, but she liked to look at colorful things. She liked to serve pinto beans in the pale blue bowl. And cornbread on the dark blue plates. She liked to serve the bacon on the yellow platter. I never knew that old Fiestaware was worth anything. I just wanted it because my momma loved it. Now I could just about buy a car with what I could get for that Fiestaware. Makes you wonder how we decide what's of value from the old stuff, what's worth keeping and what should go to the Goodwill, the county dump. Who decides the Barbie doll is worth collecting and not the lesser-known Babette?

There's often much comfort in useless things like the choice of pinto beans in a pale blue bowl and not the white. And I was thinking maybe Roy was right that I think too much. My momma, she said the same thing, said Darly worked too much and I thought too much, and why couldn't we just sit still, be happy, just be?

I was thinking about whether we'd ever find Katy Connor, and those thoughts just led me to Darly, her car on the side of the road, her bones scattered in the North Georgia mountains, how I made that detective show me the sight, how I made him give me answers: her head was here, her body there. And then my mind started spinning with what had happened to Darly between that phone booth by the side of the road and those North Georgia mountains, and I made myself sick just from thinking.

Roy calls it my *hyperbolic imagination*. And you probably wonder where some small-time county sheriff learned to talk like that. He reads. He reads anything you put in front of him. The fine print on a can of beans, *Popular Mechanics*, *Psychology Today*, manuals on small-engine repair. "Hyperbolic imagination," he says when I see things like bones and build the awful all around them. I'm only looking for the answers to the hows and whys of things. Darly's bones. Her head was here. Her body there. The words looped in my brain like a stuck record. I was thinking if I could follow those words long enough, somehow they'd lead me to Katy, thinking that in a flash I'd know exactly where she was with the ease of remembering where I'd misplaced my keys. But I wasn't seeing keys in my mind. I was seeing some girl's broken body in a field. Someone would find her in time. They find so many bodies these days. Let's just say I was in a bad place that night even with the breeze and the honeysuckle filling the air.

I call it the black turn my mind takes. Most days I can keep my mind steady, and most nights I can make myself bigger than all the pain out there, and I can stand everything that passes in this world the way the mountains back home can look down on so much sorrow and say nothing. Most times I can make my mind big and steady and solid as a mountain, but that night my heart was small and my mind just sick of things, tangled up in Billy's words, *This is fucked*. I saw what Billy did to that girl in the bar. Might as have well have punched her in the face when he spoke those words. Corn. Who would think a simple word like *corn* could turn into something mean. But I suppose anything can hurt depending on how you hold it, how you throw it, what you do.

So there I was, sick of the world and breathing that night breeze, wishing it would calm my thinking into something peaceful, as if the sweetness in the air could turn that bitter feeling to something else. What I wanted was a cold beer, but I knew one beer led to five more with the way I was feeling, and I needed to be clear the next morning when I took Livy to meet Roy. It was when I turned my house into the REV center that I promised myself to never drink alone. Not in that house. Not with all those faces of the missing tacked on the bulletin boards in the front room, not with what should be a living room a shrine to the missing and the all-too-often dead. I couldn't shake the awful feeling coiled inside.

And it was just when I decided *what the hell* and stood to go risk the one beer that my cell phone rang that "Ode to Joy" tune it rings. It was Bitsy made me pick that ring tone. I looked and saw the caller. Roy.

All I had to do was say, "Hey, Roy," and he knew where my mind was.

"You brooding?" he said. I told him I was planning on knocking off a six-pack.

He said it the way he always says it, like a light thing, but there was a heaviness in his voice: "Friends don't let friends drink alone." I told him to come on over, and I headed for the bathroom to splash cold water on my face and make my hair look like something. Not that he would care. He's seen me at my worst, covered in sweat and dirt and more sorrow than most could stand. Even then, he'll step back and look at me like I'm Venus on the half shell and say, "You're something else, Shelby Waters." And I always pretend not to notice where he's going on like that because I don't have time for all that. I was looking at my face in the mirror and wondering when I started looking old when my phone rang again. I pulled it from my pocket. Roy again. I said, "You can't wait to get here to talk to me." I was trying to sound playful but knew he heard the weariness. He said, "You still wanting those remains?" And my head went swimmy, and I was thinking of Darly's remains. But we claimed Darly years ago. I heard him saying, "Shelby, Shelby," and then I heard him saying, "Patricia England." And I said, "Damn, Roy, you scared me. I was thinking something else."

"I knew you were brooding," he said. I wanted to tell him I was sick of all the dying, and why was it so many women we found? Pretty women. Like it was open season on pretty women, and men could set their sights on them the way a hunter went for deer. "I'm in your driveway," he said. "I was downtown and thought I'd stop by before I headed out to the lake. I saw your truck in the drive but no lights on in the house. I figured you were on the back porch. It's one of those black-turn kind of nights, right?" I heard the weariness in him then. Something I'd never heard. So I headed for the front door, I asked was he all right, but he'd hung up. I opened the door to see him holding a grocery bag with one hand while the other hand slipped his phone into his pocket. He walked in, raised the bag, and I could see the shape of the cardboard box inside. "You said you wanted her remains if nobody claimed her." He looked around the front room. All those faces of the missing staring out. Kids. Old people, teenaged boys. And women, all ages, lots of women lost somewhere out there. He shook his head, went for the kitchen. "I don't know how you live with this."

I followed him. He hadn't met my eyes yet. I knew there was something more on his mind than the unclaimed remains of a woman who'd wanted to be Patricia England. "Why didn't you come on around back if you knew I was home? Why sit in my driveway?"

He put the bag on the counter, went for the fridge. "I didn't know if you'd want company. And I'm not in the best place myself, Shelby. I figured we could use the beers." He opened our beers, gave me mine, took a long pull on his, and went to the bag on the counter. We usually clink our beers, even on the bad days. He focused on taking the cardboard box from the Bi-Lo bag like it was something fragile. But I saw that there was something in *him* fragile. That was why he was being so careful. "I know you have a way of wanting to keep things." He gestured toward the front room. "Like those pictures in there. The ones you've found, the ones you want to find, the ones you never will. But why want the unclaimed remains of a stranger?"

"She wasn't a stranger by the end of the day," I said. But I didn't want to go near the box. I looked at the label, knew without reading that it would say "Jane Doe" and some number marking her place in a long list of unclaimed remains.

He put the box back in the bag as if I might want him to take it away after all. He carefully wrapped the plastic around it, tied the handles into a little bow as if it were a present. There was a little trembling to his fingers as he pushed the box away. "I don't get why you want to cling to so much sadness."

"She helped me find those kids," I said. "She gave me a day with a happy ending. I couldn't let her be stacked with all those others in some dark storage room."

He nodded, his eyes still focused on the floor. I knew he hadn't come and sat in my driveway just for me. I wasn't the only one brooding.

"Out back?" I said and led the way to the back porch.

"What you gonna do with Jane Doe?" he asked.

"Patricia England."

"That's not Patricia England."

"She's not Jane Doe either," I said, sitting on the wicker couch, hoping he'd sit beside me. "I'm calling her by the name she wanted to be." He sat but leaned forward, looked out at the dark. There was a wincing kind of tension in his face as if he hurt somewhere. "I'll just keep her here with me. Maybe one day someone will want to claim her. Maybe I'll put her in a pretty vase. She seemed the kind of woman who appreciated nice things."

"Yeah, put her in that front room with all those other unclaimed souls in there." I heard the edge in his voice, let it go, knowing that whatever was stinging at his insides would come out. He shook his head. "As if it's not enough to surround yourself with those missing people, you gonna start a collection of the remains of the dead ones too?"

I wouldn't answer that. It would lead to the old fight. About my need to fill my life with other people's sorrows so I wouldn't have to face my own. But I knew my own all right. There was no running from it. If I spoke, I knew I'd say, *What's wrong with a life of serving the world? What's the harm in helping others?* And he'd say, *What's the harm in living your own life too? What's wrong with going out and listening to music now and then, seeing a movie, letting somebody who's not dead or who might could be dead into your life?* He thinks I live for Darly, and I know he just wants me to make room for him. I've told him at least a dozen times that it does no good to argue with the living about the dead they carry around. People talk about this thing called the death grip like it's the dead ones trying to hang on to living. But it's the living can't let go. So maybe I do have to hang on to Darly, her sweetness, her trusting of the world, to keep living in this world something I can stand.

He still wasn't looking at me. "We should go somewhere," he said.

He'd tried that before. Tried to get me to go to Tybee Island, Pauley Island. Even Savannah. Told me I might be interested in the graveyards there. He'd said that with a smile. Roy has a way of smiling. Even when he was giving you shit. He was always trying to get me out of town, as if leaving could get me out of me and into a new me who doesn't look back, a new me who could look ahead only to the next round of fun the way Roy did. I never was one of those happy, giggling girls—that was Darly. Momma used to try to get me outside playing and tell me, "The good Lord didn't mean for you to be such a deep child." She called my way of thinking about things *questioning the good Lord's mysteries.* In her mind we were supposed to embrace mysteries—her word for the bad shit that happens to good people. We were supposed to have faith in the Lord's will. Like Job. She was always talking about Job. But I'm guessing Job never walked into a crack house. My guess is Job's daughter never had half her face chewed off by a Rottweiler when she tried to blow the dog for a dealer who said if she did it, he'd give her a rock of crack to smoke.

I realized that Roy was still talking about the idea of going somewhere, and his words were hanging in the air like some kind of smoke signal that was rising, fading away. I hadn't answered, and he just stared out at the dark like there was nothing but darkness between us. I noticed he wasn't drinking his beer. And he wasn't teasing at me the way he usually did when I needed steering away from the black turn and onto a brighter road. I was wondering if he didn't want to meet Livy Baines, didn't want to face another mother who'd lost a daughter somewhere. Maybe he was tired of all those dark roads I kept pulling him down. It's not like there was much crime in the small town of Lake Waccamaw. That was why he liked his job there. He liked being happy, and I guess that was why I liked having him around. But I couldn't let him out of meeting Livy. She was aching to meet the man who'd found Katy's truck. She was convinced that Roy had the secret that could lead us to Katy.

I kept watching his face, waiting for him to feel my watching, to look at me, but it seemed the longer he stared out at the darkness, the more he could see. And whatever it was he was looking at, it was bad.

Sometimes the hardest part of my job is listening. Sometimes I have the urge, like we all do, to fill and empty space with words, as if words are like little cushions to take the nervous edge off. But silence is a big space, and if you sit still and open your ears to it, you can hear all kinds of things that go missed most times. I was hearing his hurting inside. And I knew to sit quiet until he could find the words to tell me why.

He finally moved, sipped his beer. "You believe in evil, Shelby?"

I looked out at the darkness and thought about those black

turns my mind takes. If you look at darkness long enough, you can start to believe evil things are hiding in the shadows. And I was thinking, was it a man or evil that did things such as snatching a woman off the side of a road? Then a gusty breeze blew up, filling the air with that honeysuckle smell that wraps around your skin, softening everything and filling your head with nothing but the sweetness of things. I couldn't declare a belief in evil. Not with that sweet air all around me and the goodness of Roy beside me. "On bad days," I said. "Not always. And today was feeling like a bad day until you came along."

Without seeing his face, I knew he was smiling. I can always feel him smiling, even when he's on the phone. He turned to me and shook his head. "There was a girl in Land Fall." He looked back at the dark, and his words played again in my head like the beginning of a story. This was the bad thing hiding behind the hurting in his face. Land Fall. I knew where Land Fall was. I didn't know anybody there, but I had this feeling that what he had to say would have something to do with me. So I asked him what had happened to the girl in Land Fall.

He went to the screen door. "It's hard to believe a man could do the things he did to this girl." I thought of Darly. I thought of all the girls who had been and still would be damaged by some man turned monster. You know, we all know it happens every day. He didn't tell me what this man had done to the girl in Land Fall. Just said it in three clipped words: *rape and assault*. He said it was a rape and assault like he'd never seen. And I sat thinking about those words *rape*, *assault*, like Band-Aids, little plastic sticky things we paste over some wounds to hide the damage done. The words can never speak the truth.

He finished his beer and put the bottle on the table, and I could see the hard trembling in his hand. I reached, took his hand, and pulled him back to sit with me. I thought of lighting a candle to bring some softness to the porch, but I didn't want to move away from him. It seemed he'd fly apart into pieces if I stopped stroking the back of his hand.

Finally he sighed, eased up enough to talk. "It's a miracle," he said. "Somehow the girl got away. Ran to the neighbors' house. They said she looked like a bloody angel, a naked, bloody angel falling in their door, said they'd never dreamed of such horrors in the world. The girl's mom, they've got her so sedated she can hardly move."

"What about the girl?" I said.

He shook his head. "Unconscious. They don't know if she'll come out of it." He let himself lean into me then. I'd never seen him broken like that, and we've seen a lot of things. I wrapped my arm around him, pulled him close. I'd always seen the cheerful, we-can-solve-it Roy, a man who could wade into any kind of mess, fix what was broken, find what was lost. That was why every county, township, city around here kept him in their loops. Cops, they get mighty territorial, but everybody welcomed the eyes and instincts of Roy.

I thought of the words people like to say at time like this: *It will be all right; we'll have to wait and see; we'll get through this; everything happens for a reason.* I hate such words. Let them go to a preacher if they want some patched-up hope based on nothing but a need. I knew he wasn't telling me everything. He knew I didn't need to hear about another girl torn apart. There's a wisdom in not telling all you know. I held Roy close, rubbed a light circle on his shoulder to soothe him the way my momma used to do. "We're gonna get out of all this mess one day," I said. He nodded, just barely. He didn't need to say what he was thinking. He was always wanting to go somewhere. I know in his mind he likes to see himself throwing a fishing line into the surf, standing in the sand barefoot, not really giving a shit if he catches something, just happy to be standing in the sun with cool water foaming and swirling around his legs. I know he sees the two of us biking on a beach. He's told me you haven't lived until you've biked on a beach with that sea air blowing all around in your hair.

He sees going to these happy places as a solution to most all things, but I know they are only distractions. They give a way of stepping out of the mess of this world until it's all over and we cross that line to the other side of living. And even then, I wonder, do we really ever get set free from this world, or does it keep calling? I'll have to live with not knowing. And like you, like all of us, I have to work to make some kind of peace with not knowing a damn thing about this world we like to think makes sense according to some grand design. I thought of Billy's words: *This is fucked up.* Then realized I'd said it out loud. Roy nodded and sank deeper into my arms. We stayed on the porch that night, dozing in and out on the wicker sofa, waiting to see if a phone would ring. But there were no calls. It seemed the whole world was worn out from the day.

A Simple Plan

Jesse woke to the sound of Luke's dog collar clanging. He sat up, saw Luke looking at him, then back to the door. "Sorry, Luke. Guess I slept too hard to hear you." He got up, opened his door, watched the dog head down the stairs for the kitchen, where he'd push through the doggie door and go outside. Jessie listened for any sounds in the house. His mom would be on a plane by now, but his dad . . . he heard his dad downstairs talking to Luke as if Luke were his favorite child. Jesse turned toward his bathroom, remembered his pants on the floor there.

He went on down the hall to the guest bathroom, then saw his dad coming up the stairs. "Your mom said you were sick last night."

Jesse dropped his head and nodded. "I'm doing better." His dad followed him into his room. "You want to see a doctor?"

Jesse shook his head, sat on his bed. "I've got crackers. Soup in the kitchen. Plenty of Coke. I'll just take it easy today, and I'll be all right."

His dad glanced toward his bathroom. "The maid will take care of things."

"She already here?"

His dad shook his head. "I told her to come after lunch. Figured you'd want to sleep in."

"Good," Jesse said. "I'd rather throw those clothes in the trash than have her clean them." He'd have to burn it all in the fire pit out back.

His dad nodded, stood, and went toward the door.

"You heading out to the marina?"

"I thought I'd stay on the boat for the weekend since your mom's gone to Dallas. Hang with some old fishing buddies of mine."

"Cool," Jesse said. "You go on and have a good time. Mom said she'd leave me some cash and her car."

His dad reached for his wallet, put a fifty on the bedside table. "Here's a little more. Call my cell if you need anything." Jesse watched his dad, head down, guilty, start to head out the door, then stop. "Be sure to set the alarm when you leave. There was a family robbed on the next block."

Jesse sat up straight. "Really?"

"Yep." His dad walked out the door.

He waited until he heard the garage door open, then close. He grabbed the backpack from his closet. He pulled out the fluffy stuffed dog.

He reached into the bag to see what might be of interest to Zeke. The lady's Rolex. Pearls, and what looked like ruby earrings. A diamond tennis bracelet. He wrapped the jewelry in a t-shirt, slipped it into the bottom of the bag. Wrapped the vase in another shirt, put it in, then shoved in a couple of books in case he got searched. He put the dog on top, its dumb little face sticking out. His phone buzzed. "Yeah."

"It's Mike."

"I know it's Mike."

"You do it?" Mike asked.

"Do what? Let's see, I've done a lot of things since I last saw you."

"The rich girl. Did you do that rich girl out there where you live?"

"Want details?"

Mike was silent.

Jesse waited. "You there?"

"Yeah," he said. "Look, Jesse, I need some cash. There's an old farmer out here. He died, and they're all going to his funeral tomorrow. I figured we could hit the house while they're all at the funeral. This old man, they say he had a gun collection. No telling what we could find. We go in, we get the stuff. Nobody gets hurt."

Jesse rubbed his neck, already going tense. "Look, man, I'm busy. I'll give some thought to that dead farmer. I'm getting some shit together to take to Zeke. Nicki Lynn had the kid. So I'm gonna go to the hospital, try to unload some stuff to Zeke."

"It's on the news," Mike said.

Jesse picked up the remote, aimed it at the TV, flicked channels, sports, infomercials, *Survivor*, and some game show. Nothing about a rape in Land Fall. Just CNN, and they were talking about some earthquake. "What's on the news?"

"That girl."

"Which girl?"

"The rich girl. My granny was watching her story on the TV, and I heard it."

Jesse flicked through the channels again. Nothing: game shows, talk shows, the usual shit. "I guess I just missed it. What'd they say?"

"Something about a girl getting assaulted."

"What else they say?"

"Just kept going on about something like this happening in Land Fall."

Jesse looked out his window to the empty street. "They'd have come by now if they thought it was me."

"They're just saying the home was robbed and the girl was assaulted in Land Fall. No leads yet, they said."

"They never say everything on the news."

"So you want in on the farmer's house?" Mike asked

"Maybe. Let me call you after I see Zeke."

"I really need some cash, man."

"I'll front you some," Jesse said. "Just let me do my business."

"When?" Mike said. "There's hardly nothing to eat in this house."

"And this means what to me?" Jesse said.

Mike sighed. "I guess I could get out there, hit the house myself."

"I guess you could do that." Jesse remembered his clothes on the bathroom floor. "Look, I got stuff to do. Sit tight."

"I'll handle it," Mike said, but his mind wasn't in it. Jessie could always tell when Mike's mind was someplace else.

"Something doesn't feel right," he said. "I gotta go." He clicked off the phone. It would take less than an hour to burn his clothes, clean the knives. Then he'd have to burn the towel that covered the knives. He'd dump the knives on the way downtown. He had a new plan, a simple plan. He'd get out of town, get a new ID, disappear before they even figured out he was gone.

Little Room for Lying

It didn't seem right to eat a dead man's food, but Mike figured he'd done worse. And the old farmer didn't have family in town, so most likely the stuff would be thrown away. Canned stuff might go to some shelter. But Mike needed it, and his granny, she deserved a good meal. He ran cold water over the frozen ham in the sink and told himself he was doing the world a kindness in some way, making a meal for his granny, even if he had to steal it from a dead man. His granny loved fried ham with her eggs. Mike smiled, thinking how she'd like the surprise. In a drawer he found white potatoes that had gone soft, but there was one good sweet potato left.

Mike left the ham in the sink to soak and went out on the back porch to have a smoke. He'd found the cigarettes on the old man's coffee table. Mike stood on his granny's back porch and looked across the fields to the old man's house, still empty, waiting for someone to come and carry the rest of the stuff away. Maybe they'd have a yard sale. That was what they did with dead people's things.

He sat and grinned, feeling the bulk of the silver dollars in his pocket. Mike had known there'd be something of use in the old man's house. He thought of running to the store and spending them on some brown sugar for the sweet potato and some of that Sara Lee pound cake his granny loved. But they'd surely be suspicious of a guy like him buying groceries with silver dollars. Still, he was tempted. He knew he should save them for the pawnshop, but the one nearby was already closed. Mike had taken stock, figuring how they'd make it with ten more days before his granny's government check was due. Two cans of soup, half a loaf of bread, grits, some peanut butter and jelly. They had plenty of eggs. They wouldn't starve with the eggs. But even his granny had said she was aching for a meal, a real meal, with meat and potatoes and some kind of green.

She'd told him if he'd get out there and kill one of the chickens, she'd be happy to dress it and fry it up, make some gravy to pour on the bread that was left. She'd told him how he could just give that chicken's head the quick, hard twist it took to break its neck. She didn't have the strength in her hands lately with her arthritis acting up. Sometimes Mike wondered if it was worth getting old. It seemed to him the body just turned on you when you got up in years.

There was a squawking in the chicken coop like the hens were fighting. He wondered what in the hell a bunch of hens would have to fight about. He looked at the coop. He thought he'd give just about anything for some crispy fried chicken, but he couldn't stand the thought of picking up that little heap of feathers and beak and claws. He'd tried it once, and it was awful the way a chicken could fight.

Mike threw the cigarette on the ground and went back into the kitchen to check the ham. It was soft. He unwrapped it, put it in a pan, and stuck in the oven, where the sweet potato was already smelling sweet. He didn't want to think about the things Jesse had done. Jesse had told him the things he'd meant to do to the girl they were talking about on the news. He heard his granny's television down the hall, the sudden switch from *Jeopardy* to the news update on the assault on a young woman in Land Fall. He moved into the hallway and listened. They were offering five hundred dollars to anyone with information. Mike had all the information they'd need. He thought of the things he could do with five hundred dollars. Groceries, gas, get the car the tune-up it needed so he could get out of town. But he'd never leave his granny. They'd put her in one of those state homes, and she deserved a whole lot better than that. Then, as if she could hear his thinking, she called, "Mikey, baby."

"Yes, ma'am." He went to her room.

She was sitting on the edge of her bed, hands gripping the walker.

He went toward her. "You planning on going somewhere, Granny? I told you to just holler if you needed something."

She studied him with the black, beady eyes that seemed to always look at him with a little suspicion, just like those hens of hers. She pulled herself up on the walker, arms trembling as she came to a stand. "That poor, poor girl," she said. "The detective said it was the most vicious assault he'd ever seen."

"She gonna live?" Mike said.

She rolled the walker ahead a little, went with it. "Critical condition. In a coma. I guess that's a mercy. They don't have any leads yet. They're just hoping she'll wake."

"That must be why they're paying for information," Mike said, looking back to the TV screen. But there was just a commercial for some new kind of mop.

His granny was heading down the hallway, said, "They don't get a lead soon, they'll double that reward. You watch."

His granny was always right about these things. Mike weighed the options. He could call and tell them exactly where Jesse Hollowfield would be: Mercy Hospital, maternity floor. He thought about it, thought maybe he should wait and see if they raised the reward. But if he waited too long, Jesse might get it in his mind to come after him. As far as Mike knew, he was the only one who knew the things Jesse had done. His granny rested, leaning on her walker.

"You need to stay in bed," Mike said.

She took his face in one hand, gave a little shake of her head, and let him go. "I need to see what's going on in my house. I'm not as deaf as you might think. I've heard things. That Jesse. I heard you on the phone this morning. I've got to find out about some of the comings and going around here." She put her hand on his shoulder, looked him in the eye, just the way she'd done when she knew he'd skipped school, sneaked a beer, stolen something, or done any of the things that had gotten him locked up in juvy.

She squeezed his shoulder. "Where did you go today? You always tell me when you're going somewhere, and you slipped out."

He took her hand, put it back on her walker. "I'm working on a surprise for you, Granny. I wish you'd just get on back to bed and let me make you a surprise."

She shook her head. "I'm not dying, Mikey. I just have a bad cold, and it got my arthritis stirred up. Soon I'll be back out there taking care of things. Got my check coming in . . ." She looked down, then up as if the number she wanted was floating somewhere in the air.

"Ten days," he said. "But I'm taking care of things."

She straightened. "I'm just saying I'm not deaf or blind, and I still have all my bodily functions. If you don't mind, just step out of my way so I can get in the bathroom and do my business and wash myself and make myself presentable for getting in that kitchen and making some kind of supper."

"Okay, Granny." He smiled and stepped aside and watched her take those slow, jerky steps down the hall. She wasn't at the edge of dying, but she wouldn't be around much longer. He wished he could do one thing to make her proud. He looked back toward her TV.

The game show was still on, but across the bottom of the screen was more news scrolling. They'd raised the reward to one thousand, just as his granny had said. Mike headed toward the kitchen. If he turned Jesse in, Jesse would be sure to put a hit on him.

He heard his granny in the bathroom. She'd turned on that gospel station on the radio she kept in there. She was private about what she called her bodily functions. Mike smiled and thought, *You are too good for this world, Granny*, as he walked toward the kitchen. She'd be proud if he turned Jesse in. He told himself no matter what happened, he'd never do another job with Jesse. He was only getting meaner, and it was only a matter of time before Jesse took Mike down.

His granny had told him, right before he'd gotten sent off to juvy, "You can do a wrong thing once or twice, or maybe even three times, and not get caught. But you keep doing a wrong thing, it's like the rat that keeps going down the same path. It leaves signs of itself, drop-pings, tracks, somebody takes notice, sets out a trap or poison. Once you know the way a rat travels, it ain't nothing to kill him on his path."

Mike was glad she never called down religion when trying to make him change his ways. The only time she ever did that was to show him how it might help him, not hurt him. Mike figured she'd tried religion on her own kids, but all that had gotten her was her daughter, his momma, shot and killed in a drug deal and her son on death row somewhere in Texas. Sometimes Mike was glad his mother had died fast. And Mike was glad he'd never known his own daddy, who was probably no better than Jesse's blood daddy. Mike had had it rough, but nothing like Jesse. He'd seen Jesse crying in his sleep. He'd never told him—hell, Jesse would probably kill anyone who said they'd seen him crying. But Mike knew there was a crying in-side, and that was why he gave Jesse room to stretch his meanness. Jesse didn't have a granny, and sometimes Mike figured that was all the difference in the world.

He heard his granny singing along with the music in the bathroom. He checked the sweet potato in the oven. It was soft, and the ham was coming along. When he straightened, the silver dollars jingled in his pocket. Most likely she wouldn't hear the sound, but sometimes she had a way of seeing, knowing, just about everything. He went to his room to hide the coins and stopped to check under the bed for the shotgun—as if there were any way it could disappear. But somehow he could imagine Jesse floating like a ghost through the walls and taking the gun, the shells, even somehow getting the coins from his pocket.

He saw himself in the mirror. He didn't look like a thief. He wished he could be like Jesse sometimes. Maybe the only thing that kept him from being like Jesse was that little bit of heart his granny gave him. In the past two days they'd both robbed a neighbor's house. They'd broken the Zeke rule—never rob a neighbor. His granny would say they were heading down the same path, and she didn't even know they'd driven down that old farm road with that girl. Mike was glad he'd never laid a hand on her. Then he remembered she had laid a hand on him. He rubbed his arm as if he could rub the feeling of her away.

He looked out his window toward the west, where the sun would soon sink past the line of trees and field. The old farmer hadn't planted for years. When Mike had gone through that house, he'd felt kind of dumb and guilty for thinking he could take anything of value off a farmer. There was no safe, no money stashed in a coffee can in the freezer. And upstairs there was no money under that mattress. Mike flinched when he shifted the pillow and saw the shotgun. What was a sawed-off shotgun doing under a dead wife's pillow? He could tell that was her side of the bed because of the Bible and the little vase of fake flowers on the bedside table. Under the farmer's pillow he found the shells. He knew that was the farmer's side of the bed because on that bedside table was the clock and a set of teeth floating in a glass of water. It didn't seem fair for a man to be buried without his teeth. Seemed the funeral home would ask for the teeth when they asked for clothes and shoes. If they put shoes on a dead man, it stood to reason they'd want his teeth. A dead man deserved more dignity than to be stuffed in a coffin while his teeth sat floating in a glass.

Mike had shoved the gun and shells into his backpack. He went to the sock drawer. People were so predictable. Women put their jewelry with their panties, and men hid their money with the socks. Mike figured there was a reason, but it was beyond his knowing. All he knew was that he liked the smooth weight of the coins. He stood there rubbing the weight of one between his fingers just for the feel it. He slipped the coins into his pocket and headed downstairs. Then, standing in the dead man's kitchen, he had a thought about all the space left in his backpack. The refrigerator's motor clanked on, and that was when he got the idea that would've made Jesse proud: groceries. He had seen a little ham in the freezer when he'd looked for the coffee can that could be holding cash. He grabbed the ham, left the open box of fish sticks. He took the bottle of beer and a jar of apple jelly. Then in the cabinets he found the bag of coffee, the can of green beans, and the sweet potato. He looked for something sweet because he knew his granny would want that. But there was nothing sweet.

He heard his granny call him. She was back in her bedroom with the TV on. He hurried to her, saw her standing there, staring at the news. She'd seen that she was right about the reward going up to a thousand bucks. She shook her head, turned to him. "Just like I told you." She was trying to read something in his face.

He turned away, said, "I got to get to making your surprise."

Back in the kitchen, his hands shook as he took the potato out of the oven, set out the butter. He had options. Jesse was meeting Zeke at the hospital, and that meant Mike could call that number on the news and tell them exactly where to pick up the man they were after. Mike's mind kept turning on what he could do with a thousand bucks. He couldn't remember if he'd ever seen that much money at once.

With a thousand bucks Mike could get the car a good tune-up and drive his granny to Raleigh, where she could stay with that cousin of hers, and he could keep going. He'd never rest easy with Jesse on his trail. Even locked up, Jesse would have somebody beat him to death. Somehow he'd get it done. It was better to work with the devil than against him because in the devil's territory, he always wins.

Mike stepped into the hallway, made sure his granny was still in her room. Back in the kitchen he called Jesse.

Jesse answered, "I'm busy. Now what?"

"I did the farmer's house," Mike said.

There was a silence. Mike heard jazz in the background. That meant Jesse was in his mother's car. The sound turned down. "You what?"

"The dead farmer. I did his house."

"Got enough to make it worth your while to walk across that field?"

"Silver dollars. The old kind."

Jesse made that little snorting sound he always made when something struck him funny but not worth the laugh. "Silver dollars. And just how many silver dollars?"

"I got seven," he said. "And they're old."

"Seven silver dollars." Jesse kind of sang the words. "Seven silver dollars from a dead man." Silence hung there.

"I got a gun too," Mike said.

"A gun that works?"

"Yeah." He thought about the gun under his bed. It had shells next to it. The old man wouldn't keep a gun that didn't work. "Yeah," he said again. "I tried it. A sawed-off shotgun. I tell you, I really tore up a tree on my way home."

Jesse laughed, a real laugh. That was good. Mike saw the can of green beans on the counter. He could smell the ham cooking; he'd have to get the beans on. "The old man, he slept with a sawed-off shotgun. Can you believe that?"

"So why you calling me?" Jesse said. "Seems to me you ought to be heading to the coin shop with those seven silver dollars. Or the pawnshop; they take coins."

"I want to meet Zeke."

"Well, Zeke don't want to meet you."

Mike opened the green beans, dumped them in a pan, glanced down the hallway. "Shit, Jesse, I need the cash. My granny's check don't come for ten more days, and I've let her down this month. I haven't been doing my part. Things so tight I had to steal a ham from that dead man."

Jesse laughed, a real laugh. "You jacked a ham from a dead man? Hope you got a little sweet potato to go on the side." Mike froze, looked around the kitchen. How did Jesse know these things? But Jesse was still laughing. "A ham from a dead man. I gotta admit, Zeke would get a kick out of that."

"So can I meet him? Come on, Jesse, I know he could fence these coins. Might even want to keep them for his kid. You seen his kid yet?"

"What you talking about?"

"You told me you were gonna go see his kid at the hospital?"

"Maybe I already did that. Maybe I'm on my way out to your house to eat some of that dead man's ham with you and your granny."

"Don't be coming out here. My granny, she's got a way of knowing things, and she didn't take too kindly to you eating all the cookies and drinking her Coke."

"Look, man, I got shit to do. I missed visiting hours today, and Zeke's gonna be pissed."

"You can see him tonight," Mike said. "They've got visiting hours at night."

Jesse laughed, a hard sound. "Would that be Mike Carter trying to tell Jesse Hollowfield what to do?"

"Just call Zeke, please. See if he has any use for these coins. He might want that gun too. You want the gun?"

"I'd bet a hundred bucks you don't even know if that gun works because you don't have the balls to go firing off a gun anywhere near where you might get caught." Mike heard his granny coming down the hall. "Am I right? You never even fired the gun."

Mike hung up the phone. She watched him. "Why you looking like that? Who was that on the phone?"

"Salesman."

"I didn't hear the phone ring."

"That's because you don't hear everything, Granny. How about you have a look at the surprise I've been working on for you?" He opened the oven, took the ham out.

She looked around the kitchen. "Praise the Lord. Baby, how'd you do this?"

"I had a little money stashed away. Now, you sit and let me serve you."

She sat and smiled. "Thank you, Lord, for the small wonders of this world."

"It's just a ham, Granny." He sliced the ham. Put some on her plate. He sliced open the potato, forked brown sugar into it. He checked the beans, trying to go through the motions like this was an everyday thing, but she was watching him.

"Why ain't you eatin'?"

"I'm not hungry just yet."

She studied him. "Sometimes we're hungry, but we don't know it. You got to eat, Mikey." He poured the beans into a bowl, set it in the table. But his granny's eyes wouldn't leave his face, so he made himself a plate and sat with her. He lifted his fork, and she reached, touched his arm. "We should say grace." He nodded, bowed his head, and wondered who'd be next on Jesse's list. That girl had touched his arm, said, *My name is Katy*. His granny squeezed his arm. "You all right?"

He cut into his ham. "It's just gonna keep on going."

"What? What are you talking about?" She was eating now. And she was liking it. At least he had done one good thing.

"I'm thinking about that old farmer across the field. What's the trouble of living when we all just die in the end?"

"There is an afterlife. There's a reward for the children of God, baby."

He looked at the clock. Visiting hours at the hospital would start in a couple hours. They'd be over at 8:30. He was wondering if Jesse would make his granny's house the next place on his list after he saw Zeke. Mike knew he was the one loose end, and Jesse was too smart to leave a loose end, especially when there was a thousand-dollar reward. He watched his granny spread some of the apple jelly on her ham, put a dab on her sweet potato.

He stood. "I need to make a phone call, Granny."

She nodded, cut another piece of ham. "Go on, baby. I'm gonna sit and keep on eating. Mercy, it's good to have something besides chicken and eggs."

He bent and kissed the top of her head. She always smelled clean, not like most old people. "If things work out, I'm gonna take you out for a shrimp dinner next week."

"How you gonna do that?"

"I'm gonna make a phone call."

She put down her fork, put both hands flat on the table, looked up at him. "You know something about that girl on the news." She looked up at him the way she used to when he'd done something wrong and she'd say, *Go cut me a switch, and it better be a good one because you don't want me cutting the switch I'm gonna take to you.*

He picked up his plate, scraped it into the trash, and put it in the sink. "I don't know nothing about that girl."

She tracked him with her eyes. "You were looking at it on the TV."

"Granny, the whole town's watching that story on TV. People don't get attacked in Land Fall. That's a gated community." He washed his plate and knife and fork and put them in the drain.

"Who you fixin' to call?" She was back at cutting into her ham. Maybe he could fool her.

"A girl," he said. He wondered how he could turn Jesse without his granny finding out. The news had said anyone turning in information could remain anonymous.

"Well, what's this about you taking me for a shrimp dinner?"

He ran the baking pan under hot water, squirted soap on it, let it sit. "This girl, she likes me. She's an assistant manager at the Golden Corral." He winked at his granny. "Just might get a girl and a job all in one week." She nodded but showed no interest in his words, was too busy scraping the bits of sweet potato from the skin. He wanted to say, *I'm sorry.* He wanted to tell the truth. He wanted to be the boy she believed he was instead of the man he'd come to be.

"You do what you'll do, Mike. Just remember what I told you about how God knows every little secret thing we do. He wanted to cry. "I'm gonna make that call now." He went down the hall, stood still, and squeezed his eyes shut. If he made the call, it would all be over. With the thousand dollars he could get out them both of town and leave the whole mess of Jesse behind. He moved into his granny's room, sat on her bed, and stared at the phone.

He dialed the number, and when a woman's voice answered, he slammed the phone down.

He could feel Jesse, hear him laughing. *You don't have the balls to fire a gun where you might get caught.* He was right. He was always right. Except for this girl. He'd meant to kill her, but somehow she'd gotten away. The world didn't always go according to Jesse's plan. He picked up the phone again, listened to the dial tone. Everything would flip if he made this call. Maybe the world would start going his way. He sat there breathing. There was a ringing in his ears. Then a ringing in the air. It was the phone. Of course they'd ID anyone who called. He picked up the phone.

The lady sounded like a cop. "Did you just make a call to this line?"

"Yes," he said. "It was an accident. I dialed the wrong number."

"Do you have any information about the assault on the girl at Land Fall?" He felt the blood rushing in his head. She was a cop. "Just say yes or no."

"No," he said. "It was an accident. I'm sorry."

"People don't call this number by accident. And we don't take kindly to pranks."

"It was a mistake." He looked down, saw the dirt he'd tracked on his granny's rug. He should have taken off his shoes when he got back from the farmer's house. He'd tracked dirt all over his granny's clean floors. Like the rat.

"Sir, we know this is the Carter residence."

"It's my granny's house."

"And you are?"

He could imagine the squad cars coming while she kept him on the phone. "I'm just visiting," he said.

"And you are."

"I'm Jimmy," he said. "From Rhode Island." Like the chickens, he thought. He wanted to beg her now, *Just please let me off the phone*.

"Jimmy," she said. "From Rhode Island." She knew he was lying. She was probably looking at his rap sheet on her computer screen.

"Do you know an Estelle Carter?"

"She's my granny," he said.

"Does she know anything about the assault?"

"How do I know, lady? Now, could I please get off the phone? I'm sure you've got other people trying to call."

"No. We don't." The silence sat there. And just like with Jesse, Mike knew if he waded out into that silence, he'd slip and fall.

He looked up, saw his granny. She was staring at the clumps of mud from his shoes on her rug. She bent, clinging hard to her walker as she picked up a piece of mud. She held it, looked at him.

"I gotta go. My granny's calling." He hung up the phone. He looked up at his granny's face. There'd be little room for lying now.

"Michael Ray Carter, I didn't raise a boy to be a stranger."

"I'll clean the rug." He wanted to stand, run from those eyes of hers, but she was standing in the doorway.

"Just who is Jimmy from Rhode Island?" She wouldn't look at him now. She was looking at the mess on her rug.

"You heard that?"

"I heard that."

And once again the silence spread like a great icy lake between them.

She straightened up, stared at him. "You know something about that girl. You could do one right thing here, Mikey."

One right thing. Mike knew he could do one right thing now, but even with the thousand-dollar reward he'd never really get out from under all the wrongs Jesse had done. He nodded, kept his eyes on his granny as he picked up the phone.

Never Had a Need to Go over This Bridge

It was a day like so many days when you think you know where you're going, and the road bucks and you get thrown to a place without a map. You look around and try to get your bearings where low, thick clouds hang all around you, keeping you from knowing which way the sun goes.

Livy, of course, was nervous about meeting Roy, just another cop in her mind. She was also already grieving about seeing the place where he'd found Katy's truck, the lake that according to everyone was Katy's happy place to be. I waited on Katy's porch while Livy paced inside, talking to her husband on the phone, moving through the house, picking up things, putting them down while she nodded, said things like "Yes," "I know," "I understand." I could only take so much of that. I moved away from the door and looked out at the lush yard, heard the songbirds, and I wondered how many more times in my life I'd be standing on *a missing* woman's, *likely a dead woman's,* porch while her flowers keep blooming and the breeze riffles through the trees.

I had Roy's voice-mail message looping in my head: "The girl woke up. The girl from Land Fall. We might have a good lead, Shelby."

It's the kind of message that drives me crazy in the way it offers something, gives nothing. He breathed a minute, that way he has when he's thinking, then said, "It's a miracle she lived. Livy Baines won't want to know the things he did to that girl." Then that breathing again while he picked his words: "I'm heading to the hospital now." I stepped out in the yard, stood under a maple tree, and admired the way Katy had arranged geraniums and asparagus ferns and plant spikes in pots on the front steps. She was so careful with making pretty things. And I tried to tell myself there was a chance Katy had just run off, but with the weeks crawling by and not a word from her, I was having deep doubts about a happy ending. My talent's giving hope to other people, but that can be hard when you're feeling your own hope flickering, just on the edge of going out.

I went back up on the porch to remind Livy I was waiting. We were supposed to meet Roy out by Lake Waccamaw. If it weren't for Roy, I knew Wilmington police would still be thinking Katy Connor had run off to Fort Lauderdale. Livy thought she was just meeting him to thank him and to show him Katy's scrapbook, but I knew from Roy's message that she was about to learn something more.

We were late, but the lunch crew at the Lake Waccamaw Inn would keep the place open for Roy. It's like his satellite office out there. They have loyalties to him and me. It was about two years before Katy disappeared that we'd found Sam, the fry cook's, daughter. Her name is Desiree. Seems to me any parent naming a girl Desiree is asking for trouble. But then again, trouble comes to any name you could choose. She was fifteen and just never came home one night.

She was gone for three months, and the cops had given up on looking, but I wouldn't. I knew she wasn't dead. I could see it in Sam's eyes. He knew his girl was alive out there. Sam, he had hunter's eyes, not the grieving gaze I see so often on a parent's face. His eyes were steady, deep and brown and always scanning the horizon for where she might be. So we kept looking. I'd seen Desiree before, figured she had a reckless streak. Her mom had left her with her dad and run off to Vegas when Desiree was only three. Sam tried, but he couldn't cure the girl's what-the-hell attitude. Seemed like there was just a hard spot in the girl's heart where her mom used to be. And that can be a danger.

After we'd searched just about every square mile of swamp and woods and back roads for thirty miles around, and after I used my sources on drug houses around Wilmington, we knew where she was most likely to be: Myrtle Beach. Roy made some calls, and Sam and I went down there and put flyers out offering a reward. It wasn't two weeks before we found her in a crack house. She was sitting in a back room, just waiting on a bed in her bra and panties, smoking a cigarette, flipping through some magazine. She screamed this little sound when we pushed the door open. It wasn't the prettiest way for a daddy to find his girl. Once she saw it was us, she came running to Sam, said, *I'm so sorry, Daddy, so sorry; just get me out of here*. She wasn't all angry and arrogant the way most of them get when you do a rescue. She seemed sincere, as if she'd just gotten lost in the woods and needed her daddy to come find her, lift her out of the brambles and the weeds.

That was one fine thing to celebrate. Sam bought Roy a case of Miller Lite and me a bunch of roses, the kind that smell like roses and not some refrigerated thing the way most store-bought roses smell. He knew I had a soft spot for roses, and Sam knew that was just the kind of pleasure I'd want. I might come off as a hard-ass— have to—but you put a sweet-smelling rose to my face, press those petals on my nose, let me breathe it in, and that thin, hard shell I keep just under my skin, it starts to melt. Roy watched me that day, breathing in those roses. He laughed a little and said, "There she

231

goes," and without a word, with just a look to each other, we knew how that night would end.

So we joined in the barbecue at the back of my house. And volunteers brought on the groceries, all right: ribs, greens, cornbread, chocolate cake, and homemade ice cream. Sam got silly-ass drunk on whiskey while the rest got nice and juiced on the rum-runners Sam's girlfriend was mixing up. We ate and drank and danced until we could hardly stand the laughing anymore. And suddenly they all left. It was like Roy gave some signal, and they started packing up and leaving until it was just Roy helping me clear up things, with that way of smiling he has. I swear you can feel the heat of his smile in the dark. So he stayed that night. And we slept on blankets we piled under the tarp that had been put up for shade during the day. Roy hates coming inside my house, and he won't sleep there. So we stayed out all night. Woke with the predawn birds. When he was leaving—as much as I wanted him every night—I told him we couldn't be doing that again. I told him I didn't have time for pleasures like that in my life. He told me I was crazy. He didn't get mad or sad, just told me with that smile he wears even when he's hurting.

I heard Livy yelling inside, and I was glad to hear her holding her ground with her husband on the phone. It would make her stronger for what was to come. I thought of Roy out there by the lake, waiting for us with information about the Land Fall girl. I leaned in the door and called, "We really ought to get going. I'm heading to the truck now." I went down the sidewalk and admired the lantana spreading past the flower beds and into the driveway, and I saw the purple wave petunias wilting in the baskets along the fence and the whole yard suffering from neglect, and I thought the first thing I'd do when we came back was water those plants. I knew Katy would want it that way.

I got in my truck, started the engine, and looked toward the house. Finally she came out, struggling with her purse and her sunglasses and the leather tote bag crammed with the scrapbook and that framed poem and who knew what else. She got in, arranged herself, and pulled her seatbelt on. "I'm sorry," she said. "My husband." She slipped on her sunglasses and looked ahead, and I could she was fighting tears. "My husband," she said again. "He's like that detective, says I should let the police do their job and come home where I belong." She sighed, shook her head. "Truth is, he just wants his dinner on the table and his breakfast made."

I put the truck in gear, hit the gas, and said, "Everybody wants breakfast made."

"He wants his wife," she said. "You know men, whether they're from Suck Creek or Lookout Mountain, they want their wives right there doing what they expect their wives to be doing: menus, dishes, laundry."

"That's why I'll never marry," I said. She looked at me with a sadness like I'd just said I had an incurable disease.

"How old are you?" she asked.

I made like I was checking my cell phone. "Old enough to know better," I said. I know I broke my mother's heart not getting married, not giving her the grandbabies she wanted. I didn't need another woman telling me I'd chosen the path of least reward, suggesting that I'd regret my selfishness one day.

We got to a red light, and she pulled the overstuffed tote to her chest as if Katy's stuff gave her comfort. "You think this Roy will help?" I looked at her clutching that tote, and I smelled her perfume, and I took in those leather pumps, jeans pressed with a crease, starched blue shirt, and string of pearls, and all I could think was *God bless you, lady*. I don't believe much in God, but you can't change your raising, and my momma raised me to say *God bless their hearts* when you saw some frail, misguided soul doing something vain or stupid or flat-out wrong. "Do you?" she asked.

"What?" I said, my eyes on the road.

"You're not telling me something," she said.

I gave her a glance to show I meant respect. "I'm just thinking." The light changed, and I remembered her question, and I said, "Roy will do all he can to help you." I didn't tell her that Roy had said she wouldn't want to know what the man had done to the girl who'd lived. And I could feel it, that shift I get inside when we're searching for clues. We were on the right track, and I had a stronger feeling that it wouldn't end at a good place. I said, "Roy always helps. "

She rummaged through her tote, said, "I meant to bring some bottled water."

I nodded toward the backseat. "You know, I've got just about anything you could want back there. Water, soda, trail mix, and whiskey. I've got some Xanax tucked away in the first-aid kit. And a Smith and Wesson, a hunting knife. Even got a snakebite kit." I looked to her. "Just reach back in the cooler and get a water."

She grabbed a water and put the cool bottle to her face. "Billy told me there are alligators out there where Katy likes to go sit and write."

I nodded.

"What do you do if you see one?"

I was thinking, *Dear God, don't let us find this girl half eaten by some alligator*. And I thought of that woman's leg they'd found. It was too short to be Katy's leg, They were figuring a Hispanic girl. And I felt Livy looking at me, wanting an answer. "You make a point to stay clear of where you might see one. Unless you're in a car or a good-sized boat. Lots of Billy Bobs around here get in deep trouble fast, thinking they can poke a gator with a stick or tease it with a chicken leg or a rib bone."

I looked over, saw her eyes skittering. "Don't worry about gators," I said. "According to Billy and the folks at the lodge, she likes to park by the lake to watch the sun set. There's no alligators in that lake. They're back in the canals."

The Cape Fear River bridge was rising like a roller coaster in the distance. Livy looked out at the bridge and went for tissues in her purse. "She should never have left home." I was trying to get in the right lane, but the semi ahead was going too slow, and the one behind was coming up too fast. I heard her say, "I've never been over this bridge," and I saw a chance to break between the trucks. I stomped the gas, scooted in and out and passed, and boom, we were ahead of the clump of traffic and zooming on in the open lane. Livy clutched her tissue with both hands and smiled at me. "That was some race-car driving, there, Shelby." I liked the way she said my name, the way my momma used to say it, all soft and drawn out and round, the way you draw out the sounds of the things you love. I blinked that thought away and said "I guess all us Southern gals got a little NASCAR driver in us just waiting to rev up and stretch on out to the passing lane."

"Not me," she said. "I'll never get used to driving those mountain roads, those sheer drops down." She sighed. "But Katy, she loves zipping along, taking those curves so fast I sit and grip the car seat like that could keep me safe on the mountain with her behind the wheel. Katy always says, 'It's just a road, Momma. What's a road gonna do to you? You're the driver. You just keep your eyes on the road, and you'll be all right.' And she knows full well people go spinning off roads all the time." She looked down at that water churning below. "That's awful looking," she said. "It's so dark."

"It's tannins," I said, "All the vegetation up the river."

"I never had a need to go over this bridge," she said. "We only visited the nice parts of town. The beaches, mainly. Sometimes we'd come in, do shopping downtown, have lunch by the river. It doesn't look so scary from back there." We were back to solid ground, and I was praying Roy would have a good lead. "This place we're going used to be nothing but farms," I said. "But Lake Waccamaw is some prime real estate these days."

She squeezed my arm. "So this sheriff. You've worked with him before?"

"Oh, yes," I said, and I felt myself smiling.

She poked at my arm, grinned. "Ohhh, you like him."

I nodded, kept my eyes on the road. "He's a friend—a good friend. The kind of man anybody likes."

"But you *really* like him," she said.

"I don't have time for that," I said, but I was still grinning. "You're gonna love Roy," I said. "All the woman love Roy. He's kind of a mix of devil and angel, has those big, soft brown eyes that make you feel warm and safe, like the world is a good place just waiting to happen if you give it a chance. Then he's got this little devil grin that makes you want to do something bad."

"Shelby Waters!" She slapped at my arm. And that was all right because I wanted to pull her out of that worrying place. "I'm a married woman!" she said, but she was grinning too.

"Yes, ma'am," I said. "I know. But that Pete, he keeps asking when you want to move into his condo."

"Quit," she said. "I wish I could leave that house, but Billy needs me around. Drives me crazy sleeping in that place. But he needs me."

"But you need the ocean air," I said. "You need to take care of you." She had no idea where her road was going. But for the moment she looked almost content.

She got busy pulling out her compact and checking her lipstick, and I thought how sometimes a little vanity can be a comforting thing.

It's the little things like that that I love about this world. Even at our worst we want to look good for somebody. And Roy would make her feel good, nothing lewd, but he'd just help her remember she was a woman, a good woman who was patient and strong. He has a way of reminding you of your best self.

And as if he could hear my thinking, my cell rang: Roy. "We're over the bridge, almost there," I said. He asked if he could tell me now, and I said, "Sure," all light and lively, as if he'd just asked if I wanted a Coke. And he told me. The man did brutal things to a girl. He liked doing it. He took his time. And he kept talking about a girl he'd jacked, a girl in a blue truck with plates from Tennessee. I just nodded and kept my eyes on the road, knowing the words before he said them. "You're gonna have to tell her," he said. I felt Livy looking at me, so I gave her a we're-working-things-out face and a little nod. Roy was saying that they were releasing only the assault story on the news and that they were offering a thousand-dollar reward to anyone with information. I asked, "You still meeting us at the inn?"

"I'm already here," he said.

"That means you were in a hurry." He didn't say anything. Roy never hurried. "I'll be right there," I said. I stepped on the gas as I hung up the phone.

She was looking at me. "What's the news?"

I looked over to a mother about to go on the worst journey of her life. "He's already there," I said. "That's all."

She knew there was something more, kept her eyes on the highway. "This is a long road," she finally said. And I could see that she was crying, just a dabbing at the eyes with her fingertip the way ladies do. I put a tissue in her hand.

"Yeah, it is a long road," I said. "There's not much out here but old family farms—they'll slowly be sold off, chopped up into residential developments. It's the way of the future. Nice brick homes and cul-de-sacs."

She took a breath, sat straighter, looked out. "What do they grow around here?"

"Mostly corn," I said. "Tobacco. In the old days it was cotton. But it's cheaper to import cotton now. Slavery, it just moves around the world. It don't ever really go away."

"Doesn't," she said.

I looked at her.

"Slavery *doesn't* ever really go away."

Now, I'm not one who minds being corrected, but that's for important things. I couldn't let her play school marm. I could have said something hard to her, but what she had going was hard enough, so I just told her I had my natural way of talking and my public way. Told her that with her I thought I could be my natural way. She touched my arm and said it didn't matter how I talked, and I knew she was saying she was sorry. "They grow corn, tobacco, soybeans, even marijuana in some parts. Those are the big cash crops these days."

"Oh, yes," she said "Lawrence told me about that. He's big on knowing where the money is, where it's been, and where it's going. He's big on knowing things. Swears by the *Wall Street Journal* the way folks used to swear by the Bible."

"It's the way of the world," I said.

She sighed, did a little tight thing with her mouth the way people do when they're not sure they want to tell you something. "Lawrence is big on knowing things and making sure you know he knows things."

I gave a laugh. "Sounds like a lot of men."

"Like that detective," she said. "The detective should know things. He is a professional, and he profiled Katy, and he said she probably was drunk and out running around. Lawrence was furious when I told him I slapped that man, said it was a serious offense, said the detective had done me a favor."

I said, "Fuck the detective." She flinched at the word, so I told her I was sorry, and she gave a little nod. I scrambled for something useful to say. "I read an article in the *New Yorker* about profiles. These profilers act like scientists, but they basically use fake psychic tricks, the leading questions, the broad questions. They're actually right 2.7 percent of the time. Call Lawrence and tell him that."

She smiled, looked at me. "He'll want to know which issue of the *New Yorker*."

"I don't know," I said, laughing. "But I'll let you know when I get back home."

She sighed and looked out at a field of blown-down trees. It was eerie-looking, had to be five to ten acres, just piles of broken tree trunks, branches, not a green leaf left. In time the kudzu, honey-suckle, weeds would take over. Or more likely one of those develop-ers with model homes in mind. I was feeling sad for all the lost wild places. Livy had told me that even Suck Creek was filling up with condos sprawled along the river. She said I wouldn't know it any-more. And knowing that made me want to go back. But my house, it was gone now. Then she asked, "When did you lose your faith?"

I knew this would be coming. They always expect a searcher to be some kind of believer. And when you're not, it hurts.

"When my sister was killed," I said. She looked at me, wanted more. "I was sick with sorrow, so I went to the pastor, and I said if Jesus had his eye on the sparrow, why wasn't he looking after Darly? And he said some of us, the best of us most often, were sacrificial souls, meant to give our lives. *Kind of like Jesus* was exactly how he put it. My daddy, he just gave a snort—a quiet man's way of saying, *To hell with you, mister*, but Momma, she held on to that line like a comfort—her daughter was made into some sacrificial lamb. I don't believe in sacrificial lambs. I believe in cruel people and good people and weak people and strong. You mix 'em up, and shit goes down. That's all."

She just looked out her window at the land going by. I was regretting my words. Finally Livy shook her head. "It's a mystery." She tightened her lips. "I've been told by two preachers and a priest that there are divine mysteries we are supposed to accept. It all works together for those who follow the Lord and believe in his word."

I could see she was struggling to hang on, but I needed her to face this world, not some idea of the next. "I went to college for a while," I said. "I studied the history of religion. The gospels. They're stories written long after Jesus was gone."

"I know that," she said. "I went to college too, Bible college. And I know they are stories, but we are supposed to believe they were divinely inspired."

"You're right," I said. And I said it again like I meant it.

She nodded and looked out her window. "There's something I didn't tell you about Katy. Lawrence, he's hard on Katy. She is rebellious, and he doesn't like that. But there are some things he doesn't know. Her daddy had a weakness. He liked guns more than a man should." She looked at me, her eyes squinting a little like she was focusing on something just out of range. "You know, it's strange," she said, "how things seem to follow you around. I left Suck Creek to get away from all the guns and rednecks ready to shoot anything in sight. So I went up on the mountain to Covenant College—about as far away from Suck Creek as a girl can get. But it was too strict up there, made the world seem like nothing but a whole lot of wrongs piling up, and the only right thing we could hope for was heaven. There was a meanness and a self-righteousness to those people. So I went to college in town, and that started to feel a little more like something I could stand. Then I met Katy's daddy; he was an engineer, but later I found out he loved shooting at things as much as any Suck Creek redneck boy. There I was, living in a gorgeous home halfway up Lookout Mountain, but I was still in Suck Creek in my own house. Some things just follow you, I guess. I have to wonder, did that meanness follow Katy to here? It scares me sometimes."

I couldn't say anything to that. I said, "There could be some situations we just don't understand yet."

Livy shifted in her seat. "When Katy was a teenager, she had a drinking problem, just a little, out of hand. I like to think she outgrew it, but Lawrence—his ex-wife was a drunk; she died of liver disease—Lawrence says you don't outgrow these things. And Lawrence is not a foolish man. He makes a point of being an authority on things, and he is an authority on this, and he's always right, and goddamn it, that drives me crazy!" She covered her mouth with her hand, but I could see the grin there. "My momma always said cussing was contagious. Just a little car ride with you, and I'm already cussing." She smiled, but her eyes stayed cold. "Lawrence says Katy got drunk and ran off, and I'm praying he's right again."

She looked out her window at all the nothing out there. "Don't you ever get tired?" she said. "All this driving around and around and back and forth, not knowing when the end will come."

"I can drive for days without sleep when I'm on a mission."

"'A mission'?"

"Yes, ma'am."

"So you do believe in things."

"I believe in a lot of things."

"Like what?"

"Like the world of the living."

"That's a start," she said. "No afterlife?"

"I believe in the living and the dead."

"Do you believe in spirits? Is that why you do this, to put lost souls to rest?"

"I do what I do to put the living to rest. I see suffering and want to ease it."

She squeezed her eyes shut. "We'll find her."

I saw the exit for Lake Waccamaw, flipped the signal, and slowed down.

"Thank God, we're there," she said.

We rounded a curve and saw the shimmering lake stretched out, clean and blue. We drove along the narrow road and saw the little stretches of shore where people could wade in and swim.

"Look." I pointed ahead to the inn. "That's Roy's cruiser in the lot. He'll be inside joking with Sam, sipping coffee like he has nothing better to do in the world." I parked, looked at her. "You ready?"

She nodded, grabbed her purse and the tote bag stuffed with Katy's things. I knew Roy didn't need them, but it would give her comfort to think she could offer him some kind of insight. But Roy already had all the insight he needed. He'd gone through Katy Connor's truck. He'd talked to a girl who'd survived the man who'd carjacked, who'd probably killed, Katy. Roy knew more than Livy Baines would ever want to hear.

I got out of the truck, walked around to her side. I opened the door.

She sat there. "I don't know where my daughter is, and it's been over a month. Do you know how crazy that is?" I took her hand and gently pulled her out of the truck. Livy looked out at the blue sky, so wide and bright and perfect over the still water. "It's a perfect reflection," she said. "You can even see that little line of clouds reflected in the water. It's hard to find water this clean. No wonder she came here."

I nodded. "It's fed by local creeks. Every day in the summer a little blue line appears down there to the south and moves north. It's a wave, and it breaks right here on this shore. And the wind pushing it comes along, wraps the town in a steady breeze. Sometimes you look out there and see the wind push a string of dark clouds from nowhere. And the lake gets rough. And that's odd because at most it's about seven feet deep. That water can tip a little fishing boat easy and give hell to the bigger ones."

"But it looks so calm."

I thought of Suck Creek. "Yeah, so people get careless. But if you go out in that water, you'd better keep your eye on the horizon and life jackets for everybody on board." She stood there, looking out at the still water. I was watching the string of clouds out there. It was too early in the day yet for a storm.

I started for the inn, and a great blue heron flew out over the lake. We watched to see if it would dive for a fish, but it just glided over the surface, then, with a thrust of wing, lifted and vanished into the distant trees. Livy took my arm, said, "Katy was a dreamer. Like Dorothy in *The Wizard of Oz*. She always loved that movie. Since she was a girl she would sit outside, look at the sky, and dream. That's what she did here."

I nodded and led the way across the gravel lot.

She stopped, said, "I've got a feeling. I don't like where this is going."

"You're going to find your daughter," I said as bravely as I could, but I was thinking, *You're about to walk through hell, Livy Baines, and you're gonna need an asbestos cloak if you want to survive.* She found strength in my words. All of a sudden she was leading the way, her head high and the purse swinging. She was going to find her daughter, and the world would just have to get out of her way.

No Sympathy for the Devil Here

The elevator door opened, making a hissing sound. Jesse stepped in and nodded at the nervous-looking man smiling from behind a big vase of flowers. The man pressed button number seven, even though it was already lit, then asked Jesse which floor he wanted. "Same," Jesse said. "Maternity floor, right?"

The man nodded. "I'm so excited I went down instead of up."

"Excuse me?" Jesse said.

"I went to the basement because I wasn't paying attention. I've got a new baby girl. Got my wife flowers." He raised the vase toward Jesse. "Think these are good enough for a woman who came through ten hours' labor?"

Jesse caught the sweet, warm scent of the stargazer lilies. "Nice," he said. He looked over the lilies, saw the roses, Japanese irises, baby's breath, the works. His mom had taught him the names for these things.

"Real nice. Must've set you back."

"It's my first." The man's eyes caught the stuffed dog Jesse had forgotten he was squeezing in his hand. "And you?"

"I'm just here to see a friend's kid. He named him after me."

The elevator stopped at the fourth floor. A woman stepped in, had on some kind of uniform, not a nurse but something. "I know where you two are going," she grinned. She smelled like strawberries, fake strawberries. Jesse hated those sweet, sticky smells women wore. The man was doing that smiley thing again and telling her about his baby. Jesse reached to punch the close button and bumped the man's arm. He looked up as if expecting an apology, and Jesse noticed his blood-shot eyes. The doors hissed shut, and the girl and the man backed away a little.

"Sorry." Jesse gave a quick smile. "Guess I'm excited too. I didn't mean to bump your flowers, man." The girl pushed for floor five. Just one floor up. "Guess you don't like taking stairs."

"No, I should, but . . ." She gave a little shrug. She had fat cheeks and black hair and big, puffy-looking boobs.

"But what?" Jesse said.

That shrug again. "I guess I'm lazy."

"Yeah, everybody's lazy these days," he said. The door opened, and Jesse watched her get off. As the doors closed, he shook his head at the man. "By the time she's forty, she'll have an ass wide as a kitchen table."

The man went blank for a bit, then grinned. "Yeah. A pretty face, though."

"Yeah." He checked out the man's clothes. Dockers, blue oxford shirt. Nice jacket thrown over one of his arms carrying the flowers, dressed like money, but there were sweat stains at his armpits. "I bet you have a pretty wife."

The man beamed. "I have a beautiful wife. And now we have a perfect baby."

"You sound like my friend Zeke. He's crazy about his wife. He's a tough guy, and now he talks all goofy about that kid of his."

"Yep, love makes you goofy. I got her a diamond bracelet in my jacket pocket here. That's how goofy I am." Jesse eyed the bulge in the pocket. Careless. If someone got on at the sixth floor, it'd be cake to boost it. The man kept talking. "My wife, she's just a little thing, in labor ten hours. Looked like it was killing her, but the doctor said she was all right. She didn't look all right to me. I'm standing there, tears running down my face, and she's panting and sweating and making these awful sounds."

Sure enough, the sixth floor. Bing. Jesse stepped back as a nurse pushed an old woman in a wheelchair in. *Good*, Jesse thought, moving behind the man with the diamonds in his pocket. He looked down, saw the urine bag hooked to the old woman's chair.

The woman looked up with a face all wrinkled and spotted, but she had bright blue eyes. "What pretty flowers you have there." She had a voice like bells. How could such a sound come from a shriveled thing?

The man smiled down at her. "My wife just had a baby girl. She's wonderful."

The woman just stared at the flowers. Her eyes fluttered closed. She breathed, looked up, said, "I always loved the stargazers best."

"You like those?" The man bent to her, the jacket pocket brushing Jesse's thigh. He was set to drop the toy dog, have an excuse to bend and reach, but the man turned to him. "Could you do me a favor?"

Jesse shrugged. "Yeah."

"Pick one of those lilies out for this lady. My wife won't mind."

He looked at the flowers, the man who couldn't stop smiling. The old lady looked up at him. Jesse picked a lily, gave it to her. She took it with both hands. "Why, thank you." She tapped the nurse's hand. "My husband used to say the world's going to hell in a hand basket, and sometimes I'd start to believe him, and then there'd be something like this: A sweet young man gives an old lady a flower for no good reason." She was smiling up at Jesse.

"It's from him," Jesse said, pointing to the man beside him, but the woman kept smiling at Jesse. "It's from him," Jesse yelled.

And bing, the seventh floor. Before the door could whoosh all the way open, he was out. He stood there, saw a doctor go by, a cop standing at the nurses' station. They looked at him, and that old metal feeling pinged in his gut. The man with the flowers brushed by him. "Sorry about the flower, man," Jesse said.

"That's fine," he called without looking back. "It was worth it to see that smile on her face."

Jesse watched him hurry down the hall, the flowers bouncing, the jewelry box still flapping in his coat pocket. He thought, *Shit, Zeke would have bought that bracelet*. He saw the cop coming toward him. Jesse put a lost look on his face, held the toy dog like a bunch of flowers, and moved to check a room number. The cop wasn't a cop, just a security guard. Zeke had said there would be guards, to be cool, they were just there to protect the babies. Jesse gave him a nod. "Could you tell me . . ."

The guard kept going. "The nurses' station there, they'll get you to the room you need."

"Thanks." Jesse knew the room number, but he headed for the nurses' station. He could feel the guard standing at the elevator door, watching him. When the nurse looked up at him, he smiled, held up the toy dog. "Nicki Lynn Daniels's room?" He gave his sweetest smile, said, "Please."

She smiled back, pointed down the hall. He said, "Thank you, ma'am," just the way his mom would like, and headed down the hall.

Just ahead, he saw a cluster of people gawking at a window. Jesse knew it was the baby showcase. A crowd was staring with goofy smiles. He went toward the babies, looked in. The babies looked all squinched and pink. Most were sleeping, swaddled in blankets and little knit caps on their heads, pink and blue. One just lay on its back, looking up at a light. One was crying on its belly, kind of rooting at the sheet. Up front and to the left was one lying on its back. It was more yellow than pink, had a pointy kind of head. But its face looked almost like a man's, and it seemed to study the gawking crowd. It was bigger than the rest, a little blond fuzz on its head. Jesse scanned the little cribs to look at the others. Yep, the big one staring out had to be Zeke's. The rest just slept, all soft and pink-looking, like the little baby rats he'd once found in an alley.

A hand landed hard and heavy on his shoulder, squeezed. Jesse jumped. "Whoa, now." It was Zeke. He kept his hand there on Jesse, holding him still. "You're supposed to be smiling when you look at my boy in there. And you got that to-hell-with-you look on your face. What's the matter with you?"

"Just a fuck of a day." The crowd turned, moved like a single body just a little away from him.

Zeke took his arm, pulled him a few steps. "Language, son."

Jesse saw another security guard coming down the hall. He gripped the dog, looked toward the babies. "What's with all the guards?"

"I told you. People boost babies like anything else." Zeke was looking in the window, his face all lit up. "You see him?" He leaned over Jesse, his strength, his weight, moving like a mountain.

Jesse nodded. "He's the big one down front on the left, right?"

Zeke just grinned, leaned in, staring at his boy. "Like you had to guess, says 'Daniels' right there on his crib."

"I didn't notice the name tags. I just looked for the big, good-looking one."

Zeke turned, slapped his shoulder. "He's big, but I know he's funny-looking. That's from being squeezed too long in the birth canal."

Jesse stepped away. "I don't want to hear that shit, man."

Zeke turned back to the window. The crowd had cleared. "Little guy's liver is catching up. The doc says that happens. He'll be fine in a couple days." He grinned at his baby. There'd be no rushing Zeke away from his kid. Jesse felt that queasy feeling in his gut, felt the gurgling. *Fuck*, he thought. He stepped toward Zeke. "Anywhere I can get a Coke around here?" Zeke looked at him, then down at the dog. Shook his head. "Sure, I can get you a Coke. Even get you some crushed ice to go with it." Again that squeeze of his hand on the shoulder. "You wait right here. They're getting Nicki Lynn ready for visitors. I'll get you a Coke, and we can go in."

Jesse watched Zeke head to the nurses' station. Every one of the women looked up, kind of sparked at the sight of him. Jesse thought he could part the damned sea with that walk of his. The water would just pull back and let him pass. With over three hundred pounds of muscle, he moved like a cat. With that blond hair and blue eyes and teeth like something out of a commercial, he could get any girl he wanted. But he didn't screw around. He loved Nicki Lynn. Jesse watched as a woman stood nodding and laughing at whatever Zeke said, and then she turned away to get his Coke. The others smiled at him. He was probably talking about his baby and Nicki Lynn. Jesse looked back at the babies. Little Jesse was doing something with his fingers like he was counting or something thoughtful; he seemed to be staring at Jesse. Jesse leaned closer to the glass, sent his thoughts at the kid: *You know something, don't you? You're Zeke's baby; you ain't stupid. You know who I am.*

He jumped when Zeke gave a little slap to his back. "You downright skittish, son. Babies make you nervous?" He gave the Coke to Jesse, led the way down the hall.

Jesse hurried to catch up, walk beside him. "Things are just kind of hot right now. I need to sell some shit, get out of town."

Zeke stopped. "So that's what you've got in that backpack. Can't you show any more respect for Nicki Lynn and my boy?"

Jesse looked up at Zeke. His mouth was grinning, but his eyes were ice. "I respect, man. I do. It's just some shit going down, and I've got to get out of town."

Zeke shook his head, grabbed the stuffed dog. He gave it a quick smell, kept walking, swinging the dog at his side. He stood at the closed door, gave a little knock.

Nicki Lynn called, "That you, Zeke?"

"Wait here," Zeke said. "I'll make sure she's ready."

Jesse sipped his Coke, told his gut to stay calm. He wondered why Zeke had snatched the dog. He wondered about the rich bitch, how in the hell she could have gotten loose. He shouldn't have drunk the booze. Then he had to get the shits. He heard Nicki Lynn and Zeke talking inside, couldn't make out what they were saying. Zeke might be pissed, but he wouldn't pass on the Rolex and pearls. And Zeke always had plenty of cash on him for just this kind of thing. With the money to drive all night Jesse figured he'd be in Atlanta by morning. Hook up with Johnny from juvy. He'd know where to drop the car. They'd get him a fake ID, and he'd lay low a while.

Zeke opened the door, gave a nod, and let him in. It wasn't like any other hospital room Jesse had seen. Soft lamps, and on the table was a bowl of fruit and cheese and crackers. Nicki Lynn was propped up with colored pillows and a quilt.

"Nice digs, Nicki Lynn." Jesse stood at the end of her bed. He realized he was holding an empty cup. "You got a trash can around here?"

Zeke took the cup, dropped it in the trash. Jesse saw that he was still holding the dog. "The polite thing to do is ask how Nicki Lynn is. To ask about the baby. Maybe say you saw the baby, and he's the most handsome little guy you ever laid eyes on."

"Yeah," Jesse said. "Sorry. I got things on my mind, Nicki Lynn. How you feeling?"

"Just fine," she said. "Ain't our boy something?"

"Smartest-looking one in the bunch," Jesse said. "And I ain't kidding. He's got Zeke's way of looking at things. Can babies that young see?"

"They see what they need to, I guess." She smiled. She looked like a little girl with no makeup on. Couldn't weigh much over a hundred pounds. Her eyes went back to Zeke.

"I've never seen a hospital room done up like this."

Nicki Lynn sipped from her cup of ice water. "They do it up now for new moms. The idea is not to make you feel like you're in the hospital." She smiled at Zeke. "And Zeke here, he had to make sure I had my favorite pillows and my granny's quilt."

"I don't know what you do to Zeke, but he sure loves fussing over you," Jesse said.

"She loves me, Jesse boy," Zeke said. Zeke went to her bedside, used a hand as big as her face to brush a strand of hair from her cheek. She had shiny black hair, and skin so white and smooth it didn't look real, and big blue eyes.

"What's on your mind, Jesse?" Zeke said.

He looked around the room, saw vases and vases of flowers. He adjusted the strap of his backpack. "I guess I'm glad I didn't bring flowers. I thought of bringing flowers. When you get out, I'll bring you flowers."

"That's all right, Jesse," Nicki Lynn said.

Zeke gave a little cough. "Thought you said you needed to leave town."

Jesse looked down at the floor. This wasn't going right. But he'd have to try to sell something to Zeke.

Nicki Lynn shook her foot under the covers to get his attention. "You all right, Jesse? Zeke, he doesn't look so good to me."

Zeke came over and with that big hand of his lifted Jesse's chin. Only man in the world could touch him like that was Zeke. He'd make a good daddy, but now Zeke was squinting, looking over Jesse's face. "Something's changed," he said. "Something's changed from the last time I saw you."

"Maybe he's hungry," Nicki Lynn said. "There's some cheese and crackers over there, Jesse."

"No, thank you. I'm all right." He slipped off the backpack, set it on a chair. "I got some stuff here, Zeke. Thought maybe you'd be interested." He reached in, pulled out the Rolex.

"This ain't a place for business, son. You put that shit away. We got family could walk in here any minute."

He pulled out the pearls. "Wouldn't Nicki Lynn like these pearls?"

Zeke grabbed his wrist. Jesse dropped the pearls. They made a little clattering sound on the floor. As he scooped them up, he heard Zeke breathing.

"All right, man, all right." He zipped the bag, stood. "I just needed some cash to get on the road."

Zeke shoved the stuffed dog in his face "You stole this, didn't you?" He smelled it quickly, shoved it at Jesse's face. "Smells like some girl, don't it? A real clean kind of girl, not your usual type. You fucked with her, Jesse." He looked at the dog. "See, it looks new but got a little dust in the fur. It's been sitting on a shelf for a long time. You jacked this shit and tried to bring some girl's old stuffed dog to my boy."

Nicki backed up in her bed. "Just have him leave, Zeke."

Zeke grabbed the bag, unzipped it, looked in. "Top-of-the-line shit here. Rolex, pearls, and that's Lalique, man, you got this . . ." He straightened, looked dead-on at Jesse. "You did that girl in Land Fall, didn't you? I should have guessed it when I saw it on the news. Your family lives in Land Fall."

Jesse reached for his backpack. "I'm leaving, man. I can see this wasn't a good idea."

Nicki was crying now. "Just make him leave, Zeke."

"Damn right he'll leave." Zeke scooped up the toy dog from the floor, opened the bag, tossed it in. "I heard what you did to that girl. And you steal her fucking dog and bring it to my boy. Get the hell out of here."

Jesse turned to leave, glad he was in a public place. He knew Zeke wanted to kick the shit out of him, and there would be no fighting with Zeke, not if he wanted to live.

Jesse went out the door to the hallway. Before he could see what hit him, he was slammed to the floor by the smack of weight on his back, his arms yanked behind him, cuffed. Cops. He couldn't count the cops standing around him yelling his name and saying, "You sorry motherfucker!" He lay still, just the way they wanted. He stared at their shoes. Someone yanked him up, shoved him against the wall, searched his shirt, his pockets, all the way down his legs to his shoes. He glanced down the hallway; no one was in sight. They must have cleared the floor. A cop slammed him against the wall. "Eyes down, you son of a bitch." He saw Zeke's boots come out the door. Zeke stood there. Jesse moved his eyes up to see Zeke's arms tight across his chest, his face red. He just stood there breathing that hard sound a man makes once he's quit a fight. The cops were shouting, "You Jesse Hollowfield? Jesse Hollowfield?"

"Yeah, that's who I am," he said. Somebody grabbed the back of his head, mashed the side of his face against the wall. He stood still, tasted blood in his mouth. He heard them going through his backpack. He glanced at Zeke, who seemed to be enjoying this.

"You set me up. Why the fuck you set me up?" Jesse said.

Zeke shook his head. "Wasn't me. But somebody popped your ass." He looked at the cops. "Get this piece of shit out of here."

Two cops shoved him down the hallway. There were others in front and behind. He tried to count how many they'd sent to get him. He picked up his pace so they wouldn't be pushing. At the nurse's station, he saw the man who'd brought the flowers. He didn't look like some smug rich dude now. He looked scared. Jesse grinned at him. "That's right," he said. "You ought to be fucking scared of me."

The cop at his side leaned close, speaking so hard that spit spattered Jesse's ear. "Shut your mouth, you son of a bitch!"

Cops stood at the elevator, waiting. A detective was chewing on a toothpick, his eyes locked on Jesse. Jesse looked right back at him. "It's all right. You just doing your job." They shoved him in the elevator. He looked at the detective, said, "And I'm just doing mine. Ain't you got no sympathy for the devil here?" The doors closed, and it came just like he knew it would, the smack at the back of his head that made his knees crumble.

Everybody Wants
to Die Sometimes

Livy stopped on the sidewalk leading to the inn when she heard Shelby's phone ring. Shelby backed up for privacy to answer it. Livy watched her. Every time that phone rang, she thought it had to be about Katy. But there were others who went missing every day, old people with Alzheimer's wandering, sometimes driving somewhere and clarity suddenly kicking in to show them they were lost, kids swiped by a parent on the losing end of divorce, teenaged boys, and women, so many women gone. Shelby was nodding, must have felt Livy's what-is-it stare. She shook her head, then called, "It's nothing to do with Katy. You can go on inside if you want." Livy went ahead, stepped up on the porch. She sat in a rocker on the porch to wait for Shelby. She didn't want to go in alone. She could hear laughter inside. She leaned forward and looked out at the lake. A blue heron squawked and rose up from a thicket of trees down the shoreline. It flapped its giant wings and swooped across the water, then rose and settled on the post of a dock way out across the lake. And all was still.

It was no wonder Katy came here. After those late nights of tending bar, breathing smoke and liquor, and dodging all those guys who always wanted some little piece of her, it must have been heaven to sit here by the lake. Livy looked down the shoreline, saw a red Jeep pull into the parking lot of a little beach. A woman got out, helped a little girl out of the backseat, who ran straight to the water, ignoring the mother's call to take off her shoes. Then a man got out, went to the back of the Jeep to unload things. One of those family outings, Livy remembered those with Katy and her father, happy times at the start until he started changing, complaining about the mosquitoes, the sun, the sand, even yelling at the charcoal when it didn't burn right.

Shelby came up on the porch, snapped her phone shut. "It's off now," she said. "Let's get inside and talk to Roy."

Shelby wasn't looking at her, just kept her eyes on the ground as she moved forward. Livy touched her arm. "What was that call? There's something you're not telling me."

Shelby gave her a steady look. There was tension in it. "There's another news break about that girl in Land Fall. They got the guy who did it."

"What's Land Fall?"

Shelby moved toward the door. "A gated community. Nothing bad's supposed to happen there."

The room went still, and a man in a uniform turned, rose, and moved toward Shelby. "There she is!" He wrapped his arms around Shelby, gave a kiss to the side of her head. His soft, dark eyes looked straight at Livy. He gave a little nod. Shelby was right. He was the kind of man any woman would like. He smelled like Old Spice. He was handsome. But not too handsome, with his teeth just a little crooked. He moved like a man who would take care of things.

Shelby held him for a quick moment, then pushed back, said, "Roy, this is—"

"Mrs. Baines," he said, holding her hand between both of his, giving a good warm shake. She liked Roy's thick blond hair that needed a cut. He looked to be in his forties but had the graceful way of a younger man. Shelby was right; there was mischief in those eyes, but also a tension, as if even when he was laughing, his mind was on getting things done. He stepped back, glanced at the floor, then looked back into her face. "I wish we were meeting under better circumstances, ma'am." He gestured toward a table, "Have a seat."

Livy sat, looked across the room to the waitress watching her. The cook came from out back and gave a nod. Roy went to the counter for his coffee cup. "This is Sam and Maura. They put up with me. I don't know why. Must be my good looks and irresistible wit."

Maura smiled and threw a dishtowel at him. "He's just a big old flirt."

He picked up the towel from the floor, threw it back at her. "And you love it."

"Yes, she does," Sam said, walking toward them. He hugged Shelby, smiled, and reached to shake Livy's hand. "You've got a good team. They found my daughter, Roy and Shelby; they found my girl in Myrtle Beach. She's doing just fine."

Livy nodded. "Shelby told me. You are a lucky man."

"Yes, I am." He stood over them, kissed the top of Shelby's head, slapped Roy on the shoulder, then gave the lightest pat to Livy's arm as if to say they were all connected now. "You're in good hands." He touched the menu. "Anything you want. It's on me."

Maura said, "I'll be right with you," and went back to changing filters in the coffee machine.

Roy leaned toward Livy. "You mind if I smoke?"

"It's fine," she said. She watched him light up, liked the smell of the match, the little flare of tobacco and paper and the smoke unfurling.

Maura called over, "And don't forget, Roy. You aren't leaving until you buy raffle tickets from me."

257

He grinned. "Now, why would I want to spend my good money on your raffle?"

"You always spend money on my raffle. Not even a smart-ass like you can resist helping those kids."

Roy nodded, smiled at Livy. "They raise money for the high school girls' softball team. Kids playing ball to stay out of trouble. They're too worn out from running around in the heat." He took a hit off his cigarette and squinted at the menu, but Livy could see something else on his mind. No one had mentioned Katy. Livy looked at the menu but couldn't really take in the words. It seemed so strange to do these normal things. Shelby was studying the menu as if she'd never seen it before. Something was up. Livy looked out the window to the blue lake stretching out. The world went on. Fish were drifting in the lake, birds flying above, and that little family on the shore were getting ready for a picnic and a swim, and no doubt across the water some father and son were out there casting their lines.

"My Katy played softball," Livy said.

Maura came over, touched Livy's shoulder. "I'm so sorry she's missing. She's in our prayers at church."

"Thank you," Livy said, just wanting to push back from the table and leave. She had a sick feeling stirring up. There was no running from the fact the Katy was gone, and as long as Katy was gone, Livy would find herself moving from stranger to stranger, both wanting and hating their help. She smelled Roy's cigarette, the soothing yet sharp odor. She remembered Katy saying how sometimes when she felt the urge to cry, she could light up and it would stop the tears from coming. Livy leaned across the table. "You mind if I have one of your cigarettes?"

"Of course," Roy said, offering her a cigarette from his pack.

"I didn't know you smoked," Shelby said.

"I don't," she said. "I tried them in college. It's nice sometimes, gives you something to do when you're nervous." She let Roy light her cigarette. She straightened up, inhaled, barely, then looked at the cigarette. "My husband would have a fit."

Shelby smiled. "He won't hear of it from me."

Livy tried another inhalation, a little deeper this time. It burned, and she coughed, her eyes tearing up as she watched Maura place tall glasses of sweet tea on the table. She put the cigarette out, managed to say, "Well, that was stupid." The coughing kept coming, deepened to a gagging sound. She felt the nausea roll up, and she rushed to the door to get outside. Just making it to the porch, she leaned over the railing and heaved nothing but water and bile into the bushes beneath.

Finally she straightened, looked out at the lake. Her head hummed, but she felt better, as if she'd gotten some kind of poison out. She stood, feeling her breath go steady.

She looked out at the lake shimmering like a blue mirror, clouds on the water reflecting clouds in the sky. She wasn't ready for the conversation that was waiting inside the restaurant. She walked toward the lake, feeling the coolness of a breeze in the air.

She heard the sound of a child's laughter, looked over to the beach, and saw a little girl in a pink one-piece backing into the water, calling, "Watch me, Mommy, watch me." The mom stood on the shore, arms crossed, and watched. A man was taking picnic things from the Jeep. The little girl crouched in the water, smacked it with her hands to make it splash. "Careful," her mom called. The girl straightened, turned, walked farther out into the water, looking back again and again to make sure the mother was watching. She looked about six. Katy had already been swimming at that age. Katy liked to pretend she was a mermaid, diving under the water, holding her breath so long Livy would always be moving toward her by the time she surfaced. The farther out the girl went, the more she looked back, making sure the mother was there. The mother slipped her sandals off and waded into the water. The dad had stopped unloading things to watch. It was a shallow lake. Almost flat, it seemed. The girl walked and walked, the water staying around her waistline. Shelby had said it was shallow, and the lake seemed to have almost no incline. It was like a giant wading pool there at the beach, but out past the buoys, it dropped deep. Livy remembered how Shelby had said the water could suddenly turn. "Look how far out I am, Mommy," the girl called. The mom was knee-deep in the water now, smiling, nodding. "You're very, very far." The girl took more steps, turned. "Look how far I am now." "Come on back in," the mother called, moving closer to her daughter. A few more steps and her shorts would get wet, but she wasn't thinking about her shorts. Her eyes and mind were all on getting closer to her girl.

"Mrs. Baines, you all right?"

She turned at Roy's voice, saw Shelby and Roy coming toward her. Roy's face was set the way her doctor's face had been when he'd told her she had precancerous cells. But they had fixed all that.

"Just tell me the news," she said. But she couldn't look at him. She turned back toward the little girl.

"We have a lead," he said.

She looked at him. "I knew that. What kind of lead?"

His face went blank, but there was a pinch to his eyes. She knew he was going to say, *I'm sorry*. She turned to watch the girl out there, splashing her mom and laughing. Livy felt dizzy. She rocked a bit, reached to grip his arm, and he let her. Shelby was ready to catch her if she fell. She turned back to Roy, felt her nails squeezing into his arm. She relaxed her grip. "You can tell me," she said.

He glanced at her, caught her eyes, then winced, looked back toward the little girl in the lake. "There was a girl in Land Fall."

She looked to Shelby. "And she has something to do with my Katy?"

"Yes," Roy said. "There was a girl in Land Fall who was attacked. In her home."

"What do you mean 'attacked'?"

Roy looked away as if he needed to see something out there in the lake. "Raped," he said. "Beaten. Bad." He shook his head.

The little girl squealed and was running farther out into the water. "Stop right there," her mother yelled. The girl stopped, turned, her head lowered, looked up at her mom.

Livy took a breath. "And did this girl live?"

"Yes," Roy said. She saw him start to say something, take it back.

She let go of his arm, held herself, arms wrapped tightly. "And what does she have to do with my Katy?"

He sighed, put his hands in his pockets, looked back out at the lake. "The man who attacked her said something about a woman in a blue truck with Tennessee plates. He carjacked her."

"Katy." She wiped away the wetness on her face. Out there in the lake, the mother held out her hand and didn't have to say a word to make the little girl come to her. "What did this man do to Katy?"

Roy sighed and looked down. "We don't have proof it was Katy."

"*Was* Katy?" Livy said. She looked back toward the inn. The building, the land, all seemed to be receding as if some current in the lake were reaching up and pulling her away from the world of solid things. She felt herself sinking to the ground. She squeezed her arms tighter, held on.

"We don't have proof, but it sounds like your daughter. The man mentioned the *POSITIV* license plates."

"What did he do to her?' She heard the pleading in her voice. She grabbed his arm again. "You said the girl lived. What did he do to my Katy?"

He shook his head, looked her straight in the face, said it. "He said he killed her." He looked to the ground. "I'm sorry. It's what he said. But sometimes guys like to say a lot of things they didn't do."

"Killed her?" Livy whispered, but it wasn't a question. Even though it sounded like a question, it was a fact. She was on the ground now, her fingers clenching the grass, nails digging in the dirt. She looked at Roy's shoes, shiny black leather. She felt Shelby on the ground beside her. She asked, "Did he say how?" The land was spinning. She dug into the dirt to hang on.

He crouched beside her, leaned close. "We don't know for certain it was Katy."

"Yes, you do." There was a wailing sound from somewhere. She looked toward the little girl, who was jumping up and down, holding her mother's hand. Was she laughing or screaming? Livy felt the wailing sound squeezing up from her chest. There was a hand on her back. It was Shelby. She looked at Shelby, saw such a sadness there. "What did he do to the woman in a blue truck? With Tennessee plates. The woman who had the word POSITIV on her Tennessee license plates. This woman. My daughter. What did he do to my girl?"

Shelby looked to Roy, gave a nod.

"The man said the woman, the woman he killed, didn't see it coming." His eyes were on Shelby now. He was scared.

Livy watched the little girl wading back to shore, now holding her mother's hand. "I don't believe this. That girl who was attacked, maybe she imagined these things. She must have been delirious, getting raped like that. Sometimes when you're upset, you imagine the worst kinds of things." She looked at Roy, then to Shelby. They both seemed to be drifting away, but they were holding her, they were touching her. But it all seemed to be flying. "I don't believe this, but I know what you're saying is true." She pulled her knees up to her chest and rocked. All she could hear was breathing. She looked out at the lake, her vision so blurred she couldn't see the line between water, land, and sky. Roy was saying something, but she couldn't hear it over the pounding in her ears. She sat still, felt the pressure of Shelby's arms wrapped around her. She was such a little woman, but her arms were powerful, as if she had been trained in holding the world together in those thin, strong arms. "You can let me go now," Livy said. "I'm not going to go crazy."

Shelby released her, then sat beside her, held her hand. Roy was walking away, answering his phone. Livy felt nausea rising again at the back of her throat, swallowed it down. There was nothing left to get out. She took in a slow breath, exhaled. "Why would he hurt Katy?"

Shelby squeezed Livy's hand, shook her head. "There is no reason."

Livy looked over at the little family. Now the girl was sitting at the picnic table, eating something. "Katy's daddy didn't like picnics. He said he didn't see the point." She cried now, hugged her knees hard to her chest and cried. She cried and cried until it was all out. She rolled over in the grass, smelled the dirt and the green. Katy had said that when she gardened, she loved the smell of dirt and green. And Livy had laughed and asked, "How can you smell green?" But Katy was right—green did have a smell. It smelled . . . green. Livy closed her eyes. "I just want to sleep a little, just a minute, just a little, please." She remembered Lawrence. Her eyes blinked wide open, seeing nothing but grass and sky. She thought, *This is how the dead see.* She jerked up to sit. Shelby watched her, waited. "I like the way you wait. You never push."

Shelby nodded. "Oh, I push. I've spent years practicing on knowing when to wait, when to push." She looked out at the water, sat there as if she had nothing better to do than watch the sun move across the sky.

"I have to call Lawrence," Livy said. "But I can't. I don't want to say the words. And we don't know for certain it was Katy. There's lots of blue trucks."

"I'll call him for you," Shelby said. She waited a minute, watched Livy. "You want me to call him now?"

"No." Livy combed her fingers through her hair, saw dirt on the knees of her pants. She looked out at the family packing up. The little girl kept looking her way. The mother kept turning her around, busying her with something. Livy nodded toward the family. "They probably think I'm crazy."

"No," Shelby said. "They probably sense something happened here, something bad. But not crazy."

"They're trying to protect their daughter," Livy said. "And she's curious because she's never seen a grown woman roll around in the grass." She sighed, her throat tightening with tears. "But you can't protect them. Not always. Katy believes in guardian angels in this world. What about the angels?"

"They're here," Shelby said.

"I thought you didn't believe in things."

"I told you, I believe in this world. Flesh-and-blood guardian angels. Like Roy, like the people who volunteer for me."

Livy watched the little family load up the car and drive away. "The day is over," she said. "Gone, gone, gone." She looked back toward the lodge. "I left my purse in there. And Katy's scrapbook."

"I locked it all in the truck. We can just sit here."

"Katy would like that." She wanted to sit there all night. She wanted to watch the sun set, the moon rise, just sleep in the grass and wake with the sun on her face. That was all she could stand. "I can't go back to that house."

"Okay," Shelby said.

"Call that man Pete about the condo." She looked at Shelby. "I'm sorry. Would you please call Pete about the condo? And Billy? Could you call Billy, please?"

Shelby nodded. The sky was going violet. A pair of egrets flew over the lake. One dipped to the water, came up empty, then soared, gaining on the other. Livy thought of Lawrence. He'd probably called. She'd told him she was meeting with the sheriff, and he'd want to know about that. But if she called him and told him what she'd learned, he'd say, *Now, Livy, you can't be sure; you can't be absolutely sure.* His words always when she was worried. But she was sure. She'd seen it on Roy's face. He knew it was Katy. She stood. "I want to see the girl." Shelby looked up at her. "The girl who lived. I want to know everything he said about that girl in the blue truck."

"We'll see her." Shelby stood beside her. "Not yet, but we'll see her when she's strong enough."

"What did he do to the girl?"

Shelby stared out at the water, shook her head.

"Where's Roy?"

"He went back to his office. I'm sure he's getting more information."

Livy thought about the missing-person flyer, Katy's face smiling. *If you have any information, please . . . "Information,"* she said. "It's a stupid word for what it's really asking. This isn't just information."

Shelby nodded and looked out at the water. Livy could see she was biting at the inside of her cheek, not hard, not nervous, just thinking.

"Did Roy tell you what he did to that girl?"

"A little," Shelby said.

"It was more than rape, wasn't it?"

Shelby nodded. The land and sky went spinning again. Livy kept seeing that blue truck, that word *POSITIV* on the Tennessee tag. It was Katy. It had to be. She grabbed Shelby's arm. "Have you ever seen a mother die from crying? I want to die, Shelby. I just want to fall down and die."

Shelby took her hand. "We all want to die sometimes. But most times we don't. We go on. You're gonna go on. And they've picked up this guy who did it. And there'll be some satisfaction in that. This one who lived, she's got lots of information, the kind of information we need. Want to walk down to the water? Might do us good to get our feet wet. It's muddy right here at the water line, but you're a Suck Creek girl. Remember how good it feels to get mud between your toes?"

Livy nodded and stood. She followed Shelby. At the water's edge, they slipped their shoes off, rolled up their pants, and waded in. Livy could hear the little girl still calling, *Look how far I am, Mom; look how far.* The tears rushed up again. She bent and splashed water on her face. Water ran down her arms and neck. She splashed again and again, knew she was getting drenched, but the water felt good running down her breasts, chilling and soothing. She felt Shelby watching. "See, I am crazy."

"No, you're not." Shelby splashed water on her face. "This is clean water here. It's good."

The sun was gone behind the line of trees now. Livy looked back toward the lodge and thought of what was beyond the parking lot, the returning to the truck, and Billy, and Lawrence, and the world. At least there was the girl who had lived. "How old is the girl? The one who lived?"

"Twenty-two," Shelby said.

"And what did he do to her?"

Shelby bent and swished at the water, touched her face with her wet fingertips. "I don't know the details yet." She moved a little deeper into the water, and Livy followed.

Here we are, she thought, *grown women, our toes in mud while the sky is going dark and my girl is gone, and it all looks normal.* She wondered if Katy had waded in this water, if her toes had pressed the mud where she was standing. She looked at Shelby, who was looking toward the parking lot. She took Shelby's hand, led the way back to the grass. "Let's go. There's a hundred things we need to do. For Katy."

"For Katy," Shelby said

Livy felt a wave lap up at her ankles. She looked up, felt the breeze in her face, and saw the dark clouds moving slowly, filling the bright sky. "Like you said, the water's turning."

Shelby nodded. "Only about four or five days a summer it doesn't do that. Hope the fishermen out there have their life jackets."

Livy looked out. She hadn't noticed them before, two little fishing boats way out on the water. "They'll be all right." She closed her eyes, lowered her head. "'The Lord didn't give us a spirit of fear, but one of power and love and soundness of mind.'" She wanted to hang on to this thought, let it hold her.

"That's good," Shelby said. "Need to put that on a sign at the office."

"It's scripture," Livy said. "From the second book of Timothy. I have it framed in my house. I had one framed for Katy too. I hope those words were with her when she was scared." Her eyes stung. She sucked in a breath, kept moving. They picked up their shoes and headed for the truck. "We've got a long road ahead, don't we?"

"Sometimes it's shorter than you think, but I always like to be ready for the long haul." Shelby took the lead now, and Livy hurried with her. There would be time for crying all the rest of her life. For now she had a list. Call Lawrence. Tell Billy. And she'd have to pull Billy up when it was his turn to fall to the ground and want to die. And she'd tell him, *Everybody wants to die sometimes*, and she'd have to try to believe that the world was still worth loving somehow. Somewhere there was something worth going on for. There had to be.

It's Touch and Go

His granny looked old in the light of the interrogation room. She had sat there glaring at Mike the way she must have glared at his daddy before they'd sent him off to Texas. He couldn't remember his daddy, a man who showed up sometimes with TVs, stereos, smoked hams, and once a big cooler of shrimp. But the shrimp went bad because his dad went off with his friends without putting the shrimp in the freezer the way Mike's granny had told him to do. Mike glanced up at her. She'd been the only momma he'd ever known, and now she wouldn't look him in the face. He couldn't re-member ever seeing his own mom. She left him at his granny's when he was four, went off to live with a drug dealer, and in a year she was dead. He liked to think his mom had loved him, had kissed the top of his head before she'd walked out the door. He liked to think she'd meant to come back and get him, but that wasn't easy to believe since she'd left his birth certificate in the diaper bag, along with the bottles and the pacifier and what his granny said was his favorite stuffed bear. He didn't remember the bear. Only the little blue checked blanket he remembered wanting to hold every night. And his granny, she'd kept it, stitched it into a quilt she'd made. She'd saved scraps from some of his favorite shirts, a couple of her dresses, and even what she'd told him was his favorite apron that she had worn. It had little red roosters. He could see that quilt folded neatly at the foot of his bed.

It would be a while before he'd see that quilt again. He knew he'd do time, the suspended shit and more. Just like Jesse. But he wanted to think that soon he'd be walking up on her porch, smelling her fried chicken, and sleeping in his own bed. He wanted to think she'd be there waiting with a smile. But in his heart he wondered if she'd ever smile again, and in his gut he knew there was a good chance she'd pass on by the time he was free. He stared at the top of his granny's lowered head, studied the thin gray hair pulled back tight. He hoped she wasn't crying. When she raised her head, he knew he'd hurt her once again, but this time he wasn't seeing sorrow, just fury at the man he had let himself become.

"Michael Ray Carter," she said, "you could have prevented this. I raised you to be a good boy. That Hollowfield boy says you knew all about his plan to hurt that girl. You knew when he did it, and you sat on that fact, holding out for the money."

"I'm sorry," he said. And he was sorry, but no one would believe that. They'd think he was sorry he'd gotten caught, that was all. They just didn't understand Jesse's way of making a man do things, making a man think of nothing but himself and the money. He remembered Jesse's words: *Amazing what some folks will do for a buck*.

"If this girl dies, you'll be . . ." His granny's shaking finger pointed at him. She couldn't remember the word for it. She looked toward the cop at the end of the table.

"Complicit," the cop said. "He'll be complicit in the murder of that girl."

Mike thought about the blue-truck girl. But the cops didn't

know about that. They just had Jesse on the Land Fall thing. With Jesse's record, he'd be locked up for years. If the girl lived. The news had said she was conscious, but it was still—how had that newsgirl put it?—"touch and go." Mike wondered why people said "touch and go" when someone was near dying. Was it like the angel of death came and touched you, then went on without carrying you away? He remembered the blue-truck girl. She'd touched his arm, and he jumped when he felt the weight of her hand.

His granny rocked back in her chair, and he realized she'd been talking, maybe to the cop. But now she was talking to him. "How could you?" she was saying. "How could you run with a boy who could do such things to that girl?"

"I didn't know what he'd do," Mike said. He figured Jesse had messed up that rich girl in ways they wouldn't talk about on TV. The detective had given him a pretty good idea of what Jesse had done. But Mike already knew the kind of things Jesse could do. He could still see the blue truck out in that field. And how Mike had stood behind that clump of trees, afraid to do a damned thing. His granny was swaying back and forth in her chair now. Whenever she got so angry she could hardly stand it, she rocked like that. She was too weak to slam a door or punch a wall and was usually too sweet to raise her hand. But she'd slapped Mike. For the first time he'd felt the pop of her hand on his face when the cop had asked about a truck out of gas. Now she was just rocking, saying, "He will get his punishment." For a blurred second Mike thought she was talking about him; then he realized she was talking about Jesse. "They have arrested that man for his crimes against God and nature!" She was talking in her preacher tone. "They'll punish him in this world, but it's the good Lord in the next world who'll make that boy truly sorry. Only something evil could do what that boy has done." Mike was thinking, *You have no*

271

idea, Granny, but the cop was listening, leaning forward as if Mike's granny were a preacher at some pulpit, speaking the gospel, when Mike was supposed to be the one there with something to say.

Mike figured the detectives had given up on his *I told you all I know*, his *I didn't think he'd really go in and hurt that girl* talk. When they asked him about a truck running out of gas, he just shrugged. He said he didn't know anything about that. It was his granny who said something about Jesse being at her house that night, yelling about some truck out of gas. Mike said maybe she'd been dreaming, maybe she'd picked up something about a truck while she was in her room watching TV and falling asleep. But they kept asking, *Do you know anything about a truck out of gas?* They kept asking like they knew the answer, just needed him to say it. He shook his head, said he'd told them all he could about Jesse and the rich girl, but a truck out of gas, he'd swear on his momma's grave that he didn't know a thing about that. That was when his granny smacked him so hard it brought tears to his eyes. And the cop didn't make a move to hold her back. The cop who was sitting there, supposed to be keeping his eye on things, hell, he'd let her beat Mike with a belt if she wanted to.

Mike knew he shouldn't have said that thing about his momma's grave. He didn't know his momma. He just knew she was dead. And the words sounded good; the words sounded true if you followed them with something like *I swear on my momma's grave*. Jesse had taught him that. Jesse had said swearing on your dead momma was a whole lot more convincing than putting your hand on a Bible in a courtroom. People had seen that so much on TV, putting your hand on a Bible didn't mean anything anymore. But they kept trying to trick him, sneaking up on that thing about the truck, and he kept saying, *I don't know nothing about that*. They knew he was lying. He couldn't do that thing Jesse could do, but they'd given up on getting anything more out of him. That was why they'd called his granny in.

He realized she had quit talking. He reached for her hand. She sat back, pulled away from him the way his granddaddy used to do, the eyes saying, *I've had about enough of you.* She even looked like his granddaddy, her thin hair combed back, her ears grown long and rubbery, and that mole. Why wouldn't she ever let him clip that whisker growing out of that mole? He said, "Don't give up on me, Granny."

She slammed her hand against the table. "You gave up on yourself, Michael Ray Carter, when you gave your trust to that boy you call your friend. I told you long ago, that boy ain't nobody's friend."

He nodded. Jesse would find a way to kill him now. He'd have somebody somewhere somehow make Mike hurt a long time before they killed him, just like that dude and the laundry pins. He wanted to cry, grab his granny's arm the way he had when he was a little kid, just cry and say he wanted to go home. And he was thinking how he could have collected that thousand dollars of reward money if it hadn't been for his granny. He'd thought she couldn't hear a thing back there in her room. But she'd seen and heard more than he'd thought she could, and she was still going on about it. "It's my own home," she told the cop. "I've been cleaning those floors and walls over fifty years. You think I'm not gonna notice some other boy's mud prints on my floor, dead leaves in the couch cushions? You think I don't hear some boy cussing in my house? I heard what that boy said. There was a truck out of gas that day."

"Granny," Mike said, "you should stop, please. I—"

She reached, took his hand. "You don't want no lawyer. You gonna cooperate with the officers here. If you don't, I will. And the Lord tells me you gonna come out better if you and me are playing on the same team."

The cop snickered then. Mike looked at him. The cop grinned. "They sure don't make mommas like they used to."

"She ain't my momma."

"Nope. You got the wrath of God coming down on you."

She turned and gave a glare to the cop, who wiped the grin right off his face. "I ain't nothing like the wrath of God, young man." She looked back at Mike. "And there you were creeping all around the house trying to make things seem all nice and normal while that hoodlum's sleeping on my couch. I heard you come in my room, try to sleep in that chair in the corner. You hardly slept a wink, Michael Ray Carter. You were scared of that boy, and don't you deny it."

Mike looked at his hands. At least he wasn't cuffed. He wasn't convicted, just a suspect for now. And all because his granny had to volunteer her own information. He was pissed about that, part of his brain thinking, *Why the hell couldn't she mind her own business?* and part of him mad at himself for bringing Jesse to his granny's house, for using his granny like bait for the girl in the blue truck. But it was Jesse who'd picked her, Jesse who had convinced her to drive. *Not me,* he thought. He felt his granny glaring at him. He didn't know which was worse, her glaring at him like that or not looking at him at all. He remembered they were talking about Jesse; they were talking about that night Mike had sneaked her walker from her room and let Jesse sleep on her couch. Mike said, "You just got to try to please Jesse when he's in one of those moods. He was angry, and you gotta go along with whatever he wants when he's angry like that."

"I knew he was angry," she said. "Any fool could have heard that. You boys was up to something that day." She poked at the back of his hand. "Don't you lie to me. You might try to lie to the law, but don't you dare try to lie to your granny. What was that boy so angry about?"

Mike sighed. "He told me he wanted to boost some car or truck to go rob a pawnshop." He saw the cop taking notes. He didn't know why the cop bothered since most likely the conversation was being taped. He'd seen how they did that on TV. He looked around at the walls. Didn't see any glass, but he'd bet there were cameras and microphones somewhere. "Not a robbery," he said. "A burglary. He wanted to break into a pawnshop and needed a car that he could count on. He told me that much. I guess the truck he got to make the hit ran out of gas."

The cop looked up from his notebook. "And you knew full well that associating with a man planning a crime is in violation of your probation."

"We didn't do it," Mike said. "You know how sometimes guys just talk."

The cop glared. "If it was just talk, why was your friend so angry? That wasn't just talk. You were in on it, weren't you?"

"Jesse wanted it, not me." It would be all right as long as they didn't get him to say anything about the blue-truck girl. "I let him use my car, made him drop me off at the Taco Shack, told him I couldn't risk going to jail 'cause I got to take care of my granny." He looked up at her, but she only gave him a hard glance and looked away. "Jesse went on and said he was just gonna have a look at the pawnshop. But when he got there, the owner was there. Jesse didn't want to risk getting close." He looked at his granny. "So nothing happened. He didn't even try to break into any store."

She reached across the table, poked at his hand the way she used to poke him in the chest as if poking could make the truth come out. "You're telling me that boy who was yelling, stomping around my house, eating all my cookies, drinking my last Coke, getting you so nervous you couldn't even sit for ten minutes with me, and you hiding my walker so I couldn't get out there to see what was going on without risking falling, breaking my hip . . ." She paused to catch her

breath. He wished he could go home with her. If they kept him over-
night, took her home, he hoped they'd make sure she was all right
and that there was food in the house.

Mike reached, squeezed her hand. "Granny. When Jesse gets angry, he can get mean. I didn't want you to see him mean. I was trying to keep him peaceful. You don't know how he can be. I was
trying to make sure he wouldn't do something to hurt you."

She shook his fingers loose, gripped the table, and stood. "I am
a child of God, and I fear no one."

Mike looked up, surprised at the strength in her voice. He saw
her leathery skin sagging; he saw the trembling in her arms, the thin
bones, the wisps of gray hairs slipping loose. He knew she wouldn't
be around much longer. The things he was putting her through made
it all the harder for her to find the strength to keep on. "I know,
Granny." He couldn't stop the tears from slipping down his face. "I'm
sorry, Granny. But I didn't do anything wrong. It's Jesse. And I did
like you told me. I called in. I didn't see anything. I just called 'cause
he talked about how he'd like to hurt that rich girl."

She sat back down, wouldn't look at him. "You risked everything I've worked for. If they lock you up, what is going to happen
to me?"

"I'm sorry," he said. "I'm really sorry, Granny. I'll make it up
to you."

She pushed back from the table. "You tell this man here everything he needs to know. You tell him every bad thing that Jesse ever
talked about; you tell even what that boy thought about, you hear
me?" He'd always thought she'd be the one who would save him from
his trouble, who'd pull him out of whatever mess he fell into. But
while he had been in one room telling the cop everything he could
about how Jesse had wanted to hurt that rich girl in his neighborhood,
while he was thinking about how he could use that thousand bucks to

get his car fixed and maybe take his granny for a nice shrimp dinner, she was in another room telling another story, telling whatever she could about Jesse Hollowfield, how she'd known Jesse was up to no good because he was always relying on her boy, who had nothing but a granny and a beat-up car. She was the one who'd asked, just the way she was always asking Mike, *Why does some boy come from all that money need to be leaning on you?* Mike would never answer that question. He'd say he figured Jesse liked him, that was all.

There was a knock on the door. The cop stood, leaned out. Mike strained to hear the words but couldn't make them out. His hearing had been off since the time he'd gotten jumped in juvy, gotten smacked in the ears so hard his eardrums busted. Next time it wouldn't be juvy. If they sent him up, he'd be young meat for anybody who wanted a piece of his ass. That was why he'd stayed close to Jesse. Jesse had never wanted that. Jesse wanted other things Mike could do for him, like cut his hair, get him extra servings in the food line, things like making him an egg sandwich in his granny's house. Mike hoped one day he'd get some of whatever it was that ran in Jesse's blood. But now he was figuring that what Jesse had, he was born with. Mike could never be what Jesse was. He was thinking maybe Jesse was the devil. He was wondering if Jesse was sitting right now in some other interrogation room saying some kind of shit about him.

The cop shut the door. "Looks like you're staying, Carter." He went to the other side of the table, gently pulled out Mike's granny's chair. "I'm sorry, ma'am, but we got to keep your boy."

"What?" Mike said. He tried to stand, but the cop pulled him back to his chair. His granny was crying. "It's all right, Granny. I'll be home soon. These men, they just doing what they got to do."

She reached for him. The cop said, "That'll be enough, ma'am." Mike saw another cop come into the room, help his granny to her walker. "This officer will get you home, Mrs. Carter."

"I need to go take care of my granny." Mike stood "You can't leave her alone."

The cop yanked him back to his chair again. His granny turned. Mike hoped she'd come pat his back the way she always did, tell him it would be all right.

She stood there. He waited for her touch. But she just poked his arm, hard, the way Jesse might do, but not enough to hurt, just enough to let him know she was done. "You should have thought about that before you got in this mess, Michael Ray." She turned to her walker and lumbered away. He saw her bent back, the hem of her skirt swaying at the back of her calves, her swollen ankles and feet pushing those shoes around. "I'm sorry, Granny," he called. "I promise I'll make this all up to you."

He waited to hear her voice. She always said, *I love you, baby*, when he was going somewhere, as if those words could remind him to be the boy she wanted him to be. He thought surely she'd say something, something like a momma would say, before she left the room. But he just heard the clumping, rolling sound of her walker. He couldn't hear her steps, but he clung to the sight of her walking away. The door closed. Mike was wondering if she'd said something like good-bye, something he just couldn't hear for the blood pounding in his head. The cop yanked him up, pushed him toward the door. Mike kept his head down the way cops liked a man to do when they were shuffling him to another room. A whipped dog was what they wanted. *Roll over and play dead*, he thought. He'd never be what Jesse wanted him to be.

As he walked down the hallway, the cop pulling at his arm to make the cuffs cut a little deeper, he thought, *Yeah, I'm a fool all right. Ratting out Jesse. He's gonna kill me first chance he gets.* He'd have to play Jesse's way. He'd have to show Jesse what he could be if he had to. No one had mentioned the girl in the blue truck. But if they did, if he had to, he'd tell them everything to keep Jesse buried under some jail. He'd tell them how he'd never touched that girl. But he'd never tell anybody how she had stood there beside him. She'd touched him as if he were the last thing in the world she could hold on to. And he had been. She'd never gotten the chance to hold the joint Jesse had offered her out in that field. Mike shook his arm as if he could shake her off. But there would be no getting free from the reach of her hand.

Some Kind of Power

Roy warned me about going to the hearing, but he knows me enough to know that a warning to me is more like an invitation than a threat. He told me seeing Jesse Hollowfield in the flesh was nothing like seeing him on tape. Roy said seeing him in person was like watching some kind of shape-shifter. He said one minute the guy was handsome, had a face like the young Elvis, had that mouth the girls loved, and then in a second his face could change, get hard and turn to too much mouth and teeth, like a wolf ready to tear apart whatever got in its way. "When you see that change," he said, "and you're right next to it, you just quiver." I'd seen Jesse's face on tape, and yeah, he gave me a sick feeling, but I figured I could take him live just fine.

Livy was beside me, leaning close. I had tried to reason with her, told her there was nothing to be gained, that seeing his face would only set her to imagining awful things, and she didn't need that. I didn't tell her what I'd seen on that tape of Jesse in the interrogation room. But I did tell her that Mike Carter's granny had said something about Jesse being at her house the day Katy disappeared. And something about a truck out of gas. In most cases that wouldn't mean much, but Katy's truck had a gas gauge that always read empty. Livy was trying to believe maybe he wasn't involved, but for Roy and me, Jesse being involved was something we knew.

So there was Livy, leaning on the edge of her seat, watching the room like something huge would happen any minute. She'd never been in a courtroom as far as I could tell. I'd told her nothing really big was going to happen. But she had said, "I need to be there, Shelby. When I see his face, I'll know."

I knew the judge was the kind who liked to give the ones he sentenced a chance to say one last thing to the courtroom before they were led away to lockup. He liked the drama, or maybe he was just curious to hear what a convicted man had to say. And I'll admit, I was curious. Along with everybody else sitting in that room.

Livy seemed relieved, as if just being near lawyers, cops, and the judge would bring her a little closer to setting things right in her world. I knew she'd never make it back to any kind of world where she thought she belonged.

It wasn't really my business to see Jesse on tape. But Roy had convinced the DA that it could be helpful for me to study the man. When Roy led me into that viewing room to watch, he paused a second, some pain moving across his eyes. He said, "You don't know what you're in for." And that was what I felt like saying to Livy that day: *You don't know what you're in for.* But nobody ever knows what might be around the corner of any day. "Bring it on," I said, the way I always say it when I know I need to face something and I just want it over.

Roy always sees through my tough talk. He just shook his head, sat beside me, and turned on the TV. The screen showed Jesse sitting there, looking at his hands shackled to the table. He looked up, scanned the room, looking for the camera. Then he caught sight of it, a tiny thing, the lens probably no bigger than a pea, but he knew what he was looking at. He made some effort to straighten in his seat, grinned. Then he said, "You tell Mike, you get the word to Mike, I hope he enjoys that reward." When he leaned back in his chair, I could hear the creaking of metal, the clank of cuffs on the table, "You tell him . . ." Then he laughed with the low, dirty sound men can make.

When the detectives came into the room, he sat up as tall as the shackles would allow and said, "You tell that bitch Mike he'd better fucking enjoy the money. It's gonna be the last he spends."

I remembered the detective grinning. He was a friend of Roy, had Roy's cool way of playing an interview. He said, "Mike?"

Jesse looked up, fearless. "You tell him I know where his fucking granny lives." His lawyer grabbed his arm, said, "Stop." The lawyer must have known Jesse, had to be a family friend. It wouldn't be any man who'd lay a hand on Jesse, try to hush him like that.

"I'm curious," the detective said. "What do you know about a truck being out of gas?"

Jesse shrugged, looked at the backs of his hands. There were scars there. I could see them. The detective asked if he knew anything about a blue truck with Tennessee plates, left abandoned, out of gas.

Jesse just smiled and said, "I want everyone to see I'm cooperating here. But I don't have an answer to this question. Why would I know anything about a blue truck? I drive my momma's car."

Then the detective asked where Jesse had been on the day he'd gone to Mrs. Carter's house.

"Mrs. who?" That grin played again on his lips.

"The grandmother of Michael Carter."

Jesse threw his head back with a little laugh. "Oh, my boy Mike. Yeah, I was hanging with Mike that day. He wants to be my bitch sometimes. But I don't need no bitch. We tried fishing in the river. We didn't catch nothing. So we went to his granny's house to find something to eat."

"That's all you did that day. Fished, caught nothing, went to his granny's house."

Jesse looked at his lawyer, smiled, said, "Somebody deaf around here?"

The lawyer reminded him that he didn't have to answer.

Jesse leaned back as best he could to look relaxed, but the shackles kept him hunched forward. "Yeah, I was with Mike. He was having car trouble, and I told him I knew a guy might fix it cheap. But the guy's shop was closed. So we tried fishing. Gave up. It was one of those days nothing goes the way you want, so we went to his granny's house."

The detective sat, leaned close. "You spent the entire day with Mike Carter."

"Yeah," Jesse said. "You tell that little bitch I said I spent the entire day with him. You tell him he knows every goddamned thing I did. Only reason he called in on this Land Fall shit is he knows that's where I live, and it pisses him off. You ask Mike what we did that day. Goddamned snitching bitch." There was spit in the corners of his lips. He had white, white teeth. It was something you didn't want to see when his smile shifted to a snarl.

I knew they should never let a man like him on the streets. I knew then that I wanted to hear the sound of Jesse Hollowfield being led from the courtroom to serve the suspended sentence he'd been given for beating up a hooker, leaving her unconscious in an alley for some drunk to find. I knew once he was locked up, he'd never get out. He'd do time for the hooker and the Flynn girl, and in time I'd see to it he'd do time for Katy Connor. I wanted to be there and watch his smug little world start tumbling down.

When they lowered the lights in that room to show the slides of the Flynn girl, Jesse leaned forward for a closer look. A grin played at his mouth when he saw the thin cut on the blue-veined throat.

I saw the lean white belly, a red knife mark tearing across, the skin, not deep enough to gut her, the bruised arms, the neck all blue and again a knife mark on her chest, thin and jagged, enough to make her bleed but not deep enough to make her bleed out and die. He leaned closer, studying the marks, no remorse, just interest, like a surgeon's interest in a cut badly made, how he might get it right next time.

"Anything you want to say?" the detective asked.

Jesse shrugged. "Seems to me whoever did that needed a sharper knife if it was real blood he was after."

"She bled plenty," the detective said.

"The way I hear it, she lived," Jesse said.

His lawyer tried to restrain him from talking. But Jesse was too proud for silence. He jerked free of the lawyer's hand on his shoulder, leaned to the detective, and said, "You ain't got nothing on me. Like I said, that shit in my backpack, I found it. I was out walking my dog and found that shit scattered on the sidewalk. My guess is whoever did this, they got spooked and ran, spilling that shit on the sidewalk. Me, I was just walking my dog and scooped it up. Ain't no crime picking up stuff off a sidewalk."

"But you kept it," the detective said. "You took it in your backpack, tried to fence it off to your buddy Zeke."

He got a little frozen look then. I could see thoughts turning, the way a man looks when he's hit a wall at the back of an alley, scans the walls for a place to grab, swing up, get the extra step, the leap, anything it takes to find a new way to run. Then he shrugged, looked at his lawyer. He turned back to the detective and grinned. "I got a fucked-up childhood, man. My daddy, he'll get me out of this. Hell, I might even be crazy. We ain't played that card yet. Crazy?" He rolled his eyes, made a gurgling, choking sound, something ugly enough to back away from when I was only looking at the recorded image of him on that screen. "I can do all the crazy I need, man."

284

The detective stayed right on him, patted his shoulder the way you pat a dog that's done just what you want. "You left evidence, Jesse."

Jesse looked at his lawyer, who told Jesse keep his mouth shut. But Jesse liked to talk. "Bullshit."

The detective leaned closer, grinned. "Oh, yeah, you were careful—condoms, kept your clothes on, and we'll find those in time."

Jesse grinned, said, "You just keep on looking."

The detective went on as if he hadn't heard his words: "And those batting gloves your daddy bought you. When was the last time you were in a batting cage?"

Jesse shrugged.

The detective went on, "You sure have worked your way through that box of batting gloves we found in your room. You're good, Jesse; no prints anywhere."

Jesse nodded. "I told you I found that stuff on the sidewalk. I was walking my dog. Ask any of my neighbors. I'm always out walking my dog."

He sat straighter then, said, "I'm a model son, I tell you. Just go ask my dad and mom. Mow the grass, rake the leaves, walk the dog. Don't know why you gotta pick on me just 'cause I did some time in juvy."

"Yeah, you were careful," the detective said. "Sat in that living room, eating Chinese food, stuffing it in that hole in the ski mask. You even got rid of the scotch bottle, the chopsticks, used condoms, took care not to leave any DNA. It's like you've really studied up on these things."

Jesse laughed, said, "Yeah, all that *CSI* I've been watching. I learn all my best tricks watching TV." The cop leaned forward, his grin just as tight and hard as the one on Jesse's face. But Jesse didn't see that. He was enjoying himself. He said, "You know, I watch a lot of those shows. *CSI*, *NCIS*. It's mostly the tits and tight asses I like to watch. 'Cause the research, man, it's fucking Disneyland if you ask me." Jesse kept his smile tight, but I could see the tension in his eyes, not putting out anything, his expression blank as he could keep it as he waited for the next words the detective would say.

The detective stood up and paced, casual, shaking his head. "Thing about TV crime, Jesse, it just ain't real. You ever notice that?" Jesse nodded, waiting for the next words. The detective went on, "Not once, not ever in my career have I seen the rapist, the sadistic fucking rapist who likes to tear girls up for the fun of it, not once have I seen him get the shits; not once have I seen him have to run from the girl all tied and naked and waiting for his next move; not once have I seen the man run to the john and sit and spray his shit. That's some projectile shittin', man." He straightened, shook his head, winked at the other cop in the room. "Man, ain't it nice to be the ones interviewing him here? I wouldn't want to be the guy had to swab that shit—and I do mean shit—from all over that toilet."

Jesse looked away, kept his eyes on his hands shackled on the table. The cop kept at it with the other cop. "You ever have to clean a rapist's shit from a crime scene? Now, I know sometimes the victim shits, hell, no wonder with the things done to her. But the man, what kind of man gets the shits at the scene?"

The lawyer stood, said something like "We're done here," the way they say it on TV. I guess he couldn't find his own words for getting out of that room.

After Roy clicked the screen off, we sat in the dim light. It took me a while to say the words: "So they'll get him for Molly Flynn?" But I was thinking about Katy. Even though they had him for Molly Flynn, I knew it would be another long road to link him to Katy. We'd need more than some granny's talk about a truck out of gas. We'd need more than Molly telling how he'd bragged about the blue-truck girl. We needed Katy, wherever she was.

Livy leaned into me, brought me back to the courtroom. She asked me how much longer they would make us wait. I watched the guards, who didn't look like they'd be up to anything anytime soon. But to give her something, I pointed to the door where they'd lead Jesse Hollowfield into the room. "When the guards head toward that door, that's when they'll be leading him in." She settled back and locked her eyes on the door as if willing him to come on and get it over.

I didn't want Livy to see him, didn't want her to hear that laugh, yet I knew she had to see him. Sometimes we can't resist walking straight toward the beast we fear. If there really was something called evil in the world, it would move like Jesse. I kept seeing Jesse Hollowfield's face on that videotape: dead eyes, mouth grinning.

Livy suddenly reached for my hand, and the courtroom went still, and I remembered where I was. One of the guards went to a side door, pushed it open to two guards leading Jesse in. He stood as straight as the shackles would allow, face cold, jaw tight. The room stayed still, leaving only the sound of his shuffling feet, the soft clanking of the shackles. I watched him pause, scan the room. Even though he was slightly bent from the chains pulling his hands toward his feet, he raised his head, turned from side to side so he could take us all in, his audience. He grinned. That was how he saw that crowd of strangers. We were his audience, and he was ready to show us the powers of Jesse Hollowfield. Even in shackles, he could hold us all frozen and waiting to see what would follow that arrogant, disgusted gaze. He shook his head as if we were hardly worthy, and he let the guard lead him to his chair.

We all knew where the hearing would go, a simple confirmation of what we knew, which was why I wanted to take Livy's arm and leave. I looked for Roy. He stood at the back of the room, his eyes on his cell phone. I'll admit that after one look at Jesse's hard and grinning face, I wanted Roy beside me. I'd never tell him that. But the sight of Jesse's face, seeing him taking his seat so easy and grinning like he knew it was all going to go his way, made me dizzy deep inside, made me want to grab on to anything steady and good. Which was why Livy's hand was squeezing my arm, her eyes locked on Jesse Hollowfield, her face tight with wondering could this be the man, could this really be the man whose hands had last touched her girl?

I heard the *all rise*, and we stood while the judge came in, not looking at anyone, eyes only on where he needed to go. He sat, shuffled through his papers as if he didn't know precisely why we were there. I watched Jesse. He kept his eyes on the judge as if this were his personal showdown. He really didn't give a damn. He leaned back in his chair and shook his head as if to say, *Enough of the bullshit now*, and grinned.

Livy took my hand and whispered, "He's not as big as I thought he'd be." It was true. He didn't look like a man capable of such violence against a girl. Put him in a polo shirt and khakis and a ball cap on his head, and he could have been any man's kid. But I saw the mean strength in his arms, the tension in his jaw. He worked hard at being what he was. Probably did push-ups while they kept him locked in his cell, probably practiced that grin of his every time he passed a mirror. He wasn't ready to give up anything easily, even while he sat shackled in a courtroom waiting for the judge to sentence him.

Roy had said Jesse's lawyers wouldn't even try to plead a way out of Jesse serving time. They'd gotten all the mileage they could on the last charge when he'd beaten that girl. He'd said she'd tried to steal his billfold, tried to grab the keys to his mother's car. He'd said something in him had just clicked and everything had gone black. He had said he couldn't even see what he was hitting, and when she'd dropped to the ground, all he'd thought to do was run.

I wondered what other assaults he'd committed. Like Katy. I knew this was more than his second offense, and I knew there'd be more to come. This was a man who would never be rehabilitated. He was far too happy with exactly who he was.

I know that behind every horror story is a horror story, but a man has to be accountable in some way for the things he's done. Even when it's some unseen hand reaching from back in time to make a man weak in spirit and then strong enough to hurt everything in reach and to feel vindicated by the pain he can cause in the world.

I heard the judge clear his throat. Livy squeezed my hand, and I tightened my grip. I watched the judge look around the room, making sure all eyes were on him and not on the man shackled in the chair.

The judge explained that there would be no bail, and there would be no leaving Jesse to his parents' custody while he awaited trial for the assault on Molly Flynn. Assault, I thought; *what an empty word*. An assault can be something as simple as slapping someone in the face. Or burglary. Or rape. What words we find sometimes for the evil a man can do.

I leaned to Livy, said, "You need to be ready." But she didn't seem to hear me, just kept her eyes locked on Jesse Hollowfield.

The grin never left his face. He shook the shackles on his hands, said, "Damn, y'all must be scared of me." Then he winked. "Don't y'all know I'm Houdini? I can get free from any chains you put on me." The judge banged his gavel, hollered for order. I thought about Houdini, how after surviving all his tricks, he died because he was a smart-ass. He died because he dared some college boys to punch him in the gut. Too much arrogance for one small man. He'd trained his pain threshold so high he couldn't feel the internal injuries, told the boys to keep punching. He died days later, gone septic from all the damage done while he stood there grinning, saying, *Hit me again*.

I sat thinking that would be a good way for Jesse Hollowfield to die: death by his own arrogance. I kept seeing those images of Molly Flynn. I saw the tightly framed photographs of the violence done to that girl. I thought of Darly, Darly. What had they done to Darly all those years ago?

Back in the courtroom, I saw Jesse still grinning. The judge had heard all he needed. I had no doubt the judge had seen the tape, at least heard of it. The judge knew what Jesse had done. He wouldn't be the judge to try the case. They were already moving to change the location of the trial. With all the news about the assault in Land Fall, it'd be hard to find anyone to serve on the jury who didn't already have their minds made up that Jesse Hollowfield was a monster who should never be let out. So he'd be serving his sentence for the old crime while awaiting the trial for what they were calling his second offense. They'd be shipping him to the work farm. He'd be locked up at night, chopping tobacco all day. It was just about the lightest sentence they could give. The crime against Katy would take time to surface. The cops, the judge, anybody who knew anything knew Jesse would have killed the Flynn girl if she hadn't kicked free and run.

The judge asked Jesse if he had anything to say before they led him away. And I was thinking, *Why give this man anything to say?* Then I remembered it's always a good idea to listen between the lines of a confident man. The firmer his stance, the more likely you'll be able to see the little cracks between those proud words. He stood, faced his parents. "I told you I was the devil. Everybody in this room ought to stand back in fear of me." He scanned the room, hoping to see the fear he could stir with his words. His eyes passed over me but locked on Livy. He made a move to look away from her, but something yanked his gaze back. He stood and stared, and she stared right back at him as if they knew each other from some other time. I could see her trembling. I squeezed her hand to bring her back to me. One of the guards nudged Jesse back toward his chair. Jesse jerked free, looked up at the judge. "Ain't nothing but a devil can do the things I do. Go on and sentence me, judge. We'll see how long that lasts. You go on and bang that gavel like you got some kind of power over me."

And Jesse's words, of course, set the judge to doing exactly what Jesse asked.

A Lucky Boat

Livy studied the blue-gray ocean rippling out on the horizon. She felt Shelby beside her but thought she'd lose all courage if she saw one more look of pity. "I know you've told me," she said, "but what is the girl's name again?" She hated the way things kept falling out of her head these days. But there was so much to hold on to, so many little facts, signs of what could have gone wrong. Anything could be a clue. The last time she had seen Katy, Katy had been nervous. She tried to hide it with a smile pasted on her face, but she kept fiddling things with her hands. The napkin she folded and folded into a little triangle just to unfold it and fold it again. The straw for her margarita, she chewed it the way she'd chewed things when she'd been a girl. They were at the marina restaurant even though Livy didn't care for the food. But Katy said she'd heard it had improved. It hadn't. The fish was dry and the salad drenched. Katy smelled like cigarettes, and Livy said something like, "I thought you gave up smoking." And Katy just sipped her drink, squinted out at the sun, chewed an ice cube. Livy wanted to tell her to stop, she'd ruin her teeth. But the cigarettes were enough. "I just do it now and then," Katy said, "when I'm drinking." And Livy thought, *You seem to be drinking a lot these days*—Katy had had three margaritas. "Don't fuss, Mom," Katy said. "Aren't you glad I came for a visit?" She kept checking the texts on her phone. She hadn't made the sudden trip home to see her mom. Girls didn't do that. A girl made sudden trips and watched for texts on a cell phone only for a man.

"She had secrets," Livy said. "I know she did."

"Who?" Shelby asked.

She glanced at Shelby, no sorrow, just confusion in her eyes.

"What were we talking about?" Livy asked.

"Molly Flynn, the girl from Land Fall," Shelby said.

Livy wasn't sure she would ever be ready for what she'd learn from the girl. She stood on the lawn of the girl's father's house: an upscale beachfront home, designed with gardens, stone paths, a pond where koi bobbed up for food. She felt Shelby waiting beside her, wanted to talk about how much water, how much dirt and work it must take to keep this beachfront property green. She said, "I don't think I can stand this."

Livy looked around at the hibiscus, the jasmine blooming. They were at the girl's father's house. The girl from Land Fall. "I was thinking about Katy. I was remembering. I know I should pay attention. It's rude not to pay attention. This girl. What is her name?"

"Molly. Molly Flynn. We're at her father's house."

"I know where we are," Livy said. "The girl who lived. We're at her father's house. She doesn't want to go back to her mother's house. I don't blame her. Who could go back to that place? This man raped her. How many times? You say he cut her legs, her belly, her throat? Her chest? He tried to choke her, but she fought him. She kicked free from the duct tape and ran out. You told me. It's a miracle, you said." A gull called, a hungry, screeching sound. She looked up to three of them circling above. "Hoping for a scrap," Livy said. "Some things always want a scrap. I hate seagulls." She felt a bead of sweat run

293

down her throat. She tapped it with a tissue. "We're going to melt if they don't let us in soon. What's taking so long?"

"Roy is making sure the girl is comfortable. And the parents. They've been through hell, you know."

"I know hell," Livy said.

"The girl doesn't have to do this. She's already made a statement. But she wanted to meet you."

"She's pretty sure it was Katy?" The words felt like stones dropped into the pockets of Livy's seersucker jacket, heaviness falling. She tried to remember, who was the writer who had waded into a river with stones in her pocket? Katy would know. Livy looked toward the house, willing Roy to come out, let them in. But there was another urge for her to get into the car, drive away, take a plane home to where she could try to pretend something, anything but this. "The girl, she must be very strong."

"She has a strong will," Shelby said. "And she's lucky. She's very lucky. Lots of things come into play in something like this. Sometimes it just makes no sense at all."

"No sense at all," Livy said.

"You need some water?" Shelby said. "We can wait in the truck. I can turn on the AC. I didn't think we'd be out here this long."

"I just want to get this over. I like to think Katy is strong, but she's not, really. Her daddy broke her spirit a long time ago. I guess he taught her how to live with fear, taught her to take it. I used to like to think learning to live with fear was a strength. But now I think it's a weakness."

Her phone buzzed in her purse. She checked, saw it was Lawrence, clicked the ringer off. She listened to his message, then set the phone to silence.

He wanted to come down. He thought nothing good could come

from meeting this girl. He said she'd just upset Livy all the more. But Livy knew she needed to hear it. The girl said the man had bragged about the things he'd done to a tall, skinny girl who drove a blue truck with Tennessee plates. He'd said she'd gone fast. Shelby had told her that much. Lawrence said to leave it to the cops. Lawrence said she couldn't solve anything. But Lawrence saw a problem out there as a simple thing: a woman missing; the cops will find her. He didn't understand the tangle of wondering what Livy had done wrong to raise a smart girl who wanted to marry a pot-head brick-layer, a girl who couldn't really tear her heart from the drug dealer named Frank.

She took out her phone, thought maybe she should talk to Lawrence, maybe he would say something sensible, maybe she'd believe whatever he said because whatever he said would be better than what she feared. When she'd told him about the other girl, he'd been doubtful. It seemed unlikely, he had said. "Too coincidental that the man who took Katy attacked this girl on the news. You're hearing what you need to hear, Livy."

She told Lawrence it was the sheriff who said this was a lead. She argued, and he kept talking over her until they were both talked out. "Just call me if you need me," he started to say, but she didn't want to hear it. She clicked her phone off. His words kept droning in her head: *You're hearing what you need to hear.* But he was wrong. She wanted to hear that Katy was fine, that she'd just run away, the very words Lawrence kept telling her. She wanted to hear them from someone else, like Katy standing in front of her saying, "I'm sorry I scared you, Mom, but I just had to run away." She tried to tell herself she would hear these words, but all she really heard was the voice deep and strong inside her whispering, *Katy is gone.*

Shelby touched her arm. "Let's move to the patio. There's shade there." As they walked, Shelby kept her eyes on the house. "This is taking longer than I thought. Maybe the girl has changed her mind about talking to you."

"Maybe Lawrence is right. Unnecessary pain."

Shelby stopped. "You don't want to hear this?"

"No, I do. But I don't. I mean all she has is a story. She must have been delirious. We don't know anything for sure. There have to be a dozen girls driving trucks from Tennessee." She heard her voice, the pitch rising with a desperate sound.

"You've got to follow every lead," Shelby said. Her eyes went back to the door.

"I don't want to hear what she says," Livy said. "But I'll go out of my mind if she turns us away." Shelby nodded. "Lawrence keeps telling me I'm overreacting. We all knew she still wanted to be with Frank back home. She had a thing for the bad boys." Livy paused, looked around her at the landscaping, the ocean view, the huge house of stone and glass that sat on the promontory. "This place is gorgeous," she said. "This Molly, she comes from money, lives in a gated community. Horrible things aren't supposed to happen to girls like that."

"Horrible things happen to anybody." Shelby was checking her phone.

"Don't you hate it when you get a call? Always some new awful thing?"

"Not always," Shelby said. "Sometimes it really is just a case of prewedding jitters. Sometimes we find a father has stolen his child for a good reason. Once we found this old woman with early-stage Alzheimer's. Lost for three days. She'd been staying with a man she liked to call her gentleman friend. We found them in an IHOP having strawberry pancakes. It's not always bad."

"This story won't have a happy ending," Livy said.

Livy heard the front door open, saw a man standing there, white shirt, gray slacks, all perfectly pressed, but his face, he was torn up inside. He nodded at Livy, looked to Shelby, and said, "She's my daughter."

Shelby nodded. "Just say the word and we'll be out of here."

The man gave a little gesture to come in, and a chill ran up Livy's back. She kept her eyes on Shelby, who was leading the way. Livy took the hard first step, kept moving, one foot, the next, and again. She didn't want to look up, but she would once she crossed that threshold. What would she say to the mother of Molly Flynn? *You are the lucky one?*

She walked into the house, not seeing anything until they were led to the living room. Livy sat, trying not to stare at the girl. The girl had picked the darkest place in the room to sit, a difficult thing to do in a room full of light with vaulted ceilings and a wall of glass that opened to a balcony overlooking the ocean. She was tiny, had the body of a little girl made smaller by the dark leather recliner. When Livy was introduced to her, she just gave a little nod. Livy couldn't remember the parents' names. Now the mother was in the kitchen. Livy could hear the clink of ice being dropped into glasses. The father was standing by the girl, his eyes giving encouraging little glances to Livy, Shelby, Roy. The girl looked at Livy, seemed to be watching her for a sign of something. Livy looked her in the eye, gave a nod—how many times had she nodded at the girl? She probably looked stiff as a doll with her head about to fall off. She forced a flicker of a smile, looked to the man, said, "You have a beautiful home here."

"Thank you," he said. He looked at his girl and lightly, so lightly, brushed his palm over the top of her head as if to make sure she was really there.

The girl leaned back, closed her eyes, and made a sighing sound. One bandaged hand rested carefully in her lap. Livy could see little cuts on the fingers. The other hand lay cupped on her chest. The left side of her face was scraped, her eye black with the bruise reaching down her jaw. Her lip was swollen, scabbed. She wore yoga tights and a hoodie over her t-shirt. She was barefoot, her toenails bubble-gum pink.

The mother brought out a tray of iced tea. The father stood, patted his ex-wife's shoulder, took a glass to his daughter. She sat and sipped small sips, careful not to bump the scab on her lip. The man went back to the mother, served them all to keep her from moving around the room. Finally he gave the mother her own glass, led her to her chair by the girl, and took the tray back to the kitchen. Livy wondered if they were always so polite. He came back into the room and went to them, touched his daughter's head, squeezed the mother's shoulder. She looked up at him smiled, patted his hand. He looked around the room. "Everyone have what you need?"

They all nodded. Roy set up a recorder. "Miss Flynn, is it still all right if I tape? Sometimes when you keep telling a story, new things come up."

"Tape everything," she said. Her voice was strong, furious. "Do whatever you can to bury that bastard in jail." Then, as if everything she had was spent, she sank back in the chair, stared at the ice in her glass. A tear slipped down her face. She wiped it away with her finger, her movement careful, as if even her own touch could hurt. She sat back in the chair and softly shook her head.

Livy couldn't hold her glass for fear she'd drop it. Her hands were numb. She put the tea down, stood, and went to the glass doors, wished she could just slip out to the balcony, breathe the sea air, but that would seem crazy. Still, she had to move to keep from crying. She looked out. "I love the way the view looks out to just sea and sky. You don't have to see the tourists on the beach."

"I do like my privacy," the man said. "No one knows Molly is here. We said she'd gone to Florida."

"But I'm here," the girl said. "I'm here." She straightened as if ready. Her eyes darted from Livy to Roy and Shelby, back to Livy, then her dad. Finally her eyes settled on her mom. It would be the mother who would get things going. The mother looked at Livy. "I'm so sorry about your daughter. You must be—" She turned, looked at her girl. "I just hope we can help you in some way." Her voice cracked.

The girl reached to comfort her mother. Livy saw the bandage on her neck, a bruise there. If the man had done all this damage to a girl who had lived, what had he done to Katy?

"Please have a seat," the mother said. "Try to make yourselves comfortable."

Livy realized her sweaty hand was pressed against the glass. She rubbed her hands on her skirt, looked at the glass, and saw her handprint smeared there. "I'm sorry," she said. She looked across the room to her chair, and she couldn't see how she could get there without falling. She saw her handprints all over the glass. She stood there, looking at the girl, then back to the sea, the girl again.

Finally Shelby took her arm. "Let me help you," she whispered. She led Livy to her seat. Livy picked up her glass, sipped her tea. It was sweet and cold and soothed her. She leaned toward the girl. "I'm so sorry for what happened to you."

The girl nodded, looked at her bandaged hand.

Livy couldn't see how any man could hurt such a delicate girl.

The girl sipped at her tea. "There are things I didn't tell the detective." She gave a glance to her mom, then looked directly at Livy. "There was someone there helping me. Someone talking to me the whole time, someone saying, *Get him to tell you the story*." She turned back toward the ocean. "It was a woman's voice. I did everything she told me. I'm sure that voice is the only reason I lived."

Livy could see that the mother was clenching her jaw. "You are a very strong young woman," Livy said. "Not many women could do what you did."

The girl blinked back tears. She took a hard breath, said, "There was someone helping me. I couldn't fight him by myself. He's a monster. I didn't know monsters were real. I didn't know anyone could be like that." She stood as if to get away from everything. Livy feared she'd run from the room, but she went to the glass doors, looked out. She stood there breathing hard little sounds that eventually eased. "See those little fishing boats way out there? They've been out since dawn. They go out in the dark. Every morning they head out into darkness. That's very brave. Not knowing if the catch will be worth the effort. But out they go. I like to watch them heading home."

Livy looked at the mom. She wished she could remember her name. She was a beautiful woman. She looked like Marisa Tomei. She sat straight now, held her hands in her lap, perfect poise. She seemed to feel Livy's gaze. She stood up. "Forgive me," she said. "I meant to offer everyone a snack." She looked at the father. "I did make those little sandwiches, didn't I?"

He nodded. "I can serve them."

"No, thank you," she said, heading toward his kitchen. "I need something to do with my hands." They all sat, listening to the sound of drawers opening, plates being pulled from cabinets. The girl went to the bookshelf, took a book, and sat with it in her lap. *The Old Man and the Sea.* She looked at Livy. "You know it?"

Livy nodded.

The girl looked at her father, tears running down her face. "They keep telling me I'm lucky." She shook her head.

Her father went to her. "You don't have to talk if you're not up to it."

She got up again, walked to the glass wall, stood looking out at the ocean. "I have to talk about it. I have to tell the story." She looked to Livy. "There was this voice in the room, a woman's voice, saying, *Get him to tell you the story.* So I asked. And he told me what he did to the other woman because he said I wasn't going to live. He said the last one was a woman in a blue truck with Tennessee plates. And this voice kept saying, *Get him to tell you the story.* He told me it went so fast she didn't know what hit her. He said she was tall and skinny. I've seen the picture of your daughter, and I have this feeling. This woman's voice. It was like she knew what he would do. She said, *Fight him like a man, Molly.* And I just have this feeling, that voice was your daughter."

Livy looked to Shelby, who sat at a table taking notes. The girl watched them, looked to Livy "They already know this part," Molly said. They looked up, mouths tight. "I told some of this to my dad, and he called Shelby Waters." The girl looked back to the ocean. "I don't know if anybody will believe this. I could just be crazy. I don't know if what I have to say will get your hopes up or down. I just know I should tell you." Livy looked at the girl, who kept her gaze on the ocean. "I'm sorry," the girl said. "He said she was tall and drove a blue truck with Tennessee plates. He said something about 'positive.' He said it was easy." The girl turned, tears running down her face. "I hope it isn't your daughter. But they told me any kind of information might help."

Livy heard the hard, sharp breaths rushing from her mouth. It felt like crying, but there was no real sound. She glanced around the room for some kind of sense to things. The mother sat across the room with her hand over her mouth. The father stood in the doorway of the kitchen. Shelby and Roy just sat watching her. "Am I all right?"

Shelby stood.

"No, don't touch me," Livy said. "Just let me . . ." She didn't know how to finish. She stared at the girl standing by the glass, the gray ocean, blue sky behind her. The girl's hand trembled on the glass. "I so appreciate your talking to me." Her voice didn't sound like her own voice. It was some other woman, a woman who'd gone to finishing school, a woman who'd been trained to be polite. "It's just I hope it's not my daughter. . . ." She thought the words, couldn't say them. "And this voice. The woman's voice." Lawrence would say, *What are the odds, really?* "What are the odds?" she said. "Really. The mind under stress, it does play tricks. The voice could have been your own voice. Your stronger voice. Sometimes I hear voices in my head. Everybody hears voices. Sometimes I've thought it was my mother. Sometimes God. And if Katy would talk to anyone, seems it would have to be me. Or Billy. Why wouldn't she talk to someone she loves?"

They all stood watching her, waiting, knowing somehow she didn't really want an answer to her question. "It's just too coincidental," she said. "I mean maybe she was the one that man . . ." She stopped. "But the voice. Katy's voice? How would she find you? You're asking me to believe in things. She wasn't the kind to fight like a man." She wanted to say, *Katy was too weak for that*, but couldn't because she was the one who had taught Katy to be weak, to tolerate things because being passive was perceived as being good. "Katy liked to talk her way out of things."

The girl nodded. "She did tell me to keep asking him questions. Keep him talking." She turned back to the fishing boats out on the horizon. "She said, *Get him to tell you the story, keep him talking, he'll get sloppy, and you'll live.* And she was right. She knew him. He got distracted. He kept drinking and talking." She turned, glanced at Livy. "Maybe you don't want to hear all I can tell you. "

"I do," Livy said. But she didn't because if what this girl said was true, Katy was dead. She was suddenly deeply tired, as if she'd been running and running and the race was over, and she had lost. She picked up her glass. "Go on," she said. "Tell me everything you can."

The girl's posture shifted, suddenly taller, stronger. She kept her eyes on the boats. "He said she thought she could talk her way out of things. He said she had an old robin's-egg-blue pickup. He said it went fast, and that she was brave all the way." The glass crashed on the floor. Livy leaned forward, bent her head to her hands to try to stop the wailing sound. The girl's father was cleaning up the mess at her feet. The girl's mother was offering a wet towel for her face. How had they gotten to her so quickly? She rocked, felt the soft grip of Shelby's hand on her shoulder. Roy sat back in his chair, shaking his head, lips sucked back as if he were fighting to keep words inside. Livy's stomach dropped. "Not my Katy; it can't be my Katy." But she knew it was true. She sat back, letting the truth settle until her mind sought another direction, desperate for something to do. Finally the room stilled, the sobbing stopped. She wiped at her face with the cloth. "What else did he say? You can tell me. Did he say anything about where she is?"

The girl was trembling, seeming to hold the glass door to steady her. "He said he forgot to rape her, before he . . . he didn't rape her, if that's something you're worried about. He said he wanted to do it right with me." The girl covered her face, sat bent over, her harsh, deep breath moving in and out. Her father stroked her back.

The words kept bobbing in her head: *He forgot to rape her.* So what was he doing while he forgot? This was the point where a mother could go crazy, but she wasn't going crazy. She clung to words Lawrence would say: *It's just too coincidental.* "But there have to be dozens of girls with Tennessee plates in Wilmington." She wanted Roy's answer. "Roy?" He looked from reading a text on his phone. "I'm asking, couldn't there be dozens of girls with trucks from Tennessee around here?"

"Could be," he said. He looked away.

She looked to Shelby, whose eyes were on Roy as he got up and went out of the room. Livy felt a heat at her neck, her blood pressure rising. "Shelby," she said, "what is Roy doing?"

Shelby sat back, her eyes now on the front door. "My guess is he's got something."

Livy stood, walked a few steps, then back. She couldn't sit.

"You gotta have faith," the girl said.

Livy wanted to scream, *In what? Cops? God? You?* But the girl looked so frail, so wounded. It wasn't her fault. Livy sat, told herself to be calm, be strong. The words *Get her to tell you the story* hummed in her head. "That voice you heard," Livy said, "the woman's voice. Was there anything else? Was she peaceful? Was she crying?"

The girl looked up, gave a deep sigh, straightened. "Not peaceful. More worried. And sad. She wanted to help me. She told me to be strong. She told me to have faith." She faced Livy. " She said . . ." She paused. "You might have heard of this. She said, *The Lord didn't give us a spirit of fear.*"

"She said that?" Livy stood, walked across the room, touched the girl's shoulder. Her heart was fluttering. "This woman's voice you heard. She said that?"

" 'The Lord didn't give us a spirit of fear.' " Molly looked at her mom. "There was more, but I couldn't remember it. So we Googled it. It's from the Bible."

"I know where it's from." She felt calmer now, just with the memory of those words. "I have the verse framed in my bedroom. I taught Katy those words. It was all we had sometimes. Those are Katy's words. I gave them to her: 'The Lord didn't give us a spirit of fear, but one of power and love and soundness of mind.'"

"I don't believe much in spiritual things," the girl said. She sighed and took Livy's hand "At least I didn't. Now I think I do. I know it's a miracle I lived. And I think it was your daughter."

Livy nodded. The knot of tears clenched in her throat relaxed. Tears slipped down her face, and she was somehow soothed by the grief spilling out.

The girl reached into the pocket of her hoodie, gave her a tissue. "It's clean," she said. "Was your daughter spiritual?" Livy shrugged. "I think she tried. She liked to believe in guardian angels, but I don't think she really believed, just liked the idea the way we like to believe in the luck of four-leaf clovers, the way we spot a rainbow and think it's a sign of something good." She closed her eyes, wondering if the pounding behind her eyes would ever go still. Would there ever be quiet in her head again? She had a sudden urge for Lawrence. She loved the way his arms wrapped around her, made her nervous mind go still. She wondered what he would say to this story. Coincidence? It wasn't that common a phrase, *The Lord didn't give us a spirit of fear.* Even he would have to wonder. She looked at the girl. "I will say this. If there is a way in the world a spirit can come back to help someone, it would be Katy."

"I know it's true," the girl said. "We can call it superstition, magical thinking. But there are some things, even crazy things, we know to be true. I think I'm standing here now, talking to you, because of your daughter." She cried. "He tried every way he could to kill me."

The father pulled her into a gentle embrace, looked at Livy. Livy knew the words he would say: "We'll let you know if anything else comes up."

Livy stepped closer to the girl. She could smell her perfume. It was Happy by Clinique. She'd bought Katy that cologne, but Katy had thought it smelled too clean. She reached to touch the girl, felt the girl soften under her touch. "But he didn't kill you," Livy said. The girl straightened, looked at Livy. "He wasn't able to kill you, Molly. Because you are strong. You couldn't die because you're meant to do something in this world. Your story will help us find my girl."

The girl nodded, sat back down, picked up her glass of tea, held it to her face. "You have her voice," she said. "That way you just spoke. It's her voice. She said that: *You are stronger than he is.*" She looked off toward the horizon. "I'm sorry about your daughter. The doctors say there are all kinds of reasons I could have heard a voice. They say it was my own voice. But I know it was someone else's. I've seen the picture of your daughter. She was pretty. At least she was spared some things." She stared at the ice in her glass.

Livy could feel the mother come behind her. She looked at Shelby. "Did the man say anything else? Anything at all that could help us find her?"

"He said they saw her at a Dollar Daze store." She paused, looked at Livy. "There must have been two of them. He said, '*We saw her park by the Dumpster.*' He said she thought he might be a regular guy. He laughed about that." The girl stopped speaking, closed her eyes. "I'm so sorry."

Livy looked to Shelby. "So they've got him. They've got him in jail. When do they arrest him for killing my Katy? When do I get to see this monster die?"

"It isn't easy." Shelby stood, came to her, touched her arm. "It's a great lead. But they'll need more evidence."

"Like what?" she said. But she knew the answer. A body, a body. They would have to find her body. She saw the sadness move over Shelby's eyes. "I feel sick." She saw them all look at her as if any minute she might vomit on that gleaming wood floor. "No, not that kind of sick, just sick. All over."

"I'm sorry," Shelby said. "He's in jail. He's been charged for what he did to Molly."

"The minimum," the father said.

Livy looked to Shelby. "So what's next?"

"The man's in jail. And he'll stay there while they continue the investigation. It's two different crimes, different counties." She shook her head. "Jurisdiction limits can slow things down."

Livy heard the front door open, watched Shelby go to Roy. "What you got?"

He stood, hands on his hips, nodding. It wasn't a smile, but there was some kind of satisfaction on his face. "They brought in the kid that gave us the lead. He's not saying much of anything. He's a kid, a nervous kid. He says he knows the guy who attacked the girl in Land Fall. All he wants is the reward. He's mad about the reward not coming yet. But we're holding up on that as long as we can." He looked to Livy. "His granny said something about Jesse Hollowfield being at her house. Him yelling about a truck out of gas. This boy knows what happened. He goes back with Hollowfield to juvy. They've got history. A good chance he was with Hollowfield when—" His eyes went to the floor. "When he took the woman with the truck."

"Katy," Livy said. "You can say it. We all know it was Katy."

"He should die," the girl said. "I know what I'm telling you. He'll go on killing as many as he can."

"He's locked up," Roy said. "Not in juvy this time. He's a man now. He's doing time."

"Until he gets out," the girl's father said. He turned to the window. Livy could see him working his jaw, clenching, unclenching, chewing back words. "You know he's lawyered up."

307

Roy turned. "We're putting pressure on the kid that tipped us off. We know he knows more than he's saying. And like I said, they go way back. He knows damn well who Jesse Hollowfield is."

The girl went back to the glass wall. "He said he was the devil." She shook her head, staring out at the ocean.

"He likes to say all kinds of things," Roy said. "No remorse." He looked to Shelby. "I've never seen anything like it. He doesn't even act worried. No regrets even when he's sitting in jail."

The girl turned to them. "The only thing he regrets is not raping that girl," she said. She looked to Livy. "I'm sorry. But he was really angry about that."

Sweat ran down Livy's back. She watched them all. The talk was going nowhere. She looked at the little triangle sandwiches arranged on a platter and the little matching plates, napkins. She couldn't remember when the girl's mother had brought them into the room. They sat there more like stage props than something anyone would eat. She tasted a metal flavor in the back of her mouth. She worked to swallow it down. She knew if she drank something, it would help, but she couldn't try to hold a glass again. She blinked, tried to see what was going on in the room. The girl was saying something to Roy. Shelby was checking her phone.

The mother was picking up glasses, putting them back on the tray. It would be time to go any minute. And all she had was more evidence that Katy was dead. But not enough evidence. The words *a body, a body* rang in her head, clanging over anything being said. She wanted to say, *Help me,* to the people in the room, but they wouldn't reach where she was. They were far, far away, their voices making a humming sound. She could hear the words, but the meaning hovered somewhere beyond her. The girl sat back in the chair, sinking into it. "Livy," someone said. "Livy." There was a word there. She thought it had something to do with her. There was a squeeze on her shoulder. She flinched, saw Shelby.

"Livy," Shelby said, "I think you should sit."

"I don't want to sit."

"Livy," Roy said, "we're making some progress here."

"We think he killed her," Livy said. She closed her eyes, forced that crying down. "My Katy."

He looked back at Shelby as if she could help. "We've got him. He's in jail. Locked up in a concrete cave. You can try to take some kind of comfort in that."

"I won't take comfort until I have my daughter back." The anger rose in her again. It felt better to be angry. She could be strong if she ran on the rage. "I won't take comfort. This girl lived. My daughter, I know she's gone, and I won't take comfort until the man who did it is dead."

The girl spoke calmly: "You'll find your daughter. I know she's out there, and you'll find her."

Livy looked at the girl, the girl's mother, her father, standing beside her as if to protect her from a fierce wind. "I'm sorry," she said. "I don't mean to yell. I'm sorry. I know it was hard to let me come to your home. It's just that I want my girl." She looked to the parents. "Not every daughter gets to come home. And I pray it wasn't Katy he killed. But he killed someone. And I don't want that for anyone. Nothing so awful should ever happen in this world."

Shelby took her hand. "We need to go and let these people rest."

Livy looked at them, a sweet family, clinging. It seemed nothing could tear them apart. She hoped somehow this awful thing that had happened to their daughter would bring them together again. But it wouldn't. She knew damage just caused damage. "I'm so glad you have each other," she said. "And I thank you." She moved to shake the mother's hand, the father's, the good hand of the girl. She lingered at the girl. "There's another line I used to say to Katy. It's from Helen Keller. You know Helen Keller?"

The girl shook her head.

"Well, you should know Helen Keller. She was deaf and blind. And she grew up to be a miracle. You should read her work. And there's one line you should hang on to. This blind woman, she once said, 'Keep your face to the sunshine and you cannot see the shadows.'"

The girl nodded, tears again running down her face.

"I don't mean to make you cry. I want you to try to turn from all this and live a happy life." She noticed the polite stillness in the room. It seemed the whole world was waiting for her next move. She looked out, saw more fishing boats heading for the shore.

"But you need to see the shadows," the girl said.

Livy turned to her. "What?"

"That blind woman, she must have lived in a safer world. If you don't see the shadows . . ." She paused, her blank gaze back on the ocean. "I'm just saying you need to see the sun *and* the shadows."

Livy stood there, letting the words sink in. The girl was right. You'd be a fool if you just kept your face to the sunlight. "You're a smart girl," Livy said. "What would a blind woman know about seeing in this world?"

"Time to go," Shelby said.

"Thank you," Livy said, looking at the family standing there. She wondered how long they had been waiting for her to go. Livy took Shelby's arm the way she might take the arm of a daughter, and they let Roy lead the way. She let herself sink a little into the strength of Shelby Waters. Her posture wasn't perfect, had a weakness to it, but it felt right to lean a little, to trust. Maybe if she gave a little, something good would come.

Faith Is in the Doing Things

Billy had never been inside. But Katy loved the church, the old brick, the gothic arches rising, and that steeple taller than anything in their part of town. Queen of the Angels Church. He figured Katy liked it for the name as much as for those arches and the stained glass. She said when she went inside, she could remember going to church, and with all that beauty, you just had to believe in things like angels and a God who really listened to your prayers. They walked by the church when they walked to the riverfront; it was just a couple blocks out of the way, and Billy didn't mind the extra steps, especially when Katy was in the mood to pause, stare up at the rising arches and the stained glass as if it were a miracle that such a holy thing could be right there in what some called the rough part of town. Billy had never been a fan of the Catholic Church, with all its land grabbing and paying no taxes—and once he'd heard about the church looking away while priests abused boys, well, he couldn't bring himself to go inside the place. "It's your place," he told Katy, "like your Lake Waccamaw." He couldn't get the thrill of sitting in a truck and looking at a lake, and he was sure he'd never feel that holy feeling people got sometimes just by walking into a church. Just like she'd never get the rush of March madness basketball, he'd never get the peace thing she was always looking for and seeming to find just sitting by a lake or in some old church.

He stood outside it, the soft morning light on the back of his head. It was a breezy kind of morning. He could have knocked out a lot of work today. But his boss had made him take the day off. After the latest news about Katy, Billy was hardly worth anything at work. He'd go in thinking the work would steady him, but then he'd find himself just standing, staring at a brick in his hand as if it could tell him what to do next. The boss had caught him staring at a brick, tapped his shoulder, said, "Take the day tomorrow, Billy; take it for yourself. Go chill, get drunk, do anything, but you take a day, mister. Don't go joining any search parties, don't go pick up another job, don't go racing that truck over any high bridges. I'd say don't you drive at all." The boss had said, "You're losing it, Billy." So Billy was taking the day. And he was taking the advice to walk. Now he was thinking it would make Katy happy if he went inside.

He went up the steps to the big wooden doors. They seemed more like the doors to the castle of the Wizard of Oz. Those were her words, the way she described such doors that suggested that nobody, no way, no how, would get in to see the wizard.

The door opened smoothly, and when he stepped into the cooler air, something in him did settle. The stained glass was soothing, just as she said. But when he walked inside the church, it was nothing like he'd expected it to be. It had been gutted of anything old. The pews were new, smooth pine with burgundy cushions, and they weren't all facing front the way they were supposed to. Some ran from the back of the room up toward the altar, and some were laid out in rows to the right and left. Maybe it was supposed to be something like a cross, the way the pews were arranged. Or maybe it was a way to give more people a better view of whatever the priest did.

And the altar, it wasn't raised up at the back of the room the way every altar he had seen in a movie was. No, this altar, or what he guessed was the altar, was much more like a buffet table–looking thing. And the cross, nothing like the crosses he'd seen in other churches, nothing at all like what they showed in Catholic churches in movies where Jesus was nailed up there, his body lean but not too lean, enough muscle to look like a handsome man. And they always showed him with his head turned aside as if he were just taking a nap to recover from all that pain they'd put him through.

Billy sat in a pew toward the back. He closed his eyes, tried to feel something like God in the room. Katy said she went there to sort her mind out, said she even sometimes went there to pray. "For what?" Billy asked her. He'd teased her once: "Did you go in there and pray for a man like me?" She'd laughed and said she'd been praying for him her whole life. There was no way he believed that. But he loved her the way any woman would want. She was all he'd ever really wanted in a woman. He felt the crying ache in his chest. He stood. How could anyone find peace just sitting in a church? It seemed to Billy that the only way to find peace was to keep moving, walking, driving his truck fast and wild on the back roads, or laying brick, getting the mortar just right and making something solid and symmetrical rise up from uneven, scrubby ground.

He saw the rows of candles in a little cubicle to the left. At least that was familiar. He'd seen that plenty of times, people lining up to light a candle, say a prayer as if a prayer needed the heat of a flame to rise. Katy would like this. He could almost feel her behind him, saying, *Go on, go on, if nothing else, just make the little gesture.*

He pulled a dollar from the crumpled bills in his pocket, folded it, and tucked it into the metal moneybox. He put a candle in the red votive, used a taper to take the flame from another candle and light the one for Katy. He watched the wick catch the flame, thought

323

of the way Katy would hold him after she hadn't seen him all day. She would wrap her arms around him, seem to breathe him in, as if she'd been holding her breath without him and now when she held him, she didn't have to struggle, she could relax and breathe. He prayed, or thought—he wasn't sure what he was doing, but he was sending the words out: *God, please bring Katy home. I'll do anything you want. Just let her be all right. I'll promise to do anything you might want. I'll build churches in Guatemala, homes in Mexico.* He closed his eyes, listened for anything like an answer, but nothing came.

He heard a door open. He looked back toward the entrance of the church and saw a man coming out of a little side room, a bucket and a rag in hand. Billy saw the man look at him, then quickly look away. Billy felt like he'd been caught doing something wrong. He wanted to tell the man, *I put my dollar in the box.* The man just went into a space behind a little swinging door. Billy studied the door and the two doors next to it, almost like little phone booths lined up against the wall. He realized they were confession booths. Finally something the way he thought a Catholic church was supposed to be. But in the movies the booths were dark and usually carved. He wondered if these booths had that little metal grate that separated the sinner from the priest. He watched the doors, flat, smooth golden pine. No one going in or coming out. He wondered if people still went to confession these days. Did people still believe it took a priest to cancel out sins with a few Our Fathers and Hail Marys? He didn't see anything holy about those doors. They could have been doors to closets or dressing rooms. He went to sit in a pew near them, wondered if he'd hear the cleaning man saying anything in there. But there was only silence, and in the distance he heard the wailing of a police car heading somewhere.

He thought maybe if he made a confession, God would answer his prayer. He wondered what sins he might confess but couldn't

314

think of anything. He wasn't a thief, and he'd never killed anybody. He was thinking of how he could be better at honoring his mother when he saw the man come out of one booth and, without a glance at Billy, head inside the next one. Billy caught the scent of Murphy's Oil Soap. He remembered how, in the good days before his mom turned bitter and mean, she'd clean all the cabinets and doors with Murphy's Oil Soap. He studied the gleaming doors of the booths, thought about the man inside wiping at fingerprints, sweat, and most likely somebody's tears. He didn't want to think about the tears of strangers. There was too much crying in the world. He looked up at the cross, white and smooth and spare, hanging by thin, invisible wires over the altar. It looked more like some kind of streamlined jet than the cross he'd known as a kid. He thought of his mother, lonely and too mad at the world to do anything about it. No, she'd rather hole up, smoke Dorals, watch TV, and wait, he figured, just wait for her life to lift up and change. He looked at the cross that didn't really look like a cross and told God he would try to do better to honor his mother. It was too late for his dad. He'd never known his dad, but he told God that whatever his dad was doing, whether his dad was dead or alive or some rich criminal or some fuckup sitting in jail, he would try to honor him too.

Katy would like that. He felt a softening in his chest, the kind of easing feeling he got whenever he looked up at her and saw that whatever he was doing or what he had just said had brought a smile to her face. He looked back to the cross, thought, *Please, God. Don't let her be taken away.*

The man came out of the booth and again with not even a glance at Billy headed into the last one. Billy was thinking to ask whether you had to make an appointment for a confession, but the man moved the way the rabbit moved when it slipped into Katy's garden and knew Billy was sitting right there watching. He'd imagine the rabbit thinking something like, *If you don't notice me, then I won't notice you.* They'd worked out a kind of agreement, he and that rabbit. The rabbit got a good taste of lettuce, and Billy got the pleasure of watching him eat. Katy didn't mind. She said rabbits were supposed to sneak into gardens. They couldn't eat all the lettuce she grew anyway.

Billy thought he'd ask the cleaning man if you had to be Catholic to make a confession. He'd never believed much in religion, but people had believed in that man who'd died on a cross for the sins of the world, had believed in the power of priests and all that business of confessions and pardons and prayers answered if you were good and played by the rules; people had believed that for over two thousand years. What could it hurt for him to try what they all did? He'd tell the priest that he smoked too much pot and drank too much beer. It wasn't exactly breaking a commandment, but he knew just about any Christian would say pot and beer were some kind of sin, so he'd tell the priest to tell God, whoever he was supposed to tell, that he was sorry.

He looked up at the clean lines of the vaulted ceilings, more like something out of *Architectural Digest* than a church. On the outside the church had looked old and solid, had a kind of eternal feel to it that made you think if you went inside those doors you'd find an older world, a more peaceful world, a place of music and prayers, a place where nobody screamed. It looked like something built by people who were a lot closer, really closer, to God than they were these days. Billy figured if people had been coming to sit in those pews, say those prayers, stand and bow, and take that communion for over a hundred years now, there had to be some kind of holiness to the place even if the holiness was a man-made and not a God-given thing.

But sitting there, looking at those clean lines that lifted his eyes up toward someplace like heaven, Billy felt cheated. He just saw a ceiling and some old rusty water stains in the corner, where there must have been a leak when it rained. Then he felt guilty. He was sure God wouldn't be happy with some pot-smoking bricklayer criticizing his church. *I'm sorry, God*, Billy thought. *It's just sometimes I can't help myself.* He sighed and looked up at the cross. If God really did know everything a man did and thought, then he'd know Billy was some kind of sinner who didn't have the sense to admire God's church. He'd never really thought of himself as a sinner; he'd laughed at the idea of needing to be saved. He just couldn't buy those sincere looks of Christians when they'd tried to save him on street corners by pushing cartoon pamphlets about hell and damnation into his hand. He'd just keep walking, saying something like, "I'm all right; I've got my own religion." And most days he did feel all right. Living was his religion, just living a good life and being a nice guy. Wasn't that enough to please a God with any kind of compassion?

I'm not a sinner, Billy thought. But maybe God thought he was. He sat there trying to think of anything he'd done wrong. Too much pot and beer. He'd never cheated on Katy. But there had been those years when he hadn't been the most honest guy with the girls. Only the silent kind of lying, where you just let them think what they needed to think and kept the truth to yourself. But everybody did that. Didn't they? He'd never stolen anything. He had even once told his boss when he'd paid Billy overtime on a job he hadn't done. The boss had been so surprised at Billy's honesty that he'd laughed and given him a beer out of that little refrigerator he kept in the office. Billy had thought he'd let him keep the extra money, but the next week, sure enough, it was docked from his pay. Katy laughed at Billy's honesty. She said that was one of the things she loved about him—he didn't even think to lie when most men would have taken the money and laughed. He knew she was thinking about Frank, who lived on lies and laughter, but he let her keep that thought to herself. He let her keep lots of her thoughts to herself. And now he sat wondering whether he might be a little closer to knowing where she was now if he'd pushed a little harder to know what she kept in her mind. He wondered what she'd think of him sitting in her favorite church, a church they couldn't get married in, but still her favorite. She'd probably laugh at the sight of him sitting there, trying to conjure up a prayer.

Since she'd disappeared, he liked to think that somehow she could see him, know what he was doing, could see that he was still loving her and trying to be good. She'd like the way he did the dishes and the laundry. And she'd like the way he'd been good to her mom even when they all knew her mom didn't think much of him. As much as she didn't want her mom to think of her as just a bartender, she would have liked him inviting Livy to the bar, where she could meet Pete, who'd be sure to lift her spirits because that was just what Pete did. Livy had liked Pete. Livy had been pleased to see that Katy was working at a nice Irish bar and not some dive. He looked up at the cross, thought, *Please let us find Katy. Alive. Please let her be alive somewhere.*

He remembered that bartender chick. Allison, that was her name. He'd made her cry that night, even though she wouldn't show it. He knew he'd made her cry inside with that smart-ass shit about her being nothing but corn. What the fuck was the matter with him, talking like that? *I'm sorry, God,* he thought. *I'm sorry, Katy.* The girl hadn't come near him since that night. Whenever he walked in, Pete jumped up and got him his beer, or somebody without a word just brought him a drink. The girl, Allison, wouldn't even look at him. He looked up at the cross, which was looking more and more like a futuristic spaceship with the brighter light of day coming through the windows. He said the words: "Okay, God, I'm sorry.

Next time I go to the bar, I'll go right up to the girl and apologize. And even if she smacks me in the face, I'll say that's all right."

The confession-booth door opened, and the cleaning man came out. He must have felt Billy staring at him. He gave a nod and a quick little smile. Billy realized he'd probably heard him talking out loud. He was probably used to people coming in there and talking to themselves, or to God, whomever it was you were really talking to when you sat in a church. Billy thought, *See me, Katy? I'm here.* He thought about the girl from Land Fall. She'd said someone had been talking to her that night. She'd said she thought it was Katy, but if it was Katy, that would mean Katy was dead. That old knot of tears clenched in his throat, and he swallowed it down. He thought, *If you can hear me, Katy, please talk to me. Please don't leave me alone with so much quiet. I don't want to be alone.*

Since Livy had moved out to the beach, he saw her only once a week. She'd invite him to dinner, make his favorite things, like steak, pork chops. He'd only given up eating meat for Katy. *I'm sorry, Katy,* he thought. He knew she'd laugh, and he could feel the warmth inside he always felt when he got Katy to laughing. She'd be nothing but tickled that her mother was cooking for him, giving him meat.

Billy watched the cleaning guy walk up to the front of the church. He wanted to call to him, but it seemed rude to yell across a church. He thought of waving the guy over, but that seemed even more rude, would be like bossing the cleaning guy around the way some people told a bartender to hurry up and bring another beer. The man stopped in front of the altar, bowed his head, and quickly crossed himself. Billy smiled. Finally something he'd seen in the movies. Even when a church was empty, people stopped in front of the altar and crossed themselves. Most times they did a quick little drop to their knees. But this man lowered his head in a firm way, as if he really meant it and wasn't just going through the motions. With the way he stood, bowed, he seemed old. Billy figured that the old man might have trouble standing again if he went to his knees. The man gave a little nod to the altar and headed for the alcove where the votive candles glowed. There would be a lot of dust there, all that metal, glass, and wax. Billy decided to go light another candle for Katy so maybe he'd get a chance to talk to the man.

He walked quietly, even though no one was in the place but the cleaning man. Or maybe the priest was hidden somewhere behind a curtain where he could watch what his congregation did when they thought he wasn't around. When Billy turned into the alcove, he saw the old man crouched, using a putty knife to scrape at the floor. He jumped, struggled up. "Excuse me, please," he said. He grabbed his bucket of cleaning supplies and turned to go.

"It's all right," Billy said. "I already lit a candle. I came to talk to you."

"Me?" The man looked confused. He wore gold wire glasses, and his head was balding, looked to be in his seventies. He had the kind of face that looked like it had gone gentle instead of hardened with age. Billy thought he looked like the old man in *Pinocchio*, the man who had made a wooden boy because he was lonely and just wanted a boy of his own. Katy loved that movie. It was her favorite Disney movie, and Billy thought that was odd since she was a girl.

The man rushed to arrange the cleaning supplies in his bucket, and his putty knife clattered to the floor. Billy bent to pick it up, saw the hardened pool of wax. He looked at the old man. "How does so much wax get spilled on the floor?" He looked at the little candles in the box, the ones arranged and flickering neatly in the red votives. Anybody with sense would put the candle into the holder, then light it. You'd have to really work at it to get so much wax on the floor.

"Kids," the man said. "You know kids, looking for any kind of

320

trouble these days." He reached for the putty knife. "Now I'll get out of your way."

Billy kept the putty knife at his side. "I'll finish cleaning this for you."

The man shifted his glasses higher on his nose and looked at Billy with a mix of doubt and patience. He'd probably seen and heard just about everything in that church. Billy crouched and jabbed at the wax, which came up in bigger, smoother chunks than the old man had been able to scrape up. "I'm sorry about the kids," Billy said.

'I've seen worse," the man said. Then he went on to tell Billy that he didn't really need to clean the mess, that he probably should just get on with his prayers and whatever else he needed to do that day.

Billy said he really didn't have anything better to do with his day and kept scraping. He pushed the wax into a little pile, then scooped it into his palm. He stood, not knowing what to do with it.

The man offered his bucket. "Just dump it here."

Billy looked into the neatly arranged bottles, brushes, carefully folded rags. "That's too clean for dirt," Billy said and shoved the wax into his front pocket, telling himself to be sure to empty his pockets before throwing the jeans in the wash. Katy had trained him to do that. The man kept looking from the floor to Billy and back to the floor again, as if some miracle had occurred. Billy spotted the citrus cleanser in the bucket. "Perfect," he said. "This is just what you need to get the trace wax up. I thought I'd need to go get some from my truck, but you've got it right here." He gave the man the putty knife, grabbed the cleanser and a rag. He bent to clean the floor. He liked that citrus smell.

Billy scrubbed harder than he needed to, felt the tightening in his face, the tears trying to rise. His throat ached. He remembered what Livy had told him: There had to be a million blue trucks in the world. He rubbed the floor harder, heard his breath going in and out, the sound of a man running or fighting, struggling to bear weight, too much noise for a man just cleaning wax off a floor.

"You all right, fella?" the man said.

Billy sat on the floor, looked up at the man, who really did look like that man who made Pinocchio. Billy shook his head.

The man looked around the church as if he could find help. "Father Welly isn't here today. You probably came for Father Welly. He'll be back tomorrow."

"Welly?" Billy smiled. "You have a priest named Welly? Heals the sick and . . ." he thought to say *raises the dead*, but wouldn't say that. He looked up at the old man juggling his bucket on his hip and thought to say, *And I guess they call you Mr. Clean*. But that would be a smart-ass who'd talk like that. It was easy to be a smart-ass when you couldn't say what you really wanted to say, when you wanted to cry and just say to someone, *Could you bring my Katy home?*

The man was looking down at him, worried now. "We have a deacon I could call if it's an emergency."

Billy stood and looked at the cleaning rag in his hand. He gave the bottle of cleanser to the man and then folded the rag into a neat square, just like the other rags in the bucket. "It's not an emergency," he said. He wiped the tears that had slipped from his eyes with the back of his hand.

The man took the rag, put it into his bucket. Then he lightly touched Billy's elbow and led him to sit in a pew. "I'd say it's something."

Billy sat, looked up at the cross. Now it looked like a new kind of space shuttle frozen in flight. "When did crosses start looking so modern, like futuristic airplanes?"

The man followed his gaze, gave a little shrug. "How long's it been since you were in a church?"

"You mean a real church?"

"Any kind of church," he said. "I suppose they're all real to somebody."

"A couple of months ago, maybe. I was at a Unitarian place. It looked more like a New Age recreation hall than a church."

The man nodded and looked up at the cross. Billy sat breathing his smell of soap and citrus and that old-man smell, not a stink but old and comforting, like the smell of a worn-out leather sofa that was all cracked and ripped in places but still the best thing to sit in. "My fiancée," Billy said, "her name is Katy. She's been missing for over three months now. It's looking like . . ." He couldn't say it. "It's not looking good."

The old man must have been trained by the priest on how to hold steady even when somebody's world was crumbling, falling down on the ground all around. He let the silence sit there, just the way Billy needed him to. Billy needed the silence to find the words that still needed to come. "I keep hoping she'll come back. But if she could come back, she'd be home by now."

"The police, what do they say?"

Billy sighed. It felt good to let the words out to a stranger, to someone who'd just listen and not throw in their own version of things. "At first they thought she'd just run off. But Katy wouldn't do that. Then they found her truck." He bit at his lip, just the way Katy did. "But there's new evidence. That girl in Land Fall. That man that attacked her. It's looking like he's the man who took Katy."

"I'm sorry." The man shook his head as if it were hurting him to hear the words. "That was an awful thing in Land Fall."

"It was worse than you think."

"It's always worse than you think. Something like that. It's always worse than anybody can say."

Billy nodded. "So I came here. Katy, she always liked this church.

We live just a few blocks away, and we'd walk by here when we headed downtown. She liked the big trees outside. The old stone. She told me she liked to come inside to feel something like peace. But I don't get it. Maybe you have to be a Catholic to feel something like peace."

The man smiled, shook his head. "No, you don't have to be Catholic. But it helps if you're open to the idea, at least the possibility, of peace. That's what Father Welly says. You can't force grace to come, he says, no more than you can force a cool breeze to come in a stuffy house. But if you keep the doors open, in time that breeze will always come along. But nothing will come if you don't keep the doors open."

Billy sighed. "I'm open, man. I've been busted wide open to anything since Katy disappeared. She goes into a store to buy clothes—that's the last thing we know."

The man nodded. "I know that story. I've seen those pictures of her all over town. She's a pretty girl." He shook himself a little, sat straighter, and patted the back of Billy's hand. "I'm so, so sorry." Tears ran down Billy's face. They just broke and spread like something busting through a crack in a dam. The man pressed a handkerchief into Billy's hand. "Don't worry. It's clean."

Billy couldn't bring himself to wipe his face with it. He just squeezed the cloth in his sweaty hand. "I came here because Katy liked this place. I thought it would be old and comforting. She likes old things. I thought there would be comfort in an old church. It's where they always go in movies, an old church. I thought there would be comfort in a place built by men's hands, a place still standing strong after a hundred years. And I walk in, see this. It looks more like a convention center than a church. I wanted it to be the kind of church where you walk in and feel it; you feel like it's the kind of place where God might actually hang around."

The man laughed. "You think God just hangs around old churches? And you aren't even Catholic?" He kept laughing in a quiet way, not shaming, just taking real pleasure in Billy sitting there next to him, giving him something to talk about. "You think God cares what a building looks like? I'd say that's the popes. They like a nice piece of architecture." He nudged Billy as if Billy could get the joke. Then he sat back, looked out at the cross, and shook his head. "I'm an old man. I've seen this world. I wasn't always a janitor, you know. I was a soldier. Based in Germany, and let me tell you, I could show you some old, old churches, hundreds of years old. Churches built because some pope or some rich man could get cheap labor to make some kind of monument—oh, they'll say it's to God. But there's always some man who takes great pride in the thing."

"I thought they were holier back then," Billy said.

The man took Billy's hand, turned it to show the callused palms. "I see you are a laborer. Those men that built those old churches, they were laborers. Sure, they were working on a monument to God, but you know what got them up and out to work every morning? It was the pay at the end of the day. It was the money for bread and meat. Faith, we like to think it's about what you believe in, but when you get my age, you'll see that faith is in the doing things. It's a verb, that's what Father Welly says. It's not a noun; it's a verb. It's about doing things."

Billy smiled. "Katy would like that. She likes doing things."

"There you go," the man said. "I could show you churches in Berlin, Venice, Rome. All those tourists rush to see Notre Dame like it's the grandest, most holy thing in France. And in truth it's not nearly as big as those postcards would have you believe. People go looking for some kind of holy. And when they come back all they talk about are the flying buttresses, the gargoyles, and that stained-glass rose window. You ask me, you can find more of God in a real rose."

"Katy would like that," Billy said.

The man went on. "It's just stuff. Old stuff. I've seen those people standing in line just to look at the relic of some of dead pope's hand. It's pretty creepy, if you ask me. Holiness in some dead man's hand—even if he was a pope." The old man paused to get his breath. He nudged Billy. "You just remember when you think about those big holy churches, it was men that laid those stones. We can tell ourselves they did it for God, but any man knows a man works for his pay. It's the work for pay that gets him through his days."

Billy nodded. And they both sat back, grinning at that cross like a plane above the altar. "Thank you," Billy said.

The man stood. "And speaking of work, it's time for me to get back to mine."

Billy watched him gather his bucket, then pause. He wasn't in a great rush. "Thank you for your time. Your words. You were a help to me. I guess I didn't really need to see a priest."

"Oh, there's times we all need a priest. But most days you can do just fine talking to God yourself. And sometimes, just a man will do."

Billy nodded, wanted to say *thank you* again, but he'd said enough of that. He looked at his hands folded in his lap the way a little boy would do, holding his own hands to keep them out of trouble. The man spoke, but Billy didn't hear the words. He looked up. "What?"

The man was out in the aisle now, heading up to the front of the church. He stopped. "If you believed in God," the man said. He shook his head. "You strike me more as an I-wish-it-could-be-true kind of man than a man who can really make that leap to believe."

"I believed in Katy. I still believe in Katy," Billy said.

The man took a few steps away and looked back. "So how long you gonna sit here and stare up at that cross like it's gonna do something for you? You've been sitting in this church for more than an hour, and the only thing that happened to you was me." The man smiled.

Billy laughed. "And that's a good thing. A very good thing."

"So go out there and find you another good thing on this lovely day."

Billy looked up at the altar. Not even in movies did God actually speak to someone while they were sitting in a church. In a comedy, maybe, but never anything serious.

The man sat in a pew a few rows up and looked back at Billy. "So you believe in Katy. You believe, I'm guessing, in the love of Katy."

Billy nodded.

"And what would your Katy like to see you doing instead of sitting here feeling sad and lonely in a church?"

Billy smiled. "She'd like me to go home and weed and water her garden. It's been so dry, you can't water it enough." He sat thinking about the garden. The tomatoes were so fat and ripe. He liked the sharp scent that flew in the air when he helped her pick yellow leaves from the tomato plants, and he loved that warm weight of the tomato in his hand. And the peppers, he liked to watch them go to red from green. Her peppers, they were red now. They'd be sweet. And the green beans, they were growing fast. They'd be too tough to cook if he didn't pick them soon. Katy would probably really like it if he took some beans and tomatoes to her mom.

He looked at the man, who was watching him the way some old men just like to sit and watch the clouds move across the horizon and guess what the weather will bring. "Her garden," Billy said, "it's thick with weeds. Even in a drought, they never stop. Weeds, they can always find a way to grow."

"So get to it," the man said.

Billy stood, finally knowing a good thing he could do with his day. "I'll bring you some of her tomatoes. She would like that. Katy

327

always liked to give people things. We could never eat everything she grew in that garden."

The man smiled. "I'll be here."

Billy turned to leave. Stopped. "I didn't ask your name. I'm Billy."

The man seemed to stand taller now. Maybe he'd needed to talk to Billy as much as Billy had needed him. "Rufus, and don't laugh." He smiled. "It was some classic Roman name. They gave me hell back in school."

"It's a good name," Billy said. "Takes a good man to carry that name. Katy always said we needed to know each other's names, even the names of strangers. She liked to think if you had a name, it would be just a little harder for that stranger to disappear."

"I like that," the man said. "Billy, you go do what Katy would want you to do this day."

"Tomorrow I'll bring you tomatoes from the garden," Billy said.

"I'll be waiting," Rufus said.

Billy walked back down the aisle, pushed open the door, and stood at the top of the steps, just breathing the breeze stirring in the air. *Katy would like this*, Billy thought. And for the first time in a long time, he was happy to be heading home.

Pain Is a
Passing Thing

Jesse lay in his bunk and stared up at the ceiling. He moved his eyes along the top row of the cinder-block wall, his gaze drifting from left to right, back to the next row down, again left to right, next row down again, as if this were doing something. Nothing to do but stare at the walls and pick at the tobacco tar stuck under his nails and try not to make noise until he was sure Fat Mack in the bunk below was asleep. *Fucking luck*, Jesse thought, *to get locked up with a freak*. But it could be worse. And at least at the work farm he could get out in the air, even if it was just to go down the rows of tobacco and pull the leaves. *Fuck this*, he thought, *fuck, fuck, fuck*. He squeezed his eyes shut, remembered he'd get nowhere with that way of thinking. He had to have a plan.

He opened his eyes and waited for Fat Mack to slip into those snoring sounds he made when he wasn't faking sleep. Fat Mack was one mean man. They said one second he was just a fat man with a lazy eye and pissed off about something, and the next second a knife punched a man between the ribs, and the man fell to the floor, and Fat Mack, he was gone. The best thing to do with Fat Mack was stay out of his way.

That was what the guards told him that first day, said, "We're locking you up with the meanest motherfucker we've got. Fat Mack hates a cellmate. We don't know what he does to them, but they always crying and begging to get switched out." They said they figured Jesse for a fighter, not a crier. They were taking bets on who'd win this one and told Jesse the money sure wasn't riding on him to win. The guard had laughed as he shoved him into his cell. The door clanged shut, and Jesse had stood there, his eyes on the heap of a fat man squeezed into the lower bunk, the slick, balding head mottled like a cantaloupe. The pasty fat face lay still on the gray pillow, the puffy eyes closed. Jesse knew fat people slept hard. They slept deep, were slow to rise. But then they said Fat Mack moved like a rhino when he wanted to. Jesse stood there watching.

Once he was sure the man was asleep, Jesse started pacing quietly, not making a sound. Back in juvy they'd called him ghost boy for the way he could sneak up. He had paced the cell until he was feeling steady and thinking everything would work his way, and when he stopped to get up on his bunk, he turned and saw Fat Mack's eyes open and dull and gray, staring just the way a gator in the shallows looks out, waiting for the prey in sight to move a little closer. Jesse didn't flinch. He just stood there smelling sweat and piss and something a little sweet and rancid, like fruit cocktail going rotten somewhere in a corner of the room. It was the smell of bodies locked up a long time, the smell of bodies leaching into the concrete, the mattresses, the paint. He just stood still and met the fat man's gaze.

They stared like that, Fat Mack still as a mountain and Jesse standing there. Jesse didn't have a choice but to be the first to move. "Fuck this," he said, and with one smooth leap he was up in his bunk. Then he heard Fat Mack laughing this low, chuckling sound that shifted to hard and breathless laughing. Fat Mack coughed and laughed. Then he spat. Jesse heard the splat of it right there on the floor. "They call me Fat Mack," he finally said. "And I don't mind being called Fat Mack." He stopped talking, was just breathing like he was working up the words. Then he punched at the bottom of Jesse's bunk. Jesse didn't know if he'd used his fist or his foot. Fat Mack said, "Don't ever underestimate a fat man, boy." There was that breathing sound, and then that punch to the bunk again. Fat Mack said, "You." Jesse lay there a few seconds trying to figure what was next. "What they call you, asshole?"

"Jesse." He spoke the name to the ceiling, hoped he hadn't already pissed the fat man off. "They call me Jesse."

"Well, all right, then," Fat Mack said. That was pretty much all they said that day. But it had been three weeks now. Three weeks of watching, waiting, holding back.

Now Jesse looked up at the ceiling. He thought of Mike. He should have guessed Mike would turn on him. Jesse would get out of this mess, and Mike would go down. Jesse had already been asking if anybody knew Mike Carter, little baby-faced, punk-ass bitch. Nobody claimed to know him, but when Jesse put together enough money for a hit, they'd be lining up. Jesse whispered, "Hey, Mike, I know where your granny lives." He lay there waiting for the sounds of Fat Mack below sinking into his sleep.

When he thought about Mike, that juice ran in his blood like electricity sparking, and he had to move. He needed to get up, but he hated the way Fat Mack's eyes stayed on him when he walked around the cell. Jesse clenched his jaw, released. Clenched his fists. His hands ached from all the pulling of those tobacco leaves. *Fuck this*. He clenched his arms, released. Legs. Released. Then his whole body clenched, five counts, released. The clenching, releasing, it helped. He listened. The snoring was steady now.

Jesse slid to the floor. Checked Fat Mack's face. Jesse crouched down to do his push-ups. He locked his legs, held his weight on his toes and his palms. He lowered slowly, then up, and down, and up. They worked his ass off out in that tobacco field, but if he didn't stay at his push-ups, sit-ups, he'd get soft. Hell, look at Fat Mack. They worked him all day, tying bags on the flower heads of those tobacco plants so they'd go to seed. They worked him, and he was still fat, a puddle of a man spreading out wherever he sat. *Not me*, Jesse thought, feeling the sweat break as he pumped up and down.

Fat Mack coughed, and Jesse stood, looked down at those gray eyes, the one drooping. They said he'd had a stroke once. Good God, he was an ugly man. He grinned, only half his face moving. "You look like you're fucking something." He shook his head. "A man's a sad case when he gotta try and fuck a floor."

Jesse stared down at him, thinking how good it would feel to kick Fat Mack in the mouth. Jesse grinned. "Shit, I get all the pussy I want."

Fat Mack pulled himself up. He smiled. "Yeah, you so bad, ain't you."

Jesse sat on the metal bench bolted to the floor, heard the buzz that reverberated off the walls, signaling that another hour had passed. They weren't allowed to have watches, clocks. One hour was as good as another. "Fuck this," Jesse said.

Fat Mack said, "What? What's the 'fuck this' for this time?"

"I don't like not knowing what time it is."

Fat Mack shifted. Jesse hated the way every time the man made a move, there had to be this breathing sound. "Well, that buzzer you just heard, it said that it's one more hour before lunch. Then the next buzzer will say lunch, and the next means time to get back out in the fields."

Jesse looked at his hands, blistered and the nails caked with tar. "What happened to the idea of convicts making license plates?"

"This ain't the movies. You in cotton county, tobacco row."

Jesse picked at his nail. "I ain't no slave."

Fat Mack made a coughing, laughing sound. "Yeah, you are."

Jesse dug a little tar loose from under his nail, flicked it to the floor. "Ought to at least give us gloves."

Fat Mack shook his head. "It's a work farm. Ain't your momma's rose garden."

Jesse gave him a look. How'd he know his momma had a rose garden? He went back to his hands, thinking of her garden, her special gardening gloves, her shears, her hat. She always had the right tools for everything she took on. Except Jesse. Jesse stood, walked a few steps across the cell, gave Fat Mack a glance. "I hate being watched."

"I know," Fat Mack said.

Jesse went back to the bench, sat down. He looked at Fat Mack. "I hear you like to cut. Get right between the ribs, and the air goes like a busted balloon. I hear you don't even blink." Fat Mack said nothing, just watched him with that flat-concrete gaze. It was the kind of face a stupid man could fall into, trying to get some kind of meaning out of it. "I get it," Jesse said. "You don't need to say nothing."

"You want me to tell my business so you can tell your shit. I ain't interested. You think you're the first one to fuck up a gal?"

"You don't know me. I'm one bad fucker. I'm—"

Fat Mack raised his hand. "Don't say it. Jesus, God. I know *you* the devil boy."

"All right," Jesse said. "Forget it." He hated it when Fat Mack called him devil boy, but he'd let him have it. He knew it'd be useful to have a partner if he wanted to make a break. And nobody wanted to mess with Fat Mack. They said he could run like a rhino. With the tobacco plants a good five to six feet high, it'd be nothing to disappear in the leaves. If there was more than one running, the guards wouldn't have a single target. It'd be useful to create a little confusion in the leaves. Jesse chewed at his nail, trying to get a little bit more of the tar out. He looked at Fat Mack watching him. "It true you move fast as a rhino when you've got the need?"

Fat Mack shrugged. "It's what they say." He grinned.

Jesse had to look away from that face. "I hear that's how you slip the shank in. Nobody expects you to move that fast."

"It's called a knife. Only in here do they call it a shank. Ain't ever been nothing but a knife to me."

Jesse kept his eyes on his hands. "I'm planning on a way to run free of this place. Down at the end of the field, there's a little dip in the land. I figure if you run through the tobacco plants, they can't get a clear view to shoot. They might see movement, but they can't see exactly where you are. If you can get down to that little dip in the land, there's a good twenty yards they can't see nothing from where they stand guard in the field."

"They don't stand guard," Fat Mack said. "The guards sit high on those horses. I do believe sitting high on those horses gives them a better view of those little dips in the land. And those guards think nothing of kicking a horse in the ribs to make it run. They'd be right on you before you got a chance to cry to momma for help."

Jesse kept talking. "I'm saying you run *through* the tobacco plants—I don't mean run down those nice clean rows where the horses can chase you down easy. You keep your head down and run across the rows of plants. The horses, I've watched them, they don't like the smack of those leaves. They always back off a little when a guard tries to take them straight through those rows. The ground goes uneven where the plants rise, and those leaves, they can smack."

"And I guess you have no trouble running in ninety-degree heat while getting whipped by those leaves."

Jesse shrugged. "Pain is a passing thing, man. I can take that." He looked at Fat Mack, who kept his eyes dead while he slowly, just barely shook his head. Jesse studied his hands as if the plan were right there. "I'll get past that," Jesse said. "Keep running until I'm clear of the leaves to that dip in the land. And I know just half a mile west is a river, and I'm home free once I hit that river."

"Home free," Fat Mack said. "Like it's some ball game out there."

"I'm just saying I've heard some have broke and run from this place. Why not me? I'm fast. And you could break with me."

Fat Mack lifted his head a little, his eyes on Jesse like he was coming into clearer focus. "So you want a diversion, a big diversion while you make your run for the river."

"Nah, man. It's not like I need you. I just heard you can run, so maybe you'd want to run with me."

Fat Mack leaned back into his bunk, his eyes fixed on Jesse. He laughed while his eyes stayed dead. Then he broke into coughing and just coughed and breathed until he got steady. He shook his head. "Nah, it's not like you need me. You'll just disappear into those leaves 'cause you're the devil. You can outrun anything." He struggled to sit up again, farted, not a sound, but the smell came creeping out.

Fat Mack grinned. "You break from the line, devil boy, they'll be on you like flies on shit. And you seem to underestimate those rifles. The guards on the horses, they the fucking elite squad. Cowboys. Marksmen. You think those guards don't practice, you think they don't sit up there just hoping for a chance to get a round off at one of you idiots thinking you can run? I've seen them at the end of the day—while we're heading in to eat, they go out to the fields for a little target practice." Fat Mack paused, looked Jesse in the face. "Hell, man, you've heard them out there, firing at the plants we've bagged. Plants six feet tall with these canvas bags tied on top, looking like a row of scarecrow heads out there in the fields. They do it for entertainment. Getting ready for the real thing. Like you on the run. Once I saw how they like shooting those things, I told them, 'Give me a marker and I draw a face on those bags for you once I tie up those flower heads.' They like that. Feels like they're blasting a man's face off when they take aim."

"Those bagged plants can't run," Jesse said. "They planted in the dirt. Ain't nothing to hit something standing still. And I can run. I'm the—"

Fat Mack drew up, looked at Jesse and raised his finger. "Don't need to try to convince me with that devil bullshit. I see what you are."

"You don't know half what I've done. If you knew, you'd know I'm not just some other asshole sitting in your cell."

Fat Mack settled back. "All right. Every man's got to tell his story. That's why I hate a cellmate. You been trying to tell me since you walked in here. Tell me about the other one. You so damned proud of it. You led her out in that field like a lamb to slaughter. You know how fucking cliché that is?"

"I did. She walked right out of that truck. She stopped, and I said, 'Don't you want to get high with me?'

"'Sure,' she said. So she came over, stood right next to me. I could see she was shaking, so I smiled, lit up, offered her the joint. She reached. I let it drop to the ground. She bent for it, and I grabbed her up by the neck and squeezed." He looked at Fat Mack. He had his attention all right. "The little bones in her neck popped like bubble wrap." Fat Mack nodded. "I threw her down, looked up, and even the trees seemed to be shaking. Little brown birds flying away. I scared the trees, the birds, even scared the fucking worms under my feet."

Fat Mack smiled. "I guess the devil could do such things."

"I finished smoking that joint. And she stared up the way dead things do. Then I noticed her neck; it was so white, little blue veins. I had her knife in my pocket, a little pocketknife. What did she think she could do with that? I made a swipe on her neck with the blade. Just a thin red line barely. And I told you I like to make things bleed."

"Yeah, you've said that."

"Mike, he was hollering, 'Ain't you done yet?' He was hiding behind a clump of trees. I told him to bring me something to finish her off. Made him bring me a screwdriver. Then he ran. I looked back to the dead girl. A black-and-yellow butterfly was on her hair, just sitting there. Can you believe that?"

Fat Mack nodded.

"So I smacked it away and stabbed at her neck with this big old screwdriver.

"I finally just got tired. Couldn't get Mike to help me drag her up under some bushes. I couldn't leave her out in that field. I needed time before somebody found her. So pussy Mike, he just stayed behind those trees, and I had to drag her myself. I looked for a good spot to dump her, saw a big butterfly going at some purple flowers like it didn't given a damn about me. So I threw her right there. I took a few steps back. All you could see was some trash scattered, those bushes, and some trees." He looked at Fat Mack to make sure he was listening, but his eyes were still up on that flickering fluorescent light. "You ever notice how easy it can be to make a thing disappear?"

"Yep," Fat Mack said.

"So I'm standing there, feeling like it's a good day, and then I feel someone watching. I look across the field and see a pair of deer. A mother and her fawn, standing still, ears twitching. I raised my hand like a gun, said, 'Pow.' And they didn't flinch. I told them, 'You ought to be scared of me,' and they stood staring. Can you believe that?"

Fat Mack kept his eyes on the light above, but he nodded.

"They watched," Jesse said. "They weren't even scared. I hate something watching me." Jesse picked at the tar under his nails. He was thinking it was a good story; at least it was when he remembered the way she'd trembled, the way she'd walked right to him, the way her neck had popped like bubble wrap. He thought it made a good story. But when he looked at Fat Mack, he was just leaning back with his eyes closed, like the only thing on his mind was going to sleep. "So what you think?"

Fat Mack opened his eyes, said, "I think you about to be a dead man. You got a little too much pride for one boy."

Jesse stood. He went to the door as if that could give him some kind of safety from Fat Mack. "Well, it didn't go perfect. It went so fast I forgot to fuck her. Didn't even get her ring."

"I ain't talking about that. There's too much of that shit in the world to hear any more about it. You think you something 'cause you can choke some girl. Cut up another. You think that's something ain't been done a thousand times before?"

Jesse looked at his hands. He'd never get clean of that tar, not in here. He hated shit under his nails. "I gotta get out of here," he said.

Fat Mack leaned forward. "You might think you can run like the devil through tobacco plants. But those guards, they been getting ready for some cocky son of a bitch like you. You go running through that field, no matter how fast you think you going, some guard sitting high on his horse gonna get a bead on you, put a bullet through the back of your head before you know what hit."

Jesse shook his head. "Nah, I got a plan." He didn't tell Fat Mack that he'd been practicing running low to the ground, moving fast along those rows of plants. He wouldn't take a straight line but zigzag, keep them wondering where he'd go next. It would be a better plan to have Fat Mack out in that field. They'd go first for the fat man who moved like a rhino. Be easier to hit his fat ass.

"You got a plan," Fat Mack said, grinning.

"Think about it," Jesse said. "When we take a water break, all that's on anybody's mind is getting a drink, taking a piss. They loosen up then."

"You know what the guards think," Fat Mack said.

"I know how people think. I spent my life watching the way people think."

"So you know everything," Fat Mack said.

Jesse paced. He could feel Fat Mack's eyes moving over him. He wanted to yell, *Quit the fuck looking at me*, wanted to slam something into that fat face, but instead he grinned. "Think about it," Jesse said. "If you run like they say you can, we can be out of here, sipping cold ones in some bar, watching some nice titties bouncing in some tight shirt. You'd like that."

"Yeah, I'd like that," Fat Mack said, but his face was still, eyes the same gray stone they always were. Not one flicker of interest in Jesse's plan. Jesse shook his head and swung up into his bed to the sound of Fat Mack laughing. After a silence, Fat Mack punched at his bunk. "Hey, devil boy," he said. "Every fucker I put down deserved it. Had it coming. There's a reckoning always. And sometimes that reckoning is me." Jesse said nothing. There was another punch. "Sounds to me like you just fuck somebody up for no good reason. That don't sound like a plan to me." And then there was more laughing. Jesse pulled the pillow over his head to try to muffle the sound of Fat Mack laughing.

There Will Always Be More Tears

In those months of searching for Katy, we followed dozens of leads. In the beginning Livy wanted to be right there beside me when we searched, but once we hit the fields she'd get faint, have to go back to the truck, so we decided to keep her back at the tables, running the volunteer list, handing out food and drinks.

One psychic—Livy insisted on a psychic—said Katy would be found near the sound of a chained and barking dog. So to satisfy Livy, we followed that lead. It wasn't much work to call the Humane Society and get a list of every dog nuisance complaint in the city and surrounding counties. The searching, that was work. We got over a hundred volunteers for that search because everybody and their momma wants to rescue a suffering dog. We didn't find Katy. But we did save some dogs. Busted up a big dog-fighting ring, and there's some comfort in that. There's a lot of comfort in that. No living creature should be used as bait to train a killing thing. Which leads me back to Katy. And I can't tell Katy's story without telling her mother's story, a woman who refused to go back to her home on a mountaintop until she found her girl. She walked away from everything. Her whole world collapsed, was reduced to one single purpose: to find Katy, bring her home.

The searching tore her down every day, weight dropping, lines deepening in her face, eyes going dull. Staying at Katy's house, much as she felt the need to be there, it sucked the life out of her like a disease. She told me once it was like living where you feel a ghost in every corner, and you turn to look at it just when it's left the room.

I didn't tell Livy everything. I didn't tell her I knew her daughter was dead. I let her cling to whatever sliver of hope she could summon up. But I've known for most my life that hope is little more than a pretty cloud we paint out there on the horizon. We decide it is pretty with the way it reflects light from the sun, and it shifts and changes and somehow remains there in brilliant color, promising something as the sun goes down. Then you're left with darkness.

Livy was fighting that darkness even on the brightest days. So I fought to make her leave Katy's house—I should say Billy's house. It was his. Livy was living, breathing, searching, doing, but the Olivia Baines she used to be was dying every day. It took Lawrence coming down. It took both of us to pack up Livy, drive her out to that condo on the beach. And the minute she stepped out onto the balcony, took in the ocean, that steady, soothing rhythm of the ocean, something loosened in her, and for the first time in months she started to breathe.

Lawrence stayed for a week, just to help make things feel a little more normal, like they were on a vacation or some such thing. They had me over one evening for a cookout. We were hoping that for a few hours we could pretend we were all gathered for pleasure, not to survive the daily grind of pain. It promised to be a perfect evening, with Livy and me in the kitchen while Lawrence was downstairs grilling steaks on the patio near the pool. We could relax a little with him out for a while. Both of us were grateful for the condo regulations that there could be no grilling on the balcony—too great a fire hazard. We were happy with that.

Losing a child tests any marriage, and losing a young child will most likely break it because so often, when the couple looks at one another, they see only reminders, the eyes, the mouth, the dimple, or a gesture maybe that makes them see not the living person who is in front of them but instead the physical, genetic reminder of the loved one lost. This wasn't the case with Katy, being she was grown, a woman, and not Lawrence's daughter. But still he resented that his wife had been yanked from their home to this beach condo, where the wind was turning cold at night and any conversation was punctuated with fear, dread of what the next phone call might bring. Livy was disappointed and resentful that Lawrence wasn't grieving enough, even though he was there. And Lawrence still wanted to believe that Katy had just run away and would turn up back on the houseboat with Frank.

I knew they were both wrong. And even though both seemed to think the world wasn't doing enough to bring back Katy, they liked having me around. It was if my presence were some kind of promise that an answer would come. So they invited me to visit them at the condo to have a night of something like normal: steaks off the grill and salad and cold beer and a wife chopping things in a kitchen.

I watched Livy from across the kitchen counter. She gave me nothing to do, said she'd missed the pleasure of having a guest in her house. She methodically opened a beer, poured it into a chilled glass, and pushed a dish of cashews toward me. There was a kind of sweet falsity to the whole thing, reminding me of the way Darly used to make me sit on the floor with her baby dolls and pretend to drink tea from her tiny cups and saucers, pretend the Little Debbie Swiss rolls sliced in little circles were her homemade secret-recipe cakes. "This is so delicious," I would always say. "I do hope one day you'll give me the recipe." She would only shake her head and smile.

So there I sat, letting Livy and Lawrence tend to me because they needed a domestic game to play. Even though I had a hundred things to do, I had chosen to put my phone on vibrate, promised myself I would answer only the most urgent calls. I would eat, drink, let myself be served, and say, *This is so delicious*, even though I would barely taste the food in my mouth for thinking of all the other places I needed to be.

Livy tore at the baby leaves of fresh spinach with the quick gestures of a woman tearing at weeds in her flowerbed. She was making the orzo dish she told me Lawrence loved and always wanted with his steaks. "The right food soothes him," she said. But I could see that the process of making the right food was anything but soothing to her. She worked with precise jerking movements, mincing the garlic, chopping tomatoes, quickly measuring and dumping balsamic vinegar and olive oil. Occasionally she'd turn and stir the boiling orzo steaming on the stove.

I leaned over the counter, teased, "You look like you're beating up dinner over there. Quit frowning. Take a breath and sip some wine."

"I like cooking," she said, frowning at the lemon before she mashed it against the grater to get the zest. As she tossed the vegetables, vinegar, and oil in a bowl, I wondered how a Suck Creek girl came to be easy with things like orzo, balsamic vinegar, and extra virgin olive oil. I knew she'd grown up on lard biscuits and fatback in her beans. She went back to stirring the pot. "I just wish he had a better attitude." She used a spoon to test a bite of orzo, gave a nod, then dumped it all into a colander, stood back, and let the steam rise. She frowned again, came back to the counter, grabbed a chunk of feta cheese, and tore at it, crumbling with furious fingers. I wanted to tell her she was lucky to have a husband willing to fly down here. I wanted to say all he really wanted was his life back to normal, his wife home, and her daughter never lost. I wanted to say he wanted what she wanted, just in a different way.

But I knew the better way was to stay on her side of any argument. Sometimes we all have to say little things we don't mean to make it go little easier. So I nodded to Livy's frowning gaze. "I understand," I said. "I know it must be maddening when your husband doesn't seem . . ." I wanted to say *terrified* but knew I should avoid any heart-pounding kind of words, so I said, "As concerned as you."

She stopped tearing at the feta cheese and went to the sink to wash her hands. She sighed, dumped the orzo into a bowl, and stirred in the vegetables, oil and vinegar, and cheese. "I'm sure he is doing the best he can."

"We all are," I said.

"But sometimes that's not good enough." She looked at me as if I were the enemy now and took a sip of her wine.

I drank from my beer. "At least he's down there grilling our steaks. I like a man who grills the steaks and brings the beer."

She nodded, gently stirred the orzo, added lemon zest and ground pepper. "He likes to grill when he's feeling useless. Back when the stock market was burning down, he was outside every night with his dirty martini and something searing on the grill." She stirred the orzo, took a bite, seemed pleased. "Want a taste?" she asked, already reaching into the drawer for a clean spoon.

I took a bite, savored the blend of tart cheese, sweet tomatoes, the freshness of the spinach, lemon zest. "You're quite the cook," I said. "No wonder Lawrence wants you home."

"Husbands always want their women home." She gathered plates, flatware, napkins and was heading for the balcony, and I thought of Billy. She had to be thinking of Billy, who'd seemed indifferent when he'd shrugged, back when I'd asked if he could list the places Katy liked to go. He said, "Shit, I don't know. Katy always goes wherever she wants to go. I can't keep up with Katy." He was angry. He was scared.

Livy called to me, "You want to help me set the table?"

I got up. "I'm sorry I'm was just sitting there, letting you do all the work."

"You do enough work," she said. "But I know how you like to feel involved. Could you bring out the glasses and that pitcher of water on the counter?"

I gathered the glasses and pitcher and went out onto the balcony, where she'd set the table with place mats, cloth napkins, and fresh flowers. "Very nice."

"I like things nice," she said. She turned to look out at the ocean, more a slate blue than gray that day. The air still held some of the day's heat, but a cooler breeze was blowing in.

"We couldn't have a more beautiful day." I said the words meaning them, but they came out false somehow.

"Yes, we could," she said, her eyes on the horizon. I saw a tear slip down her face, heard the sound of her hard swallow. "He'll be up with the steaks any minute."

"I'll get the salad and the orzo. And your wine." She said nothing, and I turned to go inside, knowing she needed the quiet and not my bullshit courteous words. I stayed quiet, just placing the serving bowls and the wine while she faced the horizon that would soon fade to another night with Katy gone.

Sometimes we need the quiet. Sometimes sorrow is best kept to ourselves. If we keep digging it up and throwing it out for others to share, they step back. They go numb to so much sorrow, can't help but turn away. Sometimes we all go numb. And I was standing in the living room, trying to think of what else I might need to bring from the kitchen but caught up thinking about the comfort of numbness, when my cell phone buzzed. I thought to ignore it because Lawrence was just walking in the door with the platter of steaks, and he was smiling and saying, "Beautiful. Would you look at these? Prime Angus beef, the best." I pulled out my phone, saw that the caller was Roy. I smiled at Lawrence as he went out to the balcony, offering the steaks as some kind of proof that the world was as it should be. He was a good man. Just a frustrated man. Probably a scared man, wondering would his wife ever again be the happy woman he'd married.

"Hey, Roy," I said, and I heard Lawrence ask if I wanted another beer or to switch to wine. "I'm fine," I said. "I'll be right out." I went back to my phone. "Tell me it's good news."

"We have a lead." It was a flat, sad sound. "A shallow grave." I stood there facing the balcony, saw Lawrence standing with his arm around Livy, both looking out at the ocean as if there were a ship out there that could bring them something. But there was nothing. Just water and sky.

Lawrence came to the sliding glass door, said, "You really ought to switch to wine with—" He stood still, stared at me while I listened to Roy's words, trying to keep my face blank. But Lawrence was a smart man. He could see. Livy came to the door, stood half behind Lawrence, as if he could protect her from any awful thing I might have to say. I hung up the phone, went for my purse, said, "I have to go."

"Shelby," Lawrence called lightly, "can it wait until after dinner? We just set out the steaks." He came closer, stood between me and the door as if he were thinking of arguing with me. I saw the hope seep from his face. He shook his head, sat down.

Livy rushed forward, squeezed my arms, and looked down on me like a mother pinning a child who won't admit a truth. "It's about Katy."

"Maybe," I said, seeing the old sight of a body half buried, dug up, the flies, the rot, the smell. She wouldn't want to see this. "There's a lead that might be something about Katy." I looked to the floor. How do you tell a mother some kids playing in the woods had found a shallow grave that might be her girl's? How can you lead her to the site, the flies, the smell?

Roy had told me it was in the woods near a construction site at a new development near Land Fall.

"You have to tell me," Livy said. She was squeezing my arms so tightly, it burned. I looked up, saw the hysteria brimming in her eyes. Lawrence stood, put his hand on her back, as if his touch could hold her steady.

I tried to pull free of her grip, but she held on. "I really have to go. I'll let you know as soon as I know something."

She clung tighter, nails digging in. "What kind of lead?"

How do you say it could be the remains of your girl? How do you say, *You don't want to be there; you'll never, ever, never forget the smell?* You don't. I pulled free of her, but only because Lawrence was pulling at her arms. He stood behind her, his arms wrapped around her, holding her still. "Shelby," he said, "you know we have a right to know of anything that might relate to Katy. Knowing sometimes can be a lot less painful than not knowing and having to imagine. You don't want to leave her here imagining every awful thing."

I turned away to find my purse. "They have a lead that might relate to Katy," I said as if those empty words would ease their minds enough to let me go. But they followed right behind me, Livy saying, "We are coming with you. We'll follow you in our car if we have to. We are coming." Lawrence was locking the glass door. I looked past him out to the balcony, saw the nice set table, the carefully prepared meal that would go to the flies and the gulls.

347

"All right. Let's go in my truck." In seconds we were down the stairs and out the door.

In the truck Livy sat beside me with Lawrence in the backseat leaning up between us. I could see he wasn't accustomed to riding in backseats, but there was no discussion. He opened the door to let Livy climb in up front and took his place in the backseat without a word. I backed up and pulled out onto the highway leading to town. The new development was near a private school. I'd searched for another girl in the woods there. Not a place I wanted to go back to, but I wanted to be there before they pulled whatever it was from the ground. I wanted to get a sense of the scene and find a way to keep Livy back before the smell of rot thickened the air. I knew I wouldn't make it in time, and I didn't know how I could keep Livy from seeing, smelling, living the awful thing no mother should bear. I could feel the fear coming off Livy like an electric hum in the air. "It might not be anything," I said, settling back, trying to look more relaxed in my seat.

"You're driving too fast for this not to be anything," Livy said, her eyes staring out at the road. We drove on in silence for a while. Livy made a wailing sound. "You've got to tell us where we are going. You've got to tell us what kind of lead."

I thought of the Xanax in the first-aid kit in the back of the truck. I knew we'd be needing that, tried to think of an excuse to pull over, how I could convince Livy to take a pill without telling her why she needed it.

"Shelby," she said. A mother's warning tone, quickly growing furious.

"Some kids found something in the woods," I said. "Could be something. Could be nothing. Roy is on his way."

"Where?" she said. The tears were already slipping down her face.

348

"Near a new housing development. Out by Land Fall."

She sat thinking. I could see the path her mind was traveling. "You say some kids found something." She squeezed my arm. "What kind of something?"

Lawrence reached, pulled her hand away. "Let her drive, Livy. She's telling us what she can." I could feel his gaze on my face. I glanced his way and could tell by the little wince in his eyes that he could see my fear. "Damn," he whispered as he took a firmer grip on Livy's arm.

"He's killed her!" Livy cried. "It's Katy! That monster got her too, dumped her body out there." She covered her face with her hands, sank in her seat, and sobbed as if something were being beaten into her, or out of her. It was an awful breaking, shattering sound. I pulled to the side of the road, stopped the truck, and went around back for the Xanax. I shook two from the bottle and grabbed two waters from the cooler. I went to her side of the truck and pulled her out, put her in the backseat with her husband. She didn't fight. She just leaned into him and cried like a little girl. I've seen enough of this kind of sorrow. I've seen more than enough grief, and I know there will always be more tears in this world. I wanted to shake her, make her stop, make her quit making that awful sound that always breaks my heart when I think no more can be broken. But it was her daughter. *No*, I thought, *it could be her daughter*. So I reached in, stroked her back, and said, "We don't know anything yet. We don't know anything. Try not to be so upset about what we don't know." I gave Lawrence the pills and the waters. "Xanax," I said. "There's one for you if you need it, but right now we need to get her as steady as we can." He nodded, gave Livy a pill, slipped the other into his pocket. He stroked the back of her head, whispered, "We need you steady, Livy." She took the pill, gulped the water down. Then she sat back with her eyes closed, tears still seeping down.

I shut the door and went around to get back behind the wheel. I got us back on the road, grateful for the silence. After a while she sat up, blew her nose. I could hear her taking deep breaths, straightening in her seat. "Just tell us what you know," she said. "I'm going to go crazy back here trying to guess what you know." I kept my eyes on the road. I said, "I'm so sorry you have to go through this."

"Through what!" The anger would keep her stronger than grief.

"Olivia," Lawrence said in that paternal voice that reminds me of why I'll never marry.

"Some kids found . . ." I shook my head, couldn't get the words out. "A shallow grave," I said. I heard her making those choking, sobbing sounds. I knew she was swallowing the need to scream. "We don't know it's Katy," I said.

"It's near Land Fall," Lawrence said. "For God's sake!"

And so we drove. I'd searched those woods before when a girl had been reported missing after volleyball practice one night. We searched with crews, dogs, everything we had, and all we found in those woods were beer bottles, pizza boxes, some girl's panties, and a used condom. They could have been any girl's panties in that woods. Later we found her, bound and gagged in the Cape Fear River. Valerie Williams was her name. I still have her picture on the wall of the missing back at my house. We found her, but she'll always be gone. Her picture smiles out toward a future she can never know.

I kept driving while Lawrence made furious sighing sounds and Livy leaned into him and whimpered. I prayed it wouldn't be Katy. And I prayed for a way to keep Livy and Lawrence in the truck while the detectives studied whatever it was half buried in the ground. There was no use in talking. She was wearing herself out just by thinking the worst possible thing. And I could only let her. I knew in time she would face the worst possible thing. And sometimes we need to practice pain just to know that somehow in the end, we will survive.

When we turned onto the road into the subdivision, I expected Livy to start wailing again, but the Xanax must have eased her a bit. I knew she was exhausted. I glanced back at them, saw her leaning into her husband's chest and staring blankly ahead while he sat staring as if he could clearly see the thing he hated most in this world. But there were no tears, only a clench in his jaw. I drove toward the line of cars, pulled to the side of the road. I was dreading the argument of how I would convince them to stay in the truck instead of jumping out and running straight to what they didn't want to see. They both leaned forward as I edged toward the line of cars. I spoke then, the useless words: "You know, it really would be better if you waited in the truck." I could see the cops out there. The detective. And a coroner's car. It had to be bad if they'd called the coroner's car. There were some kids standing around. A shallow grave dug up was the last thing a kid needed to see. I held off on parking the truck, just slowly edged forward. I picked up my phone. "Let me just try to talk to Roy." I kept edging the truck forward, refusing to stop, knowing Livy was ready to leap out the door. Roy picked up after one ring, said, "It's a dog."

"A dog?" I said. "All they found is a dog?" I glanced back at Livy, who just fell back silent against the seat.

"A big dog," Roy said. "A collie maybe. Rolled up in a carpet."

"Why the hell did they call the coroner's car for a dog?"

"Somebody was too eager to find something worse, I guess." Roy sighed. I could almost feel his breath through the phone. "You know how people can be so eager to find the worst thing. Somebody just buried their dead dog."

I looked back to Lawrence, who sat shaking his head. "That's it," I said. "Someone just buried their dead dog."

"Yep," Roy said. "How's that for a false lead?"

I couldn't help smiling. I looked to Livy, could see the giggling rising to her face. "Poor dog," I said. "He probably belonged to some family that lives near here."

"Yeah, the family is here. They're putting the dog back in the ground." He sighed again. "You don't need to see this."

"No, we don't need to see this."

They were laughing in the backseat, both of them, laughing as if they'd just heard the funniest thing in the world.

I got off the phone, and we all sat there laughing.

"The steaks," Lawrence finally said when he could speak. "Those beautiful steaks gone to waste." Then we went through another round of laughing, calling out words, "Steak, orzo, salad." And more laughing with the words, "All gone to the birds."

We didn't eat steaks that night. We went to the Mexican place near the condo. We ate bad greasy food and drank sour-sweet margaritas. And we laughed at the tears wasted on a false lead, all that grief pulled up and thrown out for a false lead. But that was all right. Sometimes we need a taste of the bad things to get ready for what's worse.

There's Always
Hell to Pay

Jesse moved down the tobacco row, pulling leaves, and dropping them on the ground where the next man would come and stack them under his arm to take them to the stringer. One job for each man. They all added up to one big harvesting machine. If each man did his one job, the machine would go. That first day they'd sized him up, height, weight, and strength. They'd measured him for the job he could do. Like a slave, Jesse thought, going to the next plant, tearing at the leaves. He looked down the row; the stacker was way behind—they called him Lightning. His name was a joke because he had this slow, dumb way of moving like he didn't know what he was doing. But he knew exactly what he was doing, getting on the guards' nerves, everybody's nerves, by the way he could slow things down. He was handing off a stack of leaves to the stringer, taking his time. The stringer pierced the leaves with something like an arrow attached to thick twine. Once a string was full, it was stacked and trucked to the barn to cure. Jesse looked over the men working like mules, the guards scowling down at them all from their horses. One guard stuck a wad of chew in his mouth, mashed in between his teeth. Soon he'd be spitting. Some of the guards liked to aim their spit to fall right at a man's feet, not hitting, but letting a man know he was down there on the ground where the spit would fall. The guard looked his way. "You got a problem there, boy?"

Jesse shook his head, bent back to work. He saw his sweat drip from his face to the black dirt at his feet. He thought, *It's the last day you'll call me boy*, but he didn't give the man a glance, knowing he was watching, making sure Jesse was doing exactly what he was supposed to do. He stayed low to the ground as he moved, wasting no effort to stand and bend to each plant. Stay low and keep moving. His legs and back were trained to this. The guards had laughed at the way he picked, arms and legs always steady and low to the ground. They'd called him monkey man for the way he seemed to move on all fours. He kept picking down the row, thinking, *I'll show you monkey man. I'm gonna break and run. I'll be out of sight just the way a wild thing moves in the woods. All you'll see is the shaking of leaves.* He knew he was picking straight toward that little dip in the land.

There was a little breeze now and then to keep the tobacco leaves stirring, and they were working the western field, that much closer to the river. When he broke, he'd be heading into the sun, and they'd have a harder time sighting him with the glare in their eyes. He picked faster now, wanting to get way out ahead of Lightning, who was taking his time. *Not much longer*, Jesse thought. He knew the water break was coming soon. He could tell by the parched tightness in his throat. He stayed low, kept picking, heard the thundering sound of a horse going by a couple rows over. The horse stopped. Jesse could hear the impatience in the hooves of the horse being reined in, stomping at the ground. "Slow down, Hollowfield," the guard called. "We're coming up on break, and you don't need to be too far out of range." Jesse grinned but kept his face to the ground. "You hear me, boy?"

He stood. "Yes, sir." The guard looked like some kind of Texas

Ranger up there on his high horse with his face shadowed by his cowboy hat. Jesse glanced at the rifle strapped to the saddlebag. It would take a few seconds to get the rifle up, get the target in sight. And Jesse needed only a few seconds to disappear. "Yes, sir," he said again as he bent, put his hands just above his knees, and stretched his back. He breathed hard to make the guard think he was whipped and catching his breath, as if he'd barely be able to make it back to the water truck.

"All right, then," the guard said as he guided the horse on down the row. They'd never suspect Jesse for a runner. He'd played them, worked hard and steady, never complained, never begged and cried to be let out of Fat Mack's cell. Hell, he could take the stare of the fat man, the stench of him, that nonstop breathing sound. He could handle Fat Mack. Even though Fat Mack gave him that dead man's gaze that made most guys whimper and duck away, Jesse stood there and gave it right back.

The break whistle screeched, and Jesse saw the guard look back his way. Jesse gave him a nod and took a few steps down the row toward the water truck, and the guard moved on to get the others in line. He'd have five seconds to step into the row of tobacco plants and disappear. Four seconds now before the guard checked to make sure he was coming. He slowed his steps, watched the guard go to Lightning to try to make him move on. Jesse slipped down, slid into the leaves. He bent and ran low to the ground, moving lightly over the humps of soil around the plants, the flattened paths between the rows. He moved just the way he'd known he would, fast and furious, nothing like a man but like something wild and used to moving fast on rough ground. He kept his feet moving, head down, leaves smacking at the top of his head, his cheeks, his arms and hands. He wouldn't let himself feel the burn, just kept moving, breathing in and out, in and out, the way he'd trained to run without pausing to catch a breath.

Keep breathing, he thought, eyes down, *keep pushing through row after row to the river. Keep breathing to the river and you're free.* He heard the shouts of guards, not even close. No gunshots fired. He knew he would get to the river. He'd had plenty of lead time. He caught a hint of a breeze moving through the leaves, cooling him a little. He grinned, knowing even the wind was following his plan.

Fat Mack sat on the tailgate of the water truck, gave the guard a wink, and sipped cold water from his cup. "You know he hates being watched."

The guard squinted at the field, looked to the other guards, who were scattering, circling the field. "Well, he's got his audience gathering now." They knew exactly where Jesse was going, and they were giving him time to get there. He was surrounded and didn't know it. Fat Mack stood and looked over the other prisoners, cuffed and facedown in the dirt road leading out to the field. Guards stood ready to blast anyone who moved. The guard poked at his arm with the butt of his rifle. "Time to cuff you too, Mack." Fat Mack turned, let himself be cuffed with the big-sized cuffs made for men over three hundred pounds. "I'd put you on the ground," the guard said, "but I'd have to order in a crane to pull you back up again."

Fat Mack nodded, looked out over the field where Jesse was running. He called out for the others to hear, "Go on, devil boy! Run like a motherfucker! Get the hell out of here!" A few of the men on the ground cheered but went quiet when the guard yelled to shut up.

The guard leaned close to him. "Nice. You keep rooting for your devil boy." He gave Fat Mack a wink, but Fat Mack just stared back, giving nothing. The guard squirmed a little and looked back out at the field as if he could see something besides tobacco plants out there. "They gonna blow his head off just the way they blast those bagged flower heads."

Fat Mack nodded. "He's bagged all right." He looked out at the field, saw the guards circling in.

Jesse felt the ground dipping under his feet. He was in the blind spot now, that little dip in the land where they could see only the leaves shaking on the plants. He could hear the horses at a distance, though. He kept his head low. The horses seemed confused somehow, kept crossing back, not coming straight on him. He heard a guard shout, "Where the fuck he go? How's a man disappear in the middle of a field?" Jesse grinned, pushed on. A tobacco leaf slashed at his face, scratched his eye, stinging, knocking his breath back. He covered his eye with his hand, pushed on, swallowing the pain. The eye burned, tears running down his face. He pushed his head down lower, tried to shield his good eye. He'd be blind if another leaf smacked his good eye like that. He kept running, thighs and back burning from the strain. He could tell by the lay of the land that he was near the river. He went left, toward it, kept running. He glanced ahead to the top branches of the line of trees. Just behind the trees would be the river. The shouting of the guards was fainter now. But he could still hear the rushing sounds of horses, the pounding of their hooves on the ground as if they were right on him. He thought of the guards, what they could see. Fat Mack had said they were aching to take a shot at a man running through the fields. He kept running, listening for the guards closing in, his skin burning wherever the leaves hit. He stood a little taller now as he ran, taking some of the strain out of his back. Still no sound of the guards. He'd lost them.

He could see the clearing just ahead, and he was out of the tobacco in the little strip of open land before the line of trees. And just

357

beyond the trees, the river. He could smell the coolness in the air. He whispered, "Home free," as he headed for the trees. The trees stood tall and thick. He could smell the river. It would soothe his burning skin. He'd dive in, swim under, moving through the river like a trout. The current would carry him fast and far away. He stretched his legs, stood tall for the longer stride, the faster run across the clearing. The trees were just ahead. He pushed on harder, the clearing wider than he thought it would be. He ran hard, thinking, *I just gotta get to the trees*. If they saw him in the clearing, they'd shoot to kill. They wanted that. He listened for them, heard only the sound of his breath and the pounding of blood in his ears and the rush of his feet across the ground. The trees, he could smell them; he could feel the coolness of them just a few yards away now. "I'm free." The sound of laughter rippled in his head. " I'm free," he panted, "free."

He heard a shout, smelled a horse. He heard a laugh, a crack rip the air. And the land snapped, burned to black.

Fat Mack stood at the end of the line, watching the men ahead filing through the door, all cuffed, heads down, docile, just the way the guards wanted. One dead man in the field was like chum in the waters. The guards would be hungry now for another shot, another chase, anything to break the monotony of day after day herding men to and from the fields. There would be a twenty-four-hour lockdown. Then back to the routine, but the talk of a man shot in the field would hang in the air like the stench of backed-up drains. Fat Mack listened to the guards just behind him, laughing at how good it had been to circle the running man, taking their time, letting him wear himself out, think he was on the brink of freedom before they took him down. He kept his eyes forward, arms loose at his sides. They'd uncuffed him for the walk back to the building. They knew it was hard for a man his size to walk with his arms cuffed. They didn't want the work of getting him up if he fell down. Back in his cell, he'd finally have the quiet. No more of the cocky little bastard yammering on about how bad he could be. Fat Mack grinned. Couldn't they ever learn to keep their mouths shut? Couldn't they ever see from his stare that he just wanted them to shut up? He looked down at the dirt path. So devil boy's blood had splattered into the dirt like any man's. He thought, *You ain't no devil, Jesse Hollowfield. You just another dead man like anyone else.*

One of the guards stepped up to walk beside him. It was the blue-eyed guard, Unger. He had little shiny blue eyes like pinpoints. He'd been the one to make the shot. Fat Mack figured if he was going to give a guard a chance to kill a man, it'd be this prick. He liked to hurt, had probably been the kind of boy who tortured bugs and drowned cats. If he weren't a prison guard, he'd probably be out there getting in knife fights, beating up whatever got in reach, fucking up whatever he could until he ended up on the inside of a locked cell. Of all the guards, he was the one you wanted on your side. He was the one Fat Mack had offered to draw faces on the bagged flower heads for. They'd had a bond after that. He jabbed Fat Mack's arm, grinned. "That was something, Mack."

Fat Mack nodded at the dirt. "Felt good, huh."

"Yeah. That wasn't no flower head I popped back there."

"Practice pays," Fat Mack said.

"Damn right." The guard walked beside him. Fat Mack knew he was aching to talk, to say something more about letting the man run in the heat, getting smacked and cut by the leaves, thinking he was running free while the whole time he was in sight. Fat Mack was puffing from the long walk in the heat. He made the sound harder than he needed to, paused a little to catch his breath, glanced up at the guard like he was really struggling. The guard stopped, motioned the

359

other guard to go ahead. "Go on," he said. "I've got Mack here. He's cuffed. He ain't running."

The other guard, a pasty, dough-faced kid, spat his chew to the ground at Fat Mack's feet. "Nah, he ain't likely to go anywhere but the food line."

Fat Mack gave a grin to the doughboy, who looked away. His name tag said, "Watson." Fat Mack would remember that. He kept his eyes on the doughboy, who kept his eyes on Unger.

"You go on," Unger said again. "We'll take it slow. I'll get Mack in."

Watson gave a nod and hurried up to the rest. Fat Mack watched him run, ass already going fat. He glanced at Unger. "How long you think that little prick gonna last?"

Unger shook his head. "You tell me."

"That ain't for me to say," Fat Mack said and moved on toward the building.

Unger slipped a wad of Skoal into his mouth, offered Fat Mack the can. Fat Mack shook his head, kept moving. "We got no hurry," Unger said. "You know how that line backs up at the door. Might as well stand back here a while." He stood there chewing and grinning. Fat Mack studied his face. A pretty-boy face, good jawline, a James Dean kind of curve to his lips, and those blue, blue eyes. Probably got every piece of ass that walked by. Especially with that cocky, king-of-the-world way he had. Girls liked those cocky kings of the world. Like Hollowfield. And now he was dead, head splattered in the dirt.

Fat Mack could see Unger was thinking about that. "So you like your job, huh?"

"Hell, yeah," Unger said, grinning. "Days like this, like coming fifty times. That's what it's all about, man. You know I've been waiting for a runner. Told you I can shoot. Wild Bill Hickok, that's me."

Fat Mack nodded, thought it best not to remind Unger that Wild Bill had died after being shot in the back. He watched the line of men stalled at the door of the building. "Gonna be nice to have quiet again."

The guard smiled. "I guess you mean it when you say you hate having a cellmate."

"I mean everything I say," Fat Mack said.

Unger gave him a wink. Fat Mack hated to have a man wink at him, as if they shared some little secret. Fat Mack didn't share a goddamned thing. He just kept his eyes on the guard, watched his mouth work the chew until he slowed, stopped, leaned to Fat Mack. "You'll be getting that private cell next week. The nice one in the new wing. It's yours."

Fat Mack nodded, kept his eyes on the guard's face as he went back to chewing. "And the television," he said.

Unger paused. "And the television. I'll get you the television. But you'll have to keep quiet about that."

"I'm always quiet. It's these other fuckers can't quit running their mouths."

Unger nodded, chewed. "There'll be hell to pay if word gets out."

Fat Mack looked at the guard, grinned the grin that made men look sick around the eyes. He'd practiced that grin in the mirror. He knew that with half his face frozen from the stroke, when he grinned it looked like a dead man coming to life, or was it a live man going dead? Either way, nobody liked to look at his face when it moved.

The guard gave a little laugh. Nervous, faking. "Ah, hell, Mack, I knew we worked a good deal. I got my man, and you'll get your television and that private cell you want. I'm just saying—"

Fat Mack moved forward in that quick, hard way no one expected. Unger stepped back. Mack gave him that quick smile again. "There's always hell to pay."

361

The Mean
Little World

Mike sat in the interrogation room and kept his eyes on his hands. He knew if he looked at the detective, it would just get the man started: *You piece of shit, what you looking at.* He'd learned back in juvy never to look a guard in the eye; it was just like looking at a dog just waiting for you to make the little motion that would get him running to chase you as far down the road as he thought you should be.

He was a criminal now. Not a kid anymore but a man charged with manslaughter, second degree. It made him sound like something as bad as Jesse. But he was nothing like Jesse. He'd be doing three years instead of the ten he'd thought he'd get, could have gotten worse. Maybe it was his granny's prayers. Still, there'd be three years of concrete cells, lockdowns, having to watch his back, having to watch his everything around him every minute. But that was all right. In a way he'd always feel free now; at least he'd be a little more free now that Jesse was dead. He blinked, looked at the dry skin around his fingertips, the dirt under his nails. He'd never thought he'd live to see Jesse dead. But it was true. Jesse was dead. Or there'd be no way in hell he'd be sitting here willing to tell about the blue-truck girl. "Katy," she had said. "My name is Katy. You need to know my name."

The detective pulled himself a little closer. There was a guard watching him from the corner of the room while another guard was walking two new people in: some chick and a cop, not a city cop. Mike figured him for county. Mike saw the badge; it looked to be a sheriff's badge. Probably from the county out by the lake where they'd dumped the truck. Yeah, he'd get a right to be here. But Mike couldn't figure the chick. She was hot in a rough kind of way. Tight jeans, boots. Definitely not a reporter. She was a little, hard-looking woman, something in her face worn out. She looked too young to look so old, a tight body but these big eyes, and curly hair like a kid. She probably looked better on a good day. The guard led her to a chair across the room. She grabbed a notepad and pen from her purse. She gave Mike a glance, not a fuck-you-punk look like everyone else was giving him these days. Maybe she was a reporter. But she didn't look hungry and nervous, the way reporters did. She glanced over him quickly, but curious, as if he were some creature she'd never seen before. Then she looked to the sheriff guy, who sat beside her, and they talked like they knew each other. Maybe she was undercover.

Mike lowered his head a little, said, "What they doing here?"

"That isn't your concern, Carter." The detective spoke like he was so pissed off, Mike could almost feel the smack in his voice. "You just sit there while we get this ready. You sit there and remember every little mile you drove, every little place you saw, every tree, fence, highway sign. Don't you give me this I-don't-know shit. You were the driver. You tell us every damn thing you saw the day you killed Katy Connor."

"I didn't kill her," Mike said. "Jesse did it. You know Jesse did it."

"I'll let you know when it's time for you to talk. I want you to just sit there and think about what you did."

Same as his granny's words. She always said that when he screwed up and she caught him. It could have been something like

363

breaking into a house and boosting some old lady's TV. Or it could have been something as simple as drinking the last Coke in the refrigerator without asking.

She was in a nursing home now, had had some kind of breakdown because of him. He was a criminal, just like his daddy. He wondered if what Jesse said about meanness being in the blood was true. Maybe he'd gotten that from his daddy, the same way he'd gotten that soft, round face, pale as an underdone biscuit. Yeah, he was like his daddy. He had made his granny cry those deep, sobbing sounds like everything in her was gonna come out. He stood on her porch, cuffed, with the cops right beside him, and wondered if she could die from crying like that. When she heard the words they charged him with, the murder of Katherine Connor, she just dropped to the floor and made a wailing noise that still sent shivers up his spine.

He stood there looking at his granny, watching the cops help her up from the floor and get her to her favorite chair, as if they knew which was her favorite. He was afraid she might die from crying, and it was then he realized just what he had done when he'd carried that screwdriver to Jesse, not wanting to, but his mind saying the lady was already dead. Jesse had done it. Mike had only been the driver. He told his granny that, but that only made her cry harder, him trying to make some kind of sense of what he had done.

And now they'd offered him a deal. "You're one lucky fuck," the detective said. "You're lucky Katy's mother wants her daughter's remains more than she wants you dead."

He hadn't thought of the blue-truck lady as having a mother. Her name was Katy. He could still feel the touch of her hand on his arm. *I'm sorry*, he thought. It was Jesse, he had told the cops. He'd told them that Jesse had a way of making you do things. The detective had just stared at him, eyes fierce, body clenched like he was just waiting for a reason to slam Mike against the wall.

The detective kicked his chair. "You ain't talking. We brought you in here to tell us where we can find that poor girl you bastards killed."

"I didn't do it," Mike said.

The detective kicked his chair again. "No, you just stood and watched. You knew what he was gonna do to that girl. Why didn't you just get in your car and drive off, go to the cops? You had your keys!"

"I couldn't leave," Mike said. He hadn't even thought of leaving. "The girl's truck was parked behind me. There was no way I could get out."

"You couldn't go to that farmhouse just on the other side of the trees, could you? No, you couldn't move your goddamned feet. You had to stand there and watch."

"I didn't watch," Mike said.

"Then you went home to your granny's house, ate fried chicken. Let that monster sleep in your granny's house. I guess you don't give a shit who gets left dead somewhere as long as you can go eat the last of your granny's fried chicken."

Mike looked up. "I turned him in. I told what he did to the Land Fall girl."

"For the money." The detective sneered. "But you didn't get the money, did you? Because there was something else you didn't tell. Like a blue truck out of gas? There was a lot you didn't tell, but you gave us enough to bust your ass. You and Jesse Hollowfield eating fried chicken at your granny's house. Yeah, you knew about the Land Fall girl, but there were two things you didn't know when you called that number. Like your granny, she ain't as deaf as you think."

"I know," Mike said.

The detective poked him in the chest. "And that blue truck you two were so hot to jack and had to dump because the gauge was sitting on empty." The detective sat back a little, smiled. "That blue truck with the Tennessee plates, it had a tank full of gas. You boys only thought it was empty. You left a truck all tuned up and a tank full of gas just sitting on the side of the road."

Mike closed his eyes. He didn't want to see that laughing sneer on the face of the detective. They'd walked away from the truck full of gas. They could have made the pawnshop easy, ahead of time, in that truck. They could have grabbed enough cash, guns, any shit they wanted and had plenty of money for Jesse to get out of town the way he aimed to and for Mike to buy a kitchen full of groceries and maybe fix his car. That was the plan before the blue-truck girl. They'd listened to the engine, and Jesse had said, "She'll ride all right." But the blue-truck girl . . . her name was Katy. That lady named Katy, well, she'd still be dead even if they'd made the pawnshop in the blue truck. The detective moved close. Mike felt his breath, could even feel the sneer on his face the same way he could always feel a look from Jesse. "It doesn't matter," Mike said. "That lady, she'd still be dead. Jesse never meant to leave her alive."

The hard little woman stood. "Goddamn it! I've heard enough of this! Tell where she is, you little shit!" The room went still as she came at him the way a cat watches a mouse in a corner, nibbling, not even thinking about the big cat that jerks up its head and leaps at the mouse, snapping its neck in one swift move. Her eyes were flashing, and she was coming straight at him. The guard took her arm, and Mike jumped up, his heart pounding while her eyes stayed right on him. The guard pulled her back, and the detective slammed Mike back into his chair. Mike looked at the detective. "Damn, man. Who is she?"

"She wants answers." The detective spread a map on the table, pointed at a circled spot. "Here's where you fuckers grabbed Katy Connor." Mike studied the map, caught the other circle stamped on the tangled lines for roads. "And here's where you left her truck.

You were in the city. You headed north. Now, you look at this and show me exactly where you went."

"I can't read maps," Mike said. "It's all a tangle to me. I can barely read."

The detective's breath started up again, hard and fast. "All right, let's say I believe your dumb ass. Is it that you're half blind or just too dumb to read?"

"I can read," Mike said, thinking most things he could read. But maps, he just got confused by all those lines that ran together.

The detective glanced at the chick, now sitting again across the room. The sheriff, he had his hand on her knee, not soft but firm, like he was making her sit in that chair. The detective knocked the back of Mike's head, not too hard, but not soft either. "Let's see if we can stir up any memories in there. You know, like a general sense of direction. Where did you last see Katy Connor alive?"

He remembered how she'd looked walking out of that store, not happy, really, not the way most chicks look when they'd just bought something. "I didn't want to do it," Mike said. His voice, it didn't sound like him. It sounded like a little boy's.

The detective kicked his chair. "Where did you last see Katy Connor alive?"

"Up near Whitwell."

"Near Whitwell, where your granny lives," the detective said.

"Not that far up. We took the exit right before Whitwell. There's some little back roads there, nothing much else. It was a good place to hide. The farms out there, nobody grows much out there no more. The school, it's closed."

"What school?"

"I don't know. It's some brick building. You can tell by looking at it, it was a school sometime."

"I need names of something. I need route numbers!"

"I never pay attention to the route numbers. It's all just roads."

The detective punched his arm again. "You need to think a little harder, you dumb shit. You need to tell me something that was on those roads."

Mike shook his head, squeezed his eyes shut. He was driving, and Jesse was right on his ass. He thought to try to outrun Jesse, but Jesse would still kill the girl and then come to kill him. So he kept driving. "There was some old power station. It was all fenced in with razor wire. It was closed. Looked like it'd been closed a long time. It was on one of the roads. I remember that. Then we turned west."

"West. How the fuck's a dumb-ass like you know east from west?"

"'Cause the sun was in my eyes. I couldn't hardly see where I was going, and I had to keep going 'cause I was leading the way."

"Where?"

"I don't know."

"Where the fuck were you going if you were leading the way?"

"I didn't know for sure. I just knew there were these abandoned farms out there. There used to be a trailer out there. That's where I used to go when I bought my weed. Then I went one day and they were gone. I didn't know if they got busted or just moved off."

"Okay, abandoned farms. Someone used to sell weed in a trailer. You have any idea how many empty farms and trailers there are out there? I need numbers, routes, street names!"

"I told you I don't know." The detective glared into his eyes as if he could pull a number out of them if he stared hard enough. Mike thought about that night. "I saw a field of blown-down trees. Like a whole bunch of trees had just been blown over, like dominoes. Must have been a storm. Something blew down all those trees. I remember driving past that."

"On your right or left?" the lady said.

"What?"

"The blown-down trees, were they on your right or left when you were driving?"

Mike thought a minute. "On my right."

The chick nodded and wrote something down.

The detective sighed. He shook the back of Mike's chair. "You got any idea how many fields of blown-down trees we have around here? This is hurricane country, you shit."

"I'm just saying what I saw." He wouldn't say he was stoned and he didn't know where the hell he was. He didn't say he was so scared of pissing Jesse off that he just kept driving, hoping some good spot would turn up. "I'm just saying I drove past those blown-down trees for a little way. Then I turned down a little dirt road, a road I didn't know."

"Right or left?"

"I don't know. I thought I was supposed to turn right, but nothing looked familiar, so I thought maybe I took the wrong right. Or maybe I took a left. I was trying to get to that road that had the trailer, but maybe they moved the trailer. Nothing was looking right to me. And then I got on this road, and I thought it would take us somewhere, and we kept going in circles. I kept driving, looking for a way out of the circle, and I just kept coming back to the same clump of trees."

"How the fuck do you know one clump of trees from another clump of trees?"

Mike closed his eyes, worked to see it. "This one, it had some old tire near it. Some old tire leaning against a tree. And there was this purple stuff growing in the field."

"Purple stuff?"

"Like weeds maybe. It didn't look planted, looked more like a clump of weeds. I'd drive forward, think I was going somewhere, but I'd keep circling back to this clump of trees."

369

"A circle road," the detective said. "You were fucking fucked up, weren't you? They don't have circle roads in fucking farm country. It's always left or right on those farm roads."

"I know," Mike said. "And yeah, I was fucked up. Just a little bit stoned, and when you're high anything can look like anything. So I was lost, and I knew Jesse was getting more pissed off every minute, so when I saw this little gap between the trees, I took it. I thought it might lead to some other road, and it was another little road. A road so fucked up and old you could barely get through it, but it was a road, and it led to a field. When we were leaving, I saw a little brick house back up behind a line of trees."

The detective looked at the floor, sighed. Mike hoped he was a little pleased with something he'd said. Then he jerked up, got in Mike's face. "A lot of fucking roads lead to fields in farmland. And little brick houses everywhere." He stood, and Mike braced for a hit to the back of the head just the way he did whenever Jesse made a sudden move.

But the room stayed still. The detective settled back in his chair. The guard stood, his face blank. And the chick and the sheriff were texting on their cell phones.

"I'm sorry," Mike said.

"I know you're sorry," the detective said. "Sorry as hell."

Hell, he thought. His granny was always praying he wouldn't go to hell. And he let her go on praying because that gave her some kind of comfort. He never told her that he didn't believe in a heaven or a hell. He thought we died and that was it, like a candle burned out. Or maybe it was like they showed in the movies; spirits just hung around because for some reason or another they didn't want to leave this world. He thought about the blue-truck lady. Katy. He knew she was still hanging around. He could still feel her sometimes, her hand on his arm, saying, "You need to know my name." Mike looked up at the detective. "Tell her momma I'm sorry. Tell her I'd do anything in the world to change what happened that day."

The woman across the room straightened in her chair. Mike thought she might jump up and come at him again, but she just said, "That's not good enough, saying you'd like to go back and change a thing. That's just some lie you say to comfort yourself because you know damn well nobody gets to go back and change a thing." She stood, and the sheriff stood with her. She glanced at the sheriff, then gave a quick look to Mike as if she could barely stand the sight of him. "I've had enough," she said. "I've got all I need."

She turned toward the door, and everybody jumped up fast to let her out all quick and easy, as if she were the boss, as if she were the woman really calling the shots here. Mike watched until he saw the back of her head go out the door, the sheriff following, nobody looking back. Then the door was shut, and the detective leaned close into him. "Think you've had enough?" he said.

"Yeah."

The detective grinned, punched his arm just the way Jesse did. "Well, I'm just getting started here. There's something I think you left out. Like how was it, looking at the dead girl in a field, leaving her there, and getting back in your car? How was it to park her truck with a tank full of gas on a road that led to that poor dead girl's favorite place to be? How was it to know what your screwdriver, or maybe it was your granny's screwdriver, what it did to the dead girl? My guess is it was your granny's screwdriver because we all know you don't really have a damn thing she didn't give you."

Mike was thinking how it was his granny's screwdriver—he'd taken it from her junk drawer to keep in his car. But he wouldn't say that. He just let the detective keep on going because there was no other choice.

"How was it to drive to your granny's house and eat the last of

371

her fried chicken, make an egg sandwich for that son of a bitch? How was it to mooch all you could from your granny's kitchen while you were thinking she was too deaf, too stupid to know a thing about what was going on in her house? She knew you two fucks were up to no good, but she didn't say anything because the poor old thing loved her Mikey, didn't she? She had no idea of the truth of what her little Mikey could do. She thought her little Mikey was really a good boy, thought he'd just been led down the wrong path by some hoodlum. That's what she called him, 'some hoodlum.' She couldn't dream up what kind of monster he could be. She didn't say he was the devil like you keep saying he is." The detective punched him again, as if he needed to punch to get Mike's attention. "If he is the devil, Mikey boy, if he really is the devil, then my guess is he ain't done with you yet. You never gonna be free from the reach of Jesse Hollowfield. That is, if he is the devil like you believe." He sat smiling. Then he looked up at the guard. "You believe this shit?"

He turned, kicked Mike's chair. "I told you, I'm just getting started. You tell me what it was like to be Mike Carter the day you left that girl to rot in the ground."

Mike looked at his hands, the skin around the nails all cracked and dry, his nails filthy, and his wrists scraped from where they liked to yank the cuffs too tight. He knew he'd never be free of Jesse, knew it just the way he felt Katy Connor right there beside him at times. There would always be Jesse, laughing, sneering, punching at him any way a spirit could. Jesse would be saying, *I might be gone from this world of yours, but I'm here, you little snitch, you ain't ever gonna get loose of me*. And there would always be that lady, tears in her eyes, saying something about how it felt like a dream. He wished it was a dream. He wished he could forget her touch on his arm, but the memory wasn't in his mind, it was there in his skin. He could cut the arm off and he'd still feel her always. Mike put his head down on the table. He wanted his granny. He wanted anybody to say any kind word. He hadn't heard a gentle word from anybody since that day he'd seen his granny wailing, making that screaming sound only some dying thing can make while she crumpled, fell to the floor.

The detective punched his arm. "Told you, I'm just getting started here." It might as well have been Jesse sitting there beside him, and it would be just the way it was with Jesse. He'd have to give the man whatever he wanted; he'd have to say the words he wanted, the words that would keep Mike sitting there, reliving it, telling every little thing he'd seen that day. He lifted his head, kept his eyes on his hands. "It all started when he spotted the lady in the blue truck. Her name was Katy. We saw Katy Connor walk into the Dollar Daze, and we waited." He took a breath. This would take a long time. He knew he'd have to tell the story again and again. It would never be over. There would always be more Jesse Hollowfields in the world. Mike knew he'd have to take it. There was no getting out of this mean little world and into the great big world where things could be different. There was no getting out of the mean little world that had no ending, the world he and Jesse had made that day.

At Least There Are Some Mercies

Her head was here, her body there is what I would come to say when the coroner, the sheriff, when all others came to claim the remains. Her head was here, her body there, I would say, declaring a truth based on the scattering of bones, mud-caked jeans, a tuft of long, dark hair. Katy. I would like to say she passed from this world as naturally, as easily as the green slips from an oak leaf in autumn. Yes, there is a season for all things, but not this. I'd like to say she melted, as her mother came to say, melted the way snow steams in the heat of sun, sinks to the earth beneath. But *broken, scattered, left to rot* are the words I thought at the sight of her, the words that still bang around in my head, but I couldn't say them, not to a mother, not to a lover, not to any of those who'd known Katy, whose smile could make anyone's day an easier thing.

I knew I'd find her beyond that thicket of trees. Mike Carter had mentioned the field of blown-down trees, the circle road, the little brick house, the thicket. He'd called it a circle road, but Roy, he'd heard of a figure-eight road out there. So I had a good idea what I was looking for. I stood looking at the scattered remains of Katy Connor, and all I could think was *I'll have to tell her mother*, but only after the coroner, the sheriff, and all the rest came to bag the remains, sift the dirt, and mark the crime scene. It wasn't Roy's county where I found her, so it was another sheriff I called.

When I set out that morning, I knew I'd find her, so I didn't tell Livy my plans, didn't tell Roy, didn't even tell the REV crew where I was going, just told them I was taking a drive. Some things I like to keep to myself. There's too many false leads that lift and break a mother's heart when you're searching, like that dog we found. I didn't want this to be another dead-dog kind of lead. Sometimes it's best to keep a hunch in your heart. The hunch gathers energy, doesn't dissipate into the hopes and fears of whoever you might be telling. Sharing a hunch sometimes is like digging up the seed to see if it's sprouting. Keep digging at things, they'll never grow. Sometimes you just got to sit back, keep your notions to yourself, and approach the thing you want with great caution and respect that all things appear in their own time. Not yours.

I knew she was out there somewhere between the highways and the old farm road. Mike Carter had told us that much, but there were miles and miles of rough country. And the dog teams had gone down enough trails for Katy; they had been shipped out to search for a kid who was missing up near Raleigh. When we've run through the dog teams and the search crews, sometimes the searching just comes down to me. So it was just me that day. I'd circled and criss-crossed that farmland with all the loose clues that stupid kid, who was riddled with too much fear, could give. But when you're on a search, you'll take most what anyone can give. When I woke that morning, it was like something called me up from sleep said, *Go.* When I get that calling to go or stay somewhere, I always listen, do just what that little voice inside says. When I got in my truck, my travel mug of coffee steaming, I knew where I was going, that field of blown-down trees and the figure-eight dirt road. All the clues just clicked into place. She was there. I just hadn't seen the path they'd led her down. I'd missed it somehow, but she was there.

There wasn't much traffic in the dawn light of a Sunday morning. So it was a smooth ride through town and up over the Cape Fear River bridge. Hardly anyone at all on the other side of that river, and then no one out there, just me and the road and the few birds riding the air and flat farmland stretching east and west. Such a beautiful world for such horrors to grow. I remembered Darly. I don't often think of Darly, but I could feel Darly that morning, so I knew I was close. I took my exit just south of Whitwell, went back to that two-lane highway, past the field of blown-down trees and on to take the right down the dirt road that led to the figure-eight road, and I drove it, looping around and around, watching for some kind of sign of something I'd missed. It's not like there are a lot of figure-eight roads in the Carolina farmlands, so this had to be it. I knew. So I drove three times looping around, seeing nothing but fields and distant thickets of trees until I was dumped back out on the main dirt road again. In the brightening light, I studied the map, which was pretty useless when it came to charting farm roads, roads just cleared by the farmers making easier routes to the back sides of their fields. Maps can be useless in counties where any man with a tractor can make a road. We'd studied satellite views of the whole county, had narrowed the search down to three farms.

I turned back to the figure-eight road, saw no brick house, no heaps of trash. I stopped, thought maybe Mike Carter was lying. Then I thought he'd been too scared to lie, a little guy with a baby face, his hands shaking, he was so scared. Even with Jesse Hollowfield dead and a reduced sentence on the table, Mike Carter still shook. His voice quivered when he spoke. I could see him, how he must have been that day, driving the little rusted-out Datsun over the rutted roads while Jesse and Katy followed behind. He couldn't have seen much from where he sat low in the seat in that car that had to be scraping ruts in the road with every turn.

Then I remembered that his granny lived around here. He'd probably walked these roads, crossed this farmland countless times to and from his granny's house before he was old enough to drive or when that beater of a car was broken down. *He walked these roads*, I thought, the words springing up in my head like some big discovery. So I drove back onto the figure-eight road, pulled the truck to the side, grabbed my walking stick, got out, and walked. Walking, you can see lots of things easy to miss from high up in that seat of a Durango. I walked the loop toward the heart of that figure eight, where the roads cross and either way leads you back to the same place, the heart of the eight, nowhere. While walking, I saw the cornflowers blooming by the side of the road. Queen Anne's lace. Purple thistle. A butterfly hung on the thistle, moved slowly as if drying its wings from the morning dew. *Katy*, I thought. Livy had told me Katy loved butterflies, any natural thing that had a lure of magic to it. *Butterflies*, I thought, watching its wings moving stronger now. I stood still, the way I knew Katy would want.

Then, in a blink, the butterfly was off, darted beyond my seeing into the trees, and then I saw it: the path. To the right was a little path mostly covered in leaves. I used my stick to push the leaves back, then saw a parallel path. This was no path; it was a farm road, just as Mike had said, a little tractor trail off the figure-eight road. No one had come here since the old farmer had died. Kids maybe, kids like Mike Carter looking for a place to get laid, get high, get any of those many things boys want when they're out of sight. Cops never bothered to drive down this road. There was nothing out here but a fallow farm and thickets of trees where anything could happen, unheard, unseen.

Using my stick, I pushed on down that rutted trail until I saw a clearing ahead. I stood still, looked back to where the ground was level before it dropped to this rutted path that led to the clearing. They would have parked there, I thought, behind that thicket of trees. And the clearing. They would have made her walk to the clearing. From here. I looked down at my boots in the dirt. She stood here, walked there. They wouldn't have wanted to risk driving the car or the truck down this rutted road. He made her walk to him there in the clearing. Her last road, I thought as I headed down the path to the clearing where she must have seen him waiting, knowing it was the end and she had no choice but to walk.

I swallowed against the crying that was aching in my throat. I thought, *Don't cry, don't cry*, the way I used to comfort Darly when some boy had broken her heart. Yes, even pretty girls get broken hearts. *Don't cry*, I told myself, and I wiped at the tears running down my face, knowing this was the end. Again.

I walked down the rutted road, feeling the old sadness seep up, thinking, *How will I tell this story; how can I tell it and try to keep the hurt back; how will I tell the hurt?* And I asked myself again, the way I always do when I find remains, *Why do I choose to walk these sorrowful trails?* I could have been so many other things. I stood still, taking that in, thinking, *This is my calling, and no one can walk away from that.* You might try, but the calling keeps calling until you go back again and do what you must do. So I stood there, looked up from the ground to the treetops, and I breathed the sweet morning smell in the air. A blue jay squawked and moved higher in a tree, and I watched as another jay swooped. Then I saw, beyond the thicket of trees, the little brick house. I was exactly where I needed to be.

I looked down, searched the ground for a sign of something, but there was only dirt and tufts of grass and weeds. I looked around for a sign of the trash heap, but it wouldn't be obvious. I knew it wouldn't be far from the clearing. He couldn't have dragged her very far if he was in a hurry to leave. Up to my left I saw a patch of undergrowth tucked between two locust trees. *There*, I thought, *she'll be there.*

I moved forward, studying the ground with each step, saw only rocks, leaves, some scattered wildflowers, clumps of thistle growing tall. No doubt the jay was after the thistle seeds. Then I saw the rusted can, a blackened bottle, old jars, and rusted lids. It was an old fire pit. In the country people used to burn their trash. I crouched down, steadied myself with my stick. I pressed my lips tight, shut my eyes, not wanting to see what I'd come for. I breathed, knowing when I opened my eyes again I would have to focus, to scan the ground for what didn't belong in an old farmer's fire pit. I opened my eyes, and saw the mud-caked jeans as if someone had just placed them there while my eyes were closed. Just a couple of feet away, the mud-caked jeans mostly buried under fallen leaves.

I stood to move toward them, eyes tearing, the old sickness in my gut. And there at my foot, right there where I could have stepped, her jawbone, a row of browned teeth. I dropped to my knees, knelt in the dirt, all the ugliness swimming up in my head. I breathed, used my stick to gently stir at the leaves to expose the brow, the empty holes where the eyes would have been, a tuft of dark hair matted with leaves. I closed my eyes, praying no and knowing yes. Just inches from my knee was Katy Connor, what remained of the girl who'd smiled to someone's camera, whose image at the moment was fluttering on a phone pole, faded on the bulletin boards of bars, libraries, and Laundromats. I studied the teeth, still perfect except for the browning from dirt and weather. She had had a movie-star smile and had come to this, browned, dirty teeth in the leaves. Nothing wanted the bones and teeth of a dead girl but me, her mother, anyone who loved her. And the courts would want the proof. And the TV. The television crews would be all over this. What a story this would make on the news.

I breathed in and out slowly, fought to keep the sickness down, thought of how one day long ago, two hunters had found Darly just like this—well, not just like this. I used my stick to push the leaves farther back from the bone, slipped some gloves on. The cops would complain, threaten me for tampering with a crime scene, but I'd leave them their scene. I just needed to push the leaves back to see what I knew I would see, a skull and perfect teeth, a tuft of hair, the rest taken by birds and worse. I looked up to the bare trees, a gray sky. I looked back to the ground. Her head was here. And there, just a few feet away, the jeans. I carefully took the two steps toward them. And her body was here. I used my stick to push the leaves back, saw the hip bones, spine, ribs, a red striped shirt. At least he hadn't raped her. When they found Darly, they never found her clothes.

I knelt on the ground again and cried, not in the loud, sobbing way they so often show in movies—woman gone mad with grief, screaming to the sky, clawing the dirt. No, grief is a silent thing, a closing down, a dead-quiet implosion where the exterior only seems to hold steady while the inevitable collapse begins. I've seen remains before. Like Darly's. They said the bones were clean when they found her. And I thought what a mercy it can be to find the bones clean. Bones cling to this world, have to be torn away, devoured by the bite, suck, and swallow of all things that need to feed. I stood and told myself it could have been worse. The jeans had just slipped loose, weren't ripped and tossed to the undergrowth like I've seen. I studied the scene, wondered how I'd tell it.

I thought of calling Roy. Knew I should call the local sheriff at least. Knew I'd have to find the words to say to Livy. I backed away, trying to find the words, any words but *her head was here, her body there*, and I thought at least the clothes were intact. Not tortured, raped like the other girl. No, here he'd just snapped her neck. He'd

380

laughed to his cellmate: "It went so fast I forgot to fuck her." He liked to brag. Thank God for that. His cellmate hated the sound of a man bragging. So Jesse Hollowfield was dead, and Livy would never have to face a courtroom. And the girl from Land Fall would be spared facing Jesse Hollowfield at a trial. At least there are some mercies.

I looked at the dirt where she'd died. I used my stick to push back more leaves to see the remains of both arms, legs, feet. Her sandals would be somewhere close.

Then I remembered Mike saying Jesse was pissed because he'd forgotten to rape her and forgotten to take her piece-of-shit engagement ring. He could have sold that. I pulled on my gloves and crouched to the hand, long finger bones almost relaxed-looking against the dirt. I used my fingers to push the leaves and dirt back, let the tears run down my face, drop to the ground. They never found Darly's rings. I dug at the dirt and saw the dull gold. I picked the ring from the dirt, squeezed it in my palm. I wouldn't leave this to the crime scene. Too much can disappear. I'd take the ring, clean it, put it safely back into Billy's hands so he could hold it, keep it until he found another girl. He would find another girl. He would fall in love again, and he would tell himself, *This is the one; this is the one I was waiting for; this is the one I truly love.* And he would marry, have babies, and the story of Katy Connor would be a sad story from the past. He'd make a new life while Katy fell away to be a sad story he'd never want to talk about. Just another sad story. That's how it always goes.

I stood and tucked the ring into my pocket, looked around the scene, so many rusted cans and so much broken glass. I stepped back to go to the clearing where he'd snapped her neck. I looked around on the ground, knew there would be a screwdriver somewhere. And those batting gloves. And I was glad we had no need for the screwdriver or batting gloves because Mike Carter had confessed for a reduced sentence and Jesse Hollowfield was dead. Mike had told it all, hoping he'd be relieved somehow from the feeling of the dead woman's hand on his arm. He remembered her name, and now he was doing everything he could to make her name go away. But memories don't disappear the way a body can go. They'll move like living things behind your eyes until they decide to let you go.

I looked up at the trees, saw a pair of cardinals calling back and forth the way they do, like old married couples who say the same thing again and again, taking comfort more than meaning from the sound. Then I realized there were lots of birds around, twittering, singing. I hadn't heard the world waking up for all the noise in my head. The day was passing by. I reached for my phone, then dropped to the ground at the sound of a gunshot. It wasn't hunting season. Then again, back in farm country there are always restless boys with their daddies' guns out to shoot squirrels, birds, anything that would be a target no one would miss. I called out, "Hello. I'm here," just to let whoever it was know I was a person, not a deer, not a wild pig. "Don't shoot."

I heard a voice call, a woman's voice, "You. You there. What you doing on my land?" I stood, went through a line of trees, saw the little brick house and a little old black woman there on the back porch, a shotgun at her side, but ready, like she knew how to use it. She leaned, squinted as if that gave her a better look. "You hunting back in there?"

"No, ma'am," I said, walking toward her.

She lifted the gun, just to be ready. "You by yourself?"

"Yes, ma'am. My name is Shelby Waters."

She lowered the gun, waved her arm. "Didn't you see that 'No Trespassing' sign?" Then she watched me coming closer, as if I were the bill collector coming to knock on her door.

"There's a woman," I said. Then I stopped, not knowing just how to say the rest. It wasn't the kind of thing to yell across an old woman's backyard.

She started to raise the gun again. "What's that you've got in your hand?"

"A stick," I said. "A walking stick. I use it to push the brush back. Wouldn't want to step on a snake or a trap."

"You got no business back in there." She stood straighter, a little more relaxed as she looked me over, just a little woman with a stick in her backyard. "What you doing back in there behind those trees? That's still my property. I know you don't work for the county. They wear uniforms. You don't look like nothing but somebody with no right being on my land. I'm tired of those hunters. Kids up to no good. One year there was somebody tried to grow that marijuana back in there."

I was just a little ways from her porch. She could still shoot me and get off for just thinking I was a danger. "I work with the sheriff," I said. "My name is Shelby Waters. You might have seen me on TV. I'm with REV."

She tightened her lips, shook her head.

"It's a volunteer organization. We search for the missing."

"Oh, Lordy," she said, sinking to a chair. "The missing. Like people? Missing people?"

I nodded.

She looked down, then back at me. "You think one of them missing people might be back in there on my land."

"Yes, ma'am," I said. "I know you don't want to hear this, but there's a woman back in there."

"A woman," she said. She looked hard at me. "You mean a dead woman?"

383

I nodded.

"Oh, Lord, help me, Jesus," she said, shaking her head. "A dead woman on my land."

"It's been a few months now. She was murdered back in there. Left there on that trash heap."

She stood but couldn't seem to move. "I got to call somebody." She sat and leaned back in her chair and looked out toward the trees. "I smelled it. Thought it was some wild pig badly shot and left to rot. It happened once before. My husband, he got some kerosene and burned it. He said if I ever smelled something like that again to just leave it, said I wouldn't want to see a thing like that. Told me just to tie a handkerchief around my nose and let it go. He said the animals would take care of it, said there was no need for me to see a thing like that." She went quiet. I saw the tears going down her face. She looked up at me. "A woman?"

I nodded.

She looked back at the trees. "And I never even heard so much as a scream." She sat there for the longest time. And I let her. She looked at the trees. "I suppose it's time to call somebody if you ain't done it yet."

I took out my phone and said, "There's going to be a lot of noise."

She stood then, opened the back door. "You call the law," she said. "I'm calling my daughter. It's time my daughter got down here and helped. She's all I got left in this world." I nodded, watched her disappear into the darkness of the house. I opened my phone, had to think of what to do. But I couldn't think of proper protocol. There's always protocol, but I couldn't think of anything but Roy.

Where to Go from Here

Livy lay on the floor, feeling the soft carpet against her arms, wishing she could sink into it, disappear. The white ceiling held steady above her, the beige walls, and to her right above the couch the sailboat painting hung static and bright, eternally promising that those white sails would race to some wonderful wild and peaceful place beyond the horizon, but the boats just hung there as always. Nothing in that painted little world would ever change. She lay there thinking, *What now? Katy is gone, her bones found, her killer dead. It should be an ending*, she thought, *but there's never an ending. Something always follows*. She looked straight up at the ceiling, asked, "Where to go from here?" She lay there, told her mind to go blank, open, ready for an answer to come rising up from within. When in doubt, weren't you always supposed to look within? All she could feel was her heart beating slowly, tired, the emptiness in her belly, and a slight ache in her back.

She jumped when the refrigerator motor kicked on, revving up to cool what was inside. *What?* she thought. *What's in my refrigerator?* That was something to think about. Some eggs, some skim milk, raspberry jam. Lawrence was coming, and he would want something more in the refrigerator. She looked at the clock that said it was half past five. He had said he'd be there by dinnertime. He was coming to take her home. That was what would happen next. "There's nothing left for you to do, Livy," he had said. "Nothing left for you to do but bring your Katy home." He'd grown softer, sweeter, since they'd found Katy, had become the kinder, more thoughtful man she had married. He spoke to her more like a child coming out of a long and dangerous fever than the wife who'd defied him with her plan of what to do with her days, weeks, months that didn't revolve around him.

She stood and went to the sliding glass door and looked out to the balcony. She'd left her coffee cup out there, and a plate. The gulls had taken the half-eaten piece of toast. And there were her sandals left under the chair. A *People* magazine was withering under the water glass she'd set on top of it to keep the wind from whipping it away. How many days had it been there? One, or two, or three? She studied the scene that looked like someone didn't care. *That's me*, she thought. Back home, in her life before Katy had disappeared, everything had always been exactly where it needed to be. But now she'd become one of those people who didn't care about dirty dishes, shoes, socks tossed anywhere. She didn't see now why it mattered whether she was messy or clean because it all disappeared in the end.

She turned, looked back toward the kitchen, where the refrigerator's motor still whirred. She had planned to make Lawrence dinner. He'd be grateful for a home-cooked meal after so much time on his own. She scooted down to sit on the floor, her back against the glass door. She wanted to get up, go to the store. She wanted to buy some nice tilapia, and pecans for the crust. Lawrence loved her pecan-crusted tilapia. She knew he'd appreciate a dinner of fish, a salad, and that lemon-garlic couscous she made with toasted pine nuts and diced red peppers. It all made a pretty meal. They could sit on the balcony, look out at the ocean going dark, maybe see the moon rise while they ate and sipped a nice chardonnay. Maybe for a few seconds, minutes maybe, they could pretend they were on vacation, a second honeymoon, try to pretend their reunion was anything but what it was, meeting to make arrangements to get Katy's ashes, take her home to bury her ashes in a plot beside her dad. Livy shook her head. Katy wouldn't want that. Livy didn't know what she would do with Katy's ashes.

She went to the refrigerator, opened it to see just what was there before she sat to make her grocery list. It was pretty much what she expected, along with a jar of mayonnaise, some butter and a shriveled lemon. She sighed, closed the door, and went to the table. She looked at her hands. At least she was clean. She'd showered, done her hair, polished her nails. Even her toenails were glossy. She had on pressed jeans and a blue blouse and had even put on her pearls. Her pearls somehow always cheered her. Then she thought of the people she would see at the grocery, people who knew her, strangers who knew her sorrows. When she thought about having to hear one more *I'm sorry about your daughter*, she sat on the floor, then lay down to stare up at the ceiling. She thought of staying there, just lying there until Lawrence came, but that would only disappoint him. *No*, she thought, *he's seen enough weakness. I've seen enough weakness. It's time to be strong.* All she needed was her sandals.

She thought of calling him to say she'd gone out to the store to buy groceries for dinner and she'd leave the key under the mat in case he came before she returned. But he would argue, say she ought to know better than to leave a key under a mat. And as for dinner, he'd say, "Don't bother cooking; I'll take you out to eat." But the *don't bother* would be a dismissive thing, not really a comfort to tell her not to go to the effort of dinner; no, the *don't bother* would be more like a reprimand that said, *Why didn't you bother to make us dinner? You've failed my expectations again.*

She sat up, shook her head, thought, no, it was Joe who had talked

387

like that. But then there were times it was Lawrence too. She wondered why she had married another man who was always disappointed with what she did. *I'll make his damned dinner*, she thought. She went out onto the balcony for her sandals, had to stop, breathe the soft sea air. She had thought it would be hot, but it was mild, the air lifting her for a moment. She'd been locked inside most of the day, breathing the conditioned air, thinking the outside air would oppress her like everything else, and here it was, lovely. She sat and slipped on her sandals. She wouldn't bother calling Lawrence. She went back inside, grabbed her purse, slipped the door key off the ring. She didn't bother to make a list. She'd just go through the aisles of the store and pick up whatever called to her, the things needed for dinner and anything else she might want.

She went out, locked the door, and slipped the key under the mat, thinking of what she might buy for herself, not Lawrence but herself, things she had loved to indulge in like chocolate ice cream with almonds. Salty peanuts, chips and onion dip, those foods she'd loved as a girl and had to give up with age. She had learned to be careful about the right amount of protein, fiber, had learned to be careful with her carbs and sweets, not only for herself but to keep her husbands from pointing out that left to her own devices, she'd eat like a teenager. "You're not a teenager," they both had said, as if happy to tell her the news. She had acquiesced for her husbands, who seemed to think the right diet could bring immortality. But nothing did. *Get what you want while you can*, she thought as she hurried down the steps. Then she smelled his cologne—Lawrence. She looked down, saw his graying hair, the little bald patch on the top of his head. He looked up. She hadn't expected to see the sadness on his face. Tears stung her eyes, and she sighed, "Lawrence. You're here."

He stood there, adjusted the grocery bags against his chest. He moved toward her, a worried look on his face, nothing like the judgmental face she had conjured in her mind when she thought of him coming through the door. "Livy," he said, "where are you going?"

She went to him, more relieved than she'd dreamed she'd be. Why had she been fighting with him in her mind all this time? She leaned into his shoulder, kissed his cheek. "You're here," she said. "You're here."

He kissed the side of her head, leaned back, and looked at her. "You all right?"

She nodded. "I was just going to the store. I wanted to make a nice dinner."

He led the way up the stairs with that old decisive way he had. "You know, you could save yourself a lot of trouble if you turned your phone on. Checked your messages."

She followed him, knew she was supposed to apologize. In the old days, she would have apologized. She stared at the back of his head, spoke the words, daring him to argue: "I'm sick of messages."

He turned, looked at her, a sadness sweeping across his eyes. "I can understand that." He nodded at the door. "Can you let us in? I'd like to get inside so you can see what I brought you."

She waited as if he could somehow be distracted while she reached under the mat. His eyes were on her. She shrugged. "Just step back. I put the key under the mat in case you came."

He shook his head. "Damn, Livy. Given what's happened." He paused. A fury whirled up at the sound of those words: *Given what's happened*. She wanted to say what happened, say it: *My daughter is dead. That's what happened*. He sighed, looked like he felt more sorry for her than pissed off. "It seems you'd be more careful, Livy." He stepped back, watched her get the key and open the door to let them in.

389

"I'm just exhausted, Lawrence. I'm sick of words, messages. I'm sick of phones. I'm sick of worrying about things like being careful."

He went to the kitchen, put the bag on the table. "I just meant that if you'd checked your messages, you'd have known I was bringing groceries so you wouldn't have to go to the store." He pulled out milk, bread, apples, oranges, cheese. She sat watching him place the items on the counter, thinking there was still the matter of dinner; what would she make for dinner from that? He stopped, reached, cupped her chin in his hand. "You're gonna like this." Then he reached in and pulled out the pint of chocolate-almond ice cream, then the bag of chips and onion dip. He stood back and grinned.

She ran her fingers over the ice cream. "You remembered my favorite brand."

"Of course I did."

She looked at him, remembering who he was. "I can't believe you did this."

He stood beside her, squeezed her shoulder. "I know you, Livy. You deny yourself things. And when you're unhappy, you're only harder on yourself, as if more suffering can make some other suffering go away." He patted her hand, looked at the refrigerator. "And what the hell, if I'm wrong and you've been living on nothing but ice cream and chips, I guess I can at least support you in your indulgences." He shrugged, said, "What the hell" again, then pulled two bottles of wine from the bag.

She stood and wrapped her arms around him. She kissed his neck and rested her face at the center of his thick, solid chest. She'd forgotten the comfort there. She wondered why it was in marriage that after a while, you forgot the person you'd married. You forgot the person you loved. Did they change, or was it you? She kissed his chest. "You're not a bad man, Lawrence Baines."

He patted her back, stepped away, said, "I suppose that's a thank-you?"

She pulled him closer. " I'm saying you're wonderful. I'm saying I missed you. I'm saying thank you for being everything you are."

He squeezed her in his arms, let her go, and looked her in the face the way he had when he was courting her. "I missed you too, Livy. And not just your cooking or the warmth of you in our bed, but you. It's time to take you home."

She nodded. And he looked pleased. "But right now, I'd say it's time for a long-overdue glass of wine. It's time to take you out to dinner."

"I wanted to make you dinner," she said.

"No, you didn't." He put the groceries in the refrigerator, turned to her. "You might have wanted to want to make me dinner, but you didn't really want to. I think what you want is for me to pour you a glass of wine, for me to open those chips you like. And the onion dip. I think we both want to go sit on that balcony. Have a little bite to eat. I brought cheese and those crackers you like. We need to drink this bottle of wine. Then we need to see about dinner and whatever comes next."

She was happy to sit and watch him open the wine, pour it, open her chips, dip. He seemed happy to get the cheese out, slice an apple, arrange it all on a plate. She'd forgotten he knew how to do these things. When had she taken over arranging all the meals? He hadn't forced her. He'd never said, *You are my wife, and here are the things you have to do to earn your place on the mountain.* She'd done it all. She'd been the one so worried that she didn't have the right to be there that she'd scurried from task to task, trying to make herself indispensible to him so he'd always need her, always be grateful. But he'd stopped noticing her, the way we all stop noticing the sounds of refrigerator motors, air conditioners, all the appliances around the house that keep doing what they were designed to do. She wondered how and when she'd decided her life was designed by Lawrence, when she had given him all that power that he didn't even know he had.

"Livy?" Lawrence said. She realized she was staring into the dark pool of her wine. Suddenly she smelled it, swirled it, sipped it. Yes, it was her favorite cabernet. She looked up at him. "Do you want to come outside? I think the air will do you good."

She nodded, followed him to the balcony, where he'd arranged the cheese and chips and fruit. "It's lovely," she said. "Before I met you, when Katy and I were living together, we'd often have suppers like this. She was the one who taught me about wine. She was the one who showed me that now and then wine and cheese and fruit and bread could be a great meal."

Lawrence nodded. He bent over the railing, resting his arms on it, and looked out. The bar just down the beach was warming up. There was a thumping of music. Some man yelled out with laughter.

"It will get louder before they wear themselves out and go home."

He looked at her, sipped his wine, gave a look to the bar as if willing it to go away. "I should have rented you that better place down the beach where it's quiet. You deserve better than this."

"It's been fine, Lawrence."

"No, you didn't need to be staying in some man's condo near some bar where kids are laughing and screaming all night."

"You don't hear it inside. And sometimes I like to look out there and see people being silly." She reached for a chip, dipped it, and enjoyed the salty, greasy crunch in her mouth. She realized she was hungry. She put down her wine and went for a slice of apple and cheese. She looked at him watching her. "And it's not 'some man's condo.'

He was Katy's boss. He was one more person in the world who really cared for Katy. And that's why he helped me."

"I know," he said. He pulled his chair closer. "I'm so sorry for doubting you."

She shrugged, took a deep drink of wine. "It's what people do. I've doubted you at times I shouldn't have. It's just sometimes we get all these ideas about people, and then we get resentful when the ideas don't match what we see." She looked down toward the bar. A girl was running out toward the beach, laughing. A guy chased her, caught her, pulled her close, and they walked, arms draped around each other's waists as they went on silently down the beach. "Katy didn't want to marry Billy. Katy didn't want a lot of things about the way her life was going. I just wish she could have been happy more of the time."

Lawrence nodded. They sat in the quiet for a long time. She knew he was sorting through the things to say. He knew not to say, *I'm sorry*, knew not to say, *You did the best you could,* not to say some silly, hopeful thing like *She's in a better place now*. She sat watching him, told herself to be calm, that he was trying, oh, God, she could see the strain of him trying to find the right words. Finally he stood, went back to the balcony railing as if he knew he needed distance. "What would make her happy now?" She looked at him, weighing what was behind the words. "I'm just saying, try to imagine, if she could look at the world, if she could look at it all right now, what would make her happy?"

Livy smiled. He was trying so hard. "She would like this. She would like you and me sitting out in the night drinking wine, eating chips, and talking about something real instead of reading magazines, watching TV."

"That's good."

Livy leaned back in her chair, looked up to the sky, and hoped

393

as she always did that she'd see stars, but there was nothing to see up there because of the ambient light of the bars, restaurants, and condos along the beach. "She would like to be back home. She was wanting to come back home on the day . . ." She couldn't finish the sentence, just said again, "She was wanting to come back home."

Lawrence didn't speak, just came over and refilled her wine, then his. He said, "There's more wine inside, and we can order in pizza. We don't have to go out at all unless you want to."

"Good," she said. She kicked off her sandals, brushed the soles of her feet against the balcony. It felt good.

"It will be good to have us home again."

She watched him. So careful. Home again. Katy wouldn't be home again. "We can pick up her ashes tomorrow. I didn't want to do it by myself. Shelby offered to go with me, but I didn't want to be alone with them."

"We'll go," he said. "We'll take her home."

"In Katy's last journal, she said she'd never be at home in this world. She said she knew she would die young because she always felt like she was floating in this world."

He nodded, and she knew he was thinking Katy was probably drunk when she wrote in her journals. Livy had seen this. She couldn't count the times when Frank had been with some other girl, and Katy would come home, sit in the living room, drink and cry, and write in her journal. Lawrence knew Katy drank too much when she was sad instead of doing something about it. It was Livy herself who had told him this. So she said the words: "But Katy wasn't always at her best when writing in her journals."

He came to her, stood behind her, and lightly rubbed her shoulders. "It might do you good to think of a time she was happy."

Livy reached, squeezed his hand. "I just can't think of where her ashes should be. She loved the ocean, but I can't leave her here.

She didn't love Billy. She was always trying to get back to Frank. And I will not scatter her ashes out by that marina. She only thought she was happy there. And there's a plot by her dad where she was supposed to be buried. But she'd never want that. Where do you scatter the ashes of your daughter who was so unhappy in this world?"

"She wasn't always unhappy," Lawrence said. "You're just remembering her unhappy because you're sad now. You'll think of a place where she was happy."

"I like your optimism."

He went back to the railing, looked out. A guy was making a whooping sound and the others laughing. He'd whoop again, then more laughing.

Livy leaned forward to try to make out what was so funny, gave up. She sat back in her chair, closed her eyes. "Do kids get more stupid every generation, or is that just me being sad again?"

"Kids always do stupid things. Doesn't mean they're stupid."

She raised her glass to him. "There you go being right again."

He kept his eyes on the bar, then looked up and down the beach. "I know where Katy was happy. She took us there once. Well, she wanted to just take you, but I came along, and she put up with it. She loved Sunset Rock. That place on the mountain where the hang gliders take off. Remember? She had that friend who ran the hang-gliding shop. He was crazy about her. And she said he was just a friend."

Livy nodded. "She used to say he was too sweet for her. She called him the Boy Scout. Mister loyal and prepared." She straightened in her chair. "She was always going there on the weekends to watch them leap. She said the guys were all so . . ." Livy had to strain to remember the word. "Ripped. She said the guys were all so ripped. And, well, they were fit all right."

"Can't be a slouch and jump off a mountain, not if you plan to live." Lawrence smiled.

"She did love that place," Livy said. "She said she always wanted to do it but was too scared, said she was afraid she'd panic and forget what she was doing and fall. But she loved it. I remember we sat there, and she told me to watch how they took that running jump, how they'd always drop a little to the fall, and then you'd hear the cloth catch the wind, lift the boy up, and he'd always whoop, or maybe it was the crowd, but there was always some kind of whooping sound when the wind caught him, lifted him, and he used those cords on his harness to catch the wind and control it while he spiraled and soared all across that valley." She looked at Lawrence. "That would make Katy happy. She always laughed when we went to watch those boys jump off mountains and have the skills to know how to live."

Lawrence raised his glass. "Here's to leaping off mountains and living to keep doing it again."

Livy stood and clinked her glass with his. "Here's to leaping off mountains." She set her glass on the railing and leaned into him, breathed the scent of the starch in his shirt, his cologne, his sweat, every bit of him. He put his glass down and wrapped his arms around her tightly, pulled her in. She hoped he wouldn't speak. It was perfect, just leaning into him, hearing his heart, feeling the strength she'd forgotten he carried. She remembered the first time she'd leaned into him and caught that comfort and hoped that somehow, in spite of her distrust of things like love, she'd marry him. She remembered she'd thought this when he'd taken her dancing. He could move with her while moving her into a grace she didn't know she had. She thought, *Remember when you used to take me dancing?* But she didn't need to say it. They were already swaying to some unheard rhythm. She closed her eyes, happy to give in, to follow his movement as they stood there swaying, gently, firmly, steadily swaying in the dark.

Some Mornings
When You Rise

There are some mornings when you wake at dawn to the sound of birds twittering high notes to the violet sky turning toward daylight. And all you know is you want to be out, walking under the trees, feet dampening in a dew-drenched meadow, or standing slightly chilled but awake on the cool mud shore of a lake. Too often you tell yourself you need your sleep, that it doesn't make sense to get up and out early unless there is an obligation. But it is precisely at that moment that you need to shake loose your covers and rise.

And there are early evenings when you're out at a park, or a beach, or by a river, or on that warm mud shore of a lake, and you watch the yellow sky fade, curl to gray, and you stare at the violet burning red at the western horizon. Strangers pack blankets, radios, suntan oil, paper sacks, and floats and fishing gear, and you know it is time for leaving. But you keep staring out at the water. In your peripheral vision you see the cars drive away, red taillights winking as they bounce down the gravel road toward home, and you think perhaps you should leave since you don't have your flashlight or firewood. So yes, it is time to go home, peel those waxy yellow potatoes, fry your burgers, drain the grease, and eat, do the dishes, and then, dozing in the gray-blue light of your television screen, settle toward sleep.

It is at that moment, when weighing the logic of leaving against the impulse to stay, that it is precisely the time to sit still. When you hear that thin whisper of a child's sorrow at having to go in from the dark, stay. Listen to the other hunger inside, the nameless one so easy to forget, the one so soft and yet so dangerous when you forget to feed its need.

Since finding Katy's bones that day, I had decided to learn to listen to my own hungers and not everyone else's needs. I thank Roy for that, and Roy's house out in the woods near Lake Waccamaw. It's a house you like waking to, a house that gives a comfort when you sleep. Since finding Katy's bones that day, I've felt the world's slow and steady wasting in a way I only thought I knew. There's something in lifting the bones of a girl from the ground that makes you feel your own bones, your own breath, your heartbeats, measured things that will all vanish in time.

With every lost one found, I always learn a little something I only thought I knew before. And it's Katy's love for the land that took me back to loving the wildness out there way back in the woods, far up streams where a tourist would never go. When I look at the trees, I think Katy, when I watch the lake go silver with fall of night, I think Katy, and this morning with the birdsong in the predawn darkness, I felt Katy's love for this world. I lay there listening to the soft sounds of Roy's breath while he slept that still, deep sleep you'd think only innocents could sleep. He says he sleeps better with me in the house. And I'll admit, even though it's hard for me to admit a need, I do sleep better with him beside me in his house by the river so far back in the woods you can hardly see the sky for the thick cover of trees. It's cooler there. Calm. And it seems just right that I can find a bit of peace there by a river that feeds into Lake Waccamaw. Katy would like that.

I just popped wide awake that morning. I knew it was too early to stir around the house with Roy sleeping so soundly and with Livy in the guest room that's really a back porch, but a nice one with a varnished floor and good screens. Roy put in good shades to keep the light out and mounted a ceiling fan so there's always a little breeze. He did it for me because there are nights I wander. Sometimes I can't stay in my bed. I have to move from room to room, trying to find someplace that will give me a sense of ease on the outside that will calm me on the inside. When my mind yanks me from sleep all jangling and awake, I can't stay in the bed, not even with the sleeping sweetness of Roy beside me. I have to bolt up, move, find something to eat in the kitchen, just some little thing that will remind me that I'm not in my dreams but in the waking, living world where a little piece of cheese or toast with jam can provide just about all the comfort a woman could need.

I lay there a while listening to the sounds of birds. I didn't want to wake Roy or Livy with my wandering through the house. I knew Livy would need to sleep as long as the night would allow. I knew she would need to be as rested as she could be that day, a year from the day that Jesse Hollowfield had snatched her daughter, broken her, and left her dead on the ground.

I slipped out of bed, walked softly across the floor. I told myself I would wait to make the coffee, but going down the hall, I could smell it in the air. I hadn't heard a sound, not the kettle, not the grinder for the beans. And I still wonder what it is about a mother's gift that she can work so silently, so unnoticed when she does those little things to please. I didn't have to call to know where she was. I went to the living room and saw her on the front porch, with two mugs and the French-press pot, the coffee steeping, waiting for me. I walked outside, and we didn't need to speak. She just smiled and pressed the coffee, poured. I had planned to say something like *Are you ready for this?* It would be a hard day, probably harder than she could guess to go to the site where her daughter had died, a little clearing that the farmer said would always be reserved for Katy. We had put a cross there, planted a lily, but Livy said she wanted to go back and make it something beautiful, something Katy would like. She had a little notebook in her lap, a list made. She waved it at me, set it on the table, and said, "Things I'll want to buy for Katy's memorial. I want specific things, not just anything, but things that would be right for Katy."

"Absolutely," I said as she handed me my coffee. She was ready, rested and ready. My job was to simply be there, the way it always is. I'd be there to hold her steady when she trembled. This is what I do. I sipped my coffee, spotted the biscotti and strawberries on a plate. "I could get used to this," I said, "walking down the hall to find the coffee made and cookies on a plate."

"I'll put in a word to Roy," she said. "I've got Lawrence bringing me coffee in bed on Sunday mornings now. If he can be trained, just think of the possibilities for Roy."

"I don't want him to change one bit," I said. "We have an agreement. We leave each other to be the person we met, the one we fell for. If it works, don't mess with it." And I thought about that phrase, *the one we fell for*, like love is some kind of accident. It's no accident at all. I wouldn't say Roy and I fell into anything. I'd say it's more like we grew the way a honeysuckle vine reaches over a fence, covers it so thick that the boundaries don't really matter because the air is so sweet. I'd say that's the way to love each other: Show up, give a little water and light, and leave room for the other one to grow.

Livy offered me biscotti. "You changed. He got you out of sleeping in that REV center every night."

"It gets a little crowded in there sometimes." I thought of those faces of the missing still tacked to the walls. It wasn't healthy to live night and day, every day, in a place where lost souls are always looking

400

out to you, calling to be found. "It's a big world," I said. "That's what Roy keeps telling me: It's a bigger world than you think." He'd told me I'd never be able to make those faces of the missing go away. There would always be the sorrow. "That room of sorrow," he said, "it's in your heart, Shelby, but you can build a bigger house around it." That was when I knew I wanted to be in his house. It was the moment he said those words to me. Then he said, "You can go to sleep and wake up, not to a room of sorrow but to the good things in this world."

"Like you?" I said, teasing.

He blushed a little at that. Then he grinned and said, "Yeah, like me."

Livy reached and stroked the back of my arm that way mothers do when they just have to reach to feel that the child they love is there. "It's going to be a good day," she said. "We'll make it a good day. It's what Katy would want. We'll make it good. You and me." Then she rose and said, "Let's get this day started, Shelby. You and me. Let's show the world what two women and some gardening tools can do to make some little patch of ground a better place."

So there I was, driving back over this road of Katy's final journey, and Livy sipped a Slurpee beside me and watched the land go by. She had said she needed something cold and sweet to drink so she wouldn't cry when we were at K-Mart buying the plants and the tools and the mulch. Like I said, she wanted to make the site pretty somehow, and I couldn't believe a mother would think to change a place of such hard dying to a place where she could stand to dig, make something grow from the very ground where her daughter had died.

I drove and smelled the topsoil, the sharp scent of mulch and the fertile smell of the plants in the backseat: lantana and creeping myrtle and blooming thyme. And a butterfly bush. Its branches bent against the roof of the truck, tangled at my hair, tickled my shoulder if I didn't sit just right. Livy had to get that butterfly bush because Katy loved butterflies. And we had to get an angel, of course, a little stone angel with long, curling hair, a coy little smile, and her hands pressed in a prayer. She just looked wishful and kind of naive to me, but I said she was perfect.

We turned off the paved road to a dirt lane shaded by trees. My truck struggled against the ruts, lurched side to side. We took another turn to what the locals called the eight road. It had been cleared for some farm kids who liked to take their four-wheelers back in there and ride, and now it was kept clear for no good reason but because it was there. I could see how it would be easy to get lost back in the kind of land that looks the same all around with nothing but blue sky above. Back home in Tennessee, you always had a good idea of where you were by the shape of Lookout Mountain rising above the river. And for the first time since I'd left Suck Creek, I missed those mountains. I had the thought of taking Roy back there. It wouldn't be such a sad place with Roy beside me. I knew he'd make me see the old beauty there.

Mud splattered the trees and shrubs that suddenly grew so thick, it seemed nature had a mind to reach, to try to hide the site where Katy died. I slowed down and looked out my mud-splattered window, saw two butterflies dart by.

"That's a sign," Livy said. "Katy knows we're here."

Livy has a need to believe in things, so I nodded. Then I thought, *What the hell do I know? Maybe it's true.*

I saw the little clearing in the trees that showed the way off the eight road, and I took the turn down that rutted little lane. And I thought of Katy, how she must have been crying inside, knowing this was the end. Livy's face was tight but not crying, just seemed to be watching the trees go by through Katy's eyes. Then up ahead, I saw the field. We got out of the truck, and I looked at the sky to watch the weather. The air was hot and thick, and I could feel it. Before the day was out, a storm would come rolling in.

We walked down the rutted road, and I saw the place where she'd died. Overgrown in patches, bare in others, just a patch of earth like anything else around here. I was thankful to see that the farmer had cleared the trash, the underbrush, and most of the weeds. There was a little white wire fence that marked the spot to be preserved. The farmer had done that. He'd bought the land cheap, he'd said. And now just beyond the place where Katy had died, the corn stood green and shimmering, acres and acres of lush corn, the wind rustling the leaves. I can only say it was beautiful to stand there on the edge of so much green.

The old lady who'd owned the land couldn't get away quick enough once she'd learned a woman had rotted on the very ground where she and her husband had planted their first stand of corn. The new farmer had said that there would always be room for Katy to be remembered there. Sometimes it can be hard for me to love much of anything in this world. But that farmer, he had a kindness you don't often expect of a stranger. It seemed people all over town had become just a little more soft, more thoughtful of each other when they realized how Katy Connor had been snatched in broad daylight while they drove by, not minding the car swerving on the Cape Fear River bridge. We got over a hundred calls from people who claimed to have seen her blue truck that day. I suppose there was a trembling all across town with the news of the Flynn girl in Land Fall, and then a flat-out sickness at the thought of what Jesse Hollowfield had done in broad daylight, miles of traffic all around.

I stayed back from the site, knew it was best to let Livy lead the way. She paused, seemed to say a little prayer, then stepped over the low fence, crouched, and moved her palm over the ground as if she could somehow feel the life there.

Me, I still saw the brush, the trash and leaves and the jawbone torn loose. The mud-caked jeans.

"We're here for you, Katy," Livy said. She sat, palms flat on the ground. I told her to be careful; there could still be glass and rusty cans left in the dirt. She just stood, looked at me, said, "Let's get to work."

We got the plants, the mulch, the topsoil, jugs of water, tools. We weeded. We raked and worked in new dirt, good dirt that was clean. I watched Livy tamp the dirt down around a lantana plant, its petals like bright confetti. She poured water, watched it seep. I asked where she wanted to put the angel, and she placed it precisely where I'd found the jawbone. There was no talk of scattered bones and mud-caked jeans. She looked at me for approval. "That's good," I said. "That works."

Thunder rolled from a distance. We looked up see the cloud thick and white mottled with gray. The thunderhead sat poised across the flat blue sky like a giant fist. There was a sudden coolness in the air. We both felt it. She stopped, said she needed some cold water to drink, asked me if I wanted any. I told her to go ahead and get a couple bottles from the cooler.

I dug at the hole for the butterfly bush. Bits of broken glass floated up. I thought of bodies, broken bottles, broken bones, floaters in the swamps. I scooped up the dirt and dug. Thunder rolled again, and I plunged the shovel hard, heard a crunch of something, and looked down and saw a shattered skull. My stomach lurched, but I didn't flinch. I just sucked back a breath and crouched for a closer look. It was a dog. My head went swimmy, and I breathed in, out, in, slowly, squinched my eyes shut, opened, focused. Yes, it was the head, the body of a dog, tufts of fur, a brown collar dangling loosely at the ver-tebrae exposed. And there. A bullet in the dirt with scattered flecks of bone. The story, I wondered. What was the story? A dog with a collar, shot. It must have been sick, must have been old. Not murdered, not shot for fun, I hoped. It happens. Neighbors shoot neighbors' dogs for sport, revenge. Sometimes a man has to shoot his own sick dog to ease the pain and suffering. "Your cell phone's ringing," Livy called. "Are you all right?"

"Fine," I said and used my hand to scoop dirt back into the hole. I felt the sting, saw the green glass in the dirt, the oozing line of blood on the side of my hand. It was a shallow cut, a little thing, but it burned. I stood, used the shovel to push more dirt back. I felt her watching me, turned, and gave a little shrug. "There's a tangle of tree roots here. We'll have to plant the bush over there instead."

"Your cell phone," she said again. I let it go to voice mail, stamped the ground solid over the dead dog. Thunder rolled again, and a cool breeze rushed with that ozone smell I like so much with storms.

"We need to hurry and finish getting these plants in the ground before the storm hits."

I dug the new hole, got the bush in the ground, watered it. I stood watching the water pool up, then sink into the ground. I was thinking of Darly. We'd never marked the spot where they'd found her. I suppose we chose to forget it, not look back, carry on. But Darly, she's always with me. Even though I never saw her there, I'll always see the picture of her bones scattered on the ground.

Livy touched my arm, and I jumped.

"Sorry," she said. "But would you look at that? Some kids have built a little tree house over there." I looked across the cornfield, saw just about six feet up in the low limbs of an oak the rough plywood boards, a hunters' blind. They must sit up there and watch for the deer to come foraging for corn. Livy, she was smiling at the sight. She'd told me how she liked to watch the kids play in the empty lot next to her house. She was seeing a happy thing. I let it go.

"Yep," I said. "We better finish up. It's going to rain."

"Sometimes storms pass over," she said.

"But this one's coming down," I said. And I knew she saw the tears. I couldn't stop the tears running down my face. I wiped at them with the back of my hand as if they were sweat. "Damn, it's hot," I said.

She grabbed a trowel, knelt with me on the ground, and we dug. The angel seemed to watch, but in truth her eyes were just a concrete stare. I planted faster, wanted to be back in the truck and safe and dry when the storm hit. I couldn't shake my thoughts of Darly. I told myself I'd go back to Georgia. And with Roy's help, we'd find the old records, I'd find a way to find the place where Darly had given the last of anything to the earth. With every plant tamped down I said a little prayer: *Let it grow; let nothing but birds and bees and butterflies touch what's blooming here.*

Livy patted the dirt, said, "I like to think her spirit will help these things grow."

"Yes, she will," I said, and I thought of blood and flesh and bone.

"We'll need to say a prayer when we're finished."

I told her, "I'm saying a little prayer with every plant."

"You?" Livy laughed. And I could see her daughter's smile, hear her daughter's laugh, feel the life of the woman Katy would have grown to be. "You don't believe in things."

"I try," I said, and then I kept working. I told myself, *We will do this, and I will do this for Darly one day*. I told myself that in a world of so much sorrow, so many lost calling to be found, we can only do what we must do. We weed. We dig. We plant. We water. We pray. And then we will do what we can only do in the end. We will stand and walk away.

Acknowledgments

I first must give my deepest thank you to Penny Carr Britton. I never would have started this venture had it not been for your astonishing grace and strength when facing and enduring the loss of your own lovely daughter, Peggy. You will always inspire me and help sustain me in my own hard times.

And then there are so many others to thank who helped bring this book along:

Thank you, once again, Kyle Minor, Bob Welly, and Page Armstrong. If you hadn't pushed me, I may have let this story stew inside for eternity. And Bob, you went way past simple support. Thank you for the many dinners out to free my days to write, and thank you for your days of tedious proofreading.

And deep thanks to my agent, Catherine Drayton, who believed in this book from the start. You've been much more than an agent. Thank you for helping me revise and reshape this story, and thank you for your heart as well as smarts in seeing this book through to print.

Many thanks to my editor, Greg Michalson, who had enough faith in this dark story to bring it to the light of day, and to readers out there. You're one fine editor, who knew just the final adjustments needed to sharpen up the storyline, and to make it a tighter, better book overall.

This novel is dedicated to the memory of Peggy Carr, Rebecca Wight, and my sister's childhood friend, Debbie. Their lives were taken far too young and with a calculated violence that will forever compel me to wonder at the nature and range of evil in the world.

And my deepest love and thanks to Susan Falco and Sarah Elder who keep me believing in the redemptive power of love.

Ten percent of the author's profits from this book are contributed to C.U.E. (Community United Effort, Wilmington, North Carolina), a generous and tenacious organization that gives steady guidance and comfort to those seeking loved ones lost.